A MESSAGE FROM CHICKEN HOUSE

So THAT'S how it all began . . . he's brilliant and he's back with another thrilling, disturbing and completely un-put-downable book! We're with our hero all the way as, against all odds, he fights the apocalypse, crazies and a deadly disease. It's true survival of the fittest, Dashner-style!

Somehow the end of the world feels nearer and nearer, makes you think!

BARRY CUNNINGHAM
Publisher
Chicken House

THE KILL
ORDER

JAMES
DASHNER

Chicken House

2 Palmer Street, Frome, Somerset BA11 1DS
www.doublecluck.com

Text © James Dashner 2012

First published in the United States by Delacorte Press, an imprint of Random
House Children's Books, a division of Random House, Inc., New York.

First published in Great Britain in 2013
This edition published in 2015
Chicken House
2 Palmer Street
Frome, Somerset BA11 1DS
United Kingdom
www.doublecluck.com

Cover and interior design by Helen Crawford-White
Cover image (figures) © diez artwork/Shutterstock
Typeset by Dorchester Typesetting Group Ltd
Printed and bound in Great Britain by
CPI Group (UK) Ltd, Croydon CR0 4YY

The paper used in this Chicken House book is made from wood
grown in sustainable forests.

5 7 9 10 8 6 4

British Library Cataloguing in Publication data available.

ISBN 978-1-910655-13-9

For Kathy Egan.
I really miss you.

PROLOGUE

Teresa looked at her best friend and wondered what it would be like to forget him.

It seemed impossible, though she'd now seen the Swipe implanted in dozens of boys before Thomas. Sandy brown hair, penetrating eyes and a constant look of contemplation – how could this kid ever be unfamiliar to her? How could they be in the same room and not joke about some smell or make fun of some clueless slouch nearby? How could she ever stand in front of him and not leap at the chance to communicate telepathically?

Impossible.

And yet, only a day away.

For her. For Thomas, it was a matter of minutes. He lay on the operating table, his eyes closed, chest rising and falling with soft, even breaths. Already dressed in the requisite shorts-and-T-shirt uniform of the Glade, he looked like a snapshot of the past – some ordinary boy taking an ordinary nap after a long day at an ordinary school, before sun flares and disease had made the world anything *but* ordinary. Before death and destruction made it necessary to steal children – along with their memories – and send them to a place as terrifying as the Maze. Before human brains were known as the killzone and needed to be watched and studied. All in the name of science and medicine.

A doctor and a nurse had been prepping Thomas and now lowered the mask on to his face. There were clicks and hisses and beeps; Teresa watched as metal and wires and plastic tubes slithered across his skin and into the canals of Thomas's ears, saw his hands twitch reflexively at his sides. He probably felt pain on some level despite the drugs, but he'd never remember it. The machine began its work, plucking images from Thomas's memory. Erasing his mum and his dad and his life. Erasing *her*.

Some small part of her knew it should make her angry. Make her scream and yell and refuse to help for one more second. But the greater part was as solid as the rock of the cliffs outside. Yes, the greater part within her was entrenched in certainty so deeply that she knew she'd feel it even after tomorrow, when the same thing would be done to her. She and Thomas were proving their conviction by submitting to what had been asked of the others. And if they died, so be it. WICKED would find the cure, millions would be saved, and life on earth would someday get back to normal. Teresa knew this in her core, as much as she knew that humans grow old and leaves fall from trees in autumn.

Thomas sucked in a hitching breath, then made a little moaning sound, shifted his body. Teresa thought for a horrifying second that he might wake up, hysterical from the agony – things were inside his head, doing who knew what to his brain. But he stilled and resumed the soft and easy breathing. The clicks and hisses continued, her best friend's memories fading like echoes.

They'd said their official goodbyes, and the words *See you tomorrow* still rang in her head. For some reason that had really struck her when Thomas said it, made what he was about to do all the more surreal and sad. They *would* see each other tomorrow, although she'd be in a coma and he wouldn't have the slightest idea who she was – other than an itch in his mind that maybe she looked familiar. Tomorrow. After all they'd been through – all the fear and training and planning – it was all coming to a head. What had been done to Alby and Newt and Minho and all the rest would be done to them. There was no turning back.

But the calmness was like a drug inside her. She was at peace, these soothing feelings keeping the terror of things like Grievers and Cranks at bay. WICKED had no choice. She and Thomas – *they* had no choice. How could she shrink at sacrificing a few to save the many? How could *anyone*? She didn't have time for pity or sadness or wishes. It was what it was; what was done was done; what would be . . . would be.

There was no turning back. She and Thomas had helped construct the Maze; at the same time she'd exerted a lot of effort to build a wall holding back her emotions.

Her thoughts faded then, seemed to float in suspended animation as she waited for the procedure on Thomas to be complete. When it finally was, the doctor pushed several buttons on his screen and the beeps and hisses and clicks sped up. Thomas's body twitched a little as the tubes and wires snaked away from their intrusive positions and back into his mask. He grew still again and the mask powered down, all sound and movement ceasing. The nurse leaned forward and lifted it off Thomas's face. His skin was red and marked with lines where it had rested. Eyes still closed.

For a brief moment, the wall holding back Teresa's sadness began to crumble. If Thomas woke up right then, he wouldn't remember her. She felt the dread – almost like panic – of knowing that they'd meet soon in the Glade and not know each other. It was a crushing thought that reminded her vividly of why she'd built the wall in the first place. Like a mason slamming a brick into hardening mortar, she sealed the breach. Sealed it solid and thick.

There was no turning back.

Two men from the security team came in to help move Thomas. They lifted him off the bed, hoisting him as if he were stuffed with straw. One had the unconscious boy by the arms, the other by the feet, and they placed him on a trolley. Without so much as a glance towards Teresa, they headed for the door of the operating room. Everyone knew where he was being taken. The doctor and the nurse went about the business of cleaning up – their job was done. Teresa nodded at them even though they weren't looking, then followed the men into the hallway.

She could barely look at Thomas as they made the long journey through the corridors and elevators of WICKED headquarters. Her wall had weakened again. Thomas was so pale, and his face was covered with beads of sweat. As if he were conscious on some level, fighting the drugs, aware that terrible things awaited him on the horizon. It hurt her heart to see it. And it scared her to know that she was next. Her stupid wall. What did it matter? It would be taken from her along with all the memories anyway.

They reached the basement level below the Maze structure, walked through the warehouse with its rows and shelves of supplies for the Gladers. It was dark and cool down there, and Teresa felt goosebumps break out along her arms. She shivered and rubbed them down. Thomas bounced and jostled on the trolley as it hit cracks in the concrete floor, still a look of dread trying to break through the calm exterior of his sleeping face.

They reached the shaft of the lift, where the large metal cube rested.

The Box.

It was only a couple of storeys below the Glade proper, but the Glade occupants were manipulated into thinking the trip up was an impossibly long and arduous journey. It was all meant to stimulate an array of emotions and brain patterns, from confusion to disorientation to outright terror. A perfect start for those mapping Thomas's killzone. Teresa knew that she'd be taking the trip herself tomorrow, with a note gripped in her hands. But at least she'd be in a comatose state, spared of that half hour in the moving darkness. Thomas would wake up in the Box, completely alone.

The two men wheeled Thomas next to the Box. There was a horrible screech of metal against cement as one of them dragged a large stepladder to the side of the cube. A few moments of awkwardness as they climbed those steps together while holding Thomas again. Teresa could've helped but refused, stubborn enough to stand there and watch, to shore up the cracks in her wall as much as she could.

With a few grunts and curses, the men got Thomas to the edge at the top. His body was positioned in a way that his closed eyes faced Teresa one last time. Even though she knew he wouldn't hear it, she reached out and spoke to him inside her mind.

We're doing the right thing, Thomas. See you on the other side.

The men leaned over and lowered Thomas by the arms as far as they could; they dropped him the rest of the way. Teresa heard the thump of his body crumpling on to the cold steel of the floor inside. Her best friend.

She turned around and walked away. From behind her came the distinct sound of metal sliding against metal, then a loud, echoing boom as the doors of the Box slammed shut. Sealing Thomas's fate, whatever it might be.

1

THIRTEEN YEARS EARLIER

Mark shivered with cold, something he hadn't done in a long time.

He'd just woken up, the first traces of dawn leaking through the cracks of the stacked logs that made up the wall of his small hut. He almost never used his blanket. He was proud of it – it was made from the hide of a giant elk he'd killed just two months ago – but when he did use it, it was for the comfort of the blanket itself, not so much for warmth. They lived in a world ravaged by heat, after all. But maybe this was a sign of change; he actually felt a little chilled by the morning air seeping through those same cracks as the light. He pulled the furry hide up to his chin and turned to lie on his back, belting out a yawn for the ages.

Alec was still asleep in the bunk on the other side of the hut – all of four feet away – and snoring up a storm. The older man was gruff, a hardened former soldier who rarely smiled. And when he did, it usually had something to do with rumbling gas pains in his stomach. But Alec had a heart of gold. After more than a year together, fighting for survival along with Lana and Trina and the rest of them, Mark wasn't intimidated by the old bear any more. Just to prove it, he leaned over and grabbed a shoe off the floor, then chucked it at the man. It hit him in the shoulder.

Alec roared and sat up straight, years of military training snapping him instantly awake. "What the—?" the soldier yelled, but Mark cut him off by throwing his other shoe at him, this time smacking his chest.

"You little piece of rat liver," Alec said coolly. He hadn't flinched or moved after the second attack, just stared Mark down with narrowed eyes. But there was a spark of humour behind them. "I better hear a good reason why you chose to risk your life by waking me up like that."

"Ummmmm," Mark replied, rubbing his chin as if he were thinking hard about it. Then he snapped his fingers. "Oh, I got it. Mainly it was to stop the awful sounds coming out of you. Seriously, man, you need to sleep on your side or something. Snoring like that can't be healthy. You're gonna choke on your own throat one of these days."

Alec grumbled and grunted a few times, muttering almost indecipherable words as he scooted off his bunk and got dressed. There was something about "wish I'd never" and "better off" and "year of hell", but not much more Mark could make out. The message was clear, though.

"Come on, Sergeant," Mark said, knowing he was about three seconds from going too far. Alec had been retired from the military for a long time and really, really, *really* hated it when Mark called him that. At the time of the sun flares, Alec had been a contract worker for the defence department. "You never would've made it to this lovely abode if it hadn't been for us snatching you out of trouble every day. How about a hug and we make up?"

Alec pulled a shirt over his head, then peered down at Mark. The older man's bushy grey eyebrows bunched up in the middle as if they were hairy bugs trying to mate. "I like you, kid. It'd be a shame to have to put you six feet under." He whacked Mark on the side of the head – the closest thing to affection the soldier ever showed.

Soldier. It might have been a long time, but Mark still liked to think of the man that way. It made him feel better – safer – somehow. He smiled as Alec stomped out of their hut to tackle another day. A real smile. Something that was finally becoming a little more commonplace after the year of death and terror that had chased them to this place high up in the Appalachian Mountains of western North Carolina. He decided that no matter what, he'd push all the bad stuff from the past aside and have a good day. No matter what.

Which meant he needed to bring Trina into the picture before another ten minutes ticked off the clock. He hurriedly got dressed and went out to look for her.

He found her up by the stream, in one of the quiet places she went to read some of the books they'd salvaged from an old library they'd come across in their travels. That girl loved to read like no one else, and she was making up for the months they spent literally running for their lives, when books were few and far between. The digital kind were all long gone, as far as Mark could guess – wiped away when the computers and servers all fried. Trina read the old-school paper kind.

The walk towards her had been as sobering as usual, each step weakening his resolve to have a good day. Looking at the pitiful network of tree houses and huts and underground burrows that made up the thriving metropolis in which they lived – all logs and twine and dried mud, everything leaning to the left or the right – did the trick. He couldn't stroll through the crowded alleys and paths of their settlement without it reminding him of the good days living in the big city, when life had been rich and full of promise, everything in the world within easy reach, ready for the taking. And he hadn't even realised it.

He passed hordes of scrawny, dirty people who seemed on the edge of death. He didn't pity them so much as he hated knowing that he looked just like them. They had enough food – scavenged from the ruins, hunted in the woods, brought up from Asheville sometimes – but rationing was the name of the game, and everyone looked like they were one meal a day short. And you didn't live in the woods without getting a smear of dirt here and there, no matter how often you bathed up in the stream.

The sky was blue with a hint of that burnt orange that had haunted the atmosphere since the devastating sun flares had struck without much warning. Over a year ago and yet it still hung up there like a hazy curtain meant to remind them for ever. Who knew if things would ever get back to normal. The coolness Mark had felt upon waking up seemed like a joke now – he was already sweating from the steadily rising temperature as the brutal sun rimmed the sparse treeline of the mountain peaks above.

It wasn't all bad news. As he left the warrens of their camps and entered the woods, there were many promising signs. New trees growing, old trees recovering, squirrels dashing through the blackened pine needles, green sprouts and buds all around. He even saw something that looked like an orange flower in the distance. He was half tempted to go and pick it for Trina, but he knew she'd scold him within an inch of his life if he dared impede the progress of the forest. Maybe his day would be good after all. They'd survived the worst natural disaster in known human history – maybe the corner had been turned.

He was breathing heavily from the effort of the hike up the mountain face when he reached the spot where Trina loved to go to escape. Especially in the mornings, when the odds of finding someone else up there were slim. He stopped and looked at her from behind a tree, knowing she'd heard him approach but glad she was pretending she hadn't.

Man, she was pretty. Leaning back against a huge granite

boulder that seemed as if it had been placed there by a decorating giant, she held a thick book in her lap. She turned a page, her green eyes following the words. She was wearing a black T-shirt and a pair of worn jeans, trainers that looked a hundred years old. Her short blond hair shifted in the wind, and she appeared the very definition of peace and comfort. Like she belonged in the world that had existed before everything was scorched.

Mark had always felt like she was his as a simple matter of the situation. Pretty much everyone else she'd ever known had died; he was a scrap left over for her to take, the alternative to being forever alone. But he gladly played his part, even considered himself lucky – he didn't know what he'd do without her.

"This book would be so much better if I didn't have some creepy guy stalking me while I tried to read it." Trina spoke without the slightest hint of a smile. She flipped another page and continued to read.

"It's just me," he said. Half of what he said around her still came out sounding dumb. He stepped from behind the tree.

She laughed and finally looked up at him. "It's about time you got here! I was just about ready to start talking to myself – I've been reading since before dawn."

He walked over and plopped down on the ground beside her. They hugged, tight and warm and full of the promise he'd made upon waking up.

He pulled back and looked at her, not caring about the goofy grin that was most likely plastered across his face. "You know what?"

"What?" she asked.

"Today is going to be a perfect, perfect day."

Trina smiled and the waters of the stream continued to rush by, as if his words meant nothing.

2

"I haven't had a perfect day since I turned sixteen," Trina said as she thumbed down the corner of her page and placed the book by her side. "Three days later and you and I were running for our lives through a tunnel that was hotter than the sun."

"Good times," Mark mused as he got more comfortable. He leaned up against the same boulder, crossed his legs in front of him. "Good times."

Trina gave him a sideways glance. "My birthday party or the sun flares?"

"Neither. You liked that idiot John Stidham at your party. Remember?"

A guilty look flashed across her face. "Um, yeah. Seems like that was about three thousand years ago."

"It took half the world being wiped out for you to finally notice me." Mark smiled, but it felt empty. The truth was kind of depressing – even to joke about – and a dark cloud was forming over his head. "Let's change the subject."

"I vote for that." She closed her eyes and leaned her head against the stone. "I don't want to think about that stuff for one more second."

Mark nodded even though she couldn't see. He'd suddenly lost any desire to talk, and his plans for a perfect day washed away with the stream. The memories. They never let him go, not even for a half hour.

They always had to rush back in, bringing all the horror.

"You okay?" Trina asked. She reached out and grabbed his hand, but Mark pulled it away, knowing it was all sweaty.

"Yeah, I'm fine. I just wish we could go one day without something taking us back. I could be perfectly happy in this place if we could just *forget*. Things are getting better. We just need to . . . let it go!" He almost shouted the last part, but he had no idea where his anger was directed. He just hated the things in his head. The images. The sounds. The smells.

"We will, Mark. We will." She reached for him again, and this time he took her hand.

"We better get back down there." He always did this. When the memories came, he always slipped into business mode. Take care of business and work and stop using your brain. It was the only thing that helped. "I'm sure Alec and Lana have about forty jobs for us."

"That have to be done *today*," Trina added. "Today! Or the world will end!" She smiled, and that helped lighten things up. At least a little.

"You can read more of your boring book later." He climbed to his feet, pulling her up along with him. Then they set off down the mountain path, heading for the makeshift village they called home.

The smells hit Mark first. It was always that way when going to the Central Shack. Rotting undergrowth, cooking meat, pine sap. All laced with that scent of burning that defined the world after the sun flares. Not unpleasant, really, just haunting.

He and Trina wound their way past the crooked and seemingly slapped-together buildings of the settlement. Most of the buildings on this side of the camp had been put up in the early months, before they'd found people who'd been architects and contractors and put them in charge. Huts made of tree trunks and mud and bristles of pine needles. Empty gaps for windows and oddly shaped doorways. In some spots there were nothing but holes in the ground, the bottom lined with plastic sheets, a few logs lashed together to cover it when the rains came. It was a far cry from the towering skyscrapers and concrete landscape of where he'd grown up.

Alec greeted Mark and Trina with a grunt when they walked through the lopsided doorway in the Central Shack's log structure. Before they could say hello, Lana came marching briskly up to them. A stout woman with black hair that was always pulled tightly into a bun, she'd been a nurse in the army and was younger than Alec, but older than Mark's parents – she and Alec had been together when Mark had met them in the tunnels below New York City. Back then, they'd both worked for the defence department. Alec was her boss; they'd been on their way to a meeting of some sort that day. Before everything changed.

"And where have you two been?" Lana asked when she came to a stop just a few inches from Mark's face. "We were supposed to start at dawn today, head out to the southern valley and scout for another branch location. A few more weeks of this overcrowding and I might get snippy."

"Good morning," Mark said in response. "You seem cheerful today."

She smiled at that; Mark had known she would. "I do tend to get straight to business sometimes, don't I? Though I have a lot of wiggle room before I get as grumpy as Alec."

"The sarge? Yeah, you're right."

On cue, the old bear grunted.

"Sorry about being late," Trina said. "I'd make up a great

excuse, but honesty's the best policy. Mark made me go up to the stream and we . . . you know."

It took a lot to surprise Mark these days, even more to make him blush, but Trina had the ability to do both. He stammered as Lana rolled her eyes.

"Oh, spare me." Lana waved and added, "Now go and grab some breakfast if you haven't already and let's get packed and marching. I want to be back within a week."

A week out in the wilderness, seeing new things, getting some fresher air . . . it all sounded great to Mark, lifting his spirits out of the hole into which they'd fallen earlier. He swore to keep his mind on the present while they travelled and just try to enjoy the hike.

"Have you seen Darnell and the Toad?" Trina asked. "What about Misty?"

"The Three Stooges?" Alec asked, followed by a bark of a laugh. The man thought the weirdest things were funny. "At least they remembered the plan. Already eaten, gone to pack. Should be back in a jiffy."

Mark and Trina were halfway through their pancakes and deer sausage when they heard the familiar sound of the other three friends they'd picked up in the tunnels of New York.

"Take that off your head!" came a whiny voice, right before a teenage boy appeared at the door with a pair of underwear pulled over his brown hair like a hat. Darnell. Mark was convinced the kid had never taken a thing seriously in his entire life. Even when the sun had been trying to boil him alive a year past, he seemed to be ready with a joke.

"But I like it!" he was saying as he entered the Shack. "Helps keep my hair in place and protects me from the elements. Two for the price of one!"

A girl walked in after him, tall and thin with long red hair, just a little older than Mark. They called her Misty, though she'd never told them whether that was her real name. She was looking at Darnell with an expression of half disgust and half amusement. The Toad – short and squat, as his nickname implied – bounded in and pushed his way past her, grabbing for the undies atop Darnell's head.

"Give me those!" he shouted, leaping as he reached. He was the shortest nineteen-year-old Mark had ever seen, but thick as an oak tree – all muscle and sinew and veins. Which for some reason made the others think it was okay to pick on him, because they all knew he could beat the crap out of them if he really wanted to. But the Toad liked being the centre of attention. And Darnell liked being goofy and annoying.

"Why would you even *want* those nasty things on your head?" Misty asked. "You do realise where that's been, right? Covering up the Toad's nether regions?"

"Excellent point," Darnell replied with his own look of feigned disgust, just as the Toad finally managed to snatch the underwear off his head. "Very poor judgment on my part." Darnell shrugged. "Seemed funny at the time."

The Toad was stuffing his recaptured possession into his backpack. "Well, I get the last laugh. I haven't washed those suckers in at least two weeks."

He started up with that laugh, a noise that made Mark think of a dog fighting over a piece of meat. Whenever the Toad let it out, every other person in the room couldn't help but join in, and the ice officially melted. Mark still couldn't tell if he was laughing at the subject matter or just at the sounds coming out of the Toad. Either way, such moments were few and far between, and it felt good to laugh, as it did to see Trina's face light up.

Even Alec and Lana were chuckling, which made Mark think maybe it was going to be a perfect day after all.

But then their laughter was cut off by a strange sound. Something Mark hadn't heard in over a year, and hadn't expected to hear ever again.

The sound of engines in the sky.

3

It was a rumbling, cranking noise that shook the Shack from top to bottom. Puffs of dust shot between the hastily stacked and mortared logs. A coughing roar swept past just overhead. Mark covered his ears until the sound faded enough that the Shack stopped shaking. Alec was already on his feet and heading for the door before anyone else could even process the turn of events. Lana was quickly at his heels, with everyone else following.

No one said a word until they were all outside, the bright morning sun beating down. Mark squinted, hand shielding the glare, as he searched the sky for the source of the noise.

"It's a Berg," the Toad announced needlessly. "What the . . .?"

It was the first time Mark had seen one of the enormous airships since the sun flares happened, and the sight of it was jolting. He couldn't think of any reason a Berg – one that had survived the disaster – would have to come flying through the mountains. But there it was, big and shiny and round, blue thrusters burning hot and loud as it lowered towards the middle of the settlement.

"What's it doing here?" Trina asked as their little group jogged through the cramped alleys of the village, following the path of the Berg. "They've always left supplies in the bigger settlements, like Asheville."

"Maybe . . . ," Misty began. "Maybe they're rescuing us or something? Taking us somewhere else?"

"No way," Darnell scoffed. "They would've done that a long time ago."

Mark didn't say anything as he ran along at the back of the group, still a bit stunned by the sudden appearance of the huge Berg. The others kept referencing some mysterious *they*, even though no one knew who *they* were. There'd been signs and rumours that some kind of central government was organising itself, but no news that was even close to reliable. And certainly no official contact yet. It was true that supplies and food had been brought to the camps around Asheville, and the people there usually shared with the outlying settlements.

The Berg stopped up ahead, its blue thrusters pointing downwards now as it hovered fifty feet or so above the Town Square, a roughly square-shaped area they'd left bare when building the settlement. The group picked up their pace and arrived in the Square to find that a crowd had already gathered, the people gawking up at the flying machine as if it were a mythical beast. With its roar and its dazzling display of blue light, it almost seemed so. Especially after such a long time since they'd seen any signs of advanced technology.

Most of the crowd had gathered in the centre of the Square, their faces pictures of expectation and excitement. Like they'd all jumped to the same conclusion as Misty – that the Berg was here for rescue, or at least some spot of good news. Mark was wary, though. After the year he'd just been through, he'd been taught many times over to never get his hopes up.

Trina pulled on his sleeve, then leaned in to talk to him. "What's it doing? There's not enough room here for it to land."

"I don't know. There aren't any markings or anything to say whose Berg it is or where it came from."

Alec was close and somehow overheard their conversation over the burning snarl of the thrusters. Probably with his super-powered soldier hearing. "They say the ones that drop off supplies in Asheville have *PFC* painted in big letters on the side. Post-Flares Coalition." He was practically shouting. "Seems strange that this one has nothing on it."

Mark shrugged back at him, not sure Alec's information really meant anything. He realised he was sort of in a daze. He looked back up, wondered who could possibly be inside the vessel and what their purpose might be. Trina squeezed his hand and he squeezed hers back. They were both sweating.

"Maybe it's God inside," the Toad said in a high-pitched voice – it always came out that way when he shouted. "Come to say he's sorry for all the sun flare business."

Out of the corner of his eye, Mark noticed Darnell taking in a breath, his mouth opening, probably to say something smart and funny back at the Toad. But the action was cut off by a loud wrenching sound from above, followed by the groan and squeal of hydraulics. Mark watched in fascination as a large, square-shaped hatch on the bottom of the Berg began to open, pivoting on hinges to lower like a ramp. It was dark inside, and little wisps of mist came swirling out as the gap grew wider.

Gasps and shouts rippled throughout the crowd; hands raised and fingers pointed upward. Mark tore his gaze from the Berg for a moment to take everything in, struck by the sense of awe surrounding him. They'd become a desperate, desperate people, living each day with the weighty feeling that the next one could be their last. And here they all were, looking towards the sky as if the Toad's joke had been more than that. There was a longing in many of the eyes he saw, like people truly thought they were being saved by some divine power. It made Mark feel a little sick.

A fresh wave of gasps spilled through the Square, and Mark snapped his head to look up again. Five people had emerged from the darkness of the Berg, dressed in outfits that sent a chill racing down Mark's spinal cord. Green and rubbery and bulky – one-piece suits that covered the strangers from head to toe. The suits had clear visors in the headpiece through which the wearers could see, but the glare and distance made it impossible for Mark to make out their faces. They stepped carefully in big black boots pulled up over the green material until the five of them lined the outer edge of the lowered hatch door, their tense body language showing the effort it took to maintain balance.

Each of them held a black tube in their hands as if it were a gun.

But the tubes didn't look like any guns Mark had ever seen. They were thin and long, with an attachment at the end that made them resemble plumbing parts someone had ripped out of an industrial pump. And once the strangers settled into their positions, they held up the tube-like things and aimed them directly at the people below.

Mark realised that Alec was screaming at the top of his lungs, pushing and shoving people to move them away. Everything around them was erupting in chaos – shouts and panic – yet Mark had fallen into a trance, watching the strangers with their odd outfits and their menacing weapons come out of the Berg as everyone else in the crowd finally woke up to the fact that these people weren't there to save anyone. What had happened to the Mark who could act fast? Who had survived the year of hell after the flares ravaged the earth?

He was still frozen, watching, as the first shot was fired from above. A blur of movement, a quick flash of something dark and small and fast bursting from one of those tubes. Mark's eyes followed the trajectory. He heard a sickening thunk, his head twisting to the side just in time to see that Darnell had a five-inch-long dart sticking out of his shoulder, its thin metal shaft planted deep within the muscle. Blood trickled down from the wound. The boy made a strange grunt as he collapsed to the ground.

That finally snapped Mark out of it.

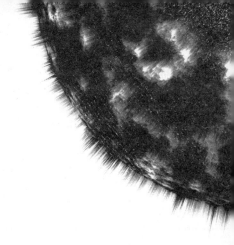

4

Screams tore through the air as panicked people fled in every direction. Mark bent down, grabbing Darnell by hooking his elbows under the boy's arms. The sound of flying darts cutting through the air to his left and right, finding targets, urged him to hurry, erasing any other thoughts from his mind.

Mark pulled on Darnell, dragging his body along the ground. Trina had fallen but Lana was there, helping her up. Both of them ran over to help, each grabbing one of Darnell's feet. With synchronised grunts they hefted him up and moved away from the Square, away from the open space. It was a miracle no one else in their little group had been struck by a dart.

Swish, swish, swish. Thunk, thunk, thunk. Screams and bodies falling.

The projectiles kept coming, landing all around them, and Mark and Trina and Lana shuffled as quickly as they could, awkwardly carrying Darnell between them. They passed behind a group of trees – Mark heard a few hard thunks as darts buried themselves in the branches and trunks – then they were in the open again. They hurried across a small clearing and into an alley between several haphazardly built log cabins. There were people everywhere, knocking frantically on doors, jumping through open windows.

Then Mark heard the roar of the thrusters and a warm wind blew across his face. The roar grew louder, the wind stronger. He looked up, following the noise, to see that the Berg had shifted position, pursuing the fleeing crowds. He saw the Toad and Misty. They were urging people to hurry, their shouts lost in the Berg's blast.

Mark didn't know what to do. Finding shelter was the best bet, but there were too many people trying to do the same thing and joining the chaos with Darnell in tow would only get them trampled. The Berg stopped again, and once more the strangers in their odd suits lifted their weapons and opened fire.

Swish, swish, swish. Thunk, thunk, thunk.

A dart grazed Mark's shirt and hit the ground; someone stepped on it, driving it deeper. Another dart hit home in the neck of a man just as he was running past – he screamed and dived forward as blood spurted from the wound. When he landed, he lay still and three people tripped over him. Mark only realised that he'd stopped, appalled by what was happening around him, when Lana yelled at him to keep moving.

The shooters above them had obviously improved their aim. The darts were hitting people left and right and the air was filled with screams of pain and terror. Mark felt utterly helpless – there was no way to shield himself from the barrage. All he could do was lamely try to outrun a flying machine, an impossible task.

Where was Alec? The tough guy with all the battle instincts? Where had he run off to?

Mark kept moving, yanking Darnell's body along, forcing Trina and Lana to match his speed. The Toad and Misty ran alongside them, trying to help without getting in the way.

Darts continued to rain down from above, more screams, more falling bodies. Mark turned a corner and lurched down the alley that led back to the Shack, sticking close to the building on his right for a partial shield. Not as many people had come this way, and there were fewer darts to dodge.

The little group hobbled as fast as they could with their unconscious friend. The structures were built practically on top of each other in this section of the settlement, and there was no room to cut through and escape into the surrounding woods of the mountains.

"We're almost at the Shack!" Trina yelled. "Hurry, before the Berg is back on top of us!"

Mark twisted his body around so that he was facing front, gripping Darnell by his shirt behind him. Shuffling backwards had strained his leg muscles to the max, and they burned with heat and were beginning to cramp. There was nothing in their way now to slow them down, so Mark sped up, Lana and Trina keeping pace, each holding one of Darnell's legs. The Toad and Misty squeezed in and each grabbed an arm, taking some of the load. They slipped through the narrow paths and alleys, over jutting roots and hard-packed dirt, turning left and then right and then left again. The roar of the Berg was coming from their right, muted by the dwellings and rows of trees in between.

Mark finally turned a corner and saw the Shack across a small clearing. He moved to make a final sprint for it, just as a horde of fleeing residents swarmed in from the other side, frantic and wild, scattering in all directions, heading for every door in sight. He froze as the Berg rushed in overhead, closer to the ground than Mark had seen it before. There were only three people standing on the hatch door of the craft now, but they opened fire as soon as the Berg settled into a hovering position.

Little silver streaks shot through the air, rained down on the people surging into the clearing. Every projectile seemed to find its mark, slamming into the necks and arms of men and women and children. They screamed and crumpled to the ground almost instantly, others tripping over their bodies in the mad rush for cover.

Mark and his little group hugged the side of the closest building and laid Darnell on the ground. Pain and weariness slogged through Mark's arms and legs, making him want to collapse beside their unconscious friend.

"We should've just left him back there," Trina said, hands on knees, struggling to catch her breath. "He slowed us down, and he's still right in the thick of things anyway."

"Dead, for all we know," the Toad's voice croaked.

Mark looked sharply at him – but the man was probably right. They might've jeopardised their own lives to save someone who had no chance in the first place.

"What's happening now?" Lana asked as she moved up to the corner of the building to look around at the clearing. She glanced back at them over her shoulder. "They're just picking people off, left and right. Why are they using darts instead of bullets?"

"Makes no sense," Mark replied.

"Can't we *do* something?" Trina said, her body trembling with what looked like frustration more than fear. "Why are we letting these people do this?"

Mark stepped up to Lana and peeked out with her. Bodies littered the clearing now, impaled darts sticking up towards the sky like a miniature forest. Still the Berg hovered overhead, its thrusters raging with blue heat.

"Where are our security guys?" Mark whispered to no one in particular. "They take the day off or something?"

No one answered, but movement over at the door of the Shack caught Mark's attention and he sighed in relief. It was Alec, waving frantically, urging them to join him. The man held what looked like two huge rifles with grappling hooks on the ends attached to big coils of rope.

Ever the soldier – even after all these years – the man had a plan, and he needed help. He was going to fight back against these monsters. And so was Mark.

Mark pulled back from the wall and looked around. He saw a piece of wood on the other side of the alley. Without telling the others what he was doing, he ran over to grab it, then sprinted out into the clearing, heading straight for the Shack and for Alec, using the wood as a shield.

Mark didn't need to look up – he could hear the distinct swoosh of darts being shot at him. Heard the solid thunk of one of them hitting the wood. He ran on.

5

Mark varied his steps, speeding up and slowing down, dodging to the left and right, making his way towards Alec. Darts thunked into the ground around his feet; a second one hit his makeshift shield. As he ran through the open space, Alec – still clutching those rifles – made a beeline for the middle of the clearing. The two of them almost crashed into each other directly under the Berg, and Mark immediately leaned in to try to protect both of them with his shield.

Alec's eyes burned with intensity and purpose. Grey hair or not, he suddenly looked twenty years younger.

"We've got to hurry!" he yelled. "Before that thing decides to take off!"

The thrusters burned overhead and the darts continued to slam into people all around them. The screams were awful.

"What do I do?" Mark shouted. The now familiar blend of adrenalin and terror surged through him as he awaited his friend's instructions.

"You cover me, with this."

Alec shifted his rifles under one arm and pulled a pistol – a dull black one that Mark had never seen before – out of the back of his pants. There was no time to hesitate. Mark took the gun with his free hand, and by the weight of the weapon he knew it was loaded. A dart slammed into the wood as he cocked the pistol. Then another one. The strangers on the Berg had taken notice of the two people scheming in the middle of the clearing. More darts thumped into the ground like a sudden hailstorm.

"Fire away, boy," Alec growled. "And aim well, 'cause you've only got twelve bullets. Don't miss. Now!"

With that, Alec spun and ran to a spot about ten feet away. Mark pointed the gun at the people on the hatch door of the Berg and fired off two quick shots, knowing he needed to get their attention immediately so they wouldn't notice Alec. The three green suits backed up and dropped to their knees, hunching down to get the metal ramp between them and the shooter. One of them turned and clambered to get back into the ship.

Mark tossed the wood shield to the side. He clutched the gun with both hands, steadied himself and concentrated. A head peeked over the edge of the hatch above and Mark quickly set it in his sights, fired a shot. His hands jumped with the recoil, but he saw the red mist, a spray of blood in the air; a body tumbled off the ramp and crashed into a group of three people below. Fresh waves of screams erupted from all directions as people saw what was happening.

An arm stretched around the Berg door above, holding the tube-weapon out to take random shots. Mark fired, heard a sharp ping as the bullet hit the metal contraption, then watched the weapon fall to the ground. A woman scooped it up and started examining it, trying to figure out how to use it to fight back. That could only help.

Mark risked a quick glance back at Alec. He was holding up the grappling-hook weapon as if he were a seaman about to harpoon a whale. A pop sounded and suddenly the hook was flying towards the Berg, the rope spinning out behind it like a trail of smoke. The hook clanged against one of the hydraulic shafts keeping the hatch door open and twisted around it, catching hold. Alec pulled the rope taut.

"Throw me the gun!" the soldier yelled at him.

Mark looked up to make sure no one had reappeared from inside to shoot another volley of darts; then he sprinted to Alec, handed him the pistol. The man had barely taken it when Mark heard a click and Alec was shooting into the sky, his device pulling him up the rope, towards the hovering Berg. He held on to the grappling-hook weapon with one hand and pointed the pistol above him with the other. As soon as he cleared the edge of the hatch door, three shots rang out in quick succession. Mark watched as the man climbed on to the ramp, his feet the last things to disappear from sight. A few seconds later, another green-suited body was launched over the edge, slamming on to empty dirt.

"The other hook!" Alec screamed down at him. "Hurry, before more come out or they take off!" He didn't wait for a reply before turning to face the main body of the Berg.

Mark's heart raced, almost hurting as it thumped rapidly against his ribs. He looked around, spotted the other hulking device on the ground where Alec had dropped it. Mark picked it up, examined it, felt a rush of panic that he wouldn't know how to use the stupid thing.

"Just aim it up here!" Alec shouted down. "If it doesn't catch, I'll tie it on myself. Hurry!"

Mark held it like a rifle and pointed it directly towards the middle of the hatch door. He pulled the trigger. The recoil was strong but he leaned into it this time, felt the bump of pain on his shoulder. The hook and trailing rope shot towards the Berg, up and over the edge of the open hatch. It clanged and slipped backward, but Alec grabbed it just in time. Mark watched as Alec hurried to one of the hydraulic shafts and wrapped the hook tightly around it.

"Okay!" Alec yelled. "Push the green retractor butt—"

He was cut off when the Berg's engines roared to a higher pitch and the vehicle vaulted into the air. Mark gripped the end of the grappling device just as it pulled him off his feet, yanking him skyward. He heard Trina shout at him from below, but the ground fell away, the people growing smaller by the second. Fear suffused Mark as he held on, squeezing his fingers so tightly they turned bone-white. Looking down made his head spin and his stomach lurch, so he forced his gaze to the hatch door.

Alec was just scrambling back over the edge of the ramp door – he'd almost been sent sailing to his death. He kicked and pulled himself to safety, using the same rope to which Mark clung for dear life. Then he flopped on to his stomach and peered down at Mark with wide eyes.

"Find the green button, Mark!" he yelled. "Push it!"

The air was rushing around Mark's body, the wind combined with the power of the thrusters. The Berg was ascending, now at least two hundred feet off the ground, and moving forward, heading for the trees. They'd clip Mark within seconds and either tear him to pieces or rip him from the rope. He held on as he frantically searched the device for the button.

There it was, a few inches down from the trigger that had shot out the hook and rope. He hated to let go, even for a second, but he focused all his strength into his right hand, clenching his fingers even tighter, then went for it with his left. His entire body flopped back and forth in the air, swaying against the wind and jolting at every bump of the Berg. The tops of the pines and oaks rushed in. He couldn't get enough control to push the button.

Suddenly there was a clank and a clanging and the squeal of metal above him and he looked up. The hatch door was closing.

6

"**H**urry!" Alec screamed at him from above.

Mark was just about to try for the button again when they reached the trees. He slapped his left hand back on the weapon and gripped it as hard as he could. He curled into a ball and squeezed his eyes shut. The top branches of the tallest pine slammed into his body as the Berg swung him into it. Needles poked his skin and the spiky points of tree limbs snagged his clothes and scratched his face. They were like skeleton hands trying to claw him free, pull him to his death. Every inch of his body seemed scraped by something.

But he made it through, the Berg's momentum and the rope jerking him from the tree's clutches. He relaxed his legs, then kicked out wildly as the ship swung around, sending him flying in a huge arc. The hatch door was halfway closed and Alec leaned out and over, trying to pull the rope up, his face almost purple from yelling. His words were lost in the noise of it all.

Mark's stomach was churning, but he knew he had only one more chance. He let go of the device with his left hand, felt along the side until he found the trigger again, fingered his way to where he knew the green button to be. His peripheral vision showed more trees coming his way, the Berg dipping lower now so that there'd be no chance of his making it through.

He found the button, pressed it, but his fingers slipped. Branches reached for him, and he tried again, pressing the device against his body for leverage, then pushing the button hard. It clicked in and he shot upwards just as his body swung into the thick foliage of the trees. He barrelled through them, vaulting towards the hatch above, branches smacking him in the face. There was a whirring sound as the rope retracted into the device, yanking him to Alec, who had a hand outstretched. The metal slab of the door was only two or three feet from sealing shut.

Mark let go of the device just before he hit the sharp corner of the slowly rising hatch door, leaping to catch Alec's hand and grab at the metal with his other. He lost his grip, but Alec held him firmly, pulling him headfirst through the narrowing gap. It was a tight fit and Mark had to squirm and kick, but he finally squeezed through just in time, though he had to yank the sole of his shoe loose from the closing jaws of the hatch. It slammed shut with a thunderous boom that echoed off the dark walls of the Berg's interior.

It was cool inside, and once the echo faded, the only thing Mark could hear was the sound of his own heavy breathing. The darkness was complete – at least for his unadjusted eyes, after being out in the blinding sun. He sensed Alec nearby, also sucking in air to catch his breath. Every last inch of Mark's body ached, and he felt blood oozing in several spots. The Berg had come to a stop, humming as it hovered in place.

"I can't believe we just did that," Mark said, his voice echoing. "But why isn't there an army of people waiting here to take care of us, throw us overboard? Shoot us with those darts?"

Alec let out a heavy sigh. "I don't know. They might have a skeleton crew, but I think there's at least one guy in there waiting on us."

"He could be aiming one of those dart guns at my head right now."

"Bah!" Alec spat. "It's my guess those guys were nobodies, sent in to do the job professionals should've done. Maybe we cleaned out their crew. Everyone except the pilot, at least."

"Or maybe there are ten guys with guns waiting outside this room," Mark muttered.

"Well, one of those two scenarios, anyway," Alec answered. "Come on, let's go." The soldier shuffled forward; Mark could only track his movement from the sounds he made. It seemed like he was crawling.

"But . . ." Mark began, then realised he had nothing to say. What else were they going to do, sit there and play blind hop-scotch until someone came out to greet them with cookies and milk? He got on his hands and knees, wincing from the beating he'd just taken, and followed his friend.

A faint light source appeared a few feet ahead, and as they got closer their surroundings began to come into focus a bit. They seemed to be in some sort of storage room, with shelves along all the walls and straps or chain-link doors to keep everything in place. But at least half of the shelves were empty.

The light was a glowing panel above a squat metal door with bolts lining its edges.

"I wonder if they locked us in," Alec said as he finally stood. He walked over to the door and tried the handle. Sure enough, it wouldn't budge.

Mark was relieved to stand up – the floor was hard against his knees – but his muscles complained as he pulled himself to his feet. It'd been a while since he'd exerted so much energy, and getting the tar beaten out of him by a bunch of trees was an absolute first.

"What's going on, anyway?" he asked. "What does anyone want with our little nothing of a village? And shooting us with *darts*? I mean, what *was* that?"

"I wish I knew." Alec pulled at the door harder, yanking on

the handle, still to no avail. "But those people sure dropped like flies once those suckers stuck in 'em." He turned away from the door with a frustrated look, then put his hands on his hips like an old lady.

"Dropped like flies," Mark repeated quietly. "One of them happened to be Darnell. You think he's okay?"

Alec shot him a look that said, *You're smarter than that.* And Mark knew it was true. His heart sank a little. Everything had been such a mad rush since the Berg had arrived that it registered only now: Darnell was probably dead.

"Why are we up here?" Mark asked.

Alec pointed a finger at him. "Because it's what you do when someone comes to *your* house and attacks *your* people. You fight back. I'm not going to let these bloodsuckers get away with that crap."

Mark thought about Darnell, about all those people hurt and confused, and he realised that Alec was right. "Okay. I'm in. So what do we do?"

"First, we've got to get this blasted door open. Help me look, see if we can find something to make that happen."

Mark wandered around the room, though the light was pitiful. "Why are we just hovering right now anyway?"

"You sure like to ask questions I got no way of answering. Just peel those eyeballs and get searching."

"Okay, okay."

At first Mark only saw junk and more junk. Spare parts, tools, boxes full of supplies – everything from soap to toilet paper. Then he saw something strapped against the wall that he knew Alec would like: a sledgehammer.

"Hey, over here!" Mark shouted. He lifted the thing out of the straps, weighing it in his hands. "It's nice and heavy – perfect for you to beat the door down with your gargantuan soldier arms."

"Not as strong as they used to be."

The old bear grinned, the faint light glinting in his eyes, as he took the wooden shaft of the hammer. He marched over to the sealed door and started whacking at it. The thing had no chance, but Mark figured it might take a good minute or two of work to break it down. He just hoped that when it opened there wasn't an army of green-suited thugs waiting on the other side.

Clang. Clang. Clang. Alec kept at it, the dents getting bigger.

Mark poked around more, hoping to find some kind of weapon for when that door finally came open. At least Alec had a huge sledgehammer to swing. Something in the darkest corner of the room caught Mark's eye, a section full of hard-cased boxes maybe two feet long and a foot high and deep that looked like they were made to protect something important. Some were open and empty; others were sealed.

He hurried over and strained his eyes to see, but it was too dark to make anything out. He picked up one of the sealed boxes – it was lighter than he would've guessed – and moved back into the light, then set the box down on the metal grate of the floor. Leaning over, he finally got a good look.

There was a warning symbol plastered across the top, the kind that indicated the contents were some sort of biohazard. A label below the symbol said:

Virus VC321xb47
Highly Contagious
24 Darts, Extreme Caution

Mark suddenly wished he hadn't touched the thing.

7

Mark straightened up and moved a few feet away. He couldn't believe he'd handled the box. He might even have opened it if he hadn't brought it into the light first. For all he knew, those darts had broken during the flight of the Berg. Maybe the virus had even seeped through the small cracks in the container. Not to mention there were open boxes on the shelves, though they appeared to be empty.

He wiped his hands on his pants, stepped away even further.
Clang. Clang. Clang.

Alec stopped, breathing heavily. "One or two more whacks and I think this baby will bust open. We need to be ready. Find any weapons?"

Mark felt sick. As if microscopic bugs had leaped from the box to his skin and were burrowing their way to his blood even as he stood there. "No, just a box holding darts filled with a deadly virus. Maybe we can throw some at them?" It was meant as a joke but somehow made him feel even worse as the words came out.

"What? A virus?" Alec repeated in a doubtful tone. He walked over and peered down at the box on the floor. "I'll be . . . So *that's* what they were shooting at us? Who *are* these people?"

Mark panicked. "What if they're waiting on the other side of that door?" he asked. "Waiting to put darts in *our* necks? What are we even doing up here?" He could hear the rising alarm in his own voice and was ashamed of it.

"Calm down, boy. We've been in a lot tougher situations than this," Alec answered. "Just find something – anything – you can get your hands on and bang away at somebody's head if they come charging. You wanna let these people get away with dart-gunning some of our friends? We're up here now. There's no turning back."

The fight in Alec's voice made Mark feel better, more sure of himself.

"Okay. I'll look."

"Hurry!"

Mark had seen a wrench strapped to the wall near the sledgehammer. He ran over and grabbed it. He'd been hoping a real weapon might reveal itself, but the foot-long piece of metal would have to do.

Alec had the sledgehammer in his hands, ready to slam it against the beaten-up handle of the door. "You're right that they might fire at us as soon as this pops open. Let's not charge through like a couple of dumb gorillas. Get over there and wait for my command."

Mark did as he was told, pressing his back against the wall on the other side of the door, holding the wrench tightly. "I'm ready." Fear pulsed within him.

"All right, then."

Alec lifted the sledgehammer high, then brought it crashing down against the handle. It took two more hits for the whole thing to finally break off with a crunch. One more swing and the door swung open, shooting outward and slamming into the wall on the other side. Almost immediately three darts cut through the air, *swoosh, swoosh, swoosh,* clanging off the far wall. Then there was the sound of something clattering against the floor, followed by footsteps running away. Just one person.

Alec held up a hand as if he thought Mark would go charging after the guy. Then he peeked around the edge of the doorframe.

"All clear. And the rat must've run out of darts, because he threw his gun on the ground. I'm beginning to think this Berg only has a few people on it. Come on, let's go and catch that weasel."

Alec leaned out into the open a bit further, sweeping his gaze back and forth one last time. Then he moved into the dimly lit area beyond. Mark took a deep breath and followed him into the hallway, kicking the dart gun away in disgust. As it clattered across the room and hit a wall, he pictured Darnell, that dart sticking straight out of his shoulder. Mark wished he had more than a wrench in his hands.

Alec held the sledgehammer in both fists, cocked at an angle as he crept through the narrow hallway. It was slightly curved, as if it followed the circular outer edge of the craft. Glowing panels like the one they'd seen in the hatch room were spaced about ten feet apart, providing the only light. They passed several doors, but each was locked when Alec tried them.

Mark battled his nerves as they walked, trying to be ready if anything jumped out at him. He was just about to ask Alec about the layout of a Berg – he remembered that the man had once been a pilot – when he heard a door slam up ahead, then more footsteps.

"Go!" Alec yelled.

Mark's heart lurched and he broke into a sprint, following Alec down the curved passage. Mark could only catch a glimpse of a running shadow up ahead, but it looked like someone in one of the green suits they'd seen earlier, without the headgear. The person yelled something, but the words were indecipherable as they echoed off the walls of the hallway. It was definitely a man. Most likely the one who'd shot at them.

Engines revved all around them and the Berg jerked into motion, blasting forwards in a rush of power. Mark lost his balance and crashed into a wall, bounced off, then tripped over Alec, who was sprawled on the floor. The two of them scrambled to their feet, grabbed their weapons.

"Cockpit's right up there," Alec yelled. "Hurry!"

He didn't wait for a reply – the man bounded down the passage and Mark followed. They reached an open area with chairs and a table just as the man they were chasing disappeared through a round hatch into what had to be the cockpit. He started pulling the door closed, but Alec threw the sledgehammer just in time. It hit the wall next to the hatch and fell to the floor, blocking the door from closing. Mark hadn't stopped – he ran past Alec and reached the cockpit first, leaning inside without letting himself stop to think about it.

He caught a quick glance of two pilot chairs, windows above wide panels full of instruments and dials and screens flashing information. One of the chairs was occupied by a woman frantically pressing buttons as the Berg shot forward, trees disappearing below them at an increasing rate. Mark had barely taken it all in when someone tackled him from the right, both of their bodies crashing to the floor.

Mark's breath was knocked out of him as his attacker tried to pin him down. Then the man was whacked in the shoulder by Alec's sledgehammer and was sent flying. He landed with a grunt of pain and Mark scrambled to his feet, struggling to suck air into his lungs. Alec grabbed the man by his green shirt and pulled him up close to his face.

"What's going on here?" the former soldier shouted, spit flying.

The pilot continued to work the controls, ignoring the chaotic scene behind her. Mark stepped up to her, not sure what to do. He steadied himself and put all the authority he could into his voice.

"Stop this thing right now. Turn it back, take us home." She acted like she hadn't heard him.

"Talk to me!" Alec was yelling at his man.

"We're nothing!" the guy said through a pitiful moan. "We were just sent to do their dirty work."

"Sent?" Alec repeated. "Who sent you?"

"I can't tell you."

Mark was listening to what was going on across the room. He was annoyed that the pilot had ignored his directions. "I said to stop this thing! Now!" He held up his wrench but felt completely ridiculous.

"Just following orders, son," the lady replied. Not a hint of emotion in her voice.

Mark was searching for a comeback when the sound of Alec punching the man on the floor tore his attention away.

"Who sent you?" Alec repeated. "What was in those darts you shot at us? Some kind of virus?"

"I don't know," the man said through a whimper. "Please, please don't hurt me." Mark's attention was fully on the man in the green suit now, and a sudden grey tinge washed over the man's face, as if he'd been possessed by some ghostly presence. "Do it," he said, almost robotically. "Take her down."

"What?" Alec said. "What is this?"

The pilot turned her head to face Mark, who stared back, perplexed. She had the same flat, dead-looking eyes as the green-suit guy. "Just following orders."

She reached out and pushed a lever, slamming it forwards until it couldn't go any further. The entire Berg lurched and plunged towards the ground, the windows of the cockpit suddenly full of greenery.

Mark flew off the floor and smashed into the control panels. Something huge shattered and the roar of engines filled his ears; there was a loud crash, followed by an explosion. The Berg jerked to a stop and something hard came flying across the room and smacked Mark in the head.

He felt the pain and closed his eyes before the blood could ooze into his vision. And then he slowly faded from consciousness as he heard Alec calling his name down a dark, endless tunnel.

A tunnel; how appropriate, he thought before he blacked out completely. That was where it had started, after all . . .

8

Mark leans his head back against the seat of the subtrans as it speeds along. He closes his eyes, smiles. School was a load that day, but it was over. Over for two weeks. Now he can relax and chill – just veg. Play the virtbox and eat outrageous amounts of food. Hang out with Trina, talk to Trina, bug Trina. Maybe he'd just say adios to his parents and kidnap her, run away. There you go.

He opens his eyes.

She's sitting across from him, completely ignoring him. She has no idea that he's daydreaming about her, or even that he's mad for her. They've been friends for a long time, by circumstance more than anything. When you live next door to a kid, that kid is your buddy by the rules of the universe. Male, female, alien – doesn't matter. But how could he have known she'd turn into this beautiful thing with the hot body and the dazzling eyes? Of course, the only problem with that is that every other dude in the school likes her, too. And Trina likes being liked. *That* is obvious.

"Hey," he says. The subtrans bullets through the tunnels beneath New York City, whisper quiet, its movement almost soothing. It makes him want to close his eyes again. "What're you thinking about over there?"

Her eyes meet his; then her face brightens into a smile. "Absolutely nothing. That's what I'm going to do for two weeks. Not think. If I start to think, I'm going to think really hard about not thinking until I quit thinking."

"Wow. That almost sounds hard."

"No. Just fun. Only brilliant prodigies know how to do it."

This is one of those moments where Mark has the ridiculous urge to say something about liking her, ask her out on an official date, reach out and take her hand. Instead, the usual dumb words come tumbling out. "O wisest of the wise, maybe you can teach me this method of thinking to not think."

Her face scrunches up a little. "You are such a dork."

Oh yeah. He has her wrapped around his finger for sure. He feels like groaning, maybe punching himself in the face.

"But I like dorks," she says to soften the blow.

And he feels good again. "So . . . what *are* your plans? You guys going anywhere, staying home, what?"

"We might go to my granny's for a few days, but we'll be home most of the break. I'm supposed to go out with Danny sometime, but nothing solid. You?"

He's been knocked down a few notches. So much up-and-down with this girl. "Um, yeah. I mean, no. We're just . . . Nothing. I'll be sitting around eating chips. Lots of burping. Lots of watching my little sister get spoiled with presents." Madison. Yeah, she's spoiled, but half of that is Mark's fault.

"Maybe we can hang out, then."

And back up the scale he goes. "That'd be awesome. How about every day?" It's the boldest statement he's ever made to her.

"Okay. Maybe we can even . . ." she looks around with exaggerated caution, then focuses back on him, ". . . sneak a kiss in your basement."

For one long second, he thinks she's serious and his heart stops completely, goosebumps rising like soldiers across his skin. A flush of feeling burns in his chest.

But then she starts laughing like a crazy person. Not really maliciously, and maybe he even notes a hint of real flirtation in there somewhere. But mostly he can tell that she sees them as lifelong buds, nothing more. That the thought of kissing in his basement is just plain silly. Mark officially decides to abandon his own notions for a while.

"You are so hilarious," he says. "I'm laughing on the inside."

She stops her giggling and uses her hand to fan her face. "I really would, ya know."

The last word has barely come out of her mouth when the lights go out.

The subtrans loses all power and begins to slow; Mark almost falls out of his seat and into Trina's lap. Any other time and maybe that would be a good thing, but now he just feels scared. He's heard stories about this sort of thing happening in the olden days, but in his lifetime the power underground never fails. They are in absolute, complete darkness. People are beginning to scream. The brain isn't wired to be plunged into such darkness without warning. It's just scary. Finally the glow from a few wristphones breaks it a little.

Trina grabs his hand and squeezes. "What in the world?" she asks simply.

He feels reassured because she doesn't seem all that scared really. And it brings him back to his senses. Even though it's never happened before, surely the subtrans is bound to break down eventually.

"Malfunction, I guess." He pulls out his palmphone – he's not rich enough for one of those fancy wrist things – but strangely, there's no service. He puts it back in his pocket.

Soft yellow emergency lights come on, strips that run down the roof of the train. They're dim but still a welcome relief after the blindness of before. People are standing up all around him, looking up and down the train, whispering furiously to each other. Whispering seems like what you're supposed to do in such a situation.

"At least we're not in a hurry," Trina says. In a whisper, of course.

Mark has lost that initial sense of panic. Now all he wants to do is ask her what she meant when she said, "I really would, ya know." But that moment has been shot down and killed for good. Of all the rotten timing.

The train shakes. Just a little. Trembling more than anything, like a heavy vibration. But it's unsettling and people scream again, move about. Mark and Trina exchange a look full of curiosity with a spark of fear.

Two men stomp over to the exit doors, working to force them apart. They finally slide open and the men jump out on to the walkway that runs the length of the tunnel. Like a bunch of rats fleeing a fire, the rest of the passengers follow them, pushing and shoving and cursing until everyone is out. In a matter of two or three minutes, Mark and Trina are left alone on the subtrans car, the pale lights glowing above them.

"Not sure that's really what we should do," Trina says, for some reason *still* whispering. "I'm sure this thing will flip back on soon."

"Yeah," Mark says. The train continues to quake slightly, and that's beginning to worry him more. "I don't know. Something seems really wrong, actually."

"You think we should go?"

He thinks about it for a second. "Yeah. If we just sit here I might go crazy."

"Okay. Maybe you're right."

Mark stands up, as does Trina. They walk to the open doors, then climb out on to the walkway. It's narrow and has no railing, which makes it seem really dangerous if the trains start again. Emergency lights have come on in the tunnel as well, but they barely do anything to break the almost tangible darkness of a place so far underground.

"They went that way," Trina says, pointing to their left. And something in her tone makes Mark think she means they should go in the opposite direction. He agrees with her.

"So . . . to the right, then," he says, giving a nod.

"Yeah. I don't want to be near any of those people. Can't even say why."

"Seemed like a mob."

"Come on."

She pulls him by his arm as she begins walking down the narrow ledge. They both run a hand along the wall, almost leaning into it to make sure they don't topple on to the tracks. The wall is vibrating, but not as strongly as the train. Maybe whatever caused the power cut has finally begun to calm. Maybe it was just a simple earthquake and everything will be okay.

They've been walking for ten minutes, not saying a word to each other, when they hear the screams up ahead. No. Not just screams. Something beyond screams. Pure terror, like people being slaughtered. Trina stops, turns to look back at Mark. Any doubts – or hopes, rather – vanish.

Something horrible has happened.

Mark's instinct is to turn and run in the opposite direction, but he's ashamed of himself when Trina opens her mouth and shows how brave she is.

"We need to get up there, see what's going on – see if we can help."

How can he say no to that? They run, as carefully and as quickly as they can, until they reach the wide platform of a substation. And then they stop. The scene before them is too horrific for Mark's mind to compute. But he knows that nothing in his life will ever, ever be the same.

Bodies litter the floor, naked and burnt. Screams and cries of pain pierce his eardrums and echo off the walls. People are limping about, arms outstretched, their clothes on fire and their faces half melted like wax. Blood everywhere. And an impossible surge of heat washes through the air, like they're inside an oven.

Trina turns, grabs his hand, a look of terror on her face that he thinks may be seared into his mind for ever. She pulls him once again, running back to where they came from.

All the while, he thinks of his parents. His little sister.

In his mind he sees them burning somewhere. He sees Madison screaming.

And his heart breaks.

9

"**M**ark!"

The vision was gone, but the memory of the tunnel still darkened his mind like some kind of seeping sludge.

"Mark! Wake up!"

That was Alec's voice. No doubt. Yelling at him. Why? What had happened?

"Wake up, dammit!"

Mark opened his eyes, blinked against the bright sun breaking through branches high above him. Then Alec's face appeared, cutting the light off, and he could see more clearly.

"It's about time," the old bear said through an exaggerated sigh. "I was starting to panic, kid."

That was when Mark was hit with the bolt of pain in his head – it had just been slower to wake than he had. The pain raged inside his skull, felt as big as his brain. He groaned and put his hands on his forehead, touched the slickness of drying blood.

"Ow," was all he could say before he groaned again.

"Yeah, you took quite the hit when we crashed. You're lucky to be alive. Lucky to have a guardian angel like me to save your hide."

Mark thought it might kill him, but he had to do it. Bracing for the agony, he sat up. He blinked back the spots in his vision and waited for the pain in his head and body to subside. Then he looked around.

They were sitting in a clearing surrounded by trees. Gnarled roots wove their way through pine needles and fallen leaves. About a hundred feet away, the wreckage of the Berg lay cradled between two giant oaks almost as if it had grown there like some sort of giant metal flower. Twisted and bent, it smouldered and smoked, though there was no sign of fire.

"What happened?" Mark asked, still disorientated.

"You don't remember?"

"Well, not since whatever it was smacked me in the head."

Alec threw his hands up in the air. "Not much to it. We crashed and I dragged your butt out here. Then I sat here and watched you roll around like you were having a bad dream. Memories again?"

All Mark could do was nod. He didn't want to think about it.

"I rummaged around in the Berg as much as I could," Alec said, changing the subject. Mark appreciated him not digging any further. "But the smoke from the engines got to be too much. Once you can walk around without going eyeball up, I want to search some more. I'll find out who these people are – and why they did what they did – if it's the last thing I do."

"Okay," Mark answered. Then a thought hit him, followed by a surge of alarm. "What about that virus stuff we saw? What if the containers and darts were broken and it's all over the place now?"

Alec held a hand out and patted Mark's chest. "I know, I know. Don't worry. Had to go through that hatch room to get out and saw the boxes – still sealed and safe."

"Well . . . how does a virus work? I mean . . . is there a chance we caught it? Would we be able to tell?" He didn't like the uncertainty. "What kind of virus do you think it is, anyway?"

Alec let out a small chuckle. "Son, those are a lot of good questions that I don't have answers to. We'll just have to ask our expert when we get back. Maybe Lana's heard of that strain before. But my guess is unless you get a bad case of the sniffles, I wouldn't worry too much about it. Remember, it knocked the others out immediately and you're still standing."

The words from the box flashed through Mark's head and he tried to relax. *Highly Contagious.* "I'll keep that in mind," he said warily. "How far from the settlement do you think we flew?"

"No idea. Might be a pretty piece gettin' back, but not too bad."

Mark lay back down on the ground and closed his eyes, put his arm over them. "Just give me a few minutes. Then I think we should search the ship. Who knows what we might find."

"You got it."

Half an hour later, Mark was back inside the Berg, kicking through debris, only now he was walking on a wall instead of the grated floor.

The Berg being on its side was disorientating – it played tricks on his mind and upset his already queasy stomach and throbbing head – but he was as determined as Alec to find something to tell them who the Berg belonged to. They were obviously no longer safe in their little mountain abode.

The biggest score would've been the computer systems, but Alec had tried that route to no avail. They were shut down, dead. Though odds were that he and Alec would find a portable phone or workpad somewhere in the wreckage – and if they got lucky it wouldn't be broken. It had been an age since Mark had seen technology like that. After the flares struck they'd been left with only whatever they had that hadn't fried, and batteries only lasted so long. But if you had a Berg, chances were you probably had batteries, too.

A Berg. He was inside a Berg. It was all really starting to hit him how much his world had changed in just over a year. At one time, seeing a Berg had been as exciting as seeing a tree. And just yesterday he would've guessed he'd never see one again. Now here he was rummaging through one that he'd helped wreck, looking for secrets. It was exciting even though all he'd seen so far was garbage, clothes, broken ship parts and more garbage.

And then he struck gold. A fully functioning workpad. It was switched on; the bright display was what caught Mark's eye. It was lodged between a mattress and the bottom of a bunk in one of the small cabins. He turned it off as soon as he pulled it out – if the battery drained on the sucker, there'd be no way to recharge it.

He found Alec in a different cabin, leaning over a personal trunk, cursing as he tried to break into it.

"Hey, lookie what I got," Mark announced proudly, holding up the workpad for the man to see. "What about you?"

Alec had straightened, his eyes lighting up at the discovery. "I didn't find a damn thing and I'm just about fed up trying. Let's go and have a look-see at that."

"I'm worried about the battery running out," Mark said.

"Yeah, well, all the more reason to study it now, don't ya think?"

"Let's do it outside, then. I'm sick of this hunk of junk."

Mark and Alec huddled over the workpad together, sitting under the shade of a tree as the sun continued to trudge its way across the sky. Mark swore that time slowed down when that thing was up there, beating down on them with its abnormally powerful rays. He had to keep wiping the sweat off his hands as he controlled the screen functions of the workpad.

Workpad. It seemed anything but. Games, books, old news programmes that predated the sun flares. There was a personal journal that could provide a ton of interesting information if it had been updated recently. But there wasn't much work-related stuff on the device.

Until they finally found the mapping feature. It obviously wasn't functioning from the old GPS satellites – they'd all been destroyed in the radiation holocaust of the sun flares. But it seemed to have a link to a tracer on the Berg, maybe controlled by old-school radar or other short-wave technology. And there was a log of every trip the now ruined ship had taken.

"Look at that," Alec said, pointing to a spot on the map. Every line tracking the Berg's flights returned to it eventually. "That's obviously their headquarters or base or whatever you want to call it. And judging by the coordinates and what I know about this ridge of hills we call home, it can't be more than fifty or sixty miles away."

"Maybe it's an old military base," Mark offered.

Alec thought about it. "A bunker, maybe. Having something like that would make sense up in the mountains. And we're going there, boy. Sooner rather than later."

"Right now?" Mark knew his brain was still jumbled up from being hit during the crash, but surely the old man didn't want to hike all that way before going back to the settlement.

"No, not right now. We need to get home and sort out what happened there. See if Darnell's okay. And the others."

Mark's heart sank at the mention of Darnell. "You know what we saw on that Berg? The boxes of darts? There's no way those people went to all that trouble to do a flyby flu ambush."

"You're right. I hate it, but you're right, kid. I don't expect much good news upon our grand return. But we need to get our butts there all the same. So come on."

Alec stood up and Mark followed suit, slipping the workpad into the back of his pants. He'd rather return to the village than search for a bunker any day.

They set off, Mark's head still woozy and achy. But the further they went, and the more his pulse quickened, the better he felt. Trees and sun and bushes and roots, squirrels and bugs and snakes. The air was warm but fresh, smelling like sap and burnt toast, filling his lungs.

The Berg had taken them a lot further from home than they'd thought, and they ended up camping in the woods for two nights, resting just long enough to feel strong again. Small game hunted by Alec and his knife provided their only food. They finally got close to the settlement in the late afternoon of the third day after the Berg attack.

Mark and the old soldier were about a mile away from the village when the stench of death hit them like a fresh wave of unbearable heat.

10

The sun was just a few hours from setting when they arrived at the base of the hill below the outlying shacks and huts.

Mark had ripped a wide strip of cloth from the bottom of his shirt to wrap around his nose and mouth. He pressed his hand against it as they came up the last rise before the village. The smell was awful. He could taste it on his tongue – dank, rotten, mouldy – all the way to his stomach, as if he'd swallowed something that had begun to decompose. Fighting the urge to throw up, he took one step after another, breathlessly waiting to see what horrors lay in the aftermath of the attack.

Darnell.

Mark had no expectations there, had accepted, with a heavy heart, that his friend might be dead. But what about Trina? Lana? Misty and the Toad? Were they alive? Or sick from some crazy virus? He stopped when Alec reached a hand out and touched Mark's chest.

"Okay, listen to me," the old man said, his voice muffled

behind his own swath of fabric. "We need to set some things straight before we get up there. We can't let our emotions rule everything. No matter what we see, our number one priority has to be saving as many people as possible."

Mark nodded, then moved to resume walking, but Alec stopped him.

"Mark, I need to know we're on the same page here." Alec spoke with a stern scowl – a look that reminded Mark of an upset schoolteacher. "If we go up there and start hugging people and crying and attempting things that make no sense with people who have no chance – all because we're distraught . . . it'll just hurt more folks in the long run. You understand? We need to think long-term. And as selfish as it sounds, we need to protect ourselves first. You get me? Ourselves. Saving the most people means we can't help anybody if we're dead."

Mark looked him in the eyes and saw something rock hard in them. He knew Alec was right. With the workpad, the map and the things they knew about the people on the Berg, it was clear there was something bigger going on.

"Mark?" Alec said, snapping his fingers to get the boy's attention. "Talk to me, buddy."

"So what're you saying?" Mark asked him. "If people look sick – if those darts really made people sick – stay away from them?"

Alec took a step back, his face pinched with an expression Mark didn't quite get. "When you say it like that, it doesn't sound so brotherly, but you're dead-on. We can't risk getting sick, Mark. We don't know what we're going to find up there – what we're dealing with. I'm just saying that we need to be prepared . . . and if there's any doubt about someone . . ."

"Leave them behind to be eaten by animals," Mark said with a coldness that he hoped would hurt Alec.

The former soldier just shook his head. "We don't even know what to expect, boy. Let's just get up there and see what we see. Find our friends. But don't be stupid, that's all I'm saying. Don't get close to anyone, certainly don't touch anyone. Keep that cloth wrapped around your pretty little head. Do you understand?"

Mark did. At the very least, it made sense to keep a distance from the people shot with darts. *Highly Contagious.* The words went through his head again and he knew Alec was right. "I understand. I won't be stupid. I promise. I'll follow your lead."

A look of compassion came across Alec's face, something Mark hadn't seen often. There was true kindness in those eyes of his. "We've been through hell and back, kid. I know it. But it's toughened us up, right? We can do what it takes to live through one more challenge." He glanced up the path towards the village.

"Let's hope our friends are okay."

"Let's hope," Mark repeated. He tightened the cloth mask around his face.

Alec gave him a stiff nod – professional again – and started up the hill. Mark pulled himself together, swearing to put emotions aside for now, and followed.

They'd just crested the hill when the source of the horrific smell came clearly into view.

So many bodies.

On the very outskirts of the village, there was a large, simple wooden structure originally meant to provide cover in a rain-storm, then – when more solid buildings were built – to store things temporarily. It had three walls and an open front. A thatched roof had been layered with mud to keep the inside as dry as possible. Everyone called it the Leaner because, despite being pretty sturdy, it looked like it was tilting down the slope of the mountain.

Someone had made the decision to put the dead in the Leaner.

Mark was horrified. He shouldn't have been – he'd seen more dead people in the last year than a hundred morticians of the past would have seen in a lifetime. But it was shocking all the same.

There were at least twenty bodies, laid out side by side, filling the entire floor. Most of them had blood covering their faces – around the nose, mouth, eyes and ears. And judging from the colour of their skin and the smell, all of them had been dead for a day or two. A quick scan revealed that Darnell wasn't in the group. But Mark didn't dare allow himself to hope. He pressed the cloth tighter to his nose and mouth and forced himself to look away from the carnage. There'd be no way he could eat anytime in the near future.

It didn't seem to faze Alec quite as much. He was still staring at the bodies with a look more of frustration than disgust. Maybe he wanted to get in there, examine the bodies and try to figure out what was going on, but knew how foolish it would be.

"Let's get into town," Mark said. "Find our friends."

"Okay," was Alec's response.

The place was a ghost town. All dust and dry wood and hot air.

Not one person could be seen on the paths or in the alleys, but Mark kept catching glimpses of eyes peering out through windows and slats and cracks in the haphazard structures. He didn't know everyone in their camp – not by a long shot – but he was sure someone had to have recognised him by now.

"Hey!" Alec shouted, startling him. "It's Alec. Somebody come out here and tell us what's happened since we left!"

A voice responded, slightly muffled, coming from somewhere up ahead. "Everyone's been inside since the morning after that Berg came. The ones who helped the people who got shot . . . most of them got sick and died, too. Just took a little longer."

"It was the darts," Alec yelled in reply, making sure everyone within earshot could hear him. "It might be a virus. We got up in that Berg – crashed it about two days from here. We found a box of the darts they shot at us. They could very well have infected the people who got hit with . . . something."

There were people murmuring now and whispers coming from inside the shelters, but no one answered Alec.

He turned to Mark. "Let's be glad they were smart enough to hole up in their homes. If there *is* some kind of virus, maybe that kept the thing from spreading like wildfire. Who knows? If everyone's been inside and no one else is sick, it could've died out with those poor saps in the Leaner."

Mark gave him a doubtful look. "I sure hope you're right."

Footsteps cut Alec off before he could respond. They both turned to face the centre of the village just in time to see Trina run around a corner, towards them. She was dirty and sweaty, her expression frantic. But her eyes lit up at the sight of Mark, and he knew that his did, too. She looked healthy, which filled him with relief. She was sprinting towards him and showing no intention of slowing down until Alec stopped her.

He stepped between her and Mark, holding both hands out. Trina skidded to a stop.

"Okay, kids," Alec said. "Let's be careful before we go around hugging each other. Can't be too cautious."

Mark expected Trina to argue a little, but she nodded, sucking in deep breaths. "Okay. I was just . . . I'm just so glad to see you guys here. But hurry, I need to show you something. Come on!" She waved her arms at them, then turned and ran back the way she'd come.

Mark and Alec followed without hesitation, sprinting through the main alley of the town. Mark heard gasps and whispers and saw fingers pointing out of the closed quarters they passed. After several minutes, Trina finally stopped in front of a small shack that had been boarded up with three wooden slats nailed across the door.

From the outside.

Someone had been imprisoned.

And that someone was screaming.

11

The screams barely sounded human.

Trina jumped back a couple of steps when she reached the boarded-up shack, then turned to face Mark and Alec. Tears were leaking from her eyes, and as she stood there taking deep breaths, Mark thought he'd never seen someone look so incredibly sad. Even after all the end-of-the-world crap they'd been through.

"I know it's terrible," she said over the screams of the prisoner. Mark could tell it was a man or boy but had no idea whether it was someone he knew. The sounds were terrifying. "But he made us do it. Said he'd slit his wrists if we didn't. And it's just been getting worse and worse since. We don't know why he didn't just die like the others. But Lana made sure from the get-go that we were careful. She was worried that there was a chance something contagious was loose. As soon as more people started getting sick, she quarantined him. It happened fast."

Mark was stunned. He opened his mouth to ask a question but shut it. He thought he knew the answer.

Alec said it for him. "It's Darnell in there, isn't it?"

Trina nodded, and a fresh wave of tears poured down her face. Mark wanted nothing else but to hug her, hold her for the rest of the day and night. But all he had now was his words.

"It's okay, Trina. It's okay. You both did the right thing. Like Lana said, Darnell knew they might've infected him with something. We all need to be careful until we know whatever this thing is has stopped spreading."

Fresh screams erupted from the hut, seeping through the cracks. It sounded like Darnell was tearing his throat apart and Mark wanted nothing more than to cover his ears.

"My head!"

Mark turned sharply, eyeing the hut. It was the first time Darnell had used actual words. Mark couldn't help himself; he hurried over to a boarded-up window with a gap about two inches wide running across the middle.

"Mark!" Alec yelled. "Get back here!"

"It's fine!" Mark replied. "I'm not gonna touch anything."

"I won't be a bit happy if you catch some nasty disease. Not a bit." Mark tried to give him a reassuring look. "I just want to see my friend." He pressed the cloth tightly against his nose and raised his eyebrows dramatically at Alec.

The man grunted and looked away. But Trina was staring him down, obviously torn between stopping Mark and joining him.

"Just stay there," he called to her before she could make a move. His voice was muffled through the mask, but she heard him clearly enough. She gave a slight nod; then her gaze fell to the ground.

Mark faced the gap between the two boards of the window. The screaming had stopped inside, but he could hear Darnell whimpering softly now, moaning those same two words every few seconds.

"My head, my head, my head."

Mark took another step forward, then another. The slit was just a few inches from his face now. He cinched the strip of cloth behind his neck, making sure his mouth and nose were entirely covered. Then he leaned forwards and peeked in.

Broken beams of the fading sunlight arrowed across the dirt floor, but it was mostly dark. He saw Darnell's feet and legs in one spot of light, tucked up tightly to his body, but his face was hidden. He had his head buried in his arms, by the looks of it.

Still the whimpering and the muttering. And he was shivering from top to bottom, as if he were caught outside in a blizzard.

"Darnell?" Mark asked. "Hey . . . it's Mark. I know you've been put through the wringer, man. I'm . . . I'm really sorry. . . Hey, we got the suckers who did this to you. Crashed their Berg and everything."

His friend didn't respond, just lay there, half in shadow, shaking and moaning. Muttering those two words.

"My head, my head, my head."

Mark's insides plummeted to some dark place and he felt hollow inside. He'd seen so much of terror and death, but looking at his friend, suffering alone . . . it killed Mark. Especially because it was so pointless. Needless. Why would someone do this to others after all the hell that happened to the world? Weren't things bad enough?

A sudden rage came over him. Mark punched the rough wood of the shack, bloodying his knuckles. He hoped somebody paid for all this one day.

"Darnell?" Mark called again. He had to say something, make it better. "Maybe . . . maybe you're stronger than the others – that's why you haven't died. Just hang tough, man. Wait it out. You'll . . ." Empty words. That was what it felt like. As if he were lying to his friend.

"Anyway, the sergeant and I, Trina, Lana, whoever – we're gonna make it right, somehow. You just—"

Darnell's body suddenly stiffened, his legs shooting straight out and his arms going rigid at his sides. Another scream, worse than before, erupted from his ravaged throat – it came out

60

sounding like the roar of an enraged animal. Mark jumped back in surprise but quickly leaned in again, his eye as close as possible to the opening without touching it. Darnell had rolled out into the middle of the floor, his face now in full view under a shaft of sunlight as he shook and shook.

Blood covered his forehead, his cheeks, his chin, his neck. Matted his hair. It was seeping from his eyes and ears, dripping off his lips. The boy finally got control of his arms and pressed them against the sides of his head, twisting this way and that as if he were trying to screw the thing right off his neck. And the screams kept coming, broken up by the only two words he seemed to know.

"My head! My head! My head!"

"Darnell," Mark whispered, knowing there was no way he could talk to his friend now. And despite how guilty and sick it made him feel, Mark also knew he couldn't possibly go in there to try and help. It would be beyond stupid.

"My *heeeeeeaaaaaad*!" Darnell shouted in one long, drawn-out wail of such ferocity that Mark stepped back again. He didn't know if he could bear to look any more.

There was the sound of movement inside, the shuffling of feet. Then a loud thunk against the door. Then another. And another.

Thunk. Thunk. Thunk.

Mark closed his eyes. He knew what that horrible sound was. Trina was suddenly there, pulling him into her arms, squeezing him tightly as she shook with sobs. Alec protested but only half-heartedly. It was too late now.

There were a few more thunks, and then a last, long, piercing scream that ended in a wet, gurgly burst. After that, Mark heard Darnell slump to the floor with an exhale of breath.

He was ashamed of himself, but all Mark felt in that quiet moment was relief that the ordeal had finally ended. And that it hadn't been Trina.

12

Mark had never thought of Alec as a gentle man. Not even remotely. But when the soldier walked over and separated Mark from Trina, he did it with a warm look on his face. Then he spoke.

"I know we've been through a lot together." Alec flicked his eyes over at the shack where Darnell was. "But that might've been the worst yet, hearing what we just heard." The man paused for a moment before he continued. "We can't give up now, though. From day one we've been about living."

Mark nodded and looked at Trina.

She wiped a tear away, giving Alec a cold look. "I'm kinda sick of surviving. At least Darnell is done with this world."

In all the years Mark had known her, she had never sounded so angry.

"Don't talk like that," he said. "I know for a fact you don't mean that."

Her gaze swept to him and softened. "When will it end? We survive months of the sun beating the tar out of the planet, find a place where we can build shelter, find food. A few days ago we were laughing! And then guys come in a Berg and shoot us with darts and people die? What is this, some kind of joke? Is someone up there laughing at us, playing us like some kind of virtgame?"

Her voice cracked and she started crying again, covering her face with her hands as she sat down on the hard-packed earth, her legs crossed under her. Her shoulders shook with her silent sobs.

Mark looked at Alec, whose eyes narrowed back at him as if to say, *She's your friend – say something.*

"Trina?" Mark said quietly. He walked over and knelt behind her, then reached out and squeezed her shoulders. "I know – just when we thought things couldn't get any worse. I'm sorry." He knew better than to make things seem less terrible than they actually were. That was a pointless trick they'd all promised to stop a long time ago.

"But I promise we'll stay together on all this," he continued. "And we'll do everything we can not to catch whatever it was that killed Darnell and the others. But if we're going to do that . . ." He rubbed her back and looked up at Alec for help.

"Then we need to be vigilant," the man said. "We need to be cautious and smart and ruthless if it comes to that."

Mark knew it might be foolish to be touching Trina. But he didn't care. If Trina died, he seriously didn't know if he could keep going.

Trina dropped her hands from her face and looked at Alec. "Mark, stand up and walk away from me."

"Trina . . ."

"Do it. Now. Go and stand near Alec so I can see both of you."

Mark did as she asked. He rejoined the man about ten feet away and turned to see that any trace of the crying, helpless, I-want-to-quit Trina was gone, replaced with the firmly resolved woman Mark was used to seeing. She got to her feet and folded her arms.

"I've been really careful since you two got up on that Berg. The suits those jerks were wearing, the darts, how quickly the people who were shot collapsed and got sick . . . Even before Lana told us anything, it was obvious something was going on. The only person I've interacted with was Darnell, but he knew to keep his distance. He was the one who barricaded himself in that place and forced me to board it up."

She paused to take a breath and eyed each of them. "My point is that I don't think I'm sick. Especially since it acted so quickly on everyone who was."

"I can see that, but—" Alec began, but Trina cut him off.

"I'm not finished," she said with a sharp glare. "I know we need to be careful. I *could* be sick. I know we've touched, but let's try not to any more. Not until we're totally sure. And all three of us need to make new masks and to wash our hands and faces like crazy."

Mark liked that she was taking charge. "Sounds good to me."

"Absolutely," Alec agreed. "Now, where are the others? Lana, Misty, the Toad?"

Trina pointed in a few directions. "Everyone is holed up somewhere, keeping their distance. Just to be safe until no one shows any signs of sickness. Maybe another couple of days."

Sitting around for a day or two sounded like the worst idea possible to Mark. "I'll go nuts if we do that. We found a work-pad with a map of where that Berg came from. Let's gather supplies and get out of here – maybe we can learn something."

"Agreed," Alec chimed in. "We should get as far as we can from this place."

"Wait – what about Darnell?" Mark asked. Though he knew what they would say, it made him feel better to at least ask. "Should we bury him?"

Trina's and Alec's eyes said it all. They couldn't risk being anywhere close to his body.

"Take us to Lana and the others," Alec said to Trina. "Then we go."

As they searched the town for their friends, Mark worried about people trying to join them. But fear had struck deep, and no one dared venture out of their home. The village was eerily quiet, but he could feel the eyes following him down the alleys and paths. It didn't surprise him, the more he thought about it. The world had punished everyone enough – why should they risk bringing anything more upon themselves?

They collected Misty and the Toad from the second floor of a log cabin on the outskirts of town, across the village from the Leaner and its bodies. Trina wasn't sure where Lana would be. They found her about an hour after they set out, sleeping behind some bushes by the river. She was upset that they'd found her sleeping, but she'd worn herself out. As soon as Mark and Alec had boarded the Berg and disappeared in the woods, she'd taken charge. Quarantining people and getting the bodies in one place – she said they'd been sure to wear gloves and masks – and helping deliver food from house to house. No one in the settlement knew exactly what had happened, but Lana had insisted from the start that care needed to be taken in case they were dealing with something contagious.

"I'm not sick," she concluded as they readied to leave the stream and go back to the village. "It happened so quickly – and the ones who got sick afterward have already died. I think I'd have symptoms by now."

"How fast?" Mark asked her. "How fast did it take effect?"

"All but Darnell were dead within twelve hours," she replied. "They woke up and showed symptoms within two or three. I really think if anyone is still alive and symptom-free right now, they're clear."

Mark took in their group: The Toad, fidgeting nervously. Misty, looking at the ground. Alec and Lana, staring at each other intently in what appeared to be a silent conversation. And

Trina, looking at Mark. Her eyes said it all – they were going to live through this just like they'd lived through everything else.

They were back at the Shack an hour later, filling backpacks with as much food and supplies as they could carry. As they worked, they kept their distance from each other. Caution seemed to come naturally now. Mark washed his hands at least three times during the packing frenzy.

They had just finished up, each of them with a loaded pack on his or her back, when Misty groaned. Mark turned to agree with her – the packs *were* heavy – but when he saw her face, his stomach sank.

She was pale and leaning on a table with both hands. Mark was stunned – the last time he'd looked at her, she was fine. But then her legs gave out and she collapsed to one knee. She touched the side of her face, tentatively, almost as if she was worried about what she'd feel there.

"My . . . head hurts," she whispered.

13

"**E**veryone get out of here!" Lana yelled. "Out! Now!"

Mark was speechless. Everything in him wanted to do the opposite of what she'd just ordered. He wanted to help his friend.

"Get outside. Then we can talk!" Lana insisted. She pointed to the door.

"Go," Misty said weakly. "Do what she says."

Mark and Trina exchanged a look, but she only hesitated a second before marching out the door. Alec was right on her heels, then Lana.

Mark turned to leave but then noticed that the Toad hadn't moved.

"Hey . . . come on, man. Let's just go out there and talk about this. Misty, tell him."

"He's right, Toadie," she said. She'd slipped her backpack to the floor and sat down next to it. Mark couldn't believe how quickly she'd gone from totally fine to literally on the ground, too weak to stand. "Go and let me figure this thing out. Maybe

6 7

I just ate something weird." But Mark could tell she didn't believe that.

"We can't just keep abandoning people," the Toad said, glaring at Mark.

"Who cares what you do if it makes you end up dead!" Misty countered. "How would you feel if it was reversed? You'd want me to leave. Now go!" That seemed to drain a good chunk of her energy – she slumped and almost lay down.

"Come on," Mark said. "We're not abandoning her. We're just going outside to talk."

The Toad stomped out of the Shack, muttering under his breath the whole way. "This is all so messed up. Totally messed up."

Mark looked at Misty, but she was staring at the floor, taking long, deep breaths. "Sorry," was all he could get out. Then he joined the others.

They decided to give her one hour. They'd see what happened. See if she got better or worse.

Or if she stayed the same.

It was a maddening hour. Mark was unable to sit still. He paced outside the Shack, worried on so many levels. The thought that a virus might be slinking its way through his system . . . it was unbearable. And Trina's, too. He wanted to *know*. Now. It was so overwhelming that he found himself forgetting that Misty could very well have it and die soon.

"I think we need to readjust our outlook here," Lana said towards the end of their allotted time. Misty hadn't improved or deteriorated – she still lay on the floor in the Shack, breathing evenly. Not moving at all. Not speaking.

"What do you mean?" Mark asked. He was grateful the silence had been broken.

"Darnell and Misty prove that whatever this is doesn't necessarily take effect right away."

Alec spoke up. "I think we should use the time we have. We

6 8

should hike to that place on the map. And we need to do it as soon as possible." He lowered his voice and added, "I'm sorry, but we have to get out of here, and what better place to go than where we can learn what's going on? Whatever was in those darts caused this – we need to go where the darts came from. Maybe there's something – some medicine that can cure this sickness. Who knows?"

It all came out sounding a little cold. Harsh. But Mark couldn't disagree with him. He felt like he had to get away from here, if nothing else.

"We can't leave Misty," Trina said. But even her statement had no strength behind it.

"We don't have a choice," Alec countered.

Lana stood from where she'd been sitting against a wall and brushed off her pants. "We don't have to bear the guilt of this," she murmured. "Let's ask Misty. She deserves that. And we'll do whatever she decides."

Mark raised his eyebrows and looked around at the others, who were doing the same.

Lana took that as agreement and walked to the open door of the Shack. Without going in, she knocked on the frame and spoke in a loud voice. "Misty? How's it going in there?"

Mark was perched on the ground where he could see inside. Misty was on her back but slowly turned to look at them.

"You guys need to go," she said weakly. "Something is seriously wrong with my head. It feels like bugs are up there, eating away at my brain." She took several deep breaths, as if saying just that much had sapped her strength.

"But, honey, how can we leave you here?" Lana asked.

"Don't make me talk any more. Just go." Another deep breath. Mark could see the pain in her eyes.

Lana turned towards the others. "Misty says we need to go."

Mark knew they'd become hardened – they'd had to, to survive the world since the sun flares struck. But this was the first time they were faced with leaving someone who still seemed so alive. Misty's decision or not, he thought the guilt would eat away at him.

When he looked at Trina his resolve hardened. Still, he let Alec be the bad guy.

The former soldier had got to his feet and slung his backpack on to his shoulders. "The best way to honour Misty right now is to get moving and learn something that could end up helping."

Mark nodded and followed suit, cinching tight the straps of his pack. Trina hesitated, then stepped up to the doorway, faced Misty.

"Misty . . . ," she began, but no more words came.

"Go!" the girl shouted, almost making Trina stumble backwards. "Go before the things in my brain jump out and bite you. Go! *Go!*" She'd risen to rest on her elbows and screamed with such ferocity that Mark thought she might've hurt herself. Might have realised that she was about to face the horror that Darnell had gone through.

"Okay," Trina said sadly. "Okay."

The Toad was by far the closest friend to Misty, and he hadn't said a word. He just stood staring at the ground, tears in his eyes. But as Mark and the others prepared to leave, the stout man didn't move. Alec finally asked him what he was doing.

"I'm not going," the Toad said.

As soon as he said it, Mark realised he'd been expecting it. No surprise at all. He also knew that there'd be no changing the guy's mind. They'd be saying goodbye to two of their friends now.

Alec argued with him, as did Lana. Trina didn't bother, obviously having come to the same conclusion as Mark. And just as Mark had predicted, the Toad didn't budge.

"She's my best friend. I'm not leaving her."

"But she *wants* you to," Lana said. "She doesn't want you to stay here and potentially die with her. She wants you to live."

"I'm not leaving her," he repeated, and gave Lana a cold

stare. Misty said nothing from inside, either not hearing or too weak to respond.

"Fine," Lana said, not bothering to hide her annoyance. "Catch up with us if you change your mind."

Mark just wanted to leave. The situation had become unbearable. He took one last look at Misty through the doorway before moving on. She was curled up into a ball, speaking in an odd voice, though it was too low to make out what she was saying. But as they walked away, he was pretty sure that the girl had been singing.

She'd snapped, he thought. She'd definitely snapped.

14

They only made it about three miles before it got too dark to continue. And Mark was more than ready to stop, exhausted from the crazy day. Alec had to have known they couldn't go far, but staying in that village was not an option. They were finally gone from it all, in the thick trees and fresh air of the woods, which helped drain some of the tension and emotional ups and downs of those last couple of hours.

No one said much as they made a simple camp and ate a dinner of packaged food brought up from the Asheville factories. Lana insisted they keep their distance from each other, so Mark lay on his side, several feet from Trina, the two of them staring at each other, wishing they could cuddle, at least. Mark almost scooted over to her about a hundred times but stopped himself. He knew she wouldn't let him, anyway. They didn't say much, just held each other's gaze.

And Mark was sure she was thinking the same things he was. How their world had fallen apart once again. How they'd just lost three friends who'd survived the trek of horror they'd made – from the devastation that was New York City to the Appalachian Mountains. And of course she was wondering about the virus. Not a whole lot of happy thoughts.

Alec ignored everyone, studying the workpad they'd retrieved from the Berg. He'd made a rough copy of the map they'd found on it with a pencil and some paper, but he wanted to see if he could unearth anything else useful. He had his compass out, was making notes, and Lana was next to him, offering pointers.

Mark realised his eyelids were drooping. Trina smiled at him. He smiled back. Pathetic or not, at least they were smiles. He fell asleep, and then the memories came rushing in once again. Never letting him forget.

Someone is on their tail.

It's only been a couple of hours since it happened in the city above them. Mark has no idea what it was, but he assumes it was a bomb set by terrorists or an explosion from a gas leak. Something that burned.

The heat is unbearable. As are the screams. He and Trina have fled through the subtrans tunnels, finding abandoned off-shoots, going deeper and deeper. But people are everywhere, most of them crazy with terror. Bad things are happening all around – theft, harassment, worse. It's like the only people who escaped the catastrophe above them are hardened criminals.

Trina found a box of instafood, left behind by someone in the chaos. Mark is carrying it now, both of them having already switched into some kind of instinctual survival mode. But others obviously have, too, and every person they look at as they run seems to know that Mark and Trina have something they want. And maybe not just the food.

No matter how many twists and turns they take in the underground labyrinth of filthy, sweltering hot passages, they can't lose the man on their tail. He's big and fast and has become like a shadow. Yet every time Mark looks back at him, he seems to disappear into some nook or cranny.

They're running down a long hallway filled with water to their ankles, splashing with every step they take. Mark's mobile phone is providing the only light, and he dreads the moment it runs out of power. The thought of being in this place, alone and clueless as to where they should go, in complete *darkness*, terrifies him. Trina suddenly stops and grabs Mark's arm, pulls him through an opening to the right that he didn't see.

They're in a small room – looks to be an old storage closet from when this part of the system was still being used, back in the old subway days.

"Turn it off!" she says in a fierce whisper as she pulls him deeper into the room and stands behind him.

Mark shuts down his phone, pitching them into the darkness he was just worrying about. His first instinct is to panic and scream and wander blindly about. But it's a brief moment of insanity and it passes. He calms his breathing and is thankful he can feel the touch of Trina's hand on his back.

"There's no way he was close enough to see us come in here," she whispers in his ear from behind. "And he can't be quiet in that water. Let's wait him out."

Mark nods, then remembers she can't see him. "Okay," he says quietly. "But if he somehow finds his way in here, I'm done running. We're going to gang up and beat him down."

"Okay. We'll fight."

Trina squeezes his arms and leans into him. Despite the absurdity of feeling such a thing at that moment, in those circumstances, he flushes from top to bottom, tingles and goosebumps all over. If only this girl knew how much he likes her. He feels a twinge of guilt that on some deep level, he's thankful for whatever tragedy has occurred, because it's forced them together.

He hears a couple of splashes in the distance. Then a few more, obviously footsteps in the water of the small tunnel outside their room. Then a steady beat of them, getting louder as their pursuer – he assumes it's their pursuer – gets closer. Mark presses against Trina and the wall behind her, wishing they could somehow disappear into the brick.

A light flicks on to Mark's right, almost making him cry out in surprise. The approaching footsteps stop. Mark squints – his eyes have already grown used to the darkness – and tries to see the source of the light. It moves and shines about the room, then settles on Mark's eyes, blinding. He looks down. It has to be someone with a torch.

"Who are you?" Trina asks. She's whispering, but her voice sounds like it came out of a bullhorn because Mark is so nervous.

The torch moves again as someone crawls out of a hole in the wall and stands up. Mark can barely make out any details, but it looks to be a man. A filthy man, his hair a mess and his clothes tattered. Another man appears behind him, and then another. They all look the same – dirty and desperate and dangerous. Three of them.

"I think we'll be askin' the questions," the first stranger says. "We were here way before you, and we don't like visitors none too much. Why are people runnin' around here like cats anyway? What happened? You two don't look like the type that comes a-callin' for the likes of us."

Mark is scared to the core. Nothing even remotely like this has ever happened to him. He fumbles for words, feeling like he needs to answer, but Trina beats him to it.

"Look, use your head. We wouldn't be down here unless something horrible happened up there. In the city."

Mark finds his voice. "Haven't you noticed how hot it is? We think it was a bomb, a gas explosion, something."

The man shrugs. "You think we care? All I care about is my next meal. And . . . maybe something nice dropped in our laps today. A little surprise for me and the boys." He eyes Trina up and down.

"You won't touch her," Mark says, the look in the man's eyes filling him with the bravery he couldn't find a few minutes earlier. "We have some food – you can take that if you'll just leave us alone."

"We're not giving him our food!" Trina snaps.

Mark turns to face her and whispers, "Better than getting our throats slit."

He hears a clicking sound, then another. When he faces the men again, he sees the light glinting off silver blades.

"Something you should learn about us," one of the men says. "We don't do much negotiatin' around this neighbour-hood. We'll take the food and whatever else we want."

They start moving forward, and then a figure suddenly flashes in from the left, coming through the doorway from the passage outside. Mark barely takes a breath as he watches a short but violent burst of chaos happen right before his eyes. Bodies spinning and arms flailing and knives being tossed aside and punches and grunts. It's like some kind of superhero has entered the room, using speed and strength to beat the hell out of the three intruders. In less than a minute they're all lying on the floor, curled up, groaning and cursing. The torch has been tossed to the floor, shining on the boots of a very large man.

The one who's been following them.

"You can thank me later," he says in a deep, grinding voice. "My name is Alec. And I think we have a much bigger problem than these losers."

15

Mark woke up with a deep ache in his side. He'd been lying on a rock for hours, by the feel of it. He rolled on to his back with a groan and looked at the lightening sky through the branches overhead . . . and remembered the dream of his past as vividly as if it had been shown to him as a movie on a screen.

Alec had saved them that day, and countless times since. But Mark felt solid knowing that he'd returned the favour on more than one occasion. Their lives were as linked together as the rocks and earth of the mountain they'd just slept upon.

The others were up within a half hour. Alec made them all a quick breakfast using some eggs he'd rustled up at the Shack. They'd have to hunt soon; Mark was glad he didn't have to be the expert on that, although he'd done his share. As they sat and ate, still staying relatively quiet and doing their best to avoid touching each other or touching things that had been touched, Mark brooded. It made him sick that someone had ruined everything just as they were on the cusp of feeling somewhat normal.

"We ready to get marching?" Alec asked when all the food was gone.

"Yeah," Mark responded. Trina and Lana just nodded.

"That workpad was a godsend," Alec said. "With this map and compass, I'm pretty sure we'll get there, straight and true. And who knows what we'll find."

They headed out, through the half-burnt trees and over the freshly grown brush.

*   *   *

They walked all day, down the face of one mountain and up another. Mark kept wondering if they'd run into another camp or village – rumour had it that there were settlements through-out the Appalachians. It was the only place fit enough after the sun flares and the risen sea levels, the massive destruction of all the towns and cities and vegetation. Mark just hoped that one day it could all go back to normal. Maybe even during his lifetime.

They'd stopped for an afternoon break by a small stream, when Trina snapped her fingers and caught his attention. When he looked at her, she motioned with her head towards the woods. Then she got up and announced she had to use the bathroom. After she left, Mark waited two long minutes, then said he had to do the same.

They met up about a hundred yards away by a big oak tree. The air smelled fresher than it had in a long time, almost green and full of life.

"What's up?" he asked. They stood about five feet apart, following orders even though no one was around to watch.

"I'm sick of being like this," she replied. "Look at us. We've barely hugged since that Berg attacked the village. We both look and feel fine, so it seems kind of silly to stay apart."

Her words filled him with relief. Even though he knew the circumstances couldn't possibly be worse, he was glad to hear she still wanted to be close to him.

Mark smiled. "So . . . let's bag this lame quarantine crap." It seemed so silly when he said it like that.

"Even if we keep it a secret from Lana so she doesn't pitch a fit." She walked up to him, put her arms around his middle and kissed him. "Like I said, I think the game is pointless anyway. We're not showing any signs, so hopefully we're in the clear."

Mark couldn't have talked if he'd wanted to. He leaned down and kissed her, and this time the kiss was much longer.

They held hands until they got close to the camp, then separated. Based on the feelings pumping through Mark at the moment, he didn't know how long he could pretend. But for now he didn't want to deal with the wrath of Lana or Alec.

"I think we can be there the day after tomorrow," Alec announced when they returned. "Maybe not until the sun poops out, but we can get there. We'll rest up and then try to figure what to do the next morning."

"Sounds good," Mark said absently as he repacked his stuff. He was still kind of floating, at least temporarily relieved from all the crap.

"Then let's quit yappin' and let's get slappin'," Alec said.

The statement didn't make much sense to Mark, but he shrugged and looked at Trina. She had a smile on her face. He hoped the other two fell asleep really early tonight.

They had to resist the urge to hold hands again as they set off after the old grizzly bear and Lana.

That night, the camp was dark and quiet except for the sound of Alec snoring and the soft sighs of Trina's breath on Mark's chest. They'd waited until Alec and Lana zonked out, then scooted together and cuddled.

Mark looked up at the branches of the trees, finding a clear spot that revealed brilliant stars overhead. His mum had taught him the constellations when he was really young, and he'd passed the valuable information on to his little sister, Madison. The stories behind the constellations were his favourite part, and he loved sharing them. Especially since it was such a rarity to see the starry sky when you lived in a huge city like New York. Every trip out to the country was a huge treat. They'd spend hours pointing out the different myths and legends hanging far above them.

He spotted Orion, the belt brighter than he'd ever seen it before. Orion. That had been Madison's favourite constellation because it was so easy to find and had such a cool story behind it – the hunter and his sword, his dogs, all of them fighting a demonic bull. Mark embellished the tale a little more each time he'd told it. The thought brought a lump to his throat, and his eyes moistened. He missed Madison so much. So much. The darker part of him almost wanted to forget her because it hurt so deeply.

He heard the crack of breaking branches out in the woods.

His thoughts of his little sister evaporated as he bolted upright, practically shoving Trina off his chest before he could think about what he was doing. She muttered something, then rolled over on to her side, falling back into her obviously deep sleep just as another crack sounded from the forest.

He put a hand on her shoulder as he got to his knees and then scanned the area around them. It was way too dark to see anything out in the thick of trees, even with the moon- and starlight. But his hearing had sharpened considerably since power and artificial lights had mostly become a thing of his past. He calmed himself and concentrated. *Listened.* He knew it could be a deer, a squirrel, lots of things. But he hadn't survived a year of the sun-ravaged world by making assumptions.

There were more snapping of twigs and cracking of branches. Heavy and definitely two-footed.

He was just about to shout Alec's name when a shadow appeared in front of him, stepping out from behind a tree. There was the scratching sound of a match being lit right before it flared to life, revealing the man who held it.

The Toad.

"What . . .?" Mark said, relief like a bursting cloud in his chest. "Toad. Sheesh, man, you about scared me to death."

The Toad dropped to his knees and held the lit match closer to his face. He looked gaunt, and his eyes were moist and haunted.

"Are . . . you okay?" Mark asked, hoping his friend was just tired.

"I'm not," the Toad answered, his face quivering as if he were about to cry. "I'm not, Mark. I'm not okay at all. There are things living inside my skull."

16

Mark shook Trina awake and scrambled to his feet, pulling her up with him. The Toad was definitely sick, and he was standing just a few feet from their camp. They didn't know anything about this sickness, but that only made it scarier. Trina seemed disorientated, but Mark didn't relent, half dragging her to the other side of the dead coals of their fire from earlier that night.

"Alec!" he shouted. "Lana! Wake up!"

As if the two were still soldiers, they were on their feet in three seconds. But neither of them had noticed the visitor yet.

Mark didn't waste time explaining. "Toad. I'm glad you came, that you're safe. But . . . are you feeling sick?"

"Why?" Toad asked, still on his knees. His face was only a shadow. "Why did you leave me like that after all we've been through?"

Mark's heart was breaking. The question had no good answer. "I . . . I . . . we tried to get you to come with us."

Toad acted as if he hadn't heard. "I have things in my skull.

I need help getting them out of there. Before they eat my brain and start heading for my heart." He whimpered, a sound that seemed to Mark more like it would come from an injured dog than from a human.

"What symptoms are you feeling?" Lana asked. "What happened to Misty?"

Mark watched as the Toad raised his hands up and pressed them against the sides of his head. Even his silhouette was creepy doing such a thing.

"There . . . are . . . *things* in my head," he repeated slowly. Deliberately. His voice was laced with anger. "Of all the people on this forsaken planet, I thought my friends of over a year would be willing to help me get them out." He got to his feet and began to shout. "Get these things out of my head!"

"Just calm down there, Toad," Alec said, the threat clear in his voice.

Mark didn't want the situation to explode into something they'd all regret. "Toad, listen to me. We're going to help you however we can. But we need you to sit down and stop shouting. Screaming at us won't help."

The Toad didn't respond, but his figure seemed rigid. Mark could tell his hands were clenched into fists.

"Toad? We need you to sit down. And then tell us everything that's happened since we left the village."

The guy didn't move.

"Come on," Mark pushed. "We want to help. Just sit down and relax."

After a few seconds, Toad obeyed, collapsing to the ground in a heap, lying there like he'd been shot. Several moans escaped him as he shifted, rocking back and forth on his side.

Mark took a deep breath, feeling like the situation was back under some kind of control. He realised that he and Trina were standing right next to each other, but neither Alec nor Lana seemed to have noticed yet. Mark took a few steps forward, to the side of the fire pit, and sat down.

"That poor kid," he heard Alec mutter behind him, thankfully not loud enough for the Toad to hear. Sometimes the old man said exactly what he was thinking.

Thankfully, Lana's nursing instincts won out and she took the reins of the conversation.

"Okay," she began. "Toad. It seems like you're in a lot of pain. I'm really sorry about that. But if we're going to help you, we need to know some things. Are you feeling well enough to talk about it?"

The Toad continued rocking and moaning softly. But he answered. "I'll do my best, guys. I don't know how long the things in my head will let me do it, though. Better hurry."

"Good," Lana responded. "Good. Let's begin from the second we left you at the village. What did you do?"

"I sat at the door and talked to Misty," the Toad said in a tired voice. "What else would I do? She's my best friend – the best friend I've ever had. I don't care about anything else. How can anyone abandon their best friend?"

"Right. I understand that. I'm glad she had someone to be there with her."

"She needed me. I could tell when it got bad for her, so I went in and held her. Held her to my chest and hugged her and kissed her forehead. Like a baby. Like my baby. I've never felt so happy as when I held her, watching her die slowly in my arms."

Mark squirmed in his seat, sickened by the Toad's words. He hoped Lana was able to learn something about what was going on.

"How did she die?" Lana asked. "Did she have a lot of pain, like Darnell?"

"Yes. Yes, Lana. She had a lot of pain. She screamed and screamed until the things left her head and crawled into mine. Then we put her out of her misery."

The forest seemed to fall deathly silent at that last remark, and Mark's breath froze in his lungs. He sensed Alec moving behind him but Lana shushed him.

"*We?*" she repeated. "What do you mean, Toad? And what're you talking about when you say things crawled into your head?"

Their friend pressed his hands against his head. "How can you be so stupid? How many times do I have to tell you? We! Me and the things in my head! I don't know what they are! Do you hear me? I . . . don't . . . know . . . what they are! You stupid, stupid kid!"

A wail escaped from his mouth, inhuman and piercingly loud, rising in pitch and volume. Mark jumped to his feet and took a couple of steps backward. It seemed as if the trees shook with the sound exploding from the Toad and every last creature within a mile fled to safety. There was only that one awful noise.

"Toad!" Lana yelled at him, but the word was lost in the shrieking.

The Toad was seesawing his head back and forth with his hands as he continued to scream. Mark looked at his friends even though he couldn't really see their faces – he had no idea what to do, and neither did Lana, evidently.

"That's it," he barely heard Alec say as the man moved forwards and past Mark, bumping him along the way. Mark stumbled, then got his balance, wondering what the former soldier had planned.

Alec walked straight at the Toad, then grabbed him by the shirt and yanked him to his feet, dragging him deeper into the woods. The screams didn't stop, just became more hitched and sporadic as he sucked in breaths and struggled to break free. Soon they were lost in the shadows of the trees, but Mark could hear the scraping of the Toad's body along the ground. The sound of his wailing faded as they got further away.

"What is that man up to?" Lana asked tightly.

"Alec!" Mark yelled after him. "Alec!"

There was no response, just the continued cries and shouts of the Toad. And then they ceased, abruptly. Cut off as if Alec had thrown him into a soundproof room and slammed the door shut.

"What the . . .?" Trina breathed behind Mark.

Soon there were footsteps marching back towards them at a determined pace. For a second Mark panicked, thinking the Toad had somehow broken free and hurt Alec, gone completely insane, and was coming back to finish off the others. Thirsting for blood.

But then Alec appeared out of the dark gloom of the trees, his face hidden in shadow. Mark could only imagine the sadness that must have been stamped in his features.

"I couldn't risk him doing anything crazy," the old man said, his voice surprisingly shaky. "I couldn't. Not if this has something to do with a virus. I . . . I need to go and wash myself in the stream."

He spread out his hands before him, looking at them for a long moment. Then he marched off towards the brook nearby. Mark thought he heard him sniffle just before he vanished back into the trees.

17

After all that, they were supposed to go back to sleep. Dawn was still hours away.

No one said a word after Alec had done . . . whatever he'd done . . . to the Toad. Mark thought he might explode, so confused was he by what had transpired over the last half an hour or so. He *wanted* to talk. But Trina turned away from him when he faced her. She slumped to the ground and curled up with a blanket, stifling some sobs. It broke Mark's heart – they'd gone several months without tears, and now it was happening all over again.

She was an enigma to him. From the beginning she'd been stronger, tougher and braver than he ever was. At first it had embarrassed and shamed him, but he loved it in her so much that he got over it. Yet she also wore her emotions on her sleeve and wasn't scared at all to let them all out in a good cry.

Lana went about her business silently, eventually lying down next to a tree on the outskirts of their small camp. Mark tried to settle into a comfortable position himself, but he was

87

wide awake. Alec finally returned. No one had anything to say, and the sounds of the forest slowly came back to Mark's awareness: insects and a soft breeze through the trees. But his thoughts still spun wildly.

What had just happened? What had Alec done to the Toad? Could it really be what Mark thought? Had it been painful? How in the world could things be so messed up?

At least he had the small blessing of a dreamless sleep after he finally drifted off.

"This virus from the darts," Lana said the next morning as they all sat, zombie-like, around a crackling fire. "I think there's something wrong with it."

It was a strange statement. Mark looked up at her. He had been staring at the flames, going over the events of the night before, until she'd spoken, and he was suddenly back in the present.

Alec voiced his thoughts bluntly. "I think there's something wrong with most viruses."

Lana gave him a sharp glare. "Come on. You know what I mean. Can't you all see it?"

"See what?" Mark asked.

"That it seems to be affecting people differently?" Trina asked.

"Exactly," Lana responded, pointing at her as if she were proud. "The people who were hit by those darts died within hours. Then Darnell and the people who'd helped the ones who were shot took a couple of days to die. Their main symptom was intense pressure in their skulls – they acted like their heads were being squeezed in vices. Then there's Misty, who didn't have symptoms for several days."

Mark remembered the moment they'd left her all too well. "Yeah," he murmured. "She was singing the last time we saw her. Curled up in a ball on the ground. She said her head hurt."

"There was just something different about her," Lana pointed out. "You weren't there when Darnell first got sick. He didn't die as fast as the others, but he started acting strangely really quickly. Misty seemed fine up until her head started hurting. But something was off up here with both of them." She tapped on her temple several times.

"And we all saw the Toad last night," Alec added. "Who knows when he got it – if he had it as long as Misty, or just got it from being with her when she died – but he was crazy like mad cow disease."

"Show some respect," Trina snapped at him.

Mark expected Alec to retaliate or defend himself, but he appeared humbled by the rebuke. "I'm sorry, Trina. Really I am. But Lana and I are just trying to assess our situation as best we can. Figure things out. And the Toad was obviously not lucid last night."

Trina didn't back down. "So you killed him."

"That's not fair," Alec said coolly. "If Misty died that quickly after her symptoms hit, it's fair to say that the Toad was going to die also. He was a threat to all of us, but he was also a friend. I did him a mercy and hopefully bought *us* another day or two."

"Unless you caught something from him," Lana said tonelessly.

"I was careful. And I immediately scrubbed myself clean."

"Seems pointless," Mark said. He was sinking further into the doldrums with every second. "Maybe we all have it and it just takes longer to kill you depending on your immune system."

Alec shifted up on to his knees. "We've strayed from Lana's point. There's something wrong with this virus. It's not consistent. I'm not a scientist, but could it be mutating or something? Changing as it jumps from one person to the next?"

Lana nodded. "Mutating, adapting, strengthening – who knows. But something. And it seems to take longer to kill you as it spreads, which – contrary to what you'd assume – actually means the virus is more effectively spreading. You and Mark weren't there, but you should've seen how quickly those first victims went. Nothing like Misty. It was bloody and brutal and awful for an hour or two, but then it was over. They convulsed and bled, which only helped it to spread to more human incubators."

Mark was glad he'd missed it. But considering what he'd seen Darnell go through at the end, those people might've been lucky that it had happened so fast. With way too much clarity, Mark recalled the sound of the boy beating his skull against the inside of the door.

"It has something to do with their heads," Trina murmured.

Everyone looked at her. She'd just voiced something obvious, but vital.

"It definitely had something to do with their heads," Mark chimed in. "They all had massive pain. And loss of sanity. Darnell was hallucinating – plain crazy. And then Misty. And the Toad . . ."

Trina posed a question. "Maybe they shot people with different things – how do we know it all started the same?"

Mark shook his head. "I went through the boxes on the Berg," he said. "They all seemed to have the same identification number."

Alec stood up. "Well, if it *is* mutating and if any of us have caught it, let's hope it gives us a week or two before we lose our wits. Come on. Let's get moving."

"Nice," Trina muttered as she got to her feet.

A few minutes later, they were on the march again.

Sometime in the middle of the afternoon they came within sight of another settlement. It was off the path Alec had scrawled on his makeshift map, but Mark spotted several wooden structures through the trees, big ones. His heart lifted at the idea of seeing large groups of people again.

"Should we go over there?" Lana asked.

Alec seemed to be weighing the pros and cons before he answered. "Hmm. I don't know. I'm eager to keep moving and follow our map. We don't know anything about these people."

"But maybe we should," Mark argued. "They might actually know something about the bunker, headquarters, whatever we're calling the place the Berg came from."

Alec looked at him, obviously considering all their options.

"I think we should check it out," Trina said. "If nothing else, we can warn them about what's happened to us."

"Okay," Alec relented. "One hour."

The smell hit them when the wind shifted, just as they were approaching the first buildings, small huts made of logs with thatched roofs.

It was the same smell that had assaulted Mark and Alec when they'd approached their own village after chasing down the Berg and marching back. The smell of rotting flesh.

"Whoa!" Alec called out. "That's it. We're turning around right now."

Even as he said it, it became clear where the stench was coming from. Further down the path several bodies had been stacked on top of each other. Then a figure appeared. A little girl was walking towards them from the direction of the dead. She must have been five or six years old, with matted dark hair and filthy clothes.

"Guys," Mark said. When the others looked at him, he nodded towards the approaching girl. She stopped about twenty feet from them. Her face was dirty and her expression sad, and she didn't say anything. Just looked at them with hollow eyes. The stench of rot hung in the air.

"Hey there," Trina called out. "Are you okay, sweetie? Where are your parents? Where are the others from your village? Are they . . ." She didn't need to finish – the stack of bodies spoke for itself.

The girl answered in a quiet voice and pointed out towards the woods behind Mark and the others.

"They all ran into the forest. They all ran away."

18

Mark didn't know what it was about her words that made him shiver, but they did, and he couldn't fight the urge to look over his shoulder towards where she was staring. There was nothing back there but the trees and the brush and the sunlight dappling the ground.

He turned to face the girl again. Trina walked towards her, which of course made Alec protest.

"You can't do this," he said, but even his gravelly rebuke didn't have any strength. It was one thing to leave adults behind, people who were able to fend for themselves. Maybe it was even one thing to put a teenager – almost an adult – out of his or her misery, like Alec had done to the Toad. But this was a child, and that made everything different. "At least try not to touch her, for all our sakes."

The girl flinched and took a few steps back when Trina got close to her.

"It's okay," Trina said, stopping. She got down on one knee. "We're friendly, I promise. We came from a village just like yours, where they had lots of kids. Do you have friends here?"

The girl nodded, then seemed to remember something. She shook her head sadly.

"They're gone now?" A nod.

Trina looked back at Mark, heartbreak in her eyes, then returned her attention to the girl.

"What's your name?" Trina asked. "Mine is Trina. Can you tell me yours?"

After a long pause, the girl said, "Deedee."

"Deedee, huh? I love that name. It's really cute."

"My brother's name is Ricky."

It seemed such a childlike thing to say, and for some reason it brought memories of Madison slamming to the forefront of Mark's thoughts. His heart ached. He wished this girl was his little sister. And as always, he tried his hardest to keep his mind from wandering down the darkest road of all. Imagining what might've happened to her when the sun flares struck.

"Where is Ricky?" Trina asked.

Deedee shrugged. "I don't know. He went with the others. Into the forest."

"With your mum and dad?"

The girl shook her head. "No. They got hit by the arrows from the sky. Both of them. They died real nasty." Tears welled up until they spilled over and washed down her dirty cheeks.

"I'm so sorry to hear that, sweetheart," Trina said, her voice full of the deepest sincerity. Mark was sure he'd never liked her as much as he did right then. "Some of our friends were . . . hurt by the same people. Nasty, like you said. I'm so, so sorry."

Deedee was crying but also rocking back and forth on her heels, something that again reminded Mark of Madison. "It's okay," she said, so sweetly that Mark didn't know how much more of this he could take. "I know it wasn't your fault. It was the bad men's fault. The ones who wear the funny green suits."

Mark pictured that day, remembered looking up at the same people on the Berg. Or friends of the same people. Who knew how many Bergs were out there, flying around with dart guns full of who knew what. Why, though? Why?

Trina kept digging, as tenderly as she could, for more information. "Why did the others leave? Why didn't you go with them?"

Deedee held up her right arm, the hand balled into a fist. She pulled up her ratty sleeve to reveal a circular wound near her shoulder, scabbed over but looking poorly cared for. She didn't say anything, just held the arm straight out for everyone to inspect.

Mark took in a quick breath. "Looks like she was shot by a dart!"

"I'm sorry about your owie," Trina said, shooting a glare at Mark. "But . . . do you know why they left? Where they went? Why didn't you go with them?"

The girl jabbed her arm out again, pointing at the wound. Mark exchanged a look with Alec and Lana, sure that they understood the deep significance as much as he did. Why was this girl okay if she'd been shot?

"I really am sorry they hurt you," Trina said. "Looks like you're one lucky girl. Do you not want to answer any more questions? It's okay if you don't."

Deedee groaned in frustration and pointed at her wound once again. "This is why! This is why they left me here! They're bad, like the green men."

"I'm really sorry, sweetie."

Mark couldn't hold it in any more. "I'll tell you what happened. They probably thought she was sick from the dart and left without her." The words sounded wrong, though. How could anyone actually do that? To a little kid?

"Is that what happened?" Trina asked her. "They left you because they thought you might be sick? Like the others?"

Deedee nodded and fresh tears streamed down her cheeks.

Trina stood up and turned to face Alec.

The soldier held a hand up. "I'll stop you before you even

95

start. I may look like I was chewed up and spit out by the meanest beast in the jungle, but I'm not heartless. We'll take the girl with us."

Trina nodded and genuinely smiled for the first time that day.

"It probably *is* true that she's infected," Lana pointed out. "It's just taking longer to manifest itself."

"Odds are we're all sick," Alec grumbled as he readjusted the straps of his backpack.

"We'll be careful with her," Trina said. "We just need to keep our hands clean and away from our nose and mouth. Wear a mask as much as possible. But I'm not letting this sweet thing out of my sight until . . ." She didn't finish, and Mark was glad for that.

"It's another mouth to feed," Alec said, "but I guess she won't eat much." He smiled to show he was joking – something that didn't happen very often. "Part of me wants to ransack this place to look for supplies, food, but whatever is taking everyone down is probably camped up nice and cosy on every dirty inch of the place. Let's get out of here."

Trina motioned to Deedee to come along, and surprisingly, she did so without any argument. Alec headed back the way they'd come, to the path he'd so carefully mapped out. As they walked, Mark tried not to think about the fact that they were going exactly where Deedee had pointed earlier.

They didn't run into anyone – living or dead – for the next few hours, and Mark almost forgot about the people who had left Deedee behind. The girl stayed quiet through the journey, never complaining as they maintained a brisk pace, up and down the rocky terrain and then up and down all over again. Trina stayed by her side, wearing a cloth over her face.

Deedee eagerly devoured her dinner, probably the first decent meal she'd had in a while. Then they hiked for another hour or two before setting up camp. Alec announced that, according to his calculations, they only had one full day of travelling to go.

Mark watched Trina with Deedee. She took such good care of the little girl – making her a spot to sleep, helping her wash up in the stream, telling her a story as darkness settled on the wooded valley.

Mark watched, and hoped for a day when life could be good and safe again. When the horrors might end and boredom became their worst problem. When a girl like Deedee could run around and laugh like kids were supposed to.

He settled down next to Trina and the little girl, thinking about the past, and drifted off to sleep, only for the darker memories to come and stamp out his foolish hopes.

19

I t takes Mark only ten minutes or so to realise that Alec is the person he wants to be close to until they're back safe and sound in their homes. Not only did he disarm three men and put them out of commission in less than thirty seconds, he is also a former soldier who wastes no time taking charge and telling them how it is.

"Sometimes you can believe the rumours and chitchat," the older man says as they slosh through the water of the passageway outside the storage closet where they encountered the armed thugs. "Most times it's some lame-brained numbskull trying to impress a lady or two. But once the majority of the rumours are saying the same thing, you better perk up and pay attention. You're probably wondering what in the hell I'm trying to say here."

Mark looks over at Trina – he can barely see her face in the dim glow from the torch that Alec is holding in front of them. She gives him a look that says, *Who* is *this guy?* She's carrying the box of food she found earlier. It's like her security blanket or something – she won't let anyone else touch it. Not yet.

"Yeah, we're wondering," Mark finally replies.

Alec stops and whirls around, quick as a striking snake. At first Mark thinks his answer came out wrong, sarcastically, and the man might punch his lights out. But instead the tough old man just holds up a finger.

"We have one hour, tops, to get out of these rat tunnels. You hear me? One hour." He turns back around and starts marching again.

"Wait, what?" Mark asks as they hurry to keep pace. "What do you mean? Why? Isn't it a bad idea to go up there until . . . well, I don't know."

"Sun flares."

He says the two words like he needs to say nothing else. Like the others should instantly know everything going on in his mind.

"Sun flares?" Trina repeats. "That's what you think happened up there?"

"Pretty sure, my lovely lady. Pretty sure."

Mark's bad feelings about it all have escalated exponentially upon the news. If it's not an isolated incident, if it's truly something as global as sun flares, then the little hope he held out for his family is gone. "How do you know?"

He hears the quaver in his voice. Alec answers with no shaking in his whatsoever.

"Because there were too many people from too many places describing the same thing before I got away from the masses. And supposedly the news agencies put out warnings right before they struck. It's sun flares, all right. Extreme heat and radiation. Double whammy. It was something the world thought it was trained and prepared for. The world was wrong, in my humble judgment."

All three of them fall silent. Alec keeps moving, Mark and Trina keep following. They turn corners, enter different tunnels, steer clear of other people when they get close. All the while, Mark's heart is sinking further and further into a dark place. He doesn't know how to handle something like this. He refuses to believe his family is gone and swears to himself that he won't rest until he finds them safe and sound. Finally Alec stops in the middle of a long passageway that looks much like all the others.

"I have a few other friends in here," he says. "Left them to go and look for food, learn some things. I've worked with Lana for years and years. We were contractors for the defence department – she's a former soldier, like me. Army nurse. The others are strays we picked up. You two max us out – we can't take one more or we'll never make it."

"Make it where?" Mark asks.

"To the world above," Alec replies, the last thing Mark expected to hear. "Back into the city, as hellacious as it may be. As long as we stay inside for a while, we should be okay. But we have to get up there before the waters flood this place and kill us all."

Mark woke up and rolled on to his side, his eyes fully open, his breathing heavy. And he hadn't even dreamed about the bad part. He didn't want to remember any of it. He didn't want to relive the terror of that day.

Please, he thought. *Please, no. Please. Not tonight. I can't.*

He didn't even know who he was talking to. Was he talking to his own brain? Maybe he'd caught the disease from the Toad and was beginning to go crazy.

He flopped on to his back, stared up at the branches and the stars above. There wasn't even the slightest hint of dawn creeping into the sky. It was dark, dark, dark. He wanted it to be morning, wanted to be done with the threat of dreams for at least a few hours. Maybe he could keep himself awake somehow. He sat up, looked around. But he couldn't see much, only the outlines of trees and the shapes of his friends lying around him on the ground.

He considered waking up Trina. She'd understand that he needed company. He wouldn't even have to tell her about his dream. But she seemed so peaceful at the moment, breathing softly. With a quiet groan to himself he gave up on the idea, knowing he'd feel too guilty about depriving her of valuable sleep. Not only did they have a lot of walking to do the next day, she had the added burden of looking after little Deedee.

Mark flopped back down, shifted around until he got comfortable. He didn't want to dream. The raging waters, the screams of people drowning. The frantic, unbearable fear of fleeing it all. Even awake he could see that room beneath New York City where they'd first met Lana and the others. Alec's weathered face as he explained to them that after surviving such massive sun flares, their biggest and most immediate worry now was the surge of a tsunami. The flares must have been devastating, inflicting catastrophic damage worldwide and unleashing the heat of hell itself.

Which meant a quick melting of the polar ice caps. Which meant sea levels rising at an alarming and apocalyptic rate. Which meant that the island of Manhattan would be a dozen feet underwater within a few hours. He explained all this to them while they huddled in a room far underground, where the water would seek out and drown everything in its path.

Back in the present, these thoughts tormented Mark for at least another hour – and he knew if he dreamed it would only get worse. He was scared of being scared.

He drifted off despite his efforts. Sleep came over him like cold, crashing waves.

20

The Lincoln Building, one of the tallest, newest, grandest buildings in New York. One of the few with direct access to the subtrans system.

That's where Alec keeps telling them they need to go. He says he has a full subtrans map saved on his phone, but he's visibly worried about them being able to make it in time. Mark was able to see, even in the dim light before they headed out, that Alec has major doubts – which is contrary to the overall persona of the hardened man he seems to be. Mark would've guessed the man could be caged with a dozen hungry lions and he'd still only have a smirk on his face as he decided which one to kill first.

The Lincoln Building, Mark tells himself. *Get there; then you can go and find your family.*

They are all running down one of the countless seemingly endless tunnels below the city. Alec in the lead, then the woman he said he's had the pleasure of working with for a dozen years: Lana. A boy about Mark's age named Darnell is next, then a girl named Misty – another teenager, but older, maybe eighteen – then a dude, also older than Mark, but short and loaded with muscles. Misty refers to him as the Toad, and he actually seems to like the moniker. Mark and Trina are next, with a boy named Baxter bringing up the rear. Baxter is the youngest of them all, maybe thirteen, but Mark can tell he's a tough little sucker. Insisted on being in the back, said he wanted to protect everyone from surprise attacks.

As they run, Mark hopes he has enough time left in life to become friends with the kid.

"I hope he knows what he's doing," Trina says quietly next to him. They are jogging along side by side and Mark finds himself having the ridiculous thought that it'd be nice if they were on a beach, the sun just setting on the water. He thanks the powers that be that Trina can't read his mind.

"He does," Mark insists. He also doesn't want her to know how he's almost trembling with fear of what might happen at any second, which is making it hard to run. Almost seventeen years of life, and he never knew what a coward he was.

"Tsunami." Trina says the word like it's the most evil thing to ever come out of her mouth. "We're in the middle of the subtrans system in New York City and that's supposed to be our biggest worry. A tsunami?"

"We're underground," Mark replies. "And our city is right by the ocean, in case you forgot. Water drains downward. Ya know, gravity and all that."

He can sense her giving him a nasty look, and he knows he deserves it. His nerves must be finally getting to him, to be such a smart aleck. He tries to save himself the only way he knows how – honesty.

"Sorry," he mutters. The run is getting to him and he's breathing heavily. "I'm just scared out of my mind. I'm really sorry."

"It's okay. I didn't really mean it like a question. I'm just . . . I don't know. Saying how crazy this is I guess. Sun flares and a tsunami. A few hours ago those words weren't even on my radar. Not by a long shot."

"It sucks," is the best Mark can come up with. He just doesn't want to talk about it any more – the more they do, the more his insides twist with distress and worry.

Alec slows down when they reach the end of the latest tunnel. He stops and turns to face them. Everyone is breathing heavily and Mark's entire body is soaked with sweat.

"We have to go through one of the newer subtrans sections now," Alec says. "There's bound to be people out there, and who knows what kind of mood they might be in. Sometimes folks get downright nasty when they think the world's about to end."

Now that their little group is calming their breathing a bit, Mark can hear faint sounds coming from behind their leader. The hum of a crowd, people talking and bustling about. A few disturbing noises mixed in as well: distant screams, crying and wailing. The isolation of their dank little storage room doesn't seem so bad now.

Lana picks up the line of conversation. "We just need to get through it. Walk fast, but don't look like you know where you're going. We can't afford to carry anything – empty your arms and pockets or we might get attacked. We'll just have to hope we can find things in the Lincoln Building."

A few of them have been carrying packets of the food Trina found earlier. They dump them on the ground. The act seems to suck some of the life out of Trina.

"We'll go through this door," Alec says as he looks at his phone – the battery has to be close to dying. "And then jump on to the tracks. If we stay off the concourse maybe we'll come across fewer people. Straight for about half a mile; then we can enter the doors of the stairwell for the Lincoln Building. That sucker goes all the way up to the ninetieth floor. It's our only shot."

Mark takes a quick look around and sees that the others are

fidgety and nervous. The Toad is hopping up and down, which seems ridiculously appropriate.

"Let's go," Alec says. "Stay close together, tight. Defend each other to the death."

Trina groans at that, and Mark really wishes the man hadn't said it.

"Go, go, go!" Lana shouts, whether from frustration or to psych them up, Mark may never know.

Alec opens the door and walks through. The others follow as a blast of heat surges past and washes over them. Mark feels as if the oxygen is being burned out of his chest; he fights for each breath until he gets used to it.

He enters the larger tunnel on Trina's heels. They're on a narrow ledge a few feet above the actual tracks for the trains – Alec and Lana have already jumped down, are reaching up to help the others. One by one they take hands, leap off the edge, land with a thump and a jolt to the legs. Mark looks up. Light is spilling in from the stairs that eventually lead up to the devastated world above them. He studies the people milling about on the landing across from where he stands, every one of them with their gaze locked on the new arrivals.

What Mark sees up there makes his heart want to stop.

The place is packed. At least half of the crowd is wounded in some way. Cuts and slashes. Terrible burns. There are people lying on the ground screaming. Children of all ages, many of them hurt, too. That's what breaks Mark inside the most. Two men are fighting brutally in one spot, pounding each other, scratching and clawing. No one even makes a move to break them up. There's a lady slumped on the edge of the landing and her face is gone, replaced by melted skin and blood. Mark feels as if he's been given a glimpse into hell.

"Walk," Alec orders once everyone is down on the tracks.

They do, staying as close together as possible. Mark has Trina on his left, the boy named Baxter on his right. The kid looks terrified and Mark wants to say something to help him feel better but can't find the words. They'd be empty anyway. Alec and Lana are right in front of Mark, their body language daring anyone to be stupid enough to confront them.

They've made it halfway across the main section of the concourse when two men and a lady jump down onto the tracks and stand directly in their path, forcing them to stop. The strangers are dirty but look unhurt. Physically, anyway. Their eyes are haunted by things they've seen.

"And where do you think you're going?" the woman asks.

"Yeah," one of her friends adds. "You seem mighty important. You know about some place to go that we don't?"

The other man steps up closer to Alec. "Not sure if you've noticed or not, but the sun decided to belch all over us. People are dead, sir. Lots of people. And I don't like how you think you can just march through here and pretend everything's okay."

A few other people are jumping down from the landing, congregating behind the first three strangers. Blocking their path.

"Let's see if they have any food!" someone shouts.

Alec rears back and punches the man standing in front of him. The guy's head snaps back and blood sprays from his nose; he collapses to the ground. It's so sudden and shocking that no one moves for a second. Then several people charge into Mark's group, screaming and shouting.

Chaos ensues. Fists are flying, feet kicking, fingers grasping hair and yanking. Mark is punched in the face just as he sees Trina yanked away by a man. Rage explodes inside of Mark and he fights back at whoever hit him, swinging his arms wildly until he connects twice. Then he pushes the guy away to see a man on top of Trina – he's struggling with her on the ground, working to get control of her arms as she desperately tries to fight him off.

Mark flies in, throwing his body at the man. They tumble off Trina and roll on to the ground. The man punches Mark and Mark punches back, barely feeling where he's been hit.

Then they're in a tangle, squirming, arms flailing, kicking. Mark breaks free, crawls away, checks to see that Trina is okay. She's got up, runs over and kicks at her attacker's face but slips when she does it, lands on her back. The stranger goes after her, but Mark's on him again, diving shoulder-first into his gut. The man grunts and curls into a ball as Mark climbs to his feet, grabs Trina by the hand. They both push out of the crowd, then look to see what's going on with the others.

Everyone's still fighting, but at least no one else has joined in from the landing above. Mark sees the Toad punch a man; Alec and Lana are fighting a man and a woman off Misty and Baxter. Two other people run away from their group. It might almost be over.

That's when it happens.

There's a rumbling sound that is low at first but begins to build in volume. The tunnel trembles slightly. All the fighting stops immediately; people get to their feet, look around. Mark's doing the same, trying to find the source of the noise. He's still holding Trina's hand.

"What is that?" she shouts.

Mark shakes his head, keeps sweeping his gaze around the tunnel. The floor vibrates below his feet and the rumbling sound gets louder, becomes an outright roar. His eyes fall upon the stairs that lead up from the subtrans concourse just as the screams erupt – countless, countless screams and the blur of panicked movement in the crowd.

A monstrous wall of filthy water is pouring down the wide steps.

21

Mark woke up. Not with a scream or a shout, and he didn't bolt upright or gasp or anything as dramatic as that. He just opened his eyes, and realised right away that they were moist with tears and his face was wet. The sun had come up, shining brightly through the trees.

The wall of water.

He'd never, never forget what it had been like to see it rushing down those stairs like some kind of living beast. And the horror of watching it sweep away the first people at the bottom.

"Are you okay?" Trina. Great.

He quickly wiped at his face and turned towards her, hoping that somehow she didn't know he'd been bawling his eyes out while sleeping. But one glance at her killed that hope. She looked like a concerned parent.

"Um, hey," he murmured. He felt so awkward. "Good morning. How's it going?"

"Mark, I'm not an idiot. Tell me what's wrong."

He looked at her, trying to communicate with his eyes that

he didn't want to talk about it. Then he saw Deedee, leaning against a tree a few feet away, peeling the bark off a twig. Her face wasn't necessarily happy, but at least that look of utter gloom was gone. That was a start.

"Mark?"

He turned back to Trina. "I just . . . I had a bad dream."

"About what?"

"You know what."

She frowned. "But what part of it? It might help to talk about it."

"I don't think so." Mark sighed, then realised he wasn't being very nice. She was just trying to help him feel better. "It was right before the water rushed in at that concourse. When we fought off those wannabe gangsters. I woke up just as the bad part began." The bad part. Like everything before that was a picnic in the park with Grandma.

Trina's gaze fell to the ground. "I wish you could stop having those dreams. We made it, and that's all that matters. Somehow you need to let go of the past." An apologetic expression came over her face. "I mean, easier said than done. I guess I just *wish* you could let go of the past. That's all."

"I know, I know. Me too."

He reached out and patted her on the knee, which seemed stupid in that situation, but Alec and Lana were just returning from getting fresh water from the stream.

"How's she doing?" he asked Trina, shooting a glance at Deedee.

"Really well, I think. She hasn't opened up yet about much, but at least she seems comfortable around me. I can't imagine the terror that poor thing was going through after she was left behind."

That stirred up the anger once again inside Mark. "How could they? I mean . . . what kind of losers . . ."

Trina nodded. "Yeah . . . but I don't know. Desperate times and all that."

"Yeah, but she can't be more than four years old!" He was doing that combination of whispering and shouting at the same time. He didn't want Deedee to hear, but he couldn't help it. It made him so angry.

"I know," Trina said softly. "I know."

Lana stepped up to them, her eyes showing that she understood how he felt.

"We better get on the road," she said. "We'll figure things out."

The day dragged and dragged.

At first Mark was wary of the people from Deedee's village, still worried about the direction she'd pointed when they'd asked her where they went. If the girl had been right, that meant they were out here somewhere, doing who knew what. He had no real reason to fear them – they were just people like anyone else. Running from an attack, running from a disease. There was just something ominous about the way Deedee had spoken of them. And he could see so clearly in his mind her pointing at her wound with such an accusatory glare. It all unsettled him.

After a few hours of not seeing any sign of them, he relaxed into the drudgery of walking, walking and then more walking. Through the forest, crossing streams and pushing through the brush. Wondering if there was any purpose in going to this place they sought.

It was mid-afternoon and they'd stopped for a break. They were eating granola bars and drinking water from a nearby river. Mark thought constantly about how there was one thing they always had. Plenty of water sources. At least there was that.

"We're getting close," Alec said as he ate. "We might have to be more careful – they could have guards surrounding the place. I bet there's a lot of people who'd like to have a nice bunker or whatever it is as their new digs. I bet the place was packed with food for emergencies."

"We sure did have an emergency," Lana muttered. "Whoever these people are, they'd better have some good explanations."

Alec took another bite and pushed it to the side of his mouth. "That's the spirit."

"Do they not teach manners in the army?" Trina asked. "You know, it's just as easy to take a bite *after* you say something as right before it."

Alec chomped on his bar. "It is?" He croaked a laugh and little pieces of granola shot out. Which made him roar even harder. He choked out a cough, composed himself, then was laughing all over again.

It was such a rare sight to see Alec acting like this, Mark didn't know how to respond at first. But then he soaked it in, chuckling right along even though he'd forgotten what was funny in the first place. Trina had a smile on her face, and little Deedee was giggling heartily. The sound of it filled Mark up and washed away the doldrums.

"You'd think someone had farted, the way you're all getting on," Lana said with a deadpan look.

That sent everyone into an even bigger fit that went on for several minutes, re-sparked every time it began to die down by Alec making fart noises. Mark laughed until his face hurt and he tried his best to stop smiling, which made him laugh even harder.

Finally it did settle down, ending with one big sigh from the former soldier. Then he stood up.

"I feel like I could run twenty miles," he said. "Let's get moving."

As they headed off, Mark realised that the dream from the night before seemed like a distant memory again.

22

Alec and Lana were much more cautious during the next part of their journey, stopping every fifteen minutes or so to listen intently, looking for telltale signs of guards or traps, keeping to the cover of the trees whenever possible.

The sun was sinking, maybe two hours from fully setting, when Alec stopped and had everyone huddle around him. At some point it seemed like the two adults had decided to stop worrying about people keeping their distance from each other. They were all in a small clearing completely surrounded by thick oak trees and towering pines – older ones that hadn't been completely consumed by the sun flares – standing on dry, brittle undergrowth. The clearing was in a little valley between two midsized hills. Mark was still in a good mood and was curious about what the older man had planned.

"I've tried to do this as little as possible," Alec said, "but it's time to look at the workpad and make sure my scribbled map is still accurate. Let's hope my ageing brain hasn't failed us."

"Yes," Lana added. "Let's hope we're not in Canada or

Mexico by now."

"Very funny."

Alec powered on the device and pulled up the maps feature, finding the one that had the Berg's voyages documented, all the lines converging in one spot. He also retrieved his compass. While everyone else stayed quiet and observed, he spent a minute or so studying the workpad, running his finger this way and that, comparing it to his handwritten copy, pausing every once in a while to close his eyes and think. Mark thought he was probably retracing their path in his mind, trying to match it to what he was reading on the maps. Finally he stood up and turned in a full circle, looking up at the sun, then checking his compass.

"Yep," he grumbled. "Yep, yep."

Then he crouched back down and studied the maps for another full minute, making some small changes to the paper version. Mark was getting impatient, mainly worried that the man had concluded they were way off course. But his next words put that to rest.

"Oh, I'm good. Seriously, after all these years, you'd think I would stop amazing myself. But here I am, still doing it."

"Oh, brother," Lana moaned.

Alec tapped the map just to the left of the spot that marked the centre of the Berg routes on the workpad screen. "Unless I've got that virus eating my brain and don't know what I'm talking about, we're standing right here. Probably five miles from the place this Berg parks every night."

"Are you sure?" Trina asked.

"I know how to read maps and I know how to read the lay of the land. And I know how to read a compass and the sun. All these mountains and hills and valleys may seem exactly the same to your pretty little eyes, but trust me. They aren't. And look here." He pointed to a dot on the map. "That's Asheville, just a few miles east. We're close. I think the next few days could be very interesting."

Mark had a feeling his good mood wouldn't last much longer.

They moved about a mile closer, heading deep into one of the thickest areas of woods they'd crossed yet. Alec wanted the cover in case the people they were planning to confront sent canvassers out at night. They settled in, had a quick dinner, then sat around an empty spot in their tight quarters – no fire for fear of being seen. There'd be no chances taken of being discovered so close to the Berg's headquarters.

So they sat in a circle, staring at each other as the light faded into dusk and the crickets began chirping out in the forest. Mark asked about plans for the next day but Alec insisted they weren't ready yet. He wanted to think, then talk things through with Lana before laying it out for the others.

"You don't think we can contribute?" Trina asked.

"Eventually," he responded gruffly. And that was that.

Trina let out an exaggerated sigh. "Just when you started getting likeable again."

"Yeah, well." He leaned back against a tree and closed his eyes. "Now let me use my brain for a while."

Trina looked to Mark for consolation, but he just smiled in return. He'd got used to the old bear's ways a long time ago. Plus, he kind of agreed with him. Mark didn't know the first thing about what they should do in the morning. How were they going to gather information from a place – and people – they knew nothing about?

"How're you doing, Deedee?" he asked. The girl was sitting with her legs crossed under her, staring at a spot on the ground. "What's going on in that head of yours?"

She shrugged and gave him a half grin.

He realised she might be worried about her role the next day. "Hey, listen, you don't need to be scared about tomorrow. There's no way we're going to let anything bad happen to you. Okay?"

"You promise?"

"I promise."

Trina leaned over and gave the girl a hug. If there'd been any doubt before that Alec and Lana had given up the battle on people getting close to each other – much less touching – they were washed away. Neither one of them said a word.

"This is all grown-up stuff," Trina said to the girl. "Don't you worry, okay? We'll put you somewhere safe and then all we're going to do is try to talk to some people. Nothing else. Everything is going to be perfectly fine."

Mark was just about to add to Trina's words of comfort when he heard a noise off in the distance. It sounded like someone singing.

"Do you hear that?" he whispered.

The others perked up – especially Alec. His eyes snapped open and he sat up straighter.

"What?" Trina asked.

"Listen." Mark held a finger to his lips and tilted his head towards the distant voice.

It was faint but definitely there. The sound of a woman singing some type of chant, not as far off as he thought at first. Chills ran up his skin – it brought back the memory of Misty singing as she began to succumb to the illness.

"What the hell is that?" Alec whispered.

No one answered; they just kept listening. It was high-pitched and lilting, would almost have been pretty if it didn't seem so completely out of place. If there really was someone out there singing like that, well . . . that was just weird. A man joined in, then a few other people, until it sounded like a full-blown chorus.

"What in the world . . .?" Trina asked. "Is there some kind of church out here or what?"

Alec leaned forward, a grave look on his face. "I hate to say this, but we need to check that out. I'll go – you guys stay here and keep quiet. For all I know this is some kind of trap."

"I'll go with you," Mark said, almost blurting it out. He couldn't stand just sitting there. Plus, he was madly curious.

Alec didn't seem so certain. He looked at Lana and then at Trina.

"What?" Trina asked him. "You don't think we womenfolk can handle ourselves? You guys go – we'll be perfectly fine. Won't we, Deedee?"

The little girl didn't look so well; the singing really seemed to have freaked her out. But she nodded up at Trina and tried her best to smile.

"Okay, then," Alec said. "Come on, Mark. Let's go and check it out."

Deedee cleared her throat and held her hands out as if she wanted to say something.

"What is it?" Trina asked her. "Do you know something?"

The girl nodded vigorously, still with a mask of fear, then burst out talking – saying more than she had in all the time since they'd found her. "The people I lived with. It's them. I know it's them. They turned weird, started . . . doing things. Saying trees and plants and animals are magic. They left me because they said I was . . . evil." She broke into a whimper on the last word. "Because I got shot and didn't get sick."

Mark and the others looked at each other – things had just got weirder.

"We better take a look, then," Lana said. "You need to at least make sure they're far enough away from us, or not heading our way. But be careful!"

Alec nodded, seeming anxious to check it out. He lightly slapped Mark's shoulder and was about to walk away when Deedee said one last thing.

"Watch out for the ugly man with no ears."

She leaned into Trina's shoulder and started sobbing. Mark looked at Alec, who shook his head not to press the girl. He gestured to Mark, and without a word, the two headed out into the forest.

23

The singing didn't stop as they marched through the woods. They tried their best to be quiet, but every once in a while Mark would step on a twig or fallen branch and break it, the crack of wood sounding like a little bomb in the relative silence of the forest. Alec gave him a sharp look each time it happened, as if such an act were the single dumbest thing a human had ever done.

All Mark could say was, "Sorry." He tried his best to step carefully but he seemed to be drawn to things that made terrible noises.

There was almost no sign of sunlight left as they crept among the trees, closer and closer to the chorus of creepy chanting. The trees became standing shadows, ominous and tall and pressing. Almost as if they leaned towards Mark no matter where he was standing or walking. And it was harder for him to stay quiet, which drew more reproachful glares from Alec. At least he couldn't see the expressions as well in the dark. He kept moving, following the old bear's lead.

They'd made their way through the woods another few hundred yards when it became obvious that there was a source of light up ahead. It was orange and flickering. A fire. A big one. And the volume of the singing had got louder and louder. As had the . . . intensity. These people were really getting into whatever it was they were doing.

Alec crept up to a fat old tree and squatted behind it. Mark was right at his back, doing his best to keep silent. They knelt side by side with plenty of room to spare.

"What do you think about the things Deedee said?" Mark whispered.

He must've said it too loudly, because the man gave him his standard *Be quiet* look, just visible in the faint light. Then, in a soft voice, he spoke back. "These could very well be the people who left her behind. And they sound like they've got scrambled eggs for brains. Now try not to make any noises, would ya?"

Mark rolled his eyes, but Alec had already turned away and was leaning forwards to peek around the edge of the tree trunk. After a few seconds he faced Mark again.

"I can't make out all of them," he said, "but there's at least four or five yahoos dancing around that fire like they're trying to call back the dead."

"Maybe that's exactly what they're doing," Mark offered. "Sounds like a cult to me."

Alec nodded slowly. "Maybe they've always been that way."

"Deedee said they called her evil. Maybe the virus or whatever it is has made them a lot worse." A cult with a disease that drove them even crazier. That sounded fun. "Gives me the creeps and I haven't even seen them yet."

"Yeah, we better get closer. I want to get one last glimpse, make sure they're not something we have to worry about."

They bent low and inched out of their hiding spot, slowly walking from tree to tree, Alec checking each time to make sure it was clear to move on to the next one. Mark was proud of himself – he hadn't made a loud noise in quite a while.

They continued until they got within a hundred yards or so – the singing was crystal clear and the shadows from the flames circled and flashed in the canopy of branches above them. Mark squatted behind a different tree from Alec this time and leaned his head out to take a look down the long slope.

The fire roared, at least ten feet wide with its tongues of flame licking far up into the air, almost threatening the lower limbs of the trees surrounding it. Mark couldn't believe how these goons were risking burning the whole forest down. Especially with how dry everything still was in the aftermath of the sun flares.

Five or six people were dancing and gyrating around the bonfire, throwing their arms up and bringing them down again, bowing towards the earth and then shuffling to the side, where they started all over again. Mark half expected them to be wearing crazy robes or be flat-out naked, but they wore simple clothes – T-shirts, tank tops, jeans, shorts, tennis shoes. A crowd of a dozen or so others were lined up in two rows on the other side of the fire, singing the weird chant that Mark had been hearing. He didn't understand a word of it.

Alec tapped him on the shoulder, making him jump.

He turned to face the man and had to restrain himself to keep his voice low. "You scared the crap out of me."

"Sorry. Look, I have a bad feeling about these people. Whether they're a threat or not – the people at this bunker we're headed for have surely noticed them by now and are going to be on high alert."

Mark wondered if maybe that would be a good thing. "But if they're a distraction, it'll be easier for us to sneak up on the place. Don't you think?"

Alec seemed to consider his words. "Yeah, I guess. We should probably—"

"*Who's up there?*"

Mark froze, as did Alec. They stared at each other with open mouths now. Mark could see the light from below flickering in the reflection in Alec's eyes.

"I said, who's up there?" It was a woman, calling from the group at the fire. "We mean you no harm. We just want to invite you to join us in our praises to nature and the spirits."

"Hoo boy," Alec whispered. "I think not."

"I definitely think not," Mark said back.

There was the crunch of footsteps and before they could do anything two people were standing over them. Their backs were to the fire, so Mark couldn't make out their faces. But it looked to be a man and a woman.

"You're welcome to dance and sing with us," the woman said. Her tone seemed way too . . . calm for the circumstances. In this new world, strangers should be met with more caution.

Alec stood up straight – there was no point in crouching there like kids spying – and Mark did the same. Alec folded his arms and stuck his chest out like a bear trying to defend its territory.

"Look," he began with his typical bark, "I'm flattered you came here with an invite, but we'll have to respectfully decline. No hard feelings, I'm sure."

Mark grimaced, thinking these two people were far too unpredictable – maybe even unstable – to risk being sarcastic or rude to them. He wished he could see their faces for a reaction, but they were still hidden in shadow.

"Why are you here?" the man asked, as if he hadn't heard the comments from Alec. "Why are you here, spying on us? I would think you'd be honoured that we offered an invitation."

Alec sucked in a short breath, and Mark sensed him tensing up.

"We were curious," Alec said evenly.

"Why did you leave Deedee behind?" Mark suddenly blurted out, having no idea where it came from. He didn't even know for sure if these people really were from the same village or not. "She's just a little girl. Why did you leave her behind like a dog?"

The woman didn't answer his question. "I have a bad feeling about both of you," she replied. "And we can take no chances. Seize them."

Before Mark could process her words, there was a rope around his neck, cinched tightly, yanking him off his feet. He croaked and threw his hands up to try to relieve the pressure as he fell on his back and the wind was knocked out of his lungs. Alec had been restrained the same way; Mark could hear him cursing through his choking sounds. Mark kicked and twisted his body, trying to turn and face his attacker, but strong hands gripped him under the arms and yanked him off the ground.

They started dragging him down the slope of the mountain.

Toward the fire.

24

Mark finally stopped struggling when someone punched him in the face, sending a burst of pain through his cheek. The effort to escape was pointless, he realised. He relaxed and let them drag him wherever it was they wanted to take him. He saw Alec struggling against two large men and watched as they tightened the rope further around his neck. The old man's choking sounds made Mark's heart want to break open.

"Stop it!" he yelled. "Alec, just stop! They're going to kill you!"

Of course the old bear paid no attention, just kept fighting.

Eventually they were dragged into the clearing where the fire still roared. Even as Mark saw it he noticed a woman step up and throw two more logs on top of the inferno. It flared and spit out glowing red sparks. His captor dragged him around the bonfire and dumped him in front of the two rows of people. They stopped chanting, and all their eyes focused on Mark and Alec.

He coughed and spit, his neck burning from the rope, then tried to sit up. A tall man – probably the guy who'd dragged him down there – put his big boot on Mark's chest and pressed him back to the ground.

"Stay down," he said. Not angry or upset; he just said it matter-of-factly, like he didn't think Mark would even consider disobeying.

It had taken two men to bring Alec down the mountain, and Mark was shocked they'd succeeded even then. They dumped him next to Mark. The soldier grunted and groaned but didn't resist because they still had the other end of the rope that was tied around his neck. He went into a long coughing fit, then spit a wad of blood into the dirt.

"Why are you doing this?" Mark asked no one in particular. He lay flat on his back and stared up at the canopy of branches and the reflection of the flames on the leaves. "We're not here to hurt you guys. We just want to know who you are, what you're doing!"

"That's why you asked about Deedee?"

He looked and saw a woman standing a few feet away. By the shape of her body he could tell it was the lady who'd spoke to them higher on the mountain.

Mark was incredulous at her lack of emotion. "So it *was* you who left her. Why? And why are we prisoners now? We just want some answers!"

Alec suddenly burst into a flurry of movement, grabbing the rope and pulling it as he leaped to his feet. It came loose from the men holding it and Alec jumped at them, hurtling forwards with his shoulder out like a battering ram. He slammed into the side of one of the men, tackling him to the ground. They landed with a heavy thump and Alec punched away, landing a couple of shots before two other men were on him, jerking him off the guy's body. Another one came in as well, and between the three of them they were able to throw Alec on his back, pin his arms and legs down. The guy he'd tackled scrambled to his feet and came at the old man, kicked him in the ribs three times in a row.

"Stop it!" Mark yelled. "Stop it!"

He jerked on his own rope and started to get up, but the boot came back, slamming him into the dirt once again.

"Do not, I repeat, do not move again," his captor said, once more using that flat monotone.

The others were still punching and kicking Alec, but the former soldier refused to give in, struggling to fight back despite his odds.

"Alec," Mark pleaded. "You need to stop or they're really going to kill you. What good will you be to us if you're dead?"

The words finally got through the man's thick, stubborn skull. He stilled, then slowly curled into a ball, his face set in a fierce grimace of pain.

Almost shaking with rage, Mark turned his attention back to the woman, who was just standing there, watching it all with that maddening lack of emotion.

"Who are you people?" he asked. It was all he could get out, but he tried to inject as much anger as he could into the words.

The woman stared at him for a few seconds before answering. "You are unwelcome intruders. And now you'll tell me about Deedee. Is the girl with you? At your camp somewhere?"

"Why do you care? You left her behind! What, are you scared she's going to sneak into your camp and make you all sick? She's *fine*. There's nothing wrong with her!"

"We have our reasons," the woman replied. "The spirits speak and we follow their orders. Since the rain of demons from the sky, we've left our village, seeking holier places. Many of our people broke away, refused to join us. They're out there somewhere, probably scheming with the demons themselves. Perhaps *you* are a spy for them."

Mark couldn't believe the absurd words coming out of this lady's mouth. "You'd leave a sweet little girl to die because she *might* be sick? No wonder the other people from your village didn't stick with you."

The woman looked genuinely confused. "Listen, boy. The others are much more dangerous than we are – they attack without warning, kill without conscience. The world is beset with evil in many forms. And we can take no risks, especially since you invoked the name of Deedee. You are prisoners, and you'll be dealt with. To release you would risk alerting those who wish us harm."

Mark stared at her, his mind spinning. He had a sudden feeling of foreboding. The more this woman spoke, the more he felt it. "Deedee told us that the darts came from the sky. We saw the dead bodies in your little settlement. The same thing happened to us. All we're trying to do is find out *why.*"

"That girl *brought* the evil upon us. Her evil ways led to it. Why do you think we left her behind? If you've rescued her and brought her near to us, then you've done something more horrible than you could dream."

"What is this load of horse crap?" Alec finally choked out. "We've got bigger problems than *you* can dream, lady."

"You need to let us go," Mark quickly added before Alec could say anything more. The man might have been the toughest guy in their group, but he was the last choice to be a negotiator. "We're just trying to find a safe place to live. Please. I promise we'll just walk away. We won't tell anyone about you and we won't bring Deedee anywhere close if you don't want us to. We can take care of her."

"It saddens me how little you grasp," the woman responded. "Truly."

Mark wanted to scream but forced himself to stay composed. "Look, let's take turns explaining things to each other, then. Would that be fair? I *want* to understand. And I really, really need you to understand us. Can you just talk instead of treating us like animals?" When she didn't respond, he grasped for something to keep the conversation going. "So . . . how about we start from the beginning? How we got to these mountains."

She had a wide, vacant look in her eyes now. "I always believed that the demons would try to be nice when they came for us. You tricked us into bringing you down here, tying you up. So you could be nice and trick us again. Demons. All of you." She gave a stiff nod to one of the men standing near Mark and Alec.

The man drew his foot back and kicked Mark in the ribs. Pain exploded in his side and he cried out, unable to help himself. The man kicked him again, this time in the back, right in the kidney. A deep ache washed through Mark, and tears stung his eyes as he cried out even louder.

Alec protested. "Stop it, you sorry son of a—" His words were cut off when one of his captors reached down and punched him in the face.

"Why are you doing this?" Mark yelled. "We're not demons! You people have lost your minds!" Another kick pierced him in the ribs, the pain unbearable. He balled up, wrapped his arms around himself. Prepared for the continued onslaught, knowing he had no chance of escape.

"Stop!"

The word rumbled through the air from the other side of the fire, the deep, bellowing voice of a man. The men beating Mark and Alec immediately jumped back from them and knelt down, their faces lowered. The woman also got to her knees and looked at the ground.

Mark, still wincing from the pain, straightened out his legs, trying to see who had spoken the simple but effective command. He caught movement through the flames and followed it as a man stepped into view and approached him. When he was within a few feet, he stopped, and Mark's eyes traced a path from his booted feet, up his denim-clad legs, his tight plaid shirt, to his face, which was hideously scarred, almost inhuman. It made Mark want to look away, but he didn't let himself. He matched gazes with the disfigured stranger, staring into those piercing, wounded eyes.

The man had no hair. And he had no ears.

25

"**M**y name is Jedidiah," the man said. His lips were yellow and malformed, twisted to one side. He had a strange lisp, and there was a . . . *tonelessness* to his voice. "But my followers call me Jed. *You* will call me Jed, because I can see that you've been mistreated and you are now my friends. Is this understood?"

Mark nodded, but all Alec did was grunt something unintelligible. Defiant to the end, the old soldier had sat up when their attackers had ordered the two of them to lie on their backs. But the men who'd been beating them just moments earlier were all kneeling as if in prayer. Mark sat up, too, hoping there would be no consequence. If anything, Jed looked pleased.

"Very good," the man said. "It looks like we're finally making some kind of peace." He walked over and sat down between them and the fire, the flames at his back. Their flickering light made the outline of his head appear wet and glistening, almost as if it were melting all over again. Melting.

That was what Mark had concluded had happened to the poor guy.

"Did the sun flares do that to you?" he asked.

Jed chuckled for a few seconds, but there was nothing pleasant or cheerful about the sound. More like disturbing. "It always tickles my funny bone when someone refers to the demon plague that way. When it occurred, yes, I thought it was merely a celestial event that happened to take place in Earth's path. *Coincidence. Misfortune. Bad luck.* Those are words that went through my head at the time."

"And now you think it was big bad demons raining from the sky?" Alec asked, his tone making it clear what a crackpot idea he thought it was. Mark shot him a glance and felt awful. Blood covered the man's face, and welts and bruises had already appeared from the brutal beating he'd been given.

"It's happened twice now," Jed replied, showing no sign that he'd noticed Alec's sarcasm. "Both times it came from the heavens – once from the sun, once from the ships. We think they may visit annually, to punish us for becoming lax and to remind us of what we need to become."

"Twice . . . sun and ships," Mark repeated. "So the sun flares and then the darts from the Berg?"

Jed's head snapped right and left, then focused on Mark again. *What in the world?*

"Yes, twice," the man said as if what he'd just done was totally normal. "And again, it both saddens and humours me that you don't see the importance of the events. It means your mind hasn't evolved yet to be able to see them for what they really are."

"Demons," Mark said, almost rolling his eyes before he stopped himself just in time.

"Demons. Yes, demons. They burned my face, melted it into what you see today. That way I can never forget my calling. And then came the little arrows from the ships, filled with their hatred. It's been two months now, and we still mourn those who lost their lives that day. It's why we build the fires and sing the songs and dance the dance. And we fear those from our village who decided not to join us. They work with the demons, undoubtedly."

"Wait, two months?" Alec asked. "What do you mean, two months?"

"Yes," Jed replied slowly, as if talking to a confused child. "We count the days solemnly, every one. It's been two months and three days."

"Whoa, whoa, whoa," Mark said. "It couldn't have been that long. It happened to us just a few days ago."

"I don't like it . . . when people doubt my words," Jed said, his tone changing drastically in the middle of his sentence. It suddenly turned threatening. "How can you sit there and accuse me of lying? Why would I lie about such a thing? I've tried to make peace with you, give you a second chance in this life, and this is how you repay me?" His voice had risen in volume with every passing word until he was shouting, his body trembling. "It . . . it makes my head hurt."

Mark could tell Alec was about to explode, so he quickly reached over and squeezed his arm. "Don't," he whispered. "Just don't." Then he returned his attention to Jed. "No, listen, please. It's not like that. We just want to understand. Our village had the . . . arrows from the ships rain down on us less than a week ago. So we assumed the same about you. And . . . you said that people died the day it happened. We saw bodies of people who seemed to have died more recently. Just help us understand."

Mark had the feeling that there was some important information to be learned from these people. He didn't think the man was lying about the time frame. There was something here.

Jed had raised his hands to place them where his ears should've been on his head and was slowly swaying from side to side. "People died right away. Then others later. More suffering as time passed. More dying. Our village split into factions. All the demons' work." He started moaning, almost chanting.

"We believe you," Mark said. "We just want to understand. Please just talk to us, tell us what happened, step by step." He tried to keep the frustration out of his voice, but he couldn't. How was he supposed to do this?

"You've made the pain come back," Jed said tightly, still swaying. His arms were rigid, his elbows sticking straight out as he continued to hold his head in his hands. It looked as if he were trying to crush his own skull. "It hurts so much. I can't . . . I have to . . .You must be from the demons. It's the only explanation."

Mark knew his time was running out. "We're not, I swear. We're here because we want to learn from you. Maybe your head is hurting because . . . you have knowledge that you're supposed to share with us."

Alec dropped his head forward.

"They came two months ago," Jed said, his voice distant somehow. "And then the death has come in waves. Taking longer each time. Two days. Five days. Two weeks. A month. And we have people from our own village – people we once called friends – trying to kill us. We don't understand what the demons want. We don't understand. We . . . don't . . . understand. We dance, we sing, we make sacrifices. . . ."

He fell to his knees, then collapsed to the ground, still pressing his hands against his head. He let out a long, pain-filled moan.

Mark had reached the end of his patience. This was complete lunacy as far as he was concerned, and there was no way to deal with it rationally. He looked over at Alec, and he could tell by the fire in the man's eyes that he was ready to take another shot at escape. Their captors were still kneeling, faces lowered in some kind of sick worship of the man writhing in pain. It was now or never.

Mark was just about to consider his next move, trying to focus over the moans and groans coming from Jed, when new sounds arose in the woods behind them. People yelling and screaming, laughing. Making bird calls and other animal noises. Accompanied by the crunch of footsteps on the dry undergrowth of the forest, the creepy sounds continued, getting louder as the people got closer. Then, more alarmingly, the noises spread in a circle around the clearing of the bonfire until it was completely surrounded by a chorus of caws and cuckoos and roars and hysterical laughter. There had to be several dozen people making the noises.

"What now?" Alec said with clear disgust.

"We warned you about them," the woman said from where she knelt. "They used to be our friends, our family. Now the demons have taken them and all they want is to torment us, to kill us."

Jed suddenly reared up on his knees again, screaming at the top of his lungs. Violently, he jerked his head down, then left and right, as if he were trying to knock something loose from his skull. Mark couldn't help but scoot backward, crab-walking until the rope around his neck grew taut. The other end was still in the hands of one of the kneeling men.

Jed let out a piercing, horrific sound that cut off all the new ones coming from the forest around them.

"They've killed me!" he yelled, the words ripping from his throat. "The demons . . . finally . . . killed me!"

His body went rigid, his arms stiff at his sides, and he fell over, a last breath rushing from his mouth. His body stilled, and blood began to seep from his nose and mouth.

26

Mark was completely frozen, staring at Jed's body lying in an unnaturally twisted position. In all his life, Mark was pretty sure he'd never endured such a strange hour as he had since arriving at this camp of madness. And as if it couldn't have got any stranger, now crazy people surrounded them out in the woods, making animal sounds and laughing hysterically.

Mark slowly looked over at Alec. The man was stunned into silence, motionless as he stared at Jed.

The movement and noises in the woods continued. Catcalls and whistles and cheering and hooting. The cricks and cracks of footsteps.

The men who'd been kneeling – and before that beating up Mark and Alec – stood up, looking at their ropes as if they weren't quite sure what to do with them. They glanced at their prisoners, then at each other, then back at the ropes. The two lines of singers behind them were doing much the same, searching about like someone should be telling them how to react. It was as if Jed had been some kind of link they all shared, and now that it had been severed, his followers were confused and unable to function.

Alec acted first, clearly wanting to take advantage of the situation. He began fumbling with the rope tied around his neck, finally getting his fingers underneath it enough to work it loose. Mark was scared that would snap the men out of their dazed state and cause them to retaliate, but they actually dropped their ends of the ropes in response. Mark immediately followed Alec's example and worked at his own noose, finally getting it loose. He pulled it up and around his head until he was free, just as Alec was slamming his to the ground.

"Let's get out of this place," the older man grumbled.

"But what about their friends out there?" Mark asked. "They have us surrounded."

He let out a big sigh. "Come on. We'll just have to fight our way through if they try to stop us. Leave them to these yahoos."

The woman who'd first spoken to them came over, her gait hurried and her face filled with worry. "All we've done is try to keep the demons at bay. Nothing more. And look how you've ruined our efforts. How could you lead our enemies here?"

She winced after saying it and stumbled a step backwards, holding a hand up to her temple. "How could you?" she whispered.

"I'm really sorry," Alec grumbled as he stepped around her and moved towards the fire. There was a long piece of wood that was half in and half out of the roaring flames. He picked up the unburnt side and held the thing up like a torch. "This ought to make 'em think twice before they try anything. Come on, kid."

Mark looked back at the woman, who was obviously experiencing head pain, and things began to click into place.

"I said come on!" Alec yelled at him.

In that moment, dozens of people came tearing out of the surrounding woods with fists raised in the air, yelling. There were women and men and children, all with the same crazed expression of rage mixed with glee. Mark – sure he'd never seen anything like it – sprang into action, following Alec's lead and grabbing a log out of the fire. Flames erupted from its tip as he swung it through the air, and he held it in front of him like a sword.

The wave of attackers crashed into the rows of singers, jumping on them with animalistic cries of battle. Two men leaped into the air and straight into the bonfire. As Mark watched in horror, their clothes and hair ignited. Screams tore from their throats as they stumbled out of the flames, but it was too late. Engulfed and burning alive, they ran out into the woods, sure to set the whole forest on fire. Mark turned back to the chanting villagers. They were being beaten and choked, he was surrounded by chaos – it was too much to take in.

"Mark!" Alec screamed from nearby. "Not sure if you noticed, but we're being attacked!"

"Please," a woman cried behind Mark, "take me with you."

He whipped around to see the lady who'd ordered them beaten, and almost burned her with the end of his torch. She seemed transformed, meek. But before he could respond they were suddenly in the middle of what seemed like a thousand-person fistfight. Mark was pushed and shoved. To his surprise, he realised that it wasn't just the new people versus the old. Many of the attackers were actually pummelling each other – he saw a woman fall into the fire, her screams filling the air.

Someone grabbed Mark by the shirt and yanked him to the side. He was just about to rear back with his weapon when he realised it was Alec.

"You have a knack for trying to get yourself killed!" the man yelled.

"I didn't know where to start or what to do!" Mark countered.

"Sometimes you just act!" He let go of Mark's shirt and they took off in the same direction – up the slope, away from the fire. But there were people all around them.

Mark swung his torch in front of him as he ran. But then someone tackled him from behind; he dropped the burning log and landed face-first in the dirt. An instant later he heard a thump and a cry of pain and the body flew off him. He looked up to see Alec bringing his foot down from a kick.

"Get up!" the man yelled. But the last word had barely come out of his mouth when *he* was slammed to the ground by a man and a woman.

Mark scrambled to his feet, grabbed the torch he'd dropped, ran to where Alec was struggling with his two attackers. He drove the burning point into the back of the man's neck – the guy screamed and grabbed his throat, falling off Alec. Then Mark hauled the log back and swung it as hard as he could, connecting with the side of the woman's head. All Mark could hear was fire burning as she toppled off Alec.

Mark reached down, grabbed Alec's hand, helped him to his feet.

More people rushed in on them. At least five or six.

Mark whipped his log around, forgetting all control and just handing himself over to instinct and adrenalin. He smacked a man, then pulled his weapon back around and hit a woman right in the nose. He drove it forwards at a man coming straight for him, thrust its tip into his stomach and watched as his clothes ignited.

Alec was next to Mark. He was punching and kicking and elbowing and picking people up, tossing them away like bags of garbage. At some point he'd lost the torch he'd grabbed, too busy using both hands to fight off the attackers. The man was every bit the soldier he'd once been.

An arm slipped around Mark's neck from behind and yanked him off his feet, started squeezing the breath out of him. Mark gripped the log in both hands, then hammered it backwards in desperation. He missed, pulled it back, then tried again, swinging it with every bit of strength he could muster while the oxygen rushed from his lungs. He felt the solid blow as he connected, heard the crunch of cartilage and the man's scream. Sweet air rushed into his chest as the arm loosened its grip.

Mark fell to the ground, sucking the life back into his lungs. Alec was bent over to catch his own breath. They had a slight reprieve, but one look showed that more people were coming their way.

Alec helped Mark to his feet. They turned up slope and half crawled, half climbed into the thicker cover of the trees. Mark heard the cries of pursuit behind them – these people didn't want anyone escaping. He and Alec hit a spot that was a little flatter and burst into an all-out sprint. And that was when Mark spotted it, about a hundred yards ahead of them.

A huge section of the forest was engulfed in flames.

Between them and their camp. Where they'd left Trina, Lana and Deedee.

27

The trees and shrubbery of the woods were already half dead – a tinder box ready to light up. It had been a few weeks since the last torrential storm, and anything that had regrown since the flares was parched. Misty tendrils of smoke bled along the ground at their feet, and the smell of burning wood laced the air.

"It's gonna spread like wildfire," Alec shouted.

Mark thought he was joking, but the man looked grave. "It *is* a wildfire!" he shouted back.

But Alec had already started running straight towards the distant flames, which seemed to have grown in the moments since it had begun. Mark set off after him, knowing they had to make it to the other side of the inferno before it got too big – they had to get to Trina and Deedee and Lana. The two of them tore through the undergrowth, kicking past thick briars, dodging trees and low-hanging limbs. The sound of pursuit still rang out from behind, but it had lessened, as if even their deranged pursuers understood it was crazy to head *into* a forest fire. But Mark could hear lingering catcalls and whistles haunting the woods.

He ran on, throwing all of his focus into making it back to Trina.

The fire got closer, crackling and spitting and roaring. A wind had picked up, fanning the flames; a huge branch toppled from far above and crashed through the canopy, throwing sparks everywhere until it finally hit the ground. Alec continued to head for the heart of the blazing section of woods, not slowing down, as if his one final goal was to run to a fiery death and end it all.

"Shouldn't we veer off?" Mark shouted up to him. "Where are you going?"

Alec answered without turning back and Mark had to strain to hear him. "I want to be as close as possible! Run along its edges so we know exactly where we are! And maybe lose those psychos while we're at it!"

"*Do* you know exactly where we are?" Mark was moving as quickly as he could, but the soldier still stayed ahead of him.

"Yes," came the curt reply. But he pulled out his compass and looked at it as he ran.

The smoke had grown thicker, making it hard to breathe. The fire took up Mark's entire field of vision now, the flames close and high and illuminating the night. The heat surged out in waves, washing across Mark's face only to be sucked away by the wind gusting from behind him.

But as they got closer, now only a few dozen feet away, the waves didn't matter any more. The temperature had skyrocketed; Mark was drenched in sweat and was so hot it felt as if his skin might melt. Just when he thought Alec might've lost his marbles after all, the man suddenly made a sharp turn to the right, running parallel to the expanding line of flames. Mark stayed as close to him as he could, putting his life in the former soldier's hands for the umpteenth time since they'd met in the subtrans tunnels.

Intense heat pulsed across his body as he ran; sweltering wind from the left, cooler air from the right. His clothes were so hot against his skin, they felt as if they might combust at any second even though they were drenched in sweat. His hair was dry, though, any moisture sucked away by the searing air. He imagined the follicles on the cusp of drying out and falling to the ground like pine needles. And his eyes. They felt as if they were being baked in their sockets; he squinted and rubbed them, tried to force tears, but there was nothing.

He ran on, mimicking Alec with every step, hoping they'd round the fire and break away from it before he died of thirst and heat exhaustion. The sound of the flames was the only thing he heard now, a constant roar like the ignited thrusters of a thousand Bergs.

Suddenly, a woman came tearing through the woods from the right just ahead, the fire a glint in the madness of her eyes. Mark prepared himself for a fight, expecting the woman to turn and attack them. But she ran across their path in front of Alec – if she'd been a little slower he would've ploughed right over her body. The woman ran, silent and determined, her feet crashing through the undergrowth. She tripped and fell, got back up. And then she disappeared in the wall of flames and her screams cut short.

Alec and Mark kept running.

Finally they reached the edge of the expanding inferno, the line of it far more distinct than Mark would've expected. They kept the same distance, but it felt good, sent a burst of fresh adrenalin through his body, to be turning towards the left, turning towards Trina and the others again. Mark ran even harder, almost tripped Alec's feet up when he caught up to him. Then they were side by side.

Every breath was a chore for Mark. The air scalded his throat as it went down, and the smoke was like poison. "We've gotta . . . get away . . . from this thing."

"I know!" Alec shouted back, bursting into a long fit of

140

coughing. He quickly glanced at the compass gripped in the palm of his hand. "Almost . . . there."

Soon they rounded another corner of the main body of flames, and this time Alec veered to the right, heading away from the fire. Mark followed, realising that he was completely disorientated now. He didn't think it was time to head straight again, but he trusted the old man. They trampled through the woods with renewed energy, going faster than ever. Mark could feel the fresher air with every breath he sucked into his lungs. The volume of the inferno's roar also died down enough that he could hear the crunching sounds of his footsteps again.

Alec stopped suddenly.

Mark ran past him a few steps before he could do the same. He turned to Alec and asked if he was okay.

The man was leaning against a tree, his chest heaving as he took in short bursts of breath. He nodded, then buried his head in the crook of his arm with a loud groan.

Mark bent over, hands on his knees, relishing the chance to rest. The wind had died down and the fire seemed at a somewhat safe distance now. "Man, you had me worried there for a while. I'm not sure that was the brightest thing ever, to run so close to a raging inferno."

Alec looked over at him, but his face was mostly hidden in shadow. "You're probably right. But it's easy to get turned around in a place like this at night. I was dead set on keeping the path we'd followed straight in my head." He checked his compass, then pointed at a spot over Mark's shoulder. "Our little camp is that way."

Mark looked around and saw nothing to distinguish that part of the woods. "How do you know? All I see is a bunch of trees."

"Just because I know."

Strange noises filled the night, mixed in with the steady roar of the fire. Screams and laughter. It was impossible to tell which direction they were coming from.

"Looks like those crazy buggers are still runnin' around looking for trouble," Alec said through a groan.

"Crazy buggers is right – I was hoping they'd all die in the fire." Mark said it before realising how terrible it sounded. But the side of him that wanted to survive at all costs – that had become ruthless over the last year – knew it was the truth. He didn't want to have to worry about them any more. He didn't want to spend the rest of the night and the next day looking over his shoulder.

"If wishes were fishes . . ." Alec said. He took a deep, long breath. "Okay. We better hurry and meet back up with the three ladies."

They started jogging, a little slower than earlier, but not much. The return of those sounds, even though they didn't seem too close at the moment, obviously had them both on edge.

A few minutes later, Alec changed course, changed again. He stopped at one point, got his bearings, poked around a bit, then pointed down a slope.

"Ah," he said. "It's right down there."

They set off that way, slipping and sliding as the descent got steeper. The wind had shifted, blowing back towards the fire, filling their lungs with fresh air and easing that concern – at least temporarily. Mark had grown so used to the light from the flames that he'd failed to notice that dawn had crept up on them – the sky through the branches above him was now purple instead of black, and he could faintly see where he was going. The landscape grew familiar and suddenly they were back at the camp. Their things were still laid out exactly as they'd left them.

But there was no sign of Trina or the others.

A little seed of panic sprouted inside Mark's chest. "Trina!" he yelled. "Trina!"

He and Alec quickly combed the surrounding area, calling their friends' names as they did.

But all was quiet.

28

Mark could barely contain himself. Of all the crap they'd been through, at least he and Trina had never really been separated before. It had only taken ten minutes of her being missing for the most sinking feeling of helplessness to hit him.

"There's no way," he said to Alec as they searched in widening circles around the camp. He heard the desperation in his own voice. "There's no way they'd just march off while we were gone. Not without at least leaving us a note or something." He ran a hand through his hair, then yelled for no reason other than anger and frustration.

Alec was doing a much better job of keeping his cool. "Calm down, boy. You need to remember two things: One, Lana is as tough as I am and a whole lot smarter. And two, you're forgetting the details."

"What do you mean?" Mark asked.

"Yes, you're right, under normal circumstances they would've stayed here until we got back. But these circumstances aren't normal. There's a forest fire raging nearby and crazy people running through the woods making horror-movie noises. Would you just sit here and twiddle your thumbs?"

That didn't make Mark feel better at all. "So . . . you think they went looking for us? What if we passed them on the way back here?" He squeezed his hands into fists and pressed them against his eyes. "They could be anywhere!"

Alec marched over to him and grabbed his shoulders. "Mark! What's come over you? Calm *down*, son!"

Mark dropped his hands and looked into Alec's eyes, which were hard and grey in the low light of dawn, but also filled with genuine concern. "I'm sorry. I'm just . . . I'm freaking out here. What're we going to do?"

"We're going to keep our wits about us and we're going to stay calm and we're going to *think*. And then we're going to go out there and find Lana and the others."

"They have a little girl with them," Mark said quietly. "What if somehow those people who attacked us got here first? Took them?"

"Then we'll get them back. But I need you to pull yourself together or that'll never happen. You got it?"

Mark closed his eyes and nodded, did his best to slow his racing heart and dampen the panic that flared in him. Alec would figure things out. He always did.

Mark finally looked at the soldier again. "Okay. I'm okay. Sorry."

"Good. That's better." Alec took a step back and studied the ground. "It's getting light enough now. We need to find any sign of what path they took – broken branches, footprints, cleared undergrowth, whatever. Start searching."

Mark did, desperate to get his mind occupied with something other than imagining every horrible scenario possible. The sounds of the fire and the occasional scream or laugh still floated through the air, but they seemed distant. At least for the moment.

He swept the area, carefully studying every spot before he dared take another step, his head swivelling up and down, side to side, like some kind of robotic scavenger unit. All they needed was one major clue and then they could probably pick up the trail more easily. Mark felt an almost competitive vibe take over him – he wanted to be the one to find something first. He had to, to make himself feel better, to feel like they'd been set on a path to relieve his panicked thoughts.

He couldn't lose Trina. Not now.

Alec was working about twenty feet further outside the camp, actually on his hands and knees and literally sniffing along like a dog. He looked ridiculous, but there was something about it that touched Mark. The old grizzly bear rarely showed the slightest hint of emotion – unless he was yelling or screaming or pounding on something . . . or some*one* – but he often showed how much he genuinely cared. Mark had no doubt the man would give his life today if it meant saving one of their three missing friends. Could Mark say the same about himself?

Both Mark and Alec came across obvious signs of passage – broken twigs, shoe impressions in the dirt, shifted branches on trees or bushes – but each time they concluded that they'd been the ones who'd caused it. After a half hour or so, this made Mark realise that they were combing the area between the camp and the direction they'd gone last night. He stopped and stood up straight.

"Hey, Alec," he said.

The man was on his hands and knees, leaning his face into the middle of a bush; he grunted something that kind of sounded like a "Yeah?"

"Why are we spending so much time on this side of where we left them?"

Alec pulled himself out of the bush and looked back at him. "Seemed logical. I'd think they either followed us out of here to find us, or they were taken by the same yahoos who attacked us. Or . . . maybe they went to investigate the fire."

Mark thought that was all barking up the wrong tree. "Or they ran *away* from the fire. Not every person on earth is as wacky-brained as you, good sir. Most people see a huge roaring inferno coming at them? They decide to cut and run. Just saying."

"No, I don't think so." Alec had shifted all his weight to his knees, stretching his back. "Lana's not a coward. She wouldn't save herself and leave us to die."

Mark was shaking his head before the soldier even finished. "You've gotta think this through. Lana has the same worship complex of you that *you* have of her. She'll think you *are* safe and taking care of yourself just fine and dandy. She'd also consider the circumstances top to bottom and decide the best course of action to take. Am I right or am I right?"

Alec shrugged, then glared at him. "So you think after all that, Lana would leave us to die at the hands of some crazies and run for her life?"

"She didn't *know* we were in the hands of people like that. We told her we were just going to take a look, remember? Then she probably heard more sounds, heard and saw the fire coming. I bet she went monster logic on us and decided she better run towards the Berg headquarters and that we'd decided the same thing. Rendezvous there. You did point out the general direction we needed to go."

Alec was nodding and grumbling, impossible to read.

"Not to mention that she has a civilian" – he made quotation marks in the air when he said that last word – "and a little girl who's probably terrified. I highly doubt Lana would leave them alone to come after us or take the others closer to danger."

Alec got to his feet and brushed the dirt off his knees. "Okay, boy, you can quit going on about it. You sold me. But . . . what's your point?" He had the slightest smile on his face, barely there. And Mark knew why. The bear was enjoying this – watching his pupil figure things out on his own.

Mark pointed to the other side of the camp, towards the spot Alec had identified the day before as the direction they needed to go. The headquarters of that Berg awaited. The place where they'd find the people who had ruined their lives once again.

"Like I said," Alec spoke with an exaggerated sigh, "you sold me. Come on, let's start looking over there." He winked at Mark as he walked past but then gave him a scowl.

Mark laughed. "You are one strange little man."

Alec stopped and faced him. "That's what my mama used to say. She'd wake me up in the morning, give me a little kiss and a hug, and she'd say, 'My sweet Alec. You are one strange little man.' Got to me every time, right here." He patted his heart, then rolled his eyes dramatically. "Let's get to work."

"See?" Mark said as he followed. "Do I need any more proof? Strange. Little. Man. Officially proven."

"You got one word right. I'm definitely a man. I'm all man, baby." He let out a strangled choking sound that might've been a laugh.

They stepped more carefully when they made it to the area Mark had indicated, and soon they were back at it, searching every square inch for a telltale sign of a trail. Mark paused to take in the sounds that had become background noise, barely there until you focused on it. The roaring, crackling, spitting forest fire, still safely distant but getting closer, and the occasional hoot or holler or laugh of their new unfriendly friends. Again, safely distant – though it was hard to tell where the sounds were coming from. The air had begun to look hazy from the smoke now that the sun was up to reveal it.

"Found something," Alec announced. "Be careful!" he yelled when Mark tramped over to see for himself.

"Oh. Sorry." He slowed down and crept over to stand next to the soldier.

Alec was on his knees, leaning back on his feet. He had a

stick in his hand and used it as a pointer. "There's about three bushes in a row that have been walked through, and by more than one person for sure. See the smashed part there, the broken branch there, the footsteps here and there." He gestured at one nearby.

Mark leaned forwards and saw it. Small. Just the right size for Deedee. "There's only one problem," Alec continued, something heavy in his voice.

"What?" Mark asked quickly.

Alec used the stick to poke a spot – just above the ground where the others had passed – of leaves clumped together. Their shiny green faces had been sprayed with small drops of blood.

29

Mark didn't allow himself to have the same panic attack this time. But he went dead silent, his insides cold and his hands slicked with sweat. He imagined that his face was pale, too. But he forced himself to remain calm as Alec stood and slowly made his way along the trail they'd found.

With growing dismay Alec pointed out more spots of blood along the path. There wasn't much, but there was enough to see. "It's hard to say how serious an injury we're talking about. I've seen bloody noses spurt this much out, but I've also seen a guy with his arm blown off who hardly bled a drop. The explosion cauterised him right clean."

"Not . . . helping," Mark muttered.

Alec shot a glance back at him. "Sorry, kid. I'm trying to say I don't think this is all bad news. Whoever's hurt might just have a bad cut. People have survived more blood loss than this many a time. If anything, maybe it'll help us keep on their trail."

Alec moved on again, his head swinging back and forth as

he walked, taking it all in. Mark followed on his heels, trying hard not to look at the trail of blood. He just couldn't. Not until his nerves settled a bit. He hoped this wasn't some kind of wild-goose chase or, worse, a trap.

"Anything else that lets us know it's definitely Trina and them?" he asked.

Alec stopped and leaned far down to examine some dirt next to a trampled bush. "Based on the pattern, I'd say it's our pretty little group that came through here – I can see their footsteps well enough. And . . ." He flicked a nervous glance backward.

"And what?"

"Well . . . I haven't seen Deedee's in a while, so my guess is that someone started carrying the poor thing back there." He jabbed a thumb over his shoulder.

"So maybe she's the one who got hurt," Mark concluded, the thought of it making his stomach fall. "Maybe . . . maybe she just fell and skinned a knee or something."

"Yeah," Alec replied numbly. "But the other thing is . . ."

Mark had never seen the man so hesitant to speak before. "Would you just spit it out, man? What's going on?"

"When they came through here," Alec said quietly, seemingly oblivious to Mark's rebuke, "they were definitely running. And running pell-mell. All the signs add up. The length of their strides, the smashed bushes, the broken shrubbery and branches." He met Mark's eyes. "Like they were being chased."

That gave Mark a lump in the back of his throat, until he remembered something. "But you just said you could only see three sets of footprints. *Is* there any sign that somebody might've been going after them?"

Alec looked up, then pointed. "Things fly around these parts, remember?"

As if they needed one more thing to worry about. "Don't you think we would've heard if a Berg came swooping in and chased our friends down the mountain?"

"In the middle of what we just got done with? Maybe not. Might've been something besides a Berg, anyway."

Mark gave another weary glance upward. "Let's just keep moving."

The two of them followed the path, Mark hoping the whole time they didn't find more blood. Or worse.

* * *

The signs of Trina, Lana and Deedee's passage continued into a long, low ravine that made its way towards an almost hidden canyon. Mark hadn't noticed the walls of the mountains to their sides getting taller, and the slope was gradual enough that he didn't really feel like they were descending very quickly. Especially being surrounded by the woods and spending most of his time studying the land for clues and traces of their friends. But one minute they were travelling along through a thick copse of trees and the next they came out into a wide clearing bordered by canyon walls of grey granite. They were so steep that only a little vegetation grew in small clumps here and there.

Alec pulled out his handwritten map and stopped. "We're here." He made Mark step back and hid the two of them behind the large trunk of an oak.

"Really?"

"Almost certain this valley is where that Berg returned after every trip."

Mark peeked around the tree and examined the tall, foreboding walls. "A little dangerous to fly down into this place, don't ya think?"

"Maybe, but also perfect to hide yourself. There has to be a landing zone somewhere close, and an entrance to wherever they call home. I still think it might be an old government bunker. Especially being this close to Asheville – the city is just on the other side of this canyon."

"Yeah." Something was troubling Mark. "So . . . what're the odds that Lana and them would get chased this far? I'm really worried they got taken."

"Maybe not. Lana knows that wandering around the mountains looking for us wouldn't amount to a hill of beans. Better to make a beeline for the one spot that's most obviously a rendezvous point. Here."

"Then where are they?"

Alec didn't answer – something had caught his attention out in the clearing.

"We might both be right," he finally whispered. His gravelly voice sounded ominous.

"What is it?"

"Stay low and follow me."

Alec got on his hands and knees and crawled out from around the tree, keeping under the line of shrubs and bushes. Mark did the same and followed him out into the clearing, certain that a Berg was going to come barrelling in with dart guns over their heads any second. They kept to the barely discernible path where Mark assumed Trina and the others had walked. At first he had thought that maybe the Bergs landed in the clearing, but there was no sign of such a spot whatsoever – the vegetation had grown pretty thick.

Alec hacked his way through it for about thirty feet, then stopped. Mark poked his head around the man and saw that there was a large spot where the bushes had been trampled and crushed. An obvious sign of struggle. His heart dropped.

"Oh, no," was all he could get out.

Alec's head hung low. He shifted to crouch even lower. "You were right. Somebody took them here, no doubt. Look – the bushes are beat to death on the other side. Like twenty people marched across it."

Mark had to push down the panic again. "So what do we do? Go back and hide or go after them?"

"Not so loud, kid. Or they're gonna be on top of us, too."

"Let's just go back," Mark whispered. "Regroup, decide what to do." He had the urge to chase after the trail, but his wiser side told him they needed to think it through first.

"We don't have time to—"

A loud clanging sound cut the man off, a metallic bang that shot through the air like a cannon. Mark dropped to his stomach, half expecting the canyon walls to come crashing down on top of him.

"What was that?" he asked.

But before Alec could answer the sound came again. A quick, ear-splitting boom that shook the ground, which continued to tremble even after the noise ceased, vibrating so much that the bushes around them danced. Mark and Alec met each other's gaze, not sure what was going on.

The noise rocked the air yet again, and the land beneath them suddenly started to rise towards the sky.

30

Mark jumped to his feet, pulling Alec's arm. The entire area around them shook as it rose, and it took all of Mark's effort not to fall again. He knew that what was happening had to be impossible, and it made him wonder about his mental state. But the ground at their feet was slowly rising, tilting as it did so. He looked around frantically, so dumbfounded and confused he didn't know what to do. Alec seemed to be in the same stupor. Mark snapped out of it first.

His mind cleared and he noticed several things at once.

First, it wasn't like the entire valley was vaulting towards the sky because of an earthquake or massive shifting of the earth's crust. It was only a small area – the clearing where they stood. The trees surrounding them were still and calm, the branches not so much as swaying with a wind. Second, the slow – but steadily increasing – tilt of the moving land made him realise that half of it was actually sinking *into* the ground. And the whole thing looked to be in the shape of a circle. Third, there was a low, metallic grinding sound.

"It's man-made!" he yelled, already on the run with Alec. "Swinging open on some kind of pivot!"

Alec nodded briskly and picked up the pace – they were both running sideways to the angle of the slope, aiming to make it to a spot where they could jump off the shifting disk of land. It was moving slowly enough that the initial burst of panic left Mark and was replaced by curiosity. They were obviously standing on some sort of massive trapdoor. But why was it so . . .

He and Alec ran the last few steps, reaching the side of the rotating section of ground at the point of the pivot, only having to jump a couple of feet to safety. They scrambled away to the line of trees and dropped down, slipping behind the same large oak as before for cover. Mark poked his head out to watch the continuation of the spectacle. The upper edge of the circular cut-out was now thirty feet in the air, the lower edge fully sunk into the ground and out of sight. It kept rotating to the grind of the labouring gears, which sounded louder now.

"Looks like a coin flipping," Alec muttered.

"A really big one. Flipping really slowly," Mark agreed.

Within another minute or so the round piece of land was exactly vertical, half in the ground and half out, still rotating. Soon the earth and bushes were descending upside down and Mark could finally see what lay on the opposite side of the coin: a flat, grey, concrete-like surface with small grooves cut across it in perfectly straight lines. It wouldn't be long before the large circle rested flat on the valley floor, facing the sky and waiting for something to land on it. Hooks and chains were scattered across the circle of grey for securing whatever did land.

A landing spot, Mark thought. A landing spot for the Berg. Or Bergs.

"Why aren't the dirt and plants sliding off the other side?" he asked. "Looks like magic."

"Probably fake as a rubber glove," answered the soldier. "Wouldn't do if they had to come out and resod the whole thing every time they used it, now, would it?"

"It sure looks real. Or did." He watched in fascination. The piece of moving land had to be a couple of hundred feet across. "Do you think they saw us? Surely they have cameras out here."

Alec shrugged. "You'd think so. All we can do is hope they're not looking real hard."

The coin of land was now at a forty-five-degree angle, and within minutes of completely sealing the hole in the earth. Mark wondered if Alec was thinking the same thing he was.

"Should we do it?" he asked him. "A Berg might be landing any second – this is our chance."

At first the man seemed surprised, as if Mark had read his mind. Then a knowing grin crept across his face. "It might be the only way to get inside, eh?"

"Maybe. It's now or never."

"Cameras and guards? It's a big risk."

"But they have our friends."

Alec nodded slowly. "Spoken like a true soldier."

"Let's go, then."

Mark got to his feet but stayed crouched down, leaning against the tree as he snuck out from behind it. He had to move before he changed his mind, and he knew Alec would be right on his heels. There was still about a fifteen-foot open space between the edges of the moving disk and the real land that surrounded it. After a deep breath to psych himself up, Mark sprinted for the left side, wondering if shots would ring out or soldiers would rise out of the darkness in the gap, waiting for them. But nothing happened.

They reached the side of the circle. Mark stopped and dropped to his knees a few feet away, then crawled forwards to peek over the edge. Alec did the same, the two of them leaning over the opening. It gave Mark a sick feeling, knowing the descending piece of land was right above him. If it suddenly dropped the last bit without warning, it'd cut them both in two.

It was dark down below, but Mark could see a walkway made of silvery metal – mostly hidden in shadow – that encircled the huge space underneath. There was no light source and no sign of people. He glanced up and was alarmed at how close the leading edge of the circle had come. They had a couple of minutes, tops.

"We need to hang our feet down and swing on to that," Mark said, pointing at the walkway – a metal ledge. "Think you can do that?" he added with a grin.

Alec was already on the move. "A lot better than you, kid," he answered with a wink.

Mark rolled onto his stomach and inched his body over the lip of the opening, lowering his feet into the abyss while he held on to the edge. He gripped the edge of the rim tightly, then began to swing his legs. Alec was two steps ahead of him. The man let go, flying forwards to land on the walkway; he crumpled to the ground with a grunt but looked okay. Mark fought off the thought that tried to lodge itself in his mind – of him missing or landing awkwardly, tumbling off to disappear into the darkness. He counted to three in his mind, timing it just right with his legs swinging backward, then letting go as they swung forward.

His momentum made his gaze shift up when he let go, and he caught a last glimpse through the small crescent gap. He saw the flaming blue thrusters of a Berg and its metal underbelly coming down from the sky above. Then he lost the view and crashed on top of Alec.

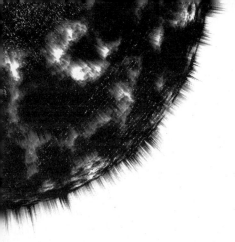

31

It took a moment for them to untangle their arms and legs. Alec was cursing and grunting, and at one point Mark started to slip off the edge and the old man pulled him back up, only to resume his cursing. Finally they were standing, straightening their clothes. And then a huge boom sounded throughout the chamber as the mechanism above them slammed shut. Complete darkness enveloped them.

"Great," Mark heard Alec say. "Can't see a thing."

"Pull out the workpad," Mark replied. "I know the battery's almost dead, but we don't have much choice."

After a grumble of agreement and a scuffling sound, the room lit up with the glow of the workpad's surface. For a second Mark was back in the tunnels of the subtrans, running with Trina by the glow of his phone. The memories began to flood in, to drown him fully in the horror of that day, but he pushed them away. He had a feeling that the next day or two might do enough to provide him with fresh ones anyway. Sighing, he wondered if he'd ever have a good night's sleep again.

"I saw a Berg dropping in at the last second before I swung down," Mark said, bringing his mind fully to the present and the task at hand. "So we know they had at least two before we crashed one of them."

Alec was shining the face of the workpad in different directions, scoping out the area. "Yeah, I could hear those thrusters. I'm guessing that the landing pad sinks down here and the Berg rolls off, then it goes back and up and rotates again. We better hurry before we have company we don't want."

Alec stopped moving the workpad, holding it up to illuminate the entrances to two chambers on opposite sides of the one in which they stood. Grooves in the floor showed where the Bergs were pulled off the landing pad once it sank down. Both cavernous spaces were dark and empty.

The walkway that encircled the abyss in the centre chamber was about four feet wide, and as they inched along, it creaked and groaned. The structure held, though Mark's heart didn't slow until he'd crossed it completely. Breathing a sigh of relief, Mark walked up to a round door with a wheel handle in the middle, like something in a submarine.

"This place was built a long time ago," Alec said as he handed the workpad over to Mark. "Probably to protect government executives in case of a world catastrophe. Too bad no one had enough time to make it here – I'm sure most of them fried like the rest."

"Nice," Mark said, holding the workpad up so he could examine the door. "You think it's locked?"

Alec had already stepped forwards and grabbed the wheel tightly with both hands, preparing as though it wouldn't budge. But when he gave it a try it spun a half circle easily, sending him lurching to the side and crashing into Mark. The two of them stumbled and fell on to the walkway, Mark on top.

"Kid," Alec said. "I've been closer to you more today than I'd hoped to be in a lifetime. Now make sure you don't fall off the edge – I need your help around here."

Mark laughed as he got to his feet, pushing off on Alec's gut a little more than he really needed to. "It's a crying shame you never had kids, old man. Just think what a good grandpa you could've been."

"Oh yeah," the former soldier replied through a grunt as he stood up. "That would've been a lot of fun imagining them all burning to death when the flares struck."

That killed the mood instantly. Mark felt his own face fall as the words made him think of his parents and Madison. Though he'd never know for sure what had happened to them, his mind was super talented at imagining the absolute worst.

Alec must have noticed. "Oh hell, I'm sorry." He reached out and squeezed Mark's shoulder. "Boy, I'm telling you right here and now, with all the sincerity an old buzzard like me can muster, that I'm sorry for what I just said. I don't envy the losses you felt that day. Not one iota. Work was my family, and it wasn't the same, I know it."

Mark had never heard the man say anything like what'd just come out of his mouth. "It's okay. Really. Thanks." He paused, then added, "Grandpa."

Alec nodded, then moved back to the wheel, spun it until there was a loud click. He swung the door open, and it clanged as it struck the wall.

The other side revealed nothing but darkness, though a rumbling hum like the sound of distant machinery grew louder.

"What is that?" Mark whispered. "It almost sounds like there's a factory or something down here." He aimed the workpad's glow through the open doorway, revealing a long hallway that disappeared into darkness.

"Generator, I'm sure," Alec responded.

"I guess they couldn't live down here without at least a little electricity. How else would this thing work?" He held the device out in front of him.

"Exactly. We've been living in the wild or in the settlements so long. It brings back memories."

"Bergs, generators . . . you think they have a ton of fuel stored here or are they bringing it in from somewhere else?"

Alec thought a second. "Well, it's been a year, and it takes a heap to keep those Bergs afloat. My guess is they're bringing it in."

"We keep going?" Mark asked, though the answer was obvious.

"Yep."

Mark stepped into the hallway first and waited for Alec to join him. "What do we do when someone sees us?" He was whispering, but his voice sounded loud in the confined quarters. "We could use a weapon or two about now."

"Tell me about it. Look, we don't have much choice here. And we don't have a whole lot to lose. Let's just keep moving and take it as it comes."

They started off down the hallway when something clanged behind them, followed by squeals and grinding gears. Mark didn't have to look to know that the landing pad – presumably with a Berg perched on top – had begun to sink into the ground.

Alec acted much calmer than Mark felt. He had to lean in to be heard over the racket. "Let's wait to see which chamber it goes into and then we'll hide in the other. We better not get caught in this hallway."

"Okay," Mark said, his heart thumping, his nerves on edge. He turned off the workpad; they didn't need it with the light spilling in from outside.

They went back through the door and pulled it shut, then crouched in the shadows of the walkway as the huge Berg descended. Luckily the cockpit was on the other side, so there was little chance of them being seen. Once it had sunk all the way down, there were more clangs and squeals and the ship started moving on tracks into the chamber to the right. Alec and Mark ran to the opposite chamber and hid in the very back, disappearing into the gloom.

The wait was agonising, but eventually the Berg found its home. When it stopped moving, the giant landing pad began to move upwards again, slowly but surely. Whoever had flown the ship had already disembarked, because Mark could faintly hear voices over the noises, then the sound of the round door being opened.

"Come on," Alec whispered into his ear. "Let's follow them."

They slipped out of the chamber and slunk along the walkway. The Berg passengers had left the door of the exit ajar, and Alec crouched next to it, leaning in to listen. He took a peek. Seemingly satisfied that they were in the clear, he gave Mark a stiff nod and slipped into the hallway once again. Mark followed just as the landing pad above him started to rotate, the bushes and earth and small trees heading back towards the sky.

Voices echoed down the passage ahead of them, but they were too distorted to understand. Alec took the workpad from Mark and slipped it inside his backpack. Then he grabbed Mark's arm and started pulling him forward, walking close to the wall, his eyes narrowed. Soon everything would be plunged back into darkness.

They crept down the hallway, step by careful step. Whoever had shown up had decided to stop and talk, because their voices became clearer as Mark and Alec continued their pursuit. It sounded like there were only two of them. Alec finally stopped as well, and suddenly Mark could hear every word.

"—just north of here," a woman was saying. "Burnt out like a brick oven. I bet it's got something to do with those people they caught last night. We'll know soon enough."

A man responded, "We better. Like things weren't bad enough without losing our other Berg. Those jacks in Alaska couldn't care less about us. Now that everything's gone weird, I bet we don't even hear from them again."

"No doubt," the woman said. "Can you say expendable?"

"Yeah, but that wasn't supposed to be *us*. It's not our fault the virus is mutating."

The landing pad clanged behind them, presumably done with its rotation. All was dark. The new arrivals started walking away, their footsteps heavy, as if they wore boots. One of them clicked on a torch, the glow from its beam bobbing up ahead. Alec grabbed Mark again and they followed, keeping a safe distance.

The two strangers didn't speak again until they reached a door. Mark heard the squeak of the hinges as it opened. Then the man said something as they stepped into a room Mark couldn't see.

"They've already got a name for it, by the way. They're calling it the Flare."

The door slammed shut.

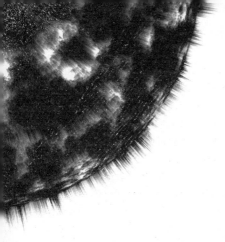

32

They hadn't heard much from the pair, but Mark didn't like the sound of it. "The Flare. He said they've started calling it the Flare. The virus."

"Yeah." Alec lit up the workpad again. The glow revealed his face – the face of a man who looked as if he'd never smiled in his life. All sags and creases. "That can't be good. If something has a nickname, that means it's big and being talked about. Not good at all."

"We need to find out what happened. Those people dancing around the fire got attacked way before us. At least their settlement did. Maybe they were some kind of test subjects?"

"Then we've got two objectives, kid: One, find Lana, Trina and that cute little whippersnapper. Two, figure out what's going on around here."

Mark couldn't have agreed more. "So let's get moving."

Alec turned off the workpad, casting the hallway into darkness. "Just run your hand along the wall," he whispered. "Try not to step on me."

They started making their way down the passage. Mark kept his footsteps light and his breathing shallow, trying to stay silent. The humming of distant machinery had grown louder, and the wall vibrated as his fingers traced an invisible line along its cool surface. They reached a spot where the slightest outline of rectangular light marked the door through which the two strangers from the Berg had gone. Alec hesitated right before it, then hurried past on his tiptoes – the least soldierly thing Mark had ever seen him do.

Mark decided to be a little braver. He stopped in front of it and leaned in, pressing his ear against the door.

"Not smart," Alec called out in a harsh whisper.

Mark didn't respond, concentrating on what he could hear. Muffled words, impossible to make out. But the discussion sounded a little heated.

"Just come on," Alec said. "I want to explore before someone locks us in a brig and throws away the key."

Mark nodded, though he doubted the man could see him very well. He moved away from the door and resumed his position next to the opposite wall, hand pressed against it. They kept walking, soon in darkness again as they left the faint light bleeding around the edges of the door.

The hallway stretched on, the world silent except for the rumble of the machinery. Mark couldn't tell when it happened exactly, but he realised he could see again. There was a hazy red glow to the air, enough that Alec looked like a creeping devil in front of him. Mark held his hand up and wiggled his fingers – they looked like they were covered in blood. Assuming Alec had noticed, too, he didn't say anything, and they continued.

They finally came upon a large door in the left wall that was slightly ajar. A red bulb covered by a wired cage hung above it. Alec stopped and stared ahead as if waiting for someone to explain what waited inside. The noises of humming and cranking machinery had escalated and now filled the air to the point that Mark couldn't whisper and be heard.

"Guess that answers the question on generators," he said. His head was really starting to ache right behind his eyes, and it hit him how exhausted he was. They'd been up through the night and half into another day. "Maybe that's where they are. Just open the stupid thing."

Alec glanced back at him. "Patience, boy. Caution. A hasty soldier is a dead soldier."

"A slow soldier means Trina and them could be dead."

Instead of responding, Alec reached out and opened the door, swinging it into the hallway. The sounds of machinery went up a notch, and a wave of heat poured from the space within, along with the stench of burning fuel.

"Oh, man," Alec said, "I forgot how bad that smells." He carefully closed the door. "Let's hope we find something more useful soon."

They came upon the next door about twenty yards further along, and there were three more past it, then finally one facing them where the hall ended. Each one of these doors also stood ajar about three inches, lit by a bulb encased in a cage just like the generator room. Except these lights were yellow and barely working.

"There's something really creepy about the doors being open," Mark whispered. "And it's so dark inside the rooms."

"What's your point?" Alec asked. "Ready to turn around and go home?"

"No. Just saying that you should go in first."

Alec chuckled. He stuck his foot out and nudged open the first door, which swung inward. It let out a metallic creak as dim yellow light spilled across the floor within, though it wasn't enough to reveal anything else. The door came to a stop with a soft thud; then there was only silence.

Alec made a harrumphing noise and walked on to the next room instead of going into the first one. He lightly kicked that door open as well, with a similar result. Mostly darkness, no sign of people, no sounds. He went to the next door and kicked it open, then to the last one at the end of the hallway. Nothing.

"Guess we better go in," he said. He turned back to Mark and jerked his head, a clear order to follow him into the last room. Mark quickly stepped up close to him, ready to do as he was told. Alec reached around the edge of the frame and searched for a light switch but came up empty, then went inside, Mark right behind him. They stood there for a moment, waiting for their eyes to adjust, searching the darkness.

Alec finally sighed and pulled out the workpad again. "What's the point of generators if none of the lights are on? This thing won't work much longer." He powered it up.

The light from the device cast a spooky blue glow across the large room – bigger than Mark would've guessed – revealing two long rows of bunks lining both walls, probably ten on each side. They were all empty except for one, almost at the end, where a slouched figure sat with its back to them; it looked to be the slumped shoulders of an older man. A chill raced through Mark at the sight of him. In the dim light, the mostly empty room, the pressing silence . . . he felt as if he were staring at the back of a ghost waiting to pronounce their doomed destiny. The person didn't move, didn't make a sound.

"Hello?" Alec called out, his voice a boom in the silence.

Mark snapped his head to look at him, shocked. "What're you doing?"

Alec's face was hidden in shadow since the workpad was pointed down the room. "Being nice," he whispered. "I'm going to ask this fella some questions." Then, louder, "Hello down there? Mind helping us out a bit?"

A low, raspy mumble – what Mark thought a man on his deathbed might sound like. The words were a jumble of lost syllables.

"What's that?" Alec asked.

The man didn't move, didn't reply. He sat on his bunk, facing away from them, a lump of a human body. Head down, shoulders slumped.

Mark suddenly had to know – *had* to – what the guy had said. He started walking down the aisle between the bunks, ignoring the short burst of protest from Alec. As he made his way towards the man, the spaces between the bunks flashing by, he heard Alec hurrying to catch up to him, the light from the workpad bobbing about and making weird shadows dance on the walls.

Mark slowed as he neared the slumped man, felt an icy tingle across his skin. The stranger was broad-shouldered and thick-chested, but his demeanour made him look frail and pathetic. Mark steered clear a few feet as he reached the man's side, saw a face covered in shadow and hanging low.

"What did you say?" Mark asked when he was in front of the man. Alec reached his side and held the workpad up to cast light on the visibly depressed stranger. The man sat forwards with elbows on knees, hands clenched together, his entire visage appearing as if it might melt and drip on to the floor.

The man slowly raised his eyes and looked at them, his head tilting on his neck like rusty machinery. His face was grave and long and wrinkled more than it should have been. His eyes were dark caverns that the light seemed unable to penetrate.

"I didn't want to give her away," he said with a raspy edge. "Oh, dear God, I didn't want to. Not to those savages."

33

Mark had so many questions he couldn't get them out fast enough.

"What do you mean?" he asked. "Who was given away? What can you tell us about this place? What about a virus? Do you know anything about two women and a little girl, maybe captured outside?" He paused to swallow the golf-ball-sized lump in his throat and slowed down. "My friend's name is Trina. Blond hair, my age. There was another woman and a girl. Do you know anything about them?"

The man lowered his gaze to the floor again and heaved a sigh. "So many questions."

Mark was so frustrated that he had to compose himself for a second. He took a deep breath and walked over to sit down on the bunk facing the raspy-voiced stranger. Maybe the old man was dotty. Bombarding him with questions probably wasn't the smartest approach. Mark looked up to see that Alec was a little astonished at his outburst, but then he shook his head and came over to join Mark on the bunk. Alec placed the

workpad on the floor so that its glow shone up and gave everyone that slightly monstrous look you get when you place a
torch under your chin.

"What can you tell us?" Alec asked in one of his gentler
tones. He'd obviously reached the same conclusion as Mark –
this guy was on edge and needed to be handled with care.
"What's happened here? All the lights are out, no one's around.
Where is everybody?"

The man merely groaned in response, then covered his face
with both hands.

Alec and Mark exchanged a look.

"Let me try again," Mark said. He leaned forward, inching
to the edge of the bunk and putting his forearms on his knees.
"Hey, man . . . what's your name?"

The stranger dropped his hands, and even in the dim light
Mark could see that his eyes were moist with tears. "My name?
You want to know my name?"

"Yeah. I want to know your name. Our lives are just as crap-
py as yours, I promise. I'm Mark and this is my friend, Alec.
You can trust us." The man made a scoffing sound, then had a
short bout of racking coughs. Finally he said, "The name's
Anton. Not that it matters."

Mark was afraid to continue. This man could hold so many
answers to so many questions, and he didn't want to screw it
up. "Listen . . . we came from one of the settlements. Three of
our friends were taken in the canyon above this place. And our
village was attacked by someone from here, we think. We just
want to . . . understand what's going on. And get our friends
back. That's it."

He sensed Alec about to say something and shot him a glare
to shut up. "Is there anything you can tell us? Like . . . what *is*
this place? What's happening out there with the Bergs and the
darts and the virus? What happened *here*? Anything you got." A
heavy weariness was starting to weigh on him, but he forced himself to focus on the man across from him, hoping for answers.

Anton took a few low, deep breaths and a tear trickled out of his right eye. "We chose a settlement two months ago," he finally said. "As a test. Not that the disastrous results changed the overall plan in the end. But the girl changed it for me. So many dead, and it was the one who lived who made me realise what a horrible thing we'd done. Like I said, I didn't want them to give her back to her people today. That's when I was truly done. Officially done."

Deedee, Mark realised. It had to be Deedee. But what about Trina and Lana? "Tell us what happened," he urged. He felt guiltier with every passing second that they weren't actively searching for their friends, but they needed information or they might never find them. "From the beginning."

Anton began to speak in a somewhat distant tone. "The Post-Flares Coalition in Alaska wanted something that spread fast, killed fast. A virus that some monsters had developed back in the good old days before the sun flares burned it all out. They say it shuts down the mind. Instant comas, they said, rendering the bodies useless but causing massive haemorrhaging that would spread it to those nearby. Transmission is by blood, but it's also airborne when the conditions are right. A good way to kill off the settlements that are forced to live in close quarters."

The man's words spilled out of him without a hitch or a change in volume. Mark's mind was growing numb from exhaustion, and he found it hard to follow the details. He knew that what he was hearing was important, but it still wasn't fitting together. How long had he been awake now? Twenty-four hours? Thirty-six? Forty-eight?

"—before they realised they'd screwed up big-time."

Mark shook his head again. He'd just missed part of what Anton had been saying.

"What do you mean?" Alec asked. "How'd they screw up?"

Anton coughed, then sniffled and wiped a hand across his nose. "The virus. It's all wrong. It didn't work right on the test subjects over the last two months, but they went ahead with the plan anyway, saying what's left of the planet's resources is being depleted. All they did was up the dosage in those darts. Those bastards are trying to wipe out half the population. Half!"

"What about the little girl?" Mark almost shouted. "Did she have two women with her?"

Anton didn't seem to be hearing a word that Mark or Alec said. "They said we'd be taken care of once the deed was done. That they'd bring us all back to Alaska and give us homes and food and protection. Let half the world die and we'd start over. But they screwed up, didn't they? That little girl lived even though she was struck with a dart. But it's more than that. The virus isn't what they thought. It spreads like wildfire, all right. Too bad it's got a mind of its own. Pardon the pun."

He let out something that was vaguely like a chuckle, but it soon transformed into a hacking cough. Suddenly he was sobbing freely. The man finally slumped over on to his side and pulled his legs up on to the bunk, curling into the foetal position, his shoulders shaking as he cried.

"I've got it," he said through the sobs. "I'm sure of it. We've all got it. You've got it, too. Have no doubts, my friends. You've got the virus. I told my co-workers I didn't want anything to do with them. Not any more. They left me up here by myself. Suits me just fine."

Mark felt like he was observing the whole scene through a fog. He couldn't concentrate. He tried to snap out of it. "Do you have any idea where our friends could be?" he asked, more calmly this time. "Where are your co-workers?"

"They're all down below," Anton whispered. "I couldn't bear it any more. I came up here to die or go crazy. Both, I guess. I'm just glad they let me."

"Down below?" Alec repeated.

"Further down in the bunker," Anton answered, his voice getting quieter as his crying subsided. "They're down there, planning. Planning to revolt in Asheville, let them know we're not happy how things ended up. They wanna take it all the way to Alaska."

Mark looked at Alec, who was just staring at Anton. It seemed like everything the poor stranger said was a little more bizarre than the statement before it.

"Revolt?" Mark asked. "Why Asheville? And who are these people?"

"Asheville is the last safe haven in the East," the man replied, his words barely perceptible now, nothing but dry, faint rasps. "Walls and everything – ramshackle as they may be. And *they* are my co-workers, all hired by the PFC – the almighty Post-Flares Coalition. My esteemed associates want to bring their bosses down before they pull out. Before they head back to Alaska through the Flat Trans."

"Anton," Alec said. "Listen to me. Is there anyone else we can talk to? And how can we find out about the friends we're looking for? The girl, two women."

The man coughed; then a little more life sprang into his voice. "Those people I work with have started to lose their minds. Do you understand? They're . . . not . . . right. They'll be down there for hours, planning and scheming. They're going to Asheville, and they'll gather an army along the way if they have to. Oh, there's talk of an antidote there, but that's a bunch of hooey. In the end, my people will make sure that others don't get what's been taken from them: life. And you know what they'll do after that. You know, don't you?"

"What?" Mark and Alec said at the same time.

Anton got up on to one elbow. The angle of light from the workpad caused one half of his face to be in shadow from the bunk, the other in that pale blue glow. The eye on the lighted side looked as if a spark had been lit inside the pupil.

"They'll go to Alaska through that Flat Trans in Asheville," the man said. "They'll go to where the governments have gathered and make sure the world ends, even though that's not their intent. They'll carry on about finding an antidote and taking down the makeshift government. But all they'll *really* do is spread the virus once and for all. Make sure they finish what the sun flares started. Fools, every last one of them."

Anton collapsed back into a heap on the bunk, and a few seconds later the sounds of his snores filled the room.

34

Mark and Alec sat in silence for a long time, listening to the wheezes and hitched breathing of Anton as he slept.

"I'm not sure we can trust much of what came out of this guy's mouth," Alec said after a while. "But I'm troubled, to say the least."

"Yeah," Mark responded flatly. His head was pounding and he felt sick to his stomach. He couldn't remember the last time he'd felt so tired. But they had to get up, get out of that room, find Trina and the others.

He didn't move.

"Boy, you look like a zombie," Alec said after twisting to face him. "And I feel like one."

"Yeah," Mark said again.

"You're not going to like what I'm about to say, but there'll be no argument."

Mark raised his eyebrows. Even that seemed to take all the energy he had. "And what's that?"

"We need to sleep."

"But . . . Trina . . . Lana . . ." He suddenly couldn't remember the little girl's name. Impossible. His head ached like a storm had erupted inside his skull.

Alec stood up. "We're not going to do our friends a bit of good if we can't function because we're too tired. We'll just catch a few winks. Maybe an hour each while the other keeps an eye out. Anton said his co-workers would be in some meeting for hours." He got up from the bed and walked quickly over to the door to the room, closed it, locked it. "Just to be safe."

Mark slumped to his side, then slowly drew his legs up on to the bunk. He folded his arms under his head. He wanted to protest but nothing came out.

Alec started talking again. "I'll take first watch, so . . ."

But Mark fell asleep before he heard any more.

The dreams came. The memories. More vivid than ever before. As if the depth of his exhaustion had created the perfect canvas for them.

35

There's that short moment that seems to last a lifetime when Mark sees the wall of water rushing down the steps of the subtrans station, like a stampede of white, frothy horses. He wonders a thousand things. How did he get there? What's happened above them in the city? Is his family dead? What does the future hold? What's it like to drown?

All these thoughts storm through his mind in the one second it takes for the water to reach the bottom of the steps. Then someone is grabbing his arm, pulling him in the opposite direction, forcing his head to turn away from the oncoming disaster. He sees Trina, yanking on him as pure terror brightens her eyes in a sick way that snaps him into motion.

He breaks into an all-out run, this time grabbing *her* arm, making sure they stay together. Alec and Lana are right ahead of them, moving quickly, passing the thugs who accosted them, a thing that now seems so silly and outrageous it angers Mark all over again. The moment passes; he keeps running down the tunnel, Trina by his side. He shoots a quick glance backward, sees Baxter, Darnell, the Toad, Misty, all keeping up, their eyes painted with the same fear as Trina's, the same fear that Mark feels himself.

There's a great rushing sound in the air that takes Mark back to his family's visit to Niagara Falls. People are screaming and things are breaking, glass shattering. Alec looks nothing like an old man as he sprints past the far edge of the station landing and slips back into the darkness of the train-sized tunnel. They can't have much time, and Mark realises with a jolt of horror that he's entrusted his entire life to the two people in front of him. That this is it. That he'll be alive or dead within minutes.

Someone cries out behind him; then he's hit hard in the shoulder, and he stumbles. He rights himself, letting go of Trina, who can't stop her momentum and keeps rushing forward. Mark looks back and sees two things: Misty has fallen to the ground, and a surging pool of water is funnelling down the tracks of the subtrans from the station. The deluge of water from the streets above is washing over the landing and spilling into the wide groove of the tunnel, and it's just a few dozen feet away.

When it washes over Misty's body, the flood is already inches deep. She pushes against the ground to get up. Mark is leaning forwards to help when Misty suddenly screams and leaps to her feet as if the water carries an electric charge.

"It's hot!" she yells as she reaches out and squeezes Mark's hand.

They turn and begin running again, water now sloshing across their feet. It soaks through Mark's shoes and socks, the bottom of his pants, and he feels its warmth, then its full heat. He jumps, like someone who has stepped into a bath with the temperature drawn too high. It's unnerving, and hot enough to burn his skin.

The group continues to run down the tunnel, doing their best to slog through the rising river. It's suddenly two feet high and Mark can't believe how quickly it's happened. It moves up past his knees and it's coming faster now – he has to plant his feet more firmly to prevent them from being swept out from under him. He catches up with Trina, the others only a few feet ahead. They're not running any more. They're struggling, using their whole bodies to push forwards step by careful step. The water is almost to Mark's upper thighs, and he knows the current is about to win the battle against all of them.

And it burns, scalding his skin. He itches from the pain of it.

"Right here!" Alec screams. Straining against the dirty, raging river, fighting the current, he's sloshed his way over to the left. There's a short set of steps there, an iron railing on both sides. It leads up to a landing and a door. "We need to get up there!"

Mark is moving in that direction, planting his feet one at a time, re-establishing his position with every step. Trina is doing the same. Lana is already there. Baxter, Misty, Darnell and the Toad are all behind Mark, making their way as well. They can't last much longer in the current. The roar of the water is deafening, broken only by Alec's words and the screams from back in the station echoing down the walls of the tunnel. Those noises have decreased dramatically, and Mark knows why. Most of the people are dead.

As if the thought must be made real, a body bumps into Mark's knee, then whips past in the river – a woman. Her face is the blue of death, framed by a floating mat of hair. She spins slowly as she rushes deeper into the black tunnel beyond. Then there are more. Some alive, most unmoving – probably dead, Mark realises. The living are flailing their arms and legs, trying to swim or gain purchase on the ground. Mark has the fleeting thought that they should try to help them, reach for their hands. But it's too late – they'll be lucky to get themselves out.

Alec has reached the stairs, has grabbed the iron railing, takes two steps up. Mark moves another sluggish step forward; the water is up to his waist now. Burning, roasting. Alec leans down and helps Lana up the stairs. Then Trina makes it, grabs his hand. Up she goes. Mark is next. He takes the last tremulous step and he's suddenly clasping forearms with the old man who keeps saving his life. His body jolts forwards as Alec pulls him hard and he's on the stairs, almost falling forwards on to his face. Trina catches him, hugs him.

The Toad makes it, then Darnell, then Misty. All of them but Alec up the short flight of stairs and on to the landing, grouping together in front of the door. The younger boy, Baxter, is struggling. Mark's suddenly struck by shame as he realises the kid's still out there – he's six feet beyond Alec's reach, the water slamming into his side, rising and rising, splashing up into his frightened face.

Mark runs back down the stairs even as Trina is calling his name. He stands next to Alec, wonders what to do. Bodies are shooting past Baxter; Mark sees a stray foot smack the kid in the shoulder. A head bobs up out of the river right next to him, spewing water, then disappears back under.

"Take a step!" Alec screams at Baxter.

The boy responds, does as he's told. Then takes another. He's almost within reach now, but the water is beating at his back, making it seem impossible that he hasn't been swept away yet.

Mark yells encouragement this time. "Just a couple more."

Baxter moves forwards and is suddenly off his feet, facedown. Alec jumps out at him, grabs the boy's arm just as the current latches on to both of them, ready to yank them away into the darkness. Marks sees it all happen so fast, reacts before he has time to think. He grips the iron railing with his left hand and lunges forwards with his right, grasping the sleeve of Alec's shirt before he's swept out of reach. The man's hand comes up and grips Mark's arm just as the material starts to rip.

Mark's body is jerked into the current but he holds on to the railing; his body is pulled out and then to the side, slamming into the concrete wall next to the track. Alec and Baxter follow, their bodies linked. Mark feels as if his arm is about to be ripped from its socket, his muscles straining, screaming. He can only focus on not letting go to ignore the pain. Water rushes into his mouth and he spits it out. It tastes like dirt and oil and burns his tongue.

He feels hands grabbing his arm, gripping his shirt and elbow, pulling. From the other side he can tell that Alec is climbing him like a rope, using both hands. Which means Baxter must be gone. Mark can do nothing, his strength spent, every part of his body aching and burning. He can only hold tight, keep the link intact. His head slips under the water and he closes his eyes, forces himself to resist the urge to suck in a breath that would kill him.

He loses all sense of movement. There is only water and heat and the rush of sound. And the pain, bursting through his body.

Then he breaks the surface, feels hands on his chest, under his arm. He's being dragged backwards up the stairs. Alec is right in front of him, having caught hold of the railing. Baxter is clasped tightly between the man's legs, like the winning grip of a wrestling match. Even as Mark looks, Baxter's face comes up and out of the river and the boy is breathing, spitting, screaming.

They made it. They all made it.

Soon they are on their feet, on the landing. All of them. The water has risen to the upper edge of the track's groove and is beginning to spill on to the landing itself.

Alec is a man whose every inch speaks of exhaustion. Soaking wet, breathing deeply and raggedly. He lurches forwards to the door, opens it. Mark has the thought that it could've been locked. Their story could've been over and done right then and there. But it's open, and Alec swings it wide.

He motions for everyone to go through.

"Get ready to climb," the old man says.

36

Mark woke up shivering in complete darkness.

His body was stiff; he shifted on the bunk and it creaked as he tried to get comfortable, find a position in which his muscles didn't ache. He heard Alec and Anton both snoring loudly. Alec obviously hadn't lasted long at first watch.

Mark finally settled on his back. Sleep had officially washed away, and there was nothing to do but wait until his friend woke up. He'd let the man get as much rest as possible – they were probably going to need it.

The dream had seemed so vivid, so lifelike. His heart was still beating from the rush of the experience, like he'd just relived it for real. He could taste the foul water, feel the burns on his skin. He remembered the exhausting climb up the endless flight of stairs afterward, the winding, the dizzying back-and-forth. Sapped of strength and hurting from the water burn, he didn't know how he'd kept up with the others. But up and up they'd gone as the water rose below them. He'd never forget the feeling of looking over the railing, down at the roiling, dirty liquid as it slowly ascended, thinking that his life had almost ended in its depths.

Alec had saved them that day. They'd spent the next two weeks in that skyscraper, realising quickly that they couldn't search for loved ones yet. The heat and radiation and rising waters were too much. That was when Mark's hopes of ever finding his family had truly begun to fade.

The Lincoln Building. A place that held plenty of its own nightmares. They'd stayed as close to the centre of the building as possible, in the structure's middle corridors, to protect themselves from the sun's ruthless radiation. Even so, they'd all been a little sick those first few months.

He heard a groan from the direction of Alec's bunk, and the thoughts floated away, pushed to the back of his mind to torment him later. But that feeling of terror he'd experienced in those last moments in the subtrans tunnel wouldn't leave, lingering like the smoke from an extinguished fire.

"Oh . . . crap," Alec said.

Mark popped up on to his elbow, looking in the direction of his friend. "What?"

"I didn't mean to fall asleep. Fine soldier I am. And I left the damn workpad on. We can forget using that thing again."

"Meh, the battery was probably almost dead anyway," Mark said. Though in truth, he'd have given anything for five more minutes of the device's glow right then.

Alec groaned and Mark heard the sounds of the bunk creaking as the older man got to his feet.

"We need to find this guy's co-workers. He said they were meeting further down in the bunker. So we need to find our way to some stairs," the man said.

"What do we do about him?" Mark pointed to Anton, forgetting for a second that Alec couldn't see him in the darkness.

"Let him sleep out his sorrows. Come on."

Mark took a moment to get his bearings, then got up and

felt his way to the end of the bunk towards the middle aisle of the room.

"How long do you think we slept?" he asked.

"No idea," Alec answered. "Maybe two hours?"

They spent the next few minutes slowly making their way through the room and out into the hallway. The light above the door still sputtered a bit, but barely enough to see by. They eventually found the stairwell Alec had been hoping for. Even the dim sight of it, mostly lines and edges of shadow descending into blackness, brought back to Mark the memory of the flood and their mad clamber up the stairs of the skyscraper. It'd been so close that day. If he'd known all that would come after, would he still have fought so hard to survive?

Yes, he told himself. Yes, he would have. And he was going to find Trina and get out of hot water again. He almost laughed at his own joke.

"Let's get on with it," Alec whispered as he started down the steps.

Mark followed him, determined to stop dwelling on the past. He had to focus on the future or he'd never reach it.

The flight of stairs only descended three levels, though there was no exit until they reached the final one. They pushed through the door and found themselves in another hallway. They'd finally come upon the section of the bunker that used the raving generators above: a line of lights along the ceiling illuminated the passage. Unlike the hallway they'd come from, this one curved.

Mark shot a glance at Alec and they started down the hall. There were doors lining the walls, but Alec suggested that they explore the length of the corridor before they tried each one. They slipped along, as quietly as possible, and it wasn't long before it became clear that the hallway was a giant crescent.

They'd traversed about half of what they could see of its length when Mark heard voices, then saw their source. Up ahead, on the left, there was a set of double doors, one propped all the way open. The sounds were coming from whatever was happening in that room. A gathering of some sort, men and women talking over each other so that Mark couldn't make out a single word being said. Anton's meeting, his co-workers.

Alec slowed as he approached the room, and carefully stepped forwards until he was right next to it, his back pressed against the closed door. He turned to look at Mark, shrugged as if to say it's now or never, then craned his neck towards the opening and leaned in for a peek. Mark held his breath, remembering all too well that they had no weapons.

Alec pulled his head back and sidled a couple feet towards Mark. "It's an auditorium. It's pretty big, seats about two hundred, maybe. They're all down at the bottom watching some guy on the stage."

"How many are there?" Mark whispered.

"At least forty. Maybe fifty. No sign of our friends, as far as I can tell. They all seem to be arguing about something, but I can't tell what they're saying."

"So what do we do?" Mark asked. "Keep going? This hall can't go on much longer."

"If we get down on our hands and knees we can crawl in there and down the back. We can hide in a corner over on the right. I think we need to hear what these people are saying."

Mark agreed. They didn't know who these people were or what they were up to, but it seemed like the only way to find out. The safest way, at least. "Okay, let's do it."

They crouched on all fours and got ready, Mark right behind Alec. The soldier leaned forwards to take a look around the edge of the door; then he started crawling into the large room. Mark followed, feeling almost naked as they entered the open air of the auditorium. But no one was close to the back – the voices were all coming from below and sounded far enough away. And judging from the fact that they all seemed to be talking at once, Mark had a feeling they weren't on the alert for intruders.

Alec crawled along the last row, his side pressed against the black plastic of the chairs, until he got all the way to the far right side of the room, where the corner was shadowed in darkness. He stopped and situated himself, his legs crossed, his body wedged into the space between the last chair and the wall. Mark moved to sit next to him. He had to tuck himself in closer than was comfortable in order to stay as hidden as possible.

Alec stretched up and peeked over the chair in front of them, then sank down again quickly.

"Can't see much. Seems like they're waiting for something to begin. Or maybe they're taking a break. I don't know."

Mark closed his eyes and leaned his head against the wall. They sat there for what seemed like for ever. At least ten excruciating minutes passed with nothing changing. Just the buzz of mixed conversation. Then, suddenly, a blur of movement made him catch his breath. A man had walked into the auditorium from the hallway, a quick flash of motion as he entered and began walking down the aisle towards the front. Mark breathed a sigh of relief that he hadn't been seen.

The crowd grew quiet and still, the room dropping into an almost eerie silence. Mark could actually hear the man's footsteps as he reached the bottom of the room and climbed a set of stairs on to the stage.

"I'll take over from here, Stanley," a deep voice said, echoing off the ceiling even though he'd said it softly. Acoustics.

"Thanks, Bruce," came the reply from Stanley, a man with a much higher voice. "Everyone give him your full attention."

There was the sound of someone descending the stairs and then the rattle of him sitting in one of the chairs. When silence fell once again, the newcomer began to speak.

"Let's get this started, people. It won't be long before we all lose our minds."

37

As if the man's opening statement wasn't bizarre enough, the crowd clapped and cheered after he said it, making Mark shiver. Bruce waited for it to die down on its own before he spoke again. Mark was anxious to hear what the guy would say next.

"Frank and Marla are back from a flyby of the areas around Asheville. Just as we thought, they've shored up those walls nice and tight. Humanity and charity, my friends? Those days are long gone. The PFC has created an army of monsters, people who used to be willing to give the shirt off their backs for a neighbour in need. No longer. Those scumbags in Alaska and North Carolina – our very own Asheville – have turned their backs on the settlements once and for all. Worse, they've turned their backs on us. *Us!*"

This elicited a chorus of angry shouts, stomping of feet and banging on the armrests of the chairs. The noises echoed through the room until Bruce started talking again.

"They sent us here!" he shouted. His voice was louder now.

"They assigned us to take part in the worst civil rights fiasco since the War of 2020. A holocaust! But they were firm that it was for the survival of the human race. They said it was to save what little resources we have, to be able to feed those people they deemed *worthy* to live. But who are they to decide who's worthy?" He paused for a moment before he continued. "Well, ladies and gentlemen, it seems that we are not worthy. They sent us here to do their dirty work and now they've decided to cut us off. Who are *they*, I ask all of you!"

He practically screamed the last sentence and once again sent the crowd into a fit of near hysterics. People screamed and stomped their feet. The roar made Mark's temples throb and the inside of his forehead ache. He thought it might never end, but it did, abruptly. He imagined that Bruce had made a gesture to silence them.

"Here's where we stand," the man said, much calmer. "The test subjects are getting more fanatical in their odd little religious cult by the day. We've made a deal with them. They wanted the little girl back. Seems that they want to sacrifice her to their newfound spirits. I think they've passed the point of no return. They're beyond any help we could give them. They can barely go a day without fighting each other, reorganising factions, starting over until they battle again. But we made a deal with the few who still seem to be operating on some sane level – I'm sick and tired of worrying who's going to jump out of a tree and attack me every time I walk outside."

He paused, allowed a long, lingering moment of silence. "We gave them the little girl and the two women we found with her. I know it's harsh, but it buys us a little time where we don't have to worry about those people. I don't want to waste the precious ammo we have left defending ourselves against a cult."

Mark suddenly had a rushing sound in his ears. The little girl. The two women. *Gave them.* The things Anton had said back in the bunk room. It all thudded in his mind, made him tremble. He thought back to how crazy those people at the bonfire were, and a situation he'd thought couldn't get worse did just that. They'd wasted all this time in the bunker and their friends weren't even there any more.

Bruce was still talking, but Mark couldn't focus on the words. He leaned in to speak in Alec's ear. "How could they have given them to those . . . *people*? We have to go. Who knows what those psychos will do to them!"

Alec held a hand out to urge calm. "I know. We will. But remember the reason we came here. Let's hear what this man has to say, then we'll go. I promise. Lana means as much to me as Trina does to you."

Mark nodded, leaned back into the wall again. Tried to listen to what Bruce was saying down on the stage.

"—fire is out, thanks to the latest storm that rolled in a couple of hours ago. The sky's black, but the flames are dead. We're going to be dealing with mudslides all over the place. The test subjects all fled to the half-burnt mountain homes, by the looks of it. Hopefully they'll stay put awhile before they get desperate and march on Asheville for food. But I think we're safe to head over to the city in the next day or two. Force our way in, demand our rights. We'll go by foot and hope to surprise them."

There were a few worried murmurs before he continued. "Look, we can't deny that we're dealing with our own outbreak now. We've all seen the symptoms, right here in our *safe* house. There's just no way our superiors would've agreed to unleash this virus without having something to reverse its effects. And I say that they'll give it to us or they'll all die. Even if we have to go all the way to Alaska to do it. We know they have a Flat Trans at their headquarters. We'll go through it and make them give us what we deserve!"

More cheers and pounding feet thundered through the air.

Mark shook his head. These people were obviously unstable. There was a wild energy in the room, like they were a nest of vipers, tensing to strike. Whatever the reason for spreading this virus, it was clear what it did to people: it made them crazy, and it appeared to be taking more time to do it as it spread. And if Asheville, the largest surviving city within hundreds of miles, really had erected walls to keep itself safe from the disease, things must be bad. Then the last thing anyone needed was a bunch of infected soldiers running through the streets. And the Flat Trans . . .

Mark's head still pounded and throbbed and it was hard to sort out his thoughts. He knew he had to focus on Trina, getting her back. But what about all this new information? He elbowed Alec, gave him a look that said his patience was running out.

"Soon, boy," the man whispered. "Never skip a chance to get intel. Then we'll go and find our friends. I swear it."

Mark wasn't willing to sacrifice Trina for information. Not after what they'd been through to survive this long. He couldn't wait much longer.

The room had grown quiet again.

"The *Post- . . . Flares . . . Coalition.*" Bruce pronounced every word with exaggerated diction and spite. "Who do these people think they are? Gods? They can just choose to wipe out the entire eastern half of the United States? Like the PFC has more right to live than anyone else?"

There was another long pause after that. Mark couldn't take it any more. He crawled around Alec and slowly peeked over the chair to take a look. Bruce was a large man with a bald head that shone in the dull light, his face pale and scruffy with a few days' worth of beard. The muscles of his arms and shoulders bulged against a tight black shirt as he stood with hands clasped in front of him, staring at the floor. If Mark hadn't heard all the things the man had just said, he'd think he could be praying.

"Don't feel bad, friends. We couldn't have said no to what they asked us to do," Bruce said, slowly raising his eyes to gaze at his captive audience again. "We had no choice. They used the very resources they're trying to preserve against us. We have to eat, too, right? It's not our fault the virus wasn't quite what they expected. All we can do is what we've done since the sun flares struck the Earth: fight tooth and nail to *live*. Darwin taught about survival of the fittest in the natural world. Well, the PFC is trying to cheat nature. It's time to stand up for ourselves. We . . . will . . . *live*!"

Another raucous round of cheers and whistles and clapping and foot pounding went on for a good minute or two. Mark slunk back to sit next to Alec, feeling stronger than ever that they had to get moving. He was just about to say something when the crowd fell silent and Bruce's voice filled the room like the amplified hiss of a snake.

"But first, my friends, I need you to do something for me. We have two spies in the back of this auditorium. They could very well be from the PFC. I want them bound and gagged by the time I count to thirty."

38

Mark was jumping to his feet almost before the man had finished his sentence, and Alec was close behind him.

A vicious roar erupted from the crowd like a war cry as Mark paused to take them all in. The group was already on the move, springing from their chairs and stumbling over each other to be the first ones to get up the aisle to the two intruders.

Mark ran towards the double doors of the exit, unable to take his eyes off the scene below, observing it with a strange mix of horror and curiosity. Bruce was bellowing orders and pointing his finger at Mark and Alec, his pale face now red with anger. There was something childish about his movements, almost cartoonish. The urgency with which his followers were clamouring to get into the open aisle also seemed exaggerated somehow, like they were all hopped up on some kind of drug. Men and women yelling and growling like apes on a rampage. Each wanting to capture *him,* acting like their life depended on being the first to do it.

Alec reached the doors first and practically flung himself out into the hallway. Mark skidded to a stop, his focus so intent on the onrushing crowd that he almost ran past the exit. That odd and misplaced sense of curiosity at their behaviour winked out finally, replaced by the horrific thump of realisation that he was about to be captured for the second time in so many days. Their cries of pursuit tore through the air and scared him, and with a quick sideways glance as he exited the room he saw the first of their group charging up the main aisle of the auditorium with bloodlust in their eyes.

He slipped on the floor of the hallway, caught his balance. Alec had reached out and closed the door after Mark came through, maybe buying them a couple of seconds. The light was dim, but Mark could tell Alec had forgotten which way they'd come from.

"It's this way!" Mark yelled, already running. He heard Alec's footsteps behind him until there was the loud bang of the door slamming back open, followed by the rush of bodies and their continued battle cries.

Mark ran hard, trying his best not to imagine their pursuers or what they'd do if they caught him. Bruce had said to bind and gag them, but the look Mark had seen on their faces told him that was only the beginning. He glanced back to make sure Alec was keeping up, saw the old bear pumping his arms and pounding his feet, then focused ahead again, sprinting along the slow curve of the hallway. He was heading for the stairs because he didn't know where else to go but up.

Adrenalin shot through Mark and hunger gnawed at his stomach. He couldn't remember the last time he'd eaten. He could only hope he had enough energy to escape back into the woods above them. The stairwell came into view up ahead and he burst forwards with a little more speed. The shouts from their pursuers echoed and tore through the narrow space of the hall, reminding Mark of that almost muffled screeching sound the approaching trains of the subtrans made as they sped along the tracks of their tunnels.

Mark reached the stairs, was already leaping on to the second one by the time Alec made it. He heard the man's heavy breathing mixed with his own, the solid thumps of their feet pounding the steps. Mark grabbed the railing at each switch-back, throwing himself forwards and on to the next set. He and Alec charged up the three levels, reaching the top just as Mark heard their pursuers reach the bottom. The hollow echo of their frantic cries sent chills across his sweaty skin.

He ran out into the upper hallway, which was still cloaked in darkness, something he could only hope would help them. A sudden moment of indecision hit him, causing a burst of panic.

"Which way?" he yelled at Alec. A part of him thought they should hide somewhere – maybe in the room that held the generators. Searching for an exit meant they'd be out in the open and just waiting for capture if they didn't find one, but hiding would only delay being found.

Instead of answering, Alec started running to the right, back in the direction of the huge, pivoting landing pad of the Berg. Mark followed him, relieved that his friend had taken charge again.

They ran through the darkness at a reckless speed. Mark ran his hand against the wall to keep his bearings, but he knew that if he came across something on the floor he was a goner. They passed the generator room, its struggling red bulb of faint light giving them a brief break from the pitch-black, the hum of machinery like the drone of bees. Both the glow and the noise faded as they sprinted past. It was at that moment that Mark noticed something that almost made him stop.

The sounds of the people chasing them had ceased. Completely. As if they'd never made it up the stairs.

"Alec," he whispered, barely hearing his own voice over their heaving breathing and footsteps. He repeated it a little louder.

His friend came to a halt, and Mark passed him before he could stop too. Sucking in deep breaths, Mark turned back to face Alec, wishing desperately for a little light.

"Why'd it stop?" he wondered aloud.

"I don't know," Alec responded. "But we should keep moving." Mark heard the man feeling his way along the walls of the corridor. "You do the right side, I'll stick to the left. Maybe there's another exit we don't know about."

Mark started searching; the walls were cool to the touch. He remembered the door with the faint rectangle of light from before – but there was no sign of it now. It was maddening to be in such darkness, and not knowing what had happened to the people chasing them put him on edge. It didn't sit right with him.

They reached the end of the hallway, where the round submarine-like door led back into the chamber below the Berg landing pad. He heard Alec step through the opening, then come back out.

"Can't see a thing in there, either."

"There's nowhere else to go," Mark replied. "Let's just get in there and shut that door until we figure something out. Maybe we can keep it—"

Alec shushed him, cutting off his sentence. "Did you hear that?" he whispered.

The question alone made Mark shiver. He grew completely still and held his breath. At first he heard nothing; then there was a rustling sound, faint, but coming from down the hallway. It continued, and oddly, the noise played tricks, seeming to be close one second and far the next. Suddenly Mark was struck by the feeling that they weren't alone.

Terror lit up his nerves. He moved to grab Alec, to push him through the doorway, knowing it was their only shot. Getting in there and slamming the thing closed, spinning the wheel handle, keeping it shut. But Mark had only taken one step forwards when there was a click, followed by the blinding beam of a torch pointed directly at Mark and Alec. Whoever held it was only a few steps away.

"We didn't say you could leave yet," a woman said.

39

There was a sudden rush of movement, the sound of other torches being clicked on, their beams crisscrossing and bobbing in a chaotic dance through the air. Bruce's people were charging forward, reigniting their shouts and cries of attack. Mark turned towards Alec, who was already reaching out, grabbing his shirt and pulling him towards the open portal.

Alec was halfway through, his fist still clutching Mark's shirt, when the storm of lights reached them. Their beams were blinding. Someone grabbed Mark's foot and heaved it up into the air, and he crashed to the floor, the back of his head smacking down hard. Mark was suddenly jerked along the floor by his leg. He slid, bumping against people as he thrashed, trying to kick himself loose.

Alec shouted his name but Mark could barely hear him over the mass of angry people. They surrounded Mark and someone kicked him in the ribs; a woman let out a shrill cry and punched him in the stomach. He groaned and tried to curl into a ball, twisting his foot so hard that it sprang free from his captor's grip. Taking advantage of the moment, he flipped on to his stomach and started crawling back towards the door. He was a flurry of arms and legs, frantically trying to stay out of everyone's reach.

A roar cut through the melee: a booming growl, a noise that might come out of a she-bear protecting a cub. It was Alec – and suddenly bodies were flying everywhere. The man had charged forwards and leaped into the fray, taking down half the people trying to get to Mark. In the frenzy, someone fell on Mark's leg, someone else on his back. He twisted around and then there was someone sitting on his face. There was a moment when everything seemed absolutely ridiculous, like Mark had fallen into a clown act in a circus, and he almost laughed.

Then someone slapped him on the cheek, clearing that image right out of his head. Mark screwed up his fist and punched back but missed, tried again and again without connecting, his arms flailing like a blind boxer's. On the fourth or fifth try he smashed his fist into someone's chin and they cried out. He caught a glimpse of Alec fighting like a lion, pushing people and elbowing faces and throwing bodies to the floor. There was the clank of a torch falling, then the tinny scrape of it rolling until it came to rest against the wall. Its light shone across the floor and illuminated the circle of the door to the chamber, maybe a dozen feet away. Mark knew they had to somehow fight their attackers off and get through there or they were done for.

Mark had climbed to his hands and knees but someone jumped on to his back, taking him down again. An arm slipped around his neck, started squeezing. Mark gagged, gasping for breath as his airway was cut off. His lungs ached. He got his hands underneath himself and pushed off the floor, twisting to the side, throwing the attacker off. He spun and kicked the assailant in the face, realising at the last second that it was a woman. Her head cracked to the right and blood flew from her nose.

Two other people rushed Mark from behind and grabbed his arms, pulled him to his feet. He tried to break free but their holds were too tight. A man stepped in front of him, a vicious grin crossing his face. He drew back his arm, slammed his fist into Mark's stomach. Mark doubled over at the explosion of pain and nausea. He retched but had nothing in his stomach to throw up.

He heard another roar come from Alec and then the man tackled one of the people holding Mark. As soon as that arm was free Mark swung back hard and smashed his elbow into the chin of the other person, freeing his other arm. He lunged forwards and took the man who'd punched him to the ground, where he landed with an "oomph".

Mark didn't bother with him any more. He scrambled to his feet, then dived towards the stray torch he'd seen roll up against the wall. He slid across the floor and grabbed it, gripped it tightly in his fist. Then he stood up and swung its hard metal end in an arc before even looking at who might be coming at him. He connected, hitting some guy in the ear; the man cried out and crumpled to the ground. Alec, who'd stolen someone else's torch, was just getting up from a tussle he'd had with two or three people who lay unmoving at the man's feet. Mark ran to him and they slowly turned in a circle to face the remaining attackers, who still greatly outnumbered them. Packed together into two groups, one on each side of the hallway, the people seemed to be readying for one last charge to smash Mark and Alec in the middle.

Mark shone his light and noticed that the group between them and the door of the chamber was the smaller of the two, maybe eight people total. At least chance had given them that much. As if he and Alec were communicating telepathically, they roared and charged the small group at the same time. They crashed into them, sending bodies flying and tumbling all over each other. Mark went ballistic in a fit of desperation, kicking and kneeing and swinging the butt end of his torch at anything that moved. Scrambling and crawling and pushing, twisting away anytime someone tried to latch on to his limbs or clothes, he moved forward, barrelling through the crowd of people.

Somehow Mark reached the other side, with a free path to the open door. Alec fought his way through as well, falling with one last surge but quickly leaping back to his feet. And then they were both running to the circular opening, climbing through. In seconds Alec was on the door, pushing to swing it shut. Several arms slipped through the gap, blocking the door from closing.

"Come and help me!" he yelled.

Mark beat at hands and fingers with his torch; then Alec pulled back on the door and pushed it forwards again, crushing it against those still trying to fight their way in. There were yelps and screams, and several pulled out. But another surge pressed ahead and almost made Alec topple over.

Mark abandoned his torch to help Alec. Together they held the outer rim of the door and jerked it open, then rammed it against those trying to break in. More arms pulled out, only to be replaced by new ones just as Mark and Alec swung the door out and slammed the edge against the assailants again. More cries of anguish, fewer arms left. They did it again. And again. Quicker, with more force, and a little closer each time.

"One more big one!" Alec yelled.

Mark braced himself, pulled the door out, then screamed and threw his body and all his strength into it. The slab of metal crunched bones and smashed fingers, and every body part disappeared from view.

Alec leaned into the door and closed it with a booming metallic ring.

Mark spun the wheel.

40

The deafening silence that filled the room was broken by the squeal of the wheel handle as Mark wrenched it tighter and tighter. Alec helped him when the people on the other side tried to spin it back. The tighter they could turn it, the easier it was to prevent the attackers from doing the opposite.

"Just hang on to that puppy," Alec finally said when they couldn't turn it any further. He took a step back and Mark gripped the right portion of the ring with both hands and hung on it. The chamber in front of him, where the landing pad rotated before lowering down into the ground, was empty and vast. Mark's head pounded with pain, along with the rest of his body, after the scrum in the bunker hallway.

Alec was just picking up the torch he'd dropped, which was right next to Mark's. The soldier shone the bluish light towards the chamber to the right, finding the massive shape of the Berg nestled there. Dust motes danced in the beam as he swung it back and forth, revealing scarred metal and rows of bolts and protruding edges and ridges. In the relative darkness, the whole thing looked like some alien vessel rising from the abyss of the ocean.

"It feels a lot bigger inside," Mark said. His arms were getting tired, but he could feel tension on the handle, the wheel inching up, then dropping back down again. "Any chance of getting out of here in that thing?"

Alec was slowly walking around the ship, searching the Berg for something, probably the hatch door. "Best idea you've had all day."

"Good thing you're a pilot." There were low, dull thumps on the door and Mark imagined Bruce's people half out of their minds wanting to get through, beating on it in frustration.

"Yeah . . . ," Alec was saying absently. Soon his voice came from the other side of the Berg, echoing off the walls. "The hatch door is over here!"

Their pursuers suddenly stopped their efforts, grew quiet.

"They gave up!" Mark said, embarrassed at the kidlike excitement in his voice.

"Which means they're up to something," Alec replied. "We need to get inside this beast and get her ready to fly. And get that landing pad open."

Mark looked up at the wheel and slowly let go of it, ready to grab it again if the thing moved. He got to his feet, his eyes glued to the handle.

He jumped when a loud clang cracked through the air, followed by the wrenching sound of metal screeching against metal. He whipped around to see what had happened, but the bulk of the Berg was between him and the source of the noise. Somehow Alec must've got the hatch door to open. Mark took one last look at the wheel handle, satisfied that it was okay for the moment, then made his way to the Berg to join Alec. On the far side of the ship, the man was standing with his hands on his hips like a proud mechanic as the huge ramp of the hatch door slowly swung towards the ground.

"Shall we board, co-captain?" Alec asked with a wry grin. "I'm sure we can control this landing pad from inside."

Mark could see it in the man's eyes: he was anxious to be at the controls of a Berg again, flying it fast and free through the sky. "As long as by 'co-captain' you mean the guy who sits around watching you do everything."

Alec let out a huge, boisterous laugh, like he didn't have a care in the world. It sounded good to Mark's ears, and for a second or two he forgot just how awful everything was. But then he thought of Trina, and at the same time his hunger pains roared in his belly. So much for that.

Alec jumped on to the hatch door just as it thumped to a stop, wide open, and climbed up the ramp, disappearing into the darkness of the ship. Mark ran back out into the main chamber to check the door again. Once he saw that they were safe, the wheel not moving, he went back and followed Alec's path.

He paused on the upper lip of the hatch door and took a second to shine his torch around inside. The Berg was spooky and dark and dusty. It looked much like the one he and Alec had boarded back in their settlement, albeit emptier. Alec was walking back and forth, investigating.

Mark stepped into the craft with a metallic thud. It echoed throughout the dark room, and the sound triggered memories of an old movie – something about astronauts boarding an abandoned alien vessel. Which, of course, had been full of aliens that liked to eat humans. He hoped he and Alec fared better in this thing.

"I don't see any signs of the dart boxes we saw on the other Berg," Alec said, pointing his light at a row of empty shelves.

Mark noticed something tucked away in the corner of the farthest shelf. "Hey, what's that?" he said. He walked over, shone his light, then picked up a stack of three workpads that had been tied down with elastic straps.

"Look at this!" he called to Alec. "Workpads!"

"Do they, um, work?" the man replied, not seeming very impressed.

Mark wedged his torch in the crook of his elbow and tried one of the devices. Its face lit up, showing a welcome screen that required a numerical password for access.

"Yeah, it works, all right," Mark said. "But we might need your old superhuman soldier brain to hack it."

"Get back over—" Alec's words were cut off when the entire Berg jolted and shook for a second. Mark almost dropped the workpad in his attempt to keep his balance. The torch slipped out of his arm and clanked across the floor, clicking off.

"What was that?" Mark asked, though he had a feeling he knew.

The words had barely left his mouth when the noise of cranking gears and scraping metal filled the air, coming through the hatch door. One of Bruce's people must have pushed a button somewhere. The landing pad in the central chamber was rotating open once again.

41

"**Q**uick, you need to close the hatch!" Alec yelled at Mark. "The controls are right next to it. I'll be getting this baby started up. We'll crash it through the ground above us if we have to!"

Alec ran out of the compartment without waiting for a response, going deeper into the ship. Unfortunately the light disappeared with him, leaving Mark in the creepy blackness all alone. But the faintest hint of light was already appearing from the opening crack of the rotating landing pad, and Mark spotted his torch.

He picked it up, then ran over to where he'd found the workpads and strapped them back in, hoping he lived long enough to see what information they held. He clicked the torch to life and took a quick look around the room with the bright beam. He heard voices – shouts – over the cranking of the landing pad, and his mind slammed back to cold reality.

They already had visitors, probably readying to drop from above like he and Alec had done earlier. He had to get that hatch closed before people tried to climb aboard.

He ran over to it and started searching. The door was surrounded by things like cabling, hooks and the plates that linked the bare-bones machinery of the door hydraulics with the more aesthetic wall coverings of the large cargo room. He found the controls on the left side and studied them, picking out the correct button and pushing it. The motor turned on, and with a crank and a squeal, the ramp door began to close, slowly pivoting upward.

He heard more voices, closer now. It looked like he'd have to fight their pursuers off until the door was fully closed. He moved out of direct view and leaned on the wall, looking around as if some magical weapon might appear in front of him. But he quickly accepted reality: all he had was the torch and his fists.

The ramp seemed to be taking for ever to close – it had only gone up halfway. Its hinges squealed as the large square of metal crept along, angling shut like the slow-motion capture of a Venus flytrap. Mark braced himself, sure that the intruders would make it to him before the thing sealed completely. He gripped the torch, wielding it like a short sword, ready to fight. The room outside was much lighter than before, meaning the landing pad was probably about vertical in its rotation.

Two people jumped on to the rising ramp and started climbing aboard. A man and a woman. Mark tensed his muscles and swung his arm around, aiming for the man, but he missed and the guy grabbed his shirt, then yanked his entire body forward. Mark lost his grip on the torch, which went tumbling end over end outside; a clang and the crack of glass signalled its demise. Mark slammed on to the metal of the hatch and stared into the man's face – he had absolutely no expression, not even a sign of fatigue or strain from the climb he'd just made.

"You're a bloody spy," the stranger said, as calmly as if they'd just sat down for a cup of coffee together. "And to make it worse, you're trying to steal our Berg. And strike three, you're an ugly son of a gun, aren't you?"

"I was just going to say the same thing about you," Mark replied. Everything had turned surreal.

The man acted as if he hadn't heard. "I've got him," he called to the other person. "Get inside, stop the door from closing."

It registered with Mark who these two people were. The pilots. He'd heard them speaking earlier.

"Sorry, man," Mark said. The sense of surreality had turned into an odd flutter in his chest, making him feel almost outside himself. His head thumped with pain. "I'm afraid I can't let you on without proper identification."

The man looked a little taken aback. His partner was further away, right on the edge of the door, crawling to get in before it closed. Something had snapped inside of Mark. He didn't understand what it was, but something felt different, and there was no way he was going to let these people on board.

Mark gripped the man's shirt and kicked out viciously with his left foot at the woman. He planted it right in her midsection; she yelped and jolted backwards, flailed to grab hold of her partner. But it was too late. She tumbled and fell off the rising ledge, her head smacking the other pilot's knee. Mark heard her crumple on the ground of the chamber.

The hatch door was almost closed now, a five-foot gap at most, moving painfully slowly. The man had leaned over the edge of the door to see if his friend was okay, but he turned now to face Mark again, full of rage. Mark felt rage, too. Like nothing he'd ever felt before. Like a storm erupting within.

He reached out and grabbed his foe's shirt, squeezed it in his fist, then growled two words that somehow calmed the storm within him.

"Your turn."

42

"You're going to die," the man wheezed back through an angry breath. "You're going to die right now."

"No," Mark answered. "I'm not."

He balled his hand into a fist and smashed it into the pilot's cheek. The man cried out, then threw his hands forward, grabbing at Mark's hair and face and clothes. He finally caught Mark's shirt and his shoulder and yanked him into a wrestler's hold. They rolled against the hatch door. A metal ridge cut into Mark's back as the pilot pressed on him from above, leaning forwards with his forearm dug into Mark's neck, cutting off the air to his windpipe.

"You messed with the wrong man today," the pilot said in a low, vicious voice. "I've had enough people tick me off without you trying to steal my ship. I'm going to take my anger out on you, boy. And I'm going to do it over a very long period of time. Do you understand?"

He eased back on his arm and Mark sucked in a breath, filling his lungs. Then the pilot grabbed him by the shirt and sat up, putting all his weight on Mark's stomach. The man reached high and swung down with a fist, hitting Mark square in the jaw. It felt as if something cracked in his face. The pilot punched him again and the pain doubled. Mark closed his eyes, tried to tamp down the rage that was building inside him like a nuclear reaction. How much could he take in one day?

"Better not let that door close for good, now," the man said, clearly confident that he'd already won the battle. "As much as it'd be fun to hold your head out there and watch it get squeezed like a grape, I think I'd rather take a little more time."

He slipped off Mark's body and got to his feet, then walked over to the controls and pressed something. There was a lurch that Mark felt in his back, then a squeal, then the continued slow wrenching sound as the door started opening once again. He could see the chamber growing lighter than ever. The landing pad must've fully rotated and was now sinking into the ground. In a few minutes they'd be open to the entire horde of Bruce's people, open to them charging aboard and ending it all.

Fighting the urge to move, Mark waited, letting the fury inside him continue to grow.

The pilot stepped up to Mark, then reached down and grabbed his feet, lifted them with a grunt. "Come on, now. Let's get you in a good position." He started to swing Mark's body around as he walked sideways deeper into the cargo room of the Berg. "I'll make sure you're nice and comfy before—"

Mark sprang to life, screaming and kicking out as he twisted himself to jerk free from the pilot's grip. The man stumbled backwards until his back hit the wall next to the reopening ramp door. Mark scrambled to stand up as he lunged forward, finally slamming his shoulder into the man's gut. The man doubled over and wrapped his arms around Mark's back, both of them crashing to the floor. They rolled and tumbled, all swinging arms and punching fists. Mark tried to knee him in the groin, but the man blocked him, then swung up and connected with Mark's chin.

Mark's head snapped back and he fell off the pilot, who leaped forward, getting on top of him once again. But Mark never stopped moving, using his momentum to spin backwards and throw the man off. Then he stood up and ran to the controls, realising with a shock of horror that the ramp door had already lowered several feet. People might swarm aboard when it was fully open, for all he knew.

He quickly pushed the retract button and the door squealed, then started closing again. He was just turning back around to face his foe when the man tackled him, their bodies crashing on to the large slab of the ramp. They slid a few feet, almost to the very edge again. Mark twisted his body and grabbed the pilot's shirt with both hands, trying to fling him off and through the gap of the door, but the man put his feet down and was able to push himself back on top of Mark.

They struggled against each other, punching and kicking. Mark was tired and hungry and weak, but he fought on, fuelled by adrenalin alone. He imagined Trina out there somewhere, being held by the bonfire people, probably even crazier with another day gone and the debacle of the forest fire. He had to live. He had to find her. He couldn't let this man stand in his way. That ball of spinning rage – the churning reactor of heat and fire and pain that had been building and building within his chest – finally exploded once and for all.

He lurched with a strength he didn't know he had, throwing the pilot off his body. He was on top of the man before he could right himself, pushing him down on to his back, punching him. Hard. There was blood. The horrific sound of things crunching. Mark felt disconnected from his own body – he almost couldn't see straight. Tiny bright lights danced before his eyes, his body trembled and he felt the blood boiling in his veins.

He was aware on some level that the ramp door was almost closed. On some level he noticed the walls of the chamber, people screaming and yelling, readying to attack the Berg. But Mark had lost all control.

He looked down, was surprised to see himself dragging the guy's body to the edge of the ramp, shoving him halfway out so that the man's head and shoulders hung over the lip of the ramp into open air. He'd tried to free himself from Mark's grip, but Mark didn't let him. He reached out and punched the man again. The pilot yelled and squirmed violently, obviously aware of what Mark intended.

Maybe even more aware than Mark himself. He held on, kept the man in position – half in, half out. Something had changed for Mark. His thoughts were purely focused on the man in his grip and on making him pay for everything. The anger was like a fog that had filled his head. And he couldn't stop himself.

Something had snapped.

The ramp door closed on the pilot's chest. Squeezed him as it strained to come fully closed. The screams that erupted from the man were horrific and pierced Mark to the core, jolting him out of the red-hot rage into which he'd sunk. As if he was seeing for the first time, he realised what he was doing. Torturing another human being. The sound of the man's sternum and ribs breaking, the squeal of the door's hinges as they continued to stress over the obstacle keeping the door open – Mark felt a rush of horror at himself.

He pushed on the pilot's body, but it was wedged tight in the narrowing gap. His screams seemed to vibrate the metal of the Berg, shake the entire thing through and through. Mark scrambled around and got on to his back, pressed his elbows against the ramp, then, with all his strength, kicked out with both feet, connecting against the man's middle. He budged a few inches more. Mark yelled as he kicked and kicked and kicked, pushing the body away from him, trying to end the man's misery.

With a final kick, Mark knocked the pilot free. The man disappeared through the gap and the ramp door slammed shut.

43

A deep and unnerving silence filled the cargo room, along with an almost complete darkness. The silence was interrupted seconds later by the grind of a motor, and then the Berg was moving on the tracks, jerking back to the central chamber.

Mark's eyes adjusted to the darkness and he pulled himself up and crawled to the wall, propping himself against it. He felt something inside that he didn't like.

He wrapped his arms around his knees and he buried his head there. He didn't really understand what had just happened to him. Those dancing lights, that fireball of rage, the adrenalin pumping like pistons in an old gas engine. He'd been consumed and out of control, every part of him wanting to destroy that pilot. He'd almost been happy when the man was wedged in the closing door. And then he'd come to his senses and pushed the man out.

It was like Mark had lost his . . .

He looked up when he realised the truth. He *had* lost his

mind there for a second. Completely. And just because he seemed like his normal self now didn't mean that it hadn't begun. He slowly pushed himself up along the wall until he was standing, and folded his arms. Shivered, rubbed them with his hands.

The virus. The illness. The thing that attacked the human brain the way the man named Anton had described in the barracks. Which reminded him of something else they'd heard down there, ironically from the pilot himself when he'd heard him talking earlier. A single word.

Mark had it. His every instinct told him so. No wonder his head had been hurting so much.

He had the Flare.

44

A surprising calm came over him.

Hadn't he expected this? Hadn't he come to terms with the fact that their odds of *not* catching the disease were almost zero? Trina probably had it. Lana and Alec, too. Why Deedee seemed immune to the thing – she'd actually been shot with a dart *two months ago* – was beyond him. But what was it Bruce had said? It made sense: anyone who risked unleashing a virus had to have protection for themselves. There had to be a treatment, an antidote somewhere. It just didn't make sense otherwise.

Maybe, just maybe, there was a spark of hope. Maybe.

How many times had he faced death in the last year or so? He was used to it by now. All he could do was focus on the next rung of the ladder: Trina. He had to find Trina. If for no other reason than so he could die with her.

He was startled when the Berg suddenly jolted to a stop. Then there were more sounds of cranking and grinding of gears and pulleys. The landing pad was finally rising towards the sky.

The Berg sprang to life – lights flickering overhead and engines and machinery revving.

With an unexpected burst of excitement, Mark sprinted for the door of the cargo room. If Alec was really going to fly this thing, he had to see it with his own eyes.

*　*　*

Alec looked more comfortable in the cockpit than Mark had ever seen him. He was a blur of activity – pushing buttons, flipping switches and adjusting levers.

"What in the world took you so long?" the man asked, not even pausing long enough to shoot Mark a glance.

"I ran into a little trouble." The last thing Mark wanted to do was talk about it right then. "You're really going to be able to fly us away in this thing?"

"Oh yeah. She's half filled with fuel cells and lookin' right sharp and pretty." He nodded at the windows in front of him, where Mark could see a line of trees coming into view. "But we better hurry before the nut jobs swarm over us and break in somehow."

Mark rushed forwards to take a better look. Leaning in, he could see that quite a few of Bruce's people had congregated outside at the rim of the landing station. They seemed a little out of sorts, pointing this way and that, obviously unsure of what to do. But a couple of them were really close to the ship, busy doing something, though Mark didn't have a good enough angle to see what. An alarming thought popped into his head.

"What about the hatch door?" he asked. "You were able to open it from the outside, right?"

"First thing I did was lock out that function. Don't worry." He was still busy at the controls. "We'll be launching this baby in about one minute. You might wanna perch that skinny butt of yours down in a seat and strap in."

"Okay." He wanted to get another look outside first, though. He stepped around Alec and went to the other end of the line of windows to take a peek. This side faced the wall of the canyon a little more, and the grey stone grabbed his attention before he could look down. His eyes were just running along the length of the granite walls when something flashed in the corner of his vision and he froze. The head of a huge hammer swung up and came at the glass. It made contact with a shattering thud, sending a web of cracks in every direction. Someone had climbed up the side of the Berg.

Mark jumped back as Alec yelped in surprise.

"Hurry, get us up in the air!" Mark called out.

"What do you think I'm doing?" Alec rushed his efforts even more, focusing on the central panel of the controls, holding his finger above a bright green button on the screen.

Mark looked back at the window just in time to see the hammer come down again, breaking all the way through with a horrible crunch and a shower of glass pellets across the controls – the hammer itself followed, bouncing off a panel and hitting the floor. Then a man's face appeared at the opening he'd created, followed by hands and arms as he started to climb in.

"Get rid of that guy!" Alec yelled. At the same time he tapped the green button and the Berg lurched off the ground, the sound of thrusters filling the air like the roar of angry lions.

Mark caught his balance and reached down for the hammer. Just as his fingers closed around the handle someone grabbed a handful of his hair and yanked. An alien screech tore out of his mouth at the pain and he dropped the hammer, beat his fists against the hand and arm that had taken hold of him. But the man held firm and quickly slipped his other arm around Mark's neck, then pulled back, bringing Mark with him.

Mark's head smacked the top edge of the missing window's frame and slipped through it, out into the hot air of the morning. Then half of his body was out, up to the waist – he gripped the window frame to stop himself from falling completely. All he could see were the tops of the trees and blue sky beyond, and he realised with a wave of horror that the man was literally hanging off him, still holding on to his hair and neck. For the second time that day, Mark couldn't breathe.

The Berg was rising towards the sky and Mark caught a quick glance of Alec looking at him through the window, his eyes wide in shock. Alec moved out of sight, leaving the Berg to hover just a few dozen feet above the ground; then Mark felt the man tugging on his legs, which only made the pain in his neck and head worse. A strangled, wet bark – a sound that scared Mark more than the pain – somehow escaped his own throat.

Alec pulled on him from above. The man hung from him below. It felt as if his body had been put into one of those medieval torture racks, stretching his bones and sinews. He wondered if it was possible for his head to pop off, like a cork from a bottle. He realised that with Alec holding him he could release his grip on the window frame; he beat at his captor's arms, *beat* at them, clawed them. The world was upside down, the valley floor like an earthen sky.

Mark slipped out the window several inches – a thunderbolt of pure terror flashed through him like an electric shock before his progress stopped again. Something dark blurred past his vision. A black lump followed by a thin shaft of light brown. The hammer. There was an awful thump and a crack and a scream. Alec had thrown the weapon at the guy's face.

The man's arm slipped from its grip around Mark's neck and he plummeted to the ground. Mark gasped for breath, sucking in the sweet air.

Alec slowly pulled his body up and up, back through the window, then crashed to the floor. Still heaving to get his breath, Mark touched his sore neck.

The old soldier looked at him carefully. Then, seeming to have decided Mark would live, he stood, returned to the controls and lifted the Berg towards the sky.

45

Mark's stomach didn't do so well with the sudden movement of the Berg. Alec took it straight up until it cleared the walls of the canyon, then sent it hurtling forwards like it had been launched from a slingshot. Mark's insides turned over with a surge of nausea; he crawled on his hands and knees until he finally found a bathroom. He pulled himself inside and threw up. Nothing but bile and acid. His throat burned as if he'd swallowed corrosive chemicals.

He sat for a while, until he was able to walk back to the cockpit.

"Food. Please tell me there's food," he croaked.

"And water?" Alec asked him. "That sound good, too?"

Mark nodded even though the old man couldn't see him.

"Let me get this thing landed somewhere first. I'd just hover, but we can't afford to waste all our fuel. We're gonna need it. But I bet there's something to shove down our throats in this hunk of junk. Then we'll go searching for our bonfire friends."

"Please," Mark muttered. His eyelids drooped, and not

because he was tired. He knew he was on the verge of passing out from low blood sugar. It seemed a week had gone by since his last meal. And the thirst. His mouth was a bucket of sand.

"You've had a rough go," Alec said quietly. "Just give me a minute or two."

*　　*　　*

Mark sat down on the floor again and closed his eyes.

He never quite lost consciousness.

But the world felt disconnected, as if it were a play Mark was watching from the back row, lying on the floor. With a few blankets over his head. Sounds were muffled and his stomach ached from hunger.

Finally the Berg slowed, and then there was a rough bump that shook the ship, followed by silence and stillness. Mark had a long moment when he thought for sure that sleep was coming. And with it, the memories. He fought it, didn't know if he could handle reliving the past at that moment. He heard footsteps from far away. Then Alec was speaking to him.

"Here ya go, son. Pretty much a standard military meal, but it's food and it's full of nutrients. Gonna perk you right up. I flew us to an empty neighbourhood between the bunker and downtown Asheville. All the crazies seem to have fled the fire and headed south."

Mark opened his eyes, the lids so heavy he almost had to use his fingers to lift them up. Alec was blurry at first but then came into focus. He held out a silvery foil that had chunks of . . . something on top. It didn't matter. It didn't matter at all. Mark grabbed three of them and shoved the delicious – beautifully delicious – morsels into his mouth. Salty and beefy. But when it came time to swallow he could barely get them down.

"Wa—" he began, but then he erupted into a coughing jag that sent the food he couldn't swallow into Alec's face.

His friend wiped it off. "Nice. Really nice."

"Water," Mark croaked out.

"Yeah, I know. Here." He held out a canteen and Mark could hear the liquid sloshing inside.

Mark sat up, groaning from the shock of pain that jolted through his body at the movement.

"Be careful," Alec said. "Don't drink too fast. You'll be sick."

"Okay." Mark took the canteen, paused to steady his hands, then brought it up and tipped the spout over his bottom lip. Glorious, cool water rushed into his mouth and down his throat. He fought off a cough, focused on swallowing without wasting a drop. Then he drank some more.

"That's enough," Alec warned. "Now eat a few more bites of the delicacy I brought you from the mess cabinet."

Mark did, and this time it tasted even better. Saltier and beefier. With a wetted mouth and throat, it went down easier, as well, though he had the worst sore throat of his life. A little strength seeped its way into his muscles. His headache receded a bit. The best news of all was that his nausea was gone.

He felt just good enough that he wanted to sleep.

"You look like a couple of the light bulbs in your brain flicked back on," Alec said, sitting down. He relaxed back against the wall and stuffed food into his mouth. "This crap ain't half bad, is it?"

"You shouldn't talk with your mouth full," Mark replied with a weak smile. "It's not polite."

"I know." Alec crammed even more food in and exaggerated his movements to make sure Mark saw everything he was chewing. "What kind of a person even needs to be told such a thing? I mean, didn't I have a mama?"

Mark laughed. Genuinely laughed, and it hurt his chest and throat. Made him cough. When he recovered, he asked, "So where did you take us, again?" Then he resumed eating.

"Well, the Berg's bunker was just west of Asheville. So I came a little east – there're a few fancy neighbourhoods along this mountainside. I spotted a lot of activity a couple miles south, and I think it might be where all those people from our lovely bonfire experience fled to after they set the forest ablaze. It seems quiet here."

He paused to take another bite. "We're parked in a cul-de-sac – a fancy-schmancy neighbourhood if I've ever seen one. Before it got baked in an oven, that is. Used to be a lot of rich folk outside Asheville, ya know. Most of these homes are half ruined now."

"But what about—"

Alec held up his hand to stop Mark's question. "I know. As soon as we get some strength and another few hours of sleep, we'll find our friends."

Mark didn't want to waste any more time, but he knew Alec was right. They needed to rest. "Any sign of . . . anything?"

"I thought I recognised some people when we flew over the place south of here. I'm almost positive it's the folks from Deedee's settlement. We'll just have to see if Lana and the others are there, too, like that Bruce seemed to be saying."

Mark closed his eyes for a second, not sure if that was something he should hope for.

They paused to eat and drink some more. Mark was curious to see what it looked like outside, but he was too tired to stand up and go to the window. Plus, he'd seen his fair share of the burnt-out shells folks had once called home. "You're sure we're okay to be parked here? In case you forgot, some wild dude with a hammer broke one of our windows."

"No one's approached yet. All we can do is keep an eye out. And when we go looking for Lana and them, we'll just have to hope people don't notice the extra entrance."

The thought of the man with the hammer made Mark's stomach sink. It made him think of what had come over him when he'd killed the pilot on the hatch door.

Alec noticed something was wrong. "I know you weren't exactly sipping tea and eating crumpets when I left you back in the cargo room all that time. Ready to tell me what happened?"

Mark flicked an embarrassed, almost nervous glance at his

friend. "For a few minutes it was like I lost control of myself, started acting weird. Sadistic, almost."

"Son, that don't mean jack. I've seen many a good man go south on the battlefield, and there wasn't a virus around to blame back then, either. It doesn't mean you . . . have it. Humans do crazy things to survive. Have you not spent the last year seeing that every day?"

Mark didn't feel any better. "This was . . . different. For a second it felt like it was Christmas morning, watching a guy get crushed to death."

"Really." Alec looked at him for a long time, and Mark had no idea what the man was thinking. "It's gonna be dark in a couple of hours. No good tramping around at night. Let's get us a long dose of shut-eye." Mark nodded, troubled to the core. He wondered if maybe he should've kept his mouth shut. Yawning, he got comfortable, planning to process it all, think things through for a while.

But a full stomach and a week's worth of exhaustion pulled him to unconsciousness.

Naturally, the dreams came next.

46

Mark is in a conference room in the Lincoln Building, curled up into a ball under the huge table where he guesses very important men and women used to gather and talk about very important things. His stomach aches from the now weeks-old diet of junk food and soda pop scavenged from the vending machines scattered throughout the building. It took some work to break open the things – but a couple of former soldiers like Alec and Lana were trained to break open things, weren't they? People and objects alike.

The Lincoln Building is a terrible place. Hotter than hell. Suffused with the gagging, sickening smell of rotting bodies, people who died from the initial burst of heat and radiation. They are everywhere. Mark and his new friends cleared the entire fifteenth floor, but the rank stench still permeates the air. It's something you just don't grow used to. And of course, there is nothing to do. Boredom has settled in like a cancer in the building, ready to eat away at their sanity. Not to mention the threat of radiation outside – though Alec thinks it's finally dwindling. Even so, they've kept away from the windows as much as possible.

For all that, there is one thing Mark keeps thinking that makes it all seem not quite as bad as it could be: he and Trina have grown closer than ever. Very close. He grins like a fool and is glad no one can see him.

The door opens up and shuts; then there are footsteps. A can rattles across the floor and someone swears under his breath.

"Hey," the someone whispers. Mark thinks it's Baxter. "You awake under there?"

"Yeah," comes Mark's groggy reply. "And if I wasn't I would be now. You're not very good at being quiet."

"Sorry. I was sent to find you – there's a boat heading down Broadway, driving straight towards us. Come have a look."

Mark never thought he'd hear those words – a boat coming down one of the most famous streets in the world, where cars are supposed to drive. But Manhattan has turned into a grid of rivers and streams, the fierce sun constantly reflecting off the waters in spectacular and blinding flashes. It's like they have a sky both above them and below.

"Are you serious?" Mark finally asks, realising he's been quiet for a few seconds, stunned by the news. He tries not to get his hopes up that they're about to be rescued.

Baxter scoffs. "No, I made it up. Come on."

"Guess the radiation *has* died down, unless a couple of freak shows are driving it." Mark wipes at his face and eyes, then scoots out from underneath the large table. He stands and stretches, yawns again, teasing Baxter by not hurrying. But then the curiosity finally gets to him.

They head out into the hallway, where a fresh wave of heat and stench assaults Mark's senses. After weeks of this, he still gags, willing himself not to throw up.

"Where are they?" he asks, assuming Alec and Lana are the ones who've spotted the boat and are watching it now.

"Down on five. Smells a thousand times worse down there,

but that's where the water line is. It's like rotting fish *and* humans. I hope you haven't eaten in a while."

Mark just shrugs, not wanting to think about food. He's sick of candy bars and potato chips – something he never would've thought possible.

The two of them go to the central bank of stairwells and begin the ten-storey trip down to the fifth floor. All is quiet except for the thumps and scuffles of their footsteps, and Mark finds that his excitement over who might be in the boat overcomes the growing stench as they descend. There are bloodstains on the stairs. He sees a chunk of hair and meaty mass on one of the handrails. He can't imagine the panic that ensued in this place when the sun flares struck, and the horrors that resulted. Luckily – for them, anyway – no one was alive by the time they arrived.

They reach the landing of the fifth floor and Trina is waiting at the door to the stairwell.

"Hurry!" she says, motioning with a quick nod to follow her. She breaks into a trot and talks over her shoulder as they manoeuvre down a long hallway towards the outermost wall of windows. "It's a big yacht – looks like it was nice and fancy before the flares struck. Now it seems like it was built a hundred years ago. Can't believe it floats, much less runs."

"Could you see the people on it yet?" Mark asks.

"No. They're obviously underneath. In the cockpit, the bridge, whatever you call it."

Seems like she knows as much about boats as Mark.

They turn a corner and see Alec and Lana at a section where the windows have been knocked out, the water of the sea lapping against the wall just a foot or so below them outside. The Toad and Misty are sitting on the floor, staring out. Mark hears the boat before he sees it, a coughing, choked sound of engines that have seen better days. Then the battered vessel comes into view past a small building, its back end sunk low into the water as the yacht chugs along. It's about thirty feet long, fifteen wide, with duct tape and plywood boards covering up scattered holes and split seams. A tinted window with spiderwebs of cracks is like an ominous eye, looking at them as it approaches.

"Do they know we're here?" Mark asks. He only allows himself to think that these people are coming to rescue them. Bring food and water, at least. "Did you hail them down?"

"No," Alec answers curtly. "By the looks of it, they're checking out every building. Scavenging, no doubt. But they've seen us by now."

"I just hope they're friendly," Trina whispers, as if she doesn't want the strangers to hear.

"I'll fly to the moon and back if these folks are nice," Alec replies in a completely dead voice. "Stay on your toes, boys and girls. Follow my lead."

The boat is very close now, its noises filling the air along with the smell of fuel. Mark can see the faint shadow of two people behind the darkened window now, and they both appear to be male. They both have short hair, anyway.

The engines of the yacht cut off and its tail end begins to swing around so that the boat can bump lengthwise against the building. Alec and Lana step back, and Mark notices that at some point the Toad and Misty have scooted all the way to the far wall. Trina, Baxter and Mark are standing in a tight group, the tension clear in their faces.

One of the people from the bridge appears on deck, stepping through a doorway from below. It's a man, and he's holding an enormous gun in both hands, the muzzle already pointed at the spectators inside the Lincoln Building. He's one ugly dude, greasy hair matted to his head, a scruffy beard – the kind that looks like a wild fungus on the neck – and black sunglasses. His skin is filthy and sunburnt, his clothes tattered.

Another person appears, and Mark's surprised to see it's a woman with a shaved head. She deals with securing the boat against the wall as her partner steps closer to the broken window where Alec and Lana stand.

"I want to see every single hand," the man says to them, sweeping his weapon back and forth, pausing for a brief moment on each person. "Two each, up in the air. Go on."

Most of them do as they're commanded, except Alec. Mark hopes the man doesn't do something crazy and get them all shot.

"You really think I'm bluffing?" the stranger says in a raw, scratchy voice. "Do it now or die."

Alec slowly raises his hands towards the ceiling.

The man with the gun doesn't seem satisfied. He's breathing heavier than he should, and staring at Alec through those dark sunglasses. Then he swings his weapon at Baxter and lets loose three quick bursts of fire. The explosions of sound rock the air, and Mark stumbles backwards until he slams into the wall of a cubicle. The bullets have torn into Baxter's chest, spraying red mist everywhere and knocking him on to his back with a hard thud. He doesn't even scream, death having taken him already. His torso is a mess of blood and mangled skin.

The man takes in a deep pull of air. "Now I expect you'll do what I say."

47

Mark twitched in his sleep and almost woke up. He'd always liked Baxter, liked the kid's smart-aleck nature and who-cares attitude. To see such a thing done to him . . .

It was something Mark would probably never get over. Of all the memories that came back to haunt his dreams, that one was the most frequent. And Mark wanted to wake up, wanted to leave it behind again instead of reliving the aftermath of what he'd witnessed and the craziness that followed.

But his body needed the rest and wouldn't allow it. Sleep pulled him back down into its embrace, with no intention of comforting his troubled mind.

It's one of those moments when it takes the brain a moment to catch up with the events playing out before your eyes – shock temporarily blocks the path. Mark is on the ground, leaning back at a forty-five-degree angle, his head resting against the wall. Trina has her hands folded against her chest and suddenly screams – a sound like a million frantic crows bursting out of a tunnel. The Toad and Misty have huddled together, their faces masks of terror. Lana and Alec stand straight, their hands still raised. But Mark can see the tension in their muscles.

"Shut up!" the man with the gun yells, spit flying out of his mouth. Trina does, the noise of her scream cutting off like it's been sliced with a blade. "If I hear one more god-awful sound like that I'll shoot whoever makes it. Am I understood?"

Trina is trembling, her hands now covering her mouth. Somehow she manages to nod, but her eyes are still glued to the bloody and lifeless Baxter. Mark doesn't let himself look at the boy. Instead he stares at the man who killed him, hatred clouding his vision.

"All done, boss," the woman on the boat says. She stands up and wipes her fingers on her filthy pants. She's tied the yacht to something on the outside – Mark can see the coiled end of a rope – either oblivious or insensitive to the murder her partner has just committed. Or maybe just used to it. "What now?"

"Go get your gun, idiot," the man answers with a sideways look that leaves no doubt how he has always treated the woman. "Do I need to tell you how to use the bathroom, too?"

Somehow even sadder to Mark than what the guy has just said, the object of his scorn just nods and apologises. Then she disappears back into the boat for a second, emerging with a similar gun held tightly in both hands. She takes a stance next to her partner and points the weapon at Mark and each of his friends in turn.

"Now here's how this is going to work," the man says. "You want to live, then all you have to do is obey. Easy-peasy. We're here for fuel and food. My guess is you have both, judging by the fact that you aren't a bunch of walking skeletons. And every building this big has generators. Bring us what we need, and we leave. You can even keep some for yourselves. That's how loving we are. All we want is our share."

"Real generous," Alec says in a low voice.

Mark jumps to his feet as the man brings his weapon up and

points it directly at the old man's face. "No! Stop!"

The stranger swings it to point at Mark, who throws his hands up and scoots back against the cubicle wall. "Please! Just stop it! We'll get you whatever you want!"

"That's right, you will, boy. Now move. All of you. Time to go on a little scavenger hunt." He jerks his weapon in a gesture to get people in motion.

"Be careful not to step on your dead friend," the woman says.

"Shut *up!*" her partner lashes back. "Seriously. You get dumber every day."

"Sorry, boss."

She's suddenly a meek little mouse, head hung low. Mark's heart is still beating a thousand times a minute, but he can't help feeling sorry for the lady.

The man returns his attention to the others. "Show us where it's at. I don't wanna be here all day."

Mark half expects Alec to do something crazy, but he just begins walking back towards the stairwell. As he passes Mark, he gives him a quick wink. Mark doesn't know if he should be encouraged or worried.

They march down the hallway, leaving the bloodied form of Baxter behind, prisoners in what has become their castle over the past few weeks. They reach the stairs and start climbing. Boss – that's the only way Mark can think of the man with the gun now, hearing over and over in his mind the pathetic way his partner saluted him – takes turns poking people in the back as they ascend, making sure they don't forget who's armed.

"Just remember what I did to your buddy," Boss whispers to Mark when it's his turn to get prodded.

Mark keeps moving, step by step.

* * *

They spend the next two hours scavenging the Lincoln Building, top to bottom, for food and fuel. Every inch of Mark's skin is sweating, and his muscles ache from carrying the large containers of generator fuel from the emergency supply room on the thirtieth floor down to the boat. They scour the vending machines, emptying over half of the dwindling stock throughout the many break rooms and other common areas.

The yacht is an oven inside the cabin, which only makes the smell within even worse. As Mark unloads the supplies, he wonders if Boss and his partner have bothered to so much as dip themselves in the warm waters that surround them. They literally live in bathwater – dirty as it may be – yet refuse to bathe. Mark grows more disgusted with the pair on every trip. He also wonders at the biding silence of Alec, who's worked hard without the slightest sign of rebellion.

They've filled almost every spare inch of the vessel when the entire group find themselves on the twelfth floor – part of one last sweep through the lower half of the building. Boss tells them they can have whatever's left above that.

The man, still pointing his gun at each of them in turn, is standing next to the windows. The orange sheen of the setting sun paints the glass behind him. His subordinate stands right next to him, looking as blank-minded as ever. Trina is grabbing a few last chip bags and candy bars through the busted cover of a vending machine. The Toad, Misty, Lana, Alec and Darnell are waiting for her, not much to do now. The place is emptied out and each of them is probably like Mark, just counting down the seconds until these people are gone. And hoping no one else dies.

Alec walks towards Boss, holding his hands up in a conciliatory gesture.

"Careful," the armed man warns. "Now your work's done, I wouldn't mind gettin' a little more target practice. Close-range, even."

"It's done, all right," Alec says in a half growl. "We're not idiots. We wanted to get that boat loaded first. Ya know, before . . ."

"Before what?" Boss seems to sense trouble and the muscles of his arms tense; Mark sees his finger tighten on the trigger of the gun.

"This."

Alec suddenly bursts into motion. His hand shoots forwards and smacks the weapon out of Boss's hands – the gun fires a wayward shot just as it spins away, clattering on the floor. Boss's partner turns and bolts down the hallway along the bank of windows, as quickly as she's done anything yet. Lana chases her, even though the other woman is armed. Mark barely has time to notice this before Alec throws his body forwards and tackles Boss, the two of them slamming into the glass of the large window.

Everything happens so fast. An icy splintering sound fills the room as cracks branch out from their point of impact. Then the entire pane bursts, exploding into a million pieces just as Alec is trying to get his balance and lift himself off Boss's body. Both of them begin to fall, tipping as if in slow motion, leaning towards the water below. Mark is already rushing at them, diving, then sliding across the floor so that he can brace his feet against the window frame for support while reaching for Alec's arm. He grabs it, grips his fingers, holds tight, but his feet miss and are suddenly in open air. His entire body is about to topple out with Alec and Boss.

Someone grabs him from behind, arms slipping around his chest. Mark holds on to Alec with every ounce of his strength and is looking straight down into the river-street. Boss is falling, madly flailing his arms and legs and screaming. Mark's arms feel like they may come out of their sockets, but Alec recovers his wits quickly, turns his body and puts his free hand on the bottom sill of the window, begins to hoist himself inside while whoever has captured Mark drags him in as well. It's the Toad.

Soon they are all standing again, safe. Lana comes charging back down the hallway.

"She got away," the woman says. "I bet she's hiding in some closet."

"Let's get out of here," Alec replies, already on the move. Mark and the others follow. "Plan worked perfectly. Got the boat stocked up and now it's ours for the taking. We're getting out of the city."

They find the stairwell, descend rapidly, taking two steps at a time. Mark is sweating and exhausted, and anxious about what they're planning to do. Leaving the place that has become home in the wake of the sun flares. Venturing out into the complete unknown. He doesn't know which is stronger, the excitement or the fear.

They make it to the fifth floor, sprint down the hallway, go through the missing window, board the boat.

"Get us loose," Alec yells to Mark.

Alec and Lana go into the cabin. Darnell, the Toad, Misty and Trina find places to sit up top, looking a little lost and a lot uncertain. Mark begins untying the rope the woman used to secure the yacht earlier. He finally gets the knots loose and pulls in the rope just as the engines come to life and the boat starts moving away from the Lincoln Building. Mark sits on a seat at the tail end of the vessel and twists backwards to look up at the towering skyscraper, where the dwindling glow of the day's sunshine reflects an amber sheen.

Boss suddenly leaps out of the water like a crazed dolphin, his arms slamming on to the back of the boat as he begins to frantically scramble on board. His legs kick and scissor as his hands search for anything to hold on to; he grabs a hook and his muscles bulge as he pulls himself up, water streaming off his body. He has a huge purple bruise covering half his face – the other half is red and angry to match his eyes.

"I'm gonna kill you," the man growls. "Every single one of you!"

The boat is picking up speed. Everything explodes inside Mark at once – he's not going to let this sorry excuse for a human ruin their chance to escape. Gripping a seat, he rears back his foot and launches it forward, kicking Boss in the shoulder. The man barely budges. Mark pulls back and kicks him again. Then again. He connects each time. Boss is beginning to lose his grip.

"Let . . . go!" Mark yells as he slams his foot into the man's shoulder again.

"Kill . . . ," Boss says, but he seems to have no strength left.

Mark yells with a burst of adrenalin, then throws all his strength into one last assault, this time leaping up and throwing both feet forward. He smashes them into Boss, connecting with his nose and his neck, and the man releases a strangled scream and lets go, falling back into the wake of the churning boat. His body disappears in the white bubbles.

Mark is desperately sucking in each breath. He scoots himself around and crawls up on to the lip of the seat and looks over the edge. Sees nothing but the wake and black water behind that. Then he spots movement at the open window of the Lincoln Building where Boss fell. It's receding now, growing smaller, but the woman – Boss's partner – is standing there, holding her gun. Mark slouches down, waiting for the barrage of bullets. But instead, he notices the woman aim the weapon at herself, the muzzle propped against the bottom of her chin.

Mark wants to scream, to tell her not to do it. But it's too late.

The woman pulls the trigger.

The boat drives on.

48

Mark woke up in a cold sweat, as if the spray from the water in his dream had doused him while he slept. His head hurt badly again – like something rolled around loose in his skull every time he moved. Thankfully Alec was easy on him and didn't talk much while they both ate and strengthened themselves for the day ahead. For the search for their friends.

The two of them were sitting in the cockpit, the light of late morning spilling in through the windows. A warm breeze whistled as it blew through the broken one.

"You were too dead to the world to notice," Alec said after they'd sat in silence for a while, "but I took this baby up for an observation run while you were sleeping. And . . . I confirmed what I'd suspected. Just a couple miles away, the bonfire . . . they . . . have Lana, Trina and Deedee. I saw them being herded like sheep."

That left a sick lump in Mark's stomach. "What . . . do you mean?"

"A few people were being herded from one house to another. I spotted Lana's black hair and Trina with the kid in her arms. I got closer to make sure." Alec took a deep breath before he finished. "At least we know they're alive and where they are. And now we know what we have to do."

Mark should've been relieved that his friends weren't dead. But instead he was consumed by the gnawing realisation that to get them out, they'd have to go in and fight. Two against . . . how many?

"Did you forget how to talk, kid?"

Mark had been staring at the back of the pilot's chair as if something mesmerising were painted there. "No. Just scared." He'd given up long ago trying to act brave for the old army vet.

"Scared. That's good. A fine soldier is always scared. Makes you normal. It's how you respond to it that makes or breaks you."

Mark smiled. "You've given that speech a few times. I think I got it."

"Then pour some water down your gullet and let's get hopping."

"Sounds good." Mark drank long and hard from his canteen, then stood up. The weighty burden of his dream was finally starting to fade a little. "So what's the plan?"

Alec was just wiping his mouth. He nodded in the general direction of the Berg's middle section. "Go get our friends. But first we break into the ship's weapons stash."

Mark knew nothing about Bergs, but Alec knew more than most. In the central area of the ship there was a locked storage facility that required passwords and retinal scans to open. Since they had neither the words nor the eyeballs for such access, they decided to work at it the old-fashioned way: with an axe.

Luckily the Berg was old and had seen its better days many years before, so it only took three turns each and a half hour of sweat to bust the hinges and locks off the metal door. Little shards of steel clattered across the hallway and the big door tipped over and slammed into the opposite wall. The echo seemed to reverberate through the vessel for a solid minute.

Alec had thrown the last blow of the axe to make it happen. "Let's hope there's still something inside this beast," he announced.

The storage room was dark and smelled like dust. The Berg had power, but most of the lights had been broken, except for a small red emergency bulb in the corner that made everything look like it was washed in blood. Alec started searching, but Mark could already see that most of the shelves were empty. Nothing but trash and discarded containers strewn about from the ship tipping upside down now and then. Alec swore under his breath with every disappointing discovery, and Mark was feeling it, too. How could they possibly have a chance if all they had when they went after Trina were their fists and their feet?

"There's something over here," Alec muttered, his voice strained. He was already working to get open whatever he'd found.

Mark stepped up to him and looked over his shoulder. The object was mostly in shadow, but it appeared to be a large box with several metal clasps.

"It's useless," Alec finally said when his hands slipped off the clasps for the third time. "Go get me that axe."

Mark quickly grabbed it from the hallway where Alec had dropped it after pounding the door hinges. He hefted it in his hands, ready to take a shot at getting the box open.

"*You're* gonna do it?" Alec asked, straightening up. "You sure about that?"

"Huh? What do you mean?"

Alec pointed at the box. "Boy, do you have any idea what could be inside that thing? Explosives. High-voltage machinery. Poison. Who knows?"

"And?" Mark pushed.

"Well, I wouldn't just start whacking at it or we might be

dead before noon. We need to be careful. Delicate, precise hits on the clasps."

Mark almost laughed. "Since there's not one delicate cell in your entire body, I think I'll give it a go."

"Fair enough," Alec replied, taking a step back and sweeping his hand out with a bow. "Just be careful."

Mark gripped the handle of the axe tightly and leaned in, taking little chops instead of full swings at the small but stubborn brackets. Sweat poured down his face and the thing almost slipped out of his hands a couple of times, but eventually he broke the first seal and moved on to the next one. Ten minutes later his shoulders ached like nothing else and his fingers had grown almost numb from gripping so hard. But he'd broken through every last clasp.

He stood up and stretched his back, unable to keep himself from wincing. "Man, that wasn't quite as easy as it looked."

They both laughed, which made Mark wonder where all the sudden levity had come from. The task ahead of them was treacherous and scary. But for some reason his mind refused to focus on that.

"Feels good to get yourself worked up in a sweat, doesn't it?" Alec asked. "Now let's see what we've got waiting for us. Grab that end."

Mark slipped his fingers under the small lip of the lid and waited for Alec's signal. The man counted to three and then they both lifted – it was heavy but they were able to get it up and swing it against the wall, where it crashed with a boom. All Mark could see inside the box were shiny, elongated forms that reflected the red light. The things almost looked wet.

"What *are* those?" Mark asked. He glanced over at Alec and saw a wide-eyed, almost crazy expression on the man's face. "Based on that look, I'm guessing you know exactly what they are."

"Oh, yeah," Alec said in a tight whisper. "I do. I really think I do."

"And?" Mark was almost bursting from curiosity now.

Instead of answering, Alec leaned down and grabbed one of the objects from the box. He lifted it up – the thing was the size and shape of a rifle – and examined it, turning it in his hands. It appeared to be made mostly of silver metal and plastic, with little tubes spiralling down the long shaft of its main body. One end was a gun-like butt with a trigger, and the other end looked like an elongated bubble with a spout popping out. There was a strap to sling across your shoulder.

"What *is* that thing?" Mark asked, hearing the awe in his own voice.

Alec was just shaking his head back and forth, in obvious disbelief as he continued studying the object in his hands. "Do you have any idea how much these things cost? They were way too expensive to ever make it to the actual weapons market. I can't believe I'm holding one."

"What?" Mark asked, filled with impatience. "What is it?"

Alec finally looked up and met his eyes. "This bad boy is called a Transvice."

"A Transvice?" Mark repeated. "What does it do?"

Alec held the strange weapon up as if it were some holy relic.

"It makes people dissolve into thin air."

49

"**D**issolve?" Mark said sceptically. "What is that supposed to mean?"

"Well, it won't matter much if these things don't even work." Alec inspected the box for a minute, then removed a bulky black thing with silvery latches. He took his precious items and moved past Mark, out of the storage room and into the hallway and beyond. "Come on!" he yelled when he'd disappeared.

Mark spared a last glance at the menacing, almost magical items shining inside the box, then took off to catch up with the man. He found him back in the cockpit, sitting in the captain's chair, admiring the weapon in his hands. He looked like a kid with a new toy. The black thing he'd also retrieved was sitting on the floor. It looked like a cradle for the weapon. Some kind of charging device, perhaps.

"Okay," Mark said as he sidled up to stand behind Alec. "Tell me what that thing does."

"Just a sec," Alec said as he placed his toy in the long cradle bay of the black thing. He pushed a button on a small control pad on the side. Something chirped, then hummed; then there was a grey light emanating from the entire body of the weapon itself.

"We'll charge her up and then you'll *see* what she does," Alec announced proudly. He looked up at Mark. "Ever heard of a Flat Trans?"

Mark rolled his eyes. "Of course I have. I live on planet Earth."

"Okay, wise guy. Calm your shorts. Anyway, you know how expensive those things are, right? And how they work?"

Mark shrugged and took a seat on the floor – the same spot where he'd fallen asleep at some point a million years ago, it seemed. "It's not like I've ever used one. Or even seen one. But I know it's a molecular transporter."

Alec barked a forced laugh. *"Obviously* you haven't seen one, because you don't have a billion dollars. Or work for the government. Just one of those devices costs more than you could count to in a year. But you're right, that's how they work. Breaking down molecular structures and then reassembling them at the receiver point. Well, this bad boy of a gun does the same thing, except it only does half the job."

Mark looked at the charging weapon and got the chills. "You mean it breaks people apart? Splits them into tiny little pieces?"

"Yep. That about sums it up. Throws them into the air like the tossed ashes of the dearly departed. For all I know they fly around for the rest of eternity screaming for someone to put them back together again. Or maybe it's just instant and over. No way to tell. Maybe it's not such a bad way to die."

Mark shook his head. Modern technology. The world had some pretty cool stuff, but it didn't amount to much when the sun decided to wipe out most of civilisation.

"So I guess that's it, then?" Mark asked. "Didn't seem like there was anything else in that room."

"Nope. So . . . let's hope these puppies work."

Mark told himself to make sure he didn't shoot his own foot. "How long till it charges?"

"Not long. Just enough time for us to pack up some supplies for the rescue mission." Talking like a soldier, Mark thought. "Then we'll test it out while we charge one up for you. Maybe a spare for the road."

Mark stared at the charging device until Alec dragged him to his feet to help prepare for their journey.

*   *   *

A half hour later, they had backpacks full of food and water and some clean clothes they'd found hidden away in the small barracks section. The first Transvice had been fully charged and was firmly gripped in Alec's hands, its strap across his shoulder, as they opened up the ramp door of the cargo hatch. They'd done a cursory search of their surroundings and didn't see anyone close, so they'd decided it was safe to test the new fancy weapon.

Mark winced as the hinges of the ramp squealed open, and he looked over at his proud partner.

"Holding that thing a little tightly, aren't you?" The Transvice glistened with shine and, now charged, put out a faint orange glow.

Alec gave Mark a look that said *Give me a break*. "These might look fragile, but they're far from it. We could drop it from the top of the Lincoln Building and it wouldn't break."

"That's because it'd land in the water."

Alec twisted and pulled the Transvice up so that its business end – that strange little spout coming from the long bubble – was pointing straight at him.

Mark flinched in spite of himself. "Not funny," he said.

"Especially if I pulled the trigger."

The ramp door thumped to its open position on the cracked pavement of the cul-de-sac in which they were parked. A sudden and stark silence fell over the world, broken only by the distant cries of a bird. Warm, humid air engulfed them, making it almost hard to breathe. Mark coughed when he tried to pull in a deep breath.

"Come on," Alec said, already stomping down the ramp. "Let's find us a squirrel." He swept the weapon back and forth as he walked, looking for any interlopers. "Or better yet, one of the crazies who might've strayed over here. Too bad these things have to be charged or we could get rid of this virus problem in a jiffy. Sweep these old neighbourhoods nice and clean."

Mark joined him on the ground below the Berg, wary that someone might be watching from the ruined homes surrounding them or from the burnt woods beyond those. "Your value of human life brings tears to my eyes," he muttered.

"Long-term," Alec replied. "Sometimes you gotta think long-term. But they're just words, son. Just words."

Being in the suburbs was really unsettling Mark – he'd grown used to life in the mountains, in the woods, living in a hut. This abandoned neighbourhood just made him feel odd and uncomfortable. He needed to steel up his nerves before they set out to do the real business at hand. "Let's get this test over with."

Alec started walking towards a brick mailbox that was half destroyed. It looked like someone had smashed into it with a car or truck during a frantic attempt to escape.

"All right, then," he said. "I wanted to test it on something alive – it works much better with living, organic material. But you're right . . . we need to be quick about it. I'll try zapping this pile of br—"

A door slammed open in the half-crumbled house closest to them and a man came out of it running straight for them, screaming at the top of his lungs. His words were indecipherable, and his eyes were full of madness, his hair ratty and matted; sores covered his face, as if he'd been trying to claw through his own skin. And he was completely naked.

Mark stumbled a couple of steps backwards, stunned by the

man's appearance and scared out of his mind. He was searching for something to do or say.

But Alec had already raised his weapon, pointing the Transvice directly at the quickly approaching man.

"Stop!" the vet yelled. "Stop or you're . . ." He gave up because the wild man coming at him was obviously not listening. Screaming nonsensical things, stumbling but not slowing, heading for Alec.

A sharp ping sounded, seemingly from everywhere at once, followed by a rushing, spinning sound, like the whirr of a jet engine. Mark noticed that the orange light emanating from the Transvice had brightened, visible even in the sunshine. Then Alec suddenly jerked backwards when a bolt of pure, brilliant white light shot out of the weapon and slammed into the chest of the screaming man.

His cries cut off instantly, like he'd been sealed in a tomb. His body turned grey as ash from top to bottom, all details and dimension disappearing so that he looked like a cut-out of grey cloth, shimmering and rippling. Then he exploded into a mist, evaporating into nothingness. Just like that, without leaving a single trace that Mark could see.

He turned to look at Alec, who'd lowered his weapon and was breathing heavily, his eyes still wide and staring at the spot the man had occupied just seconds earlier.

The old soldier finally returned Mark's stunned stare. "I guess it works."

50

Mark was at a loss for words. The spectacle of the Transvice dissolving a person like a cloud of smoke caught in the wind wasn't even what weighed on his thoughts the heaviest. A completely insane man had just charged out of a house, straight at them. What had he been thinking? Was he attacking or begging for help? Were others going to be as bad? As . . . crazy?

It haunted him through and through, witnessing what the disease did to people. *Was doing.* It had to be getting worse. That guy had been utterly *nuts.* And Mark had already felt something like it – the faintest trace – starting within him. There was a beast hidden inside, and soon it might come out and make him look like the man Alec had zapped with the Transvice.

"You okay over there?"

Mark shook his head and came back to his senses. "No, I'm not okay. Did you see that dude?"

"Yeah. I saw him! Why do you think I evaporated him into

oblivion?" Alec was resting the weapon against its strap, looking around for signs of more people. So far there were none.

Though it should've happened a long time ago, it finally hit Mark – like a hammer to his heart – just how much trouble Trina was in. Held prisoner by lunatics who could now be as bad as the one he'd just seen. And Mark and Alec had taken the time to sleep? To eat? To pack? He suddenly hated himself.

"We have to go and rescue her," he said.

"What's that?" Alec was walking towards him.

Mark raised his eyes and glared at his friend. "We have to go. Now."

The next hour was a mix of maddening rushing around, then equally maddening waiting.

They closed the ramp door, Alec standing by with the Transvice in case anyone tried to board during the agonising couple of minutes it took the thing to pull all the way shut. Then they made sure their packs were ready to go and Alec gave Mark a quick lesson on how to hold and shoot the Transvice. It seemed straightforward enough. Finally the soldier got the Berg up and running, its thrusters pushing them into the sky.

They flew low, Mark the key observer, searching the ground below them as they passed. As they got closer to the neighbourhood ruins in which Alec had seen Trina and the others, Mark definitely saw more signs of life. People running between homes in little groups; a few fires in yards and smoke coming from half-crumbled chimneys; carcasses of dead animals that had been stripped of meat. He even saw a few humans lying lifeless here and there – sometimes piles of them.

"We're right on the outskirts of Asheville," Alec pointed out. They were at the head of a large valley, fed into by the foothills of the mountain forests that had burned in the recent fire. Expensive developments of big houses dotted the sides of those foothills. Several of the homes had been burnt to the ground, nothing left but charred black swaths of debris.

Mark saw dozens of people milling about in packs here and there along the streets. A handful of them had seen the Berg now – some were pointing up at the ship, some running for cover. But the majority didn't seem to have noticed at all, as if they'd been struck deaf and blind. "There's a huge group of them on that street." He pointed at them. Alec nodded. "That's where I saw them put Trina, Lana, and the kid in one of the houses."

Alec banked the Berg to swoop in and get a closer look. He pulled up and hovered about a hundred feet above the spot, then joined Mark at the windows. The two of them looked down on a complete nightmare.

It was as if a mental hospital had released all its patients. There was no order to the madness that Mark witnessed below him. Here he saw a girl lying flat on her back, screaming at no one. There he saw three women beating two men who'd been tied together, back to back. In another spot, people were dancing and drinking some kind of black liquid out of a pot that boiled over a makeshift fire pit. Others were running around in circles, still others stumbling about as if drunk.

But then Mark saw the worst thing of all. And he no longer had any doubt that the people who'd gathered there were beyond any kind of help.

A small group of men and women were fighting over something that looked like it had once been a person, their hands and faces covered in blood.

Mark was simultaneously revolted and terrified that he might be looking at the remains of the only girl he'd ever loved. His whole body suddenly shook, trembling from head to toe.

"Go down," he growled. "Go down there right now! Let me out!" Alec had backed away from the window, his face as pale a thing as Mark had ever seen. "I . . . we can't do that."

A furious burst of anger shot through Mark. "We can't give up now!"

"What're you talking about, kid? We need to land in a safer

place or they'll swarm this thing. We'll need it to get back to safety. We won't go too far."

Mark couldn't believe how heavily he was breathing. "Okay . . . okay. Sorry. But . . . just hurry."

"After what we just saw?" Alec asked as he was already positioning himself at the controls. "Yeah, I think that's sound advice."

Mark stumbled, leaned against the wall. The anger inside him was being replaced by an overwhelming sadness. How could she possibly still be alive in the midst of such madness? What was this Flare virus? What possibly could've possessed any person to want to spread it? Every question only increased his anguish. And there were no answers.

The Berg came to life and banked again, turning back towards the way they'd come. Mark wondered how many of the people down below had even noticed that a huge ship was just hovering right above them. They flew for a few minutes, and when Alec seemed satisfied, he landed the Berg in a cul-de-sac surrounded by empty lots, part of some developmental expansion that had never happened. And never would.

"That whole street was full of people," Mark said as he and his friend walked back to the cargo room. They both carried a fully charged Transvice and had backpacks strapped to their shoulders. "And there were signs of them in every house. They're probably in that entire section of the neighbourhood."

"For all we know they might've moved Lana and them again," Alec replied. "It would be smart to check every house in that section. But remember – they were alive this morning. I saw them, no doubt. Don't give up hope yet, son."

"You only call me son when you're scared," Mark answered.

Alec smiled kindly. "Exactly."

They made it to the big cargo room and Alec went to the control pad, pressed the ramp buttons. The hatch began to open, announcing their presence with its screeching hinges.

"Do you think the ship will be safe while we're gone?" Mark

asked, the broken window still haunting him.

"I've got the remote control here. We'll lock her up. That's the best we can do."

The door touched down and the noises ceased. The stifling hot air enveloped them as they walked to the bottom of the metal slab. They'd just stepped off when Alec pushed a button on the pad and sent the ramp closing up again. Soon it sealed shut and all was silent.

Mark looked at Alec, and Alec looked back. Mark thought it was a tight contest as to whose eyes showed more fire.

"Let's go and get our friends," Mark said.

The two of them began walking away from the Berg, weapons hefted in their arms, marching towards the madness and chaos that waited down the street.

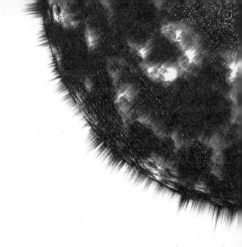

51

The air was dusty and dry.

With each step it seemed to become thicker, almost choking them. Sweat already covered every inch of Mark's body, and the breeze that swept across them now and then felt as if it came from a furnace, doing nothing to cool his skin. He pressed on, hoping his palms wouldn't become too slippery to handle the weapon properly. The sun hung above them like the eye of some hellish beast looking down, wilting the world around them.

"It's been a while since I've been out like this during the middle of the day," Mark said, the effort of speaking making him thirsty. His tongue felt swollen. "Gonna have one sweet sunburn come tomorrow." He knew what he was doing. Trying to convince himself that things weren't so bad – that he wasn't losing it up top, that his anger and headaches weren't going to hinder his concentration and focus and everything was going to be fine. But the effort seemed pointless.

They reached their first crossroads and Alec pointed to the

right. "Okay, it's just a couple of turns up that way. Let's start sticking closer to the houses."

Mark followed Alec's lead, crossing the dead lawn – now nothing but weeds and rocks – into the shadow of a home that had once been a mansion. All stone and dark wood, it had held up for the most part, though it now had a faded, sad look, as if losing its former occupants had stolen its soul away.

Alec leaned back against the wall and Mark did the same behind him. They swept their gazes – and weapons – back to where they'd just come from to see if anyone was following them. There wasn't a person in sight. Strangely, though, the breeze had stopped, so that the world seemed as lifeless as the neighbourhood itself. Mark shifted in his sticky clothes.

"We need to stay hydrated," Alec said, placing his weapon on the ground. He slipped off his backpack and pulled out one of his two canteens. After a long drink he handed it to Mark, who relished every drop as it slicked his parched mouth and throat.

"Oh, man," he said when he finished, handing the canteen back to Alec. "That was the single best drink I've ever had in my life. That one right there."

"Sayin' a lot," Alec muttered as he put the thing away and hunched into his backpack once again. "Considering all the times we've been thirsty in the last year."

"I think that crazy dude you . . . evaporated got me all worked up. But I'm ready to go now." He really did feel invigorated, as if the canteen had been full of adrenalin instead of water.

Alec picked up his weapon and slung the strap across his shoulder. "Follow me. From here on out we'll keep the houses between us and the streets."

"Sounds good."

Alec slipped out of the shade and made a beeline for the neighbouring yard, heading towards the back. Mark was right on his heels.

They kept the same routine for the next dozen or so homes: a quick sprint across the dead, lifeless yards, slipping into the shade of the buildings; then they'd slink their way around the back to the other side and Alec would peek around the corner, searching for any sign of company. Once he gave the all clear, they sprinted to the next house and started again.

They made it to the end of another street, where you could turn left or right.

"Okay," Alec whispered. "We need to head down this road and take the second left. That one runs into the big street where we saw all that partying going on."

"Partying?" Mark repeated.

"Yeah. It reminded me of some crankheads we busted in the twenties when martial law was declared. Those people were just as nuts – bloody hell-bent psychos, they were. Come on."

Crankheads. Mark had known some druggies in his life, but those were the worst. The drug had become stronger and stronger over the decades. Now it was something you never came back from. *Never.* For some reason the word stuck in Mark's mind.

"Hey!" Alec was halfway to the next house, and he turned back towards Mark. "Fine time to daydream!"

Mark shook off the cobwebs and ran after Alec. He caught up and they booked it to the side of a three-storey mansion, the shade a welcome relief as always. Even if it didn't last long. They sidled along the wall until they reached the back. Alec took a peek; then they stepped around the corner and started for the other side. Mark had only taken three or four steps when he heard a wet, cackling sound above him. He looked up, half expecting to see some kind of exotic animal, the noise had been so strange and alien.

But there was a woman perched on the roof, as ratty and filthy as any of the other infected Mark had seen recently. Her hair stuck out in every direction and her face was smeared with mud, the pattern almost ritualistic-looking.

She made that same cackling sound – somewhere between a laugh and a racking cough. She smiled, revealing a set of perfectly white teeth, but then turned it into a snarl. After another burst of cackles she rolled backwards and disappeared behind the lip of the roof's gutter – one of the few homes that still *had* a roof.

Mark shuddered. He hoped he'd be able to get the image of the woman out of his mind. He turned back and saw Alec was standing a few feet away from the house, aiming his weapon towards the roof but with no shot.

"Where'd she go?" the man asked absently.

"Let's just get out of here. Maybe she's by herself."

"Fat chance."

They shuffled along until they reached the far corner of the back side of the house. Alec leaned out for a quick look.

"All clear. We're getting closer, so buck up and look alive."

Mark nodded.

Alec took off for the next house and Mark was just stepping out to do the same when a horrific screech stopped him cold. He looked up just in time to see the woman leap off the roof, flying through the air with her arms outstretched like wings. Her face was lit with madness as she shrieked, plummeting towards Mark, who couldn't believe what he was seeing.

He turned to run but it was too late. Her body slammed into his shoulders and they both crashed to the ground.

52

She went for his eyes, as if the impact of the fall had done nothing to her. Howls poured from her mouth as if she were some kind of tortured creature. The wind had been knocked out of him, and his knees ached where they'd thumped against the hard ground. He rolled over, gasping for air as he grabbed her hands, tried to force them away from his face. She ripped free of his grasp and clawed at his ears, his nose, his cheeks, scratching and slapping. He continued to fight her off.

"Help!" he screamed to Alec.

"Push her off so I can get a clear shot!" the man yelled back.

Mark twisted his body and darted a quick glance at Alec. He was standing there, hopping around as he aimed his weapon, waiting until he could risk firing the Transvice at the woman.

"Just come get—" Mark started to yell, but her fingers were suddenly in his mouth, pulling at his lips. She hooked a finger into his cheek and pulled as if trying to rip the side of his face off, but her finger slipped out. Her hand flew up into the air, then came crashing back into his face with a clenched fist. Pain and anger burst through him like a lit chain of firecrackers.

Finally able to breathe, he got his hands underneath her body and stuck his elbows out, then pushed hard. She flew off him, crashing on to her back with an audible thud that momentarily shut her up. Then she was scrambling to get back on to her hands and knees. But Mark had righted himself first, and he lurched forward, then planted his weight on his left foot and kicked out with his right, slamming the toe of his shoe into the side of her head. She screamed and flopped over, curled up into a ball and held her face in her arms. Rocked back and forth, whimpering.

Mark quickly scrambled away from her. "Go ahead, do it!"

But Alec didn't. He calmly walked up to stand beside Mark, the end of his weapon pointed at the suffering woman. "It'd be a waste. Let's save it for bigger game."

"But what if she follows us? Goes and gets her friends? Ruins our chance at surprising them up ahead?"

Alec gave her a long look, then raised his eyes to Mark. "If it makes you feel better, then you do it." He turned and started walking towards the next house, scanning the area for potential enemies.

Mark went over to where he'd dropped his Transvice and backpack in the melee of fighting off the crazy woman. He didn't take his eyes off her as he picked both items up, slinging the pack on to his shoulders and tightening the straps, then hefting the weapon in both hands once they were free. He aimed it at the lady and walked closer until he was just a few feet away. Still she lay curled up in the foetal position, whimpering and moaning, rocking back and forth. Mark found that he felt no pity, no sorrow. She was past being human, had lost every ounce of sanity, and that wasn't his fault. And for all he knew, she had friends nearby, or was just playing weak so that they'd walk away and leave her alone.

No. There wasn't time for pity any more.

He took another step back, firmly pressed the butt of the weapon against his chest, aimed a little more precisely and pulled the trigger. A buzz and hum filled the air; then the Transvice recoiled and shot out a beam of white light that sliced into the woman's body. She didn't have time to scream before her body turned into a rippling wave of grey and exploded into a fine mist, vanishing in an instant.

Mark had stumbled two steps backward, but he was just glad he hadn't fallen down. He stared at the empty space on the ground where the woman had been lying, then finally looked up to see that Alec had stopped and was facing him, eyeing him with an unreadable expression on his face. But there seemed to be a mix of shock and unmistakable pride in there somewhere.

"Our friends," Mark said, sure that he'd never heard such a bitter voice escape his own lips before. "That's all we can think about."

He lifted the weapon, nestled it in the crook between his neck and shoulder and held it there with one hand while dropping the other to rest at his side. Then he calmly and quietly walked towards Alec.

The old soldier waited for him and didn't say a word. They moved on to the next house.

53

Mark began to hear the chaos after passing two more houses. Screams and laughter and what sounded like metal beating on metal. The screams were the most chilling, and he didn't know if he was prepared to see their source. He tried not to think about the fact that he might end up just as sick as the people he could hear. He might have already started the journey there.

After dodging and weaving past several more houses, he and Alec finally reached the street they'd seen from the sky.

Alec held up his hand to stop Mark behind the last house on the block. It faced the road yet still provided some protection from being seen. They stood in the shade of a half-crumbled awning.

"Okay," Alec said, slipping off his backpack. "This is it. Let's get ourselves fed and watered up. Then we're going in hot and heavy."

Mark was surprised at how little fear he felt, at least at that moment. Maybe it was because they were taking a short break and the situation didn't seem real yet. But if anything, it'd been building up for so long he was just anxious to get out there and let what happened happen. His head was throbbing again badly, and he knew somehow that it was only going to get worse. He couldn't afford to waste time.

They sat down and ate some of the dried, packaged food scavenged from the Berg. Mark enjoyed every swallow of the water from his canteen. He had the fleeting thought that it could be the last time he ever drank the stuff. He shook his head. The morbid thoughts were becoming harder and harder to push from his mind. He crammed the last couple of bites into his mouth and stood up.

"I can't take it any more," he said. He reached down, picked up his backpack and slung it on to his shoulders. "Let's get out there and find our friends."

Alec gave him a sharp look.

"I just meant with all the waiting. . . . I can't take it." His head ached but he tried hard to ignore it. "Come on. Let's do this."

Alec stood up and got himself packed and prepared. Once he was done, the two of them hoisted their weapons into their hands, ready for battle.

"Remember," Alec said, "there might be no defence against these Transvices. But that doesn't mean anything if we get the damn things taken from us. Do not, I repeat, *do not* let anyone get close enough to get it out of your hands. And keep the strap over your shoulder. That's our number one priority – keeping these babies for ourselves."

Mark gripped his tightly, as if someone were going to try to take it from him right then and there, and nodded. "Don't worry. I won't let anyone get close."

Alec put out his hand. "We're going to make it through this, but just in case . . ."

Mark shook the man's hand, squeezing it. "Thanks for the billion times you saved my life."

"It's been an honour serving with you, kid. Maybe today you'll save mine a couple more times."

"I'll do my best."

They hefted their weapons and turned the corner of the house. Alec looked at Mark and nodded, then burst into a full-on sprint. Mark followed his lead and ran behind him into the street.

The main pack of infected were further down the road, but there were enough people nearby for the two to be wary. One woman sat square in the middle of the road, clapping her hands in a rhythmic pattern. A few feet away from her, two men were fighting over what looked like a dead rat. Another guy was standing on the corner, singing at the top of his lungs.

Mark and Alec crossed the street and headed towards the first home. Like most of the ruins in the wealthy neighbourhood, it was huge and half burnt down. What remained had rotted. Mark followed Alec closely, stopping at the side of the house. They inched up against the wall and caught their breath. No one seemed to have noticed them yet. Of course, many hadn't even looked up when they'd been in the Berg right over their heads, thrusters burning louder than anything Mark could imagine.

"Okay," Alec said. "When I saw them, Lana and the others were being led to a house down there." He nodded towards the street to the right. "But I think we should search each one to be sure. If they've been moved, I'd rather not miss them. If we can avoid the main pack of wackos up the street, all the better."

"Might as well get started, then," Mark replied. "Right here."

Alec nodded. "Come on."

They slipped out from the protection of the wall and headed for the front door – only to run straight into a man standing in front of the entrance. He was dressed in tattered clothing and his face was dirty, a red gash taking up most of his cheek.

"Get out of the way," Alec barked. "Step away from the door and into the yard or you'll be dead in five seconds."

The man gave them a blank look. Then he raised his eyebrows once and did as he was told, stepping calmly off the porch and walking – slowly – on to the weedy, rocky front yard. And he kept walking, without a backward glance, until he reached the sidewalk, where he turned to the right and headed for the activity down the road.

Alec shook his head. "Be ready in case someone jumps out at us." Mark planted his feet and aimed his weapon.

Alec held his Transvice with one hand and reached out with the other, grabbing the door and pulling it open. He took a step back as it swung wide, giving Mark a clear shot if he needed it. But the place was empty.

"You go first so I can watch your back," Alec said, waving his arm for Mark to enter.

"Or watch me get eaten before you do."

"Trust me on this one, kid. It's better for you if I'm back here. Now get moving."

A surge of excitement was pumping through Mark's body. Fear no longer tugged at him; he was itching to do something. He gave Alec a curt nod and stepped up to the porch and entered the house, sweeping his weapon left and right as he searched the room. Everything was hot and dusty and dark, sunlight visible only through holes in the walls. The upstairs seemed much lighter, though.

The floor creaked with every step he took.

"Stop and listen for a sec," Alec said behind him.

Mark stilled his body and strained his ears. Other than the distant sounds of the chaotic dance taking place down the street, he couldn't hear a thing. The house was silent.

"Let's go top to bottom," Alec suggested.

The stairs proved to be too broken to manage. Mark gave up after his foot went completely through the third step.

Alec motioned towards a door that seemed likely to lead to the basement. "Bag that idea. I don't hear anything up there. Let's check it out down below, then move on."

Mark carefully removed himself from the stairs and went to the basement door. He gave Alec a confirming look, grabbed the handle and jerked it open. Alec swung his weapon into the gap in case anyone attacked, but nothing happened. A rush of moist, noxious air swept up and over Mark, and he gagged. He had to cough and swallow a couple of times to keep himself from throwing up.

Alec decided to go first this time, stepping through the doorway and on to the landing. He reached back and pulled his torch out of his pack, clicked it on and shone it down the steps. Mark leaned in to see dust motes dancing in the bright beam. Alec was just putting his foot forwards to start down when a voice rang out from below.

"C-c-come any closer and I'll l-l-light the match."

It was a man's voice, weak and shaky. Alec glanced back at Mark with a questioning look.

Out of the corner of his eye, Mark caught movement, at the bottom of the steps and gestured towards it with his weapon. Alec shone the light down there to reveal the person who'd spoken, who'd just appeared out of the darkness. He was trembling top to bottom and soaking wet, his dark hair matted to his head and his clothes dripping. Little puddles were already forming on the floor. The man's face was starkly pale, as if he hadn't left the basement in weeks. His eyes squinted against the brightness of the torch.

At first Mark wondered if the man was just sweating profusely. Then he wondered if maybe the guy had some kind of busted pipe or ground-water down there. But then he caught a whiff of gasoline or kerosene – some kind of fuel. And then he noticed that the guy had things in his hands, holding them tight to his waist. In one, he held a rectangular box. In the other, a single match.

"Take one more step and I'll light it," the man said.

54

Mark wanted to turn and run, but Alec hadn't moved yet. He just stood there with his weapon aimed down the stairs at the man with the match.

"We didn't come here to hurt you," Alec said carefully. "We're just looking for some friends of ours. Is anybody else down there?"

It seemed as if the man hadn't heard anything Alec had said. He just continued to stand there, trembling and dripping with fuel. "They're scared of fire, you know. Everyone is scared of fire, no matter how far your mind has gone. They don't bother me down here. Not with my matches and gasoline."

"Trina!" Mark called out. "Lana! Are you guys here?"

No one responded, and the man with the match wasn't fazed by the outburst. "It's your choice, my new friends. You can take a step towards me and I'll light the flames that'll take me away once and for all. Or you can go on your merry way and let me live another day."

Alec was slowly shaking his head. He finally started to back away from the steps, pushing against Mark until they were both in the hallway again. Without a word, Alec reached out and slowly closed the door until it clicked softly. Then he turned towards Mark.

"What kind of world has this become?"

"A really sick one." Mark was feeling it, too. Something about seeing that guy doused in fuel, holding a match. For some reason he just seemed to sum things up. "And I doubt its end will be so happy for us. All we can do is find our friends and make sure we die on our own terms."

"Well said, son. Well said."

Mark and Alec quietly exited the first house and moved on to the next.

The sounds were louder now. In a crouching run, Alec and Mark had made their way to the home across the street, planning to follow a zig-zagging route. A few stragglers noticed them and pointed but moved on quickly enough. Mark hoped their luck would hold and no one would give them too much thought. Although the shiny weapons were bound to ruin that plan.

They'd just stepped up to the porch of the next house when two small children came running out. Mark's finger was twitching on the trigger, but relief washed over him when he realised the advancing figures were only kids. They were filthy and had that strange distant look in their eyes. They giggled and ran away, but as soon as they disappeared a large woman came stomping out, screaming something about brats and threatening to tan their hides.

She didn't seem to notice the two strangers until after she'd yelled for a few good seconds, and then she only gave them a disapproving look.

"We're not crazy in this home," she said, her face suddenly red with anger. "Not yet, anyway. No need to take my kids. They're the only things keeping the monsters away. "There was a vacancy in her eyes that chilled Mark to the bone.

Alec was visibly annoyed. "Look, lady, we don't care about your kids and we're certainly not here to cart them off. All we want to do is have a quick look in your home, make sure our friends aren't in there."

"Friends?" the woman repeated. "The monsters are your friends? The ones that want to eat my children?" The vacancy was suddenly replaced by a stark terror that darkened her eyes. "Please . . . please don't hurt me. I can give you one of them. Just one. Please."

Alec sighed. "We don't know any monsters. Just . . . look, just move aside and let us in. We don't have time."

He stepped forward, muscles tensed, ready to use force if necessary, but she scrambled away, almost tripping on to the dead weeds of her yard. Mark looked at her sadly – he'd assumed the monsters were the infected people down the street, but now he realised he was wrong. This woman wasn't any more right in the head than the last guy they'd found, and he wouldn't be surprised if she really did think monsters were living under the beds.

Mark left the woman in the front yard and followed Alec inside only to be stunned by what he saw. The interior looked more like a back alley from one of the worst parts of New York City than a suburban home. Pictures had been drawn – with what looked like black crayon and chalk – all over the walls. Dark, terrifying pictures. Of monsters. Things with claws and sharp teeth and vicious eyes. They were messy, as if they'd been done in a hurry, but some had vivid details. Enough to make the hair on Mark's arms stand up.

He gave Alec a grim look and followed the older man past them, to the stairs to the basement, and went down, weapons held at the ready.

They found more children below – at least fifteen, maybe more. And they were living in filth. Most of them were huddled together in groups, cowering as if they expected some horrible punishment from the new arrivals. They were all dirty and poorly clothed and, by the looks of it, starving. Mark hardly registered the fact that the people he was looking for were nowhere to be seen.

"We . . . we can't leave them here," Mark said. He'd let go of his weapon, and it hung from the strap on his shoulder. He was dumbfounded. "There's no way we can leave them here."

Alec seemed to sense he wouldn't be able to make Mark budge on this. The soldier stepped in front of him and spoke gravely.

"I understand what you're saying, son. Where you're coming from. But listen to me. What can we do for these children? Everyone in this godforsaken place is sick, and we don't have the manpower to get them out. At least they're . . . I don't even know what to say."

"Surviving," Mark said quietly. "I thought surviving was all that mattered, but I was wrong. We can't leave these kids here."

Alec sighed. "Look at me." When Mark didn't, Alec snapped his fingers and yelled, "Look at me!"

Mark did.

"Let's go and find our friends. After that we can come back. But if we take them now, we'll have no chance. You hear me? Absolutely zero."

Mark nodded. He knew the old man was right. But something had torn in his heart at the sight of these kids, and it physically hurt. He didn't think it would ever mend.

He turned around to gather his thoughts. All he could do was focus on Trina. He had to save Trina. And Deedee.

"Okay," he finally said. "Let's go."

Mark and Alec moved from house to house, searching them from top to bottom.

It all became a big, hazy blur to Mark. The more he saw, the more numb he grew to the strangeness of the new world. This sickness that had been spread on purpose. In each house, on each block, he saw things that kept topping what he'd thought untoppable. He saw a woman jump off a roof and land, broken, on her front steps. He saw three men drawing circles in the dirt and jumping in and out of them, like kids playing a game. Except something was making them more and more upset and they finally erupted into a crazed brawl. There was a room in one of the homes where twenty or thirty people were lying in a heap in complete silence. Definitely alive, but not moving.

A woman eating a cat. A man chewing on a rug in the corner of his living room. Two kids throwing rocks at each other as hard as they could, bloodied and bruised from head to toe. Laughing all the while. People standing still in their yards, staring at the sky. Others lying facedown in the dirt, talking to themselves. Mark saw a man bull-rushing a tree, slamming himself into the trunk over and over, as if he thought eventually he'd win some battle and knock the thing down.

But on they went, quickly searching each and every home as they got closer to what Alec had called the party. The strangest thing, though, was that so far no one had attacked them. Most people actually seemed scared to death of them.

They were approaching their next house when a scream suddenly tore through the air, somehow louder than all the other sounds combined. It was piercing and raw, ripping its way along the street like a living thing.

Alec pulled up short, as did Mark, and they both looked in the direction of the noise.

About five houses down, two men were dragging a woman with black hair by her feet through the front door. Her head smacked the concrete of each step as they descended to the yard.

"Holy Mother of . . . ," Alec whispered. "It's Lana."

55

Alec didn't wait for Mark's response.

He burst into an all-out sprint, booking into the street, his feet pounding the pavement as he headed for Lana and the strangers now dragging her across the rock-filled yard of the house. He'd reacted so quickly that Mark was far behind. He tried his best to catch up, his backpack bouncing against his shoulders and his weapon threatening to slip out of his sweaty hands.

Alec was screaming at the men to stop what they were doing. He held up his Transvice, but the thugs didn't understand the threat, or didn't care. They continued pulling Lana across the yard until they reached the sidewalk, where they threw her legs down violently. She'd ceased her screaming and Mark wondered if she was still conscious. Still alive.

Alec stopped a dozen feet from where Lana lay unmoving. He was aiming his weapon, yelling at them all to freeze, when Mark caught up to him. It took him a moment to catch his breath before he could aim his own Transvice.

There were three men total, and they stood in a circle around Lana's body, all of them looking down at her. They seemed completely oblivious that people had weapons aimed at them.

"Step away from her!" Alec shouted.

Now that they were closer, Mark finally got a good look at their friend. It made his stomach turn. She was battered and bloody and covered in bruises. Much of her hair had been ripped out, and her bloody scalp showed through where it was missing. The last thing Mark noticed was that one of her ears looked like someone had tried to tear it off. The horror of it struck Mark like an anvil to his chest, and the rage he'd grown all too familiar with came boiling back up. These people were monsters, and if they'd done the same things to Trina . . .

He stepped towards them, but Alec reached a hand out and stopped him.

"Just a second," he said, then returned his attention to Lana's captors. "I'm not going to repeat myself. Step away from her or I start shooting." But instead of responding, the three men knelt to the ground, their knees touching Lana's body as they surrounded her. Frantically, she looked back and forth between them.

"Just do it," Mark said. "What're you waiting for?"

"I don't have a clear shot!" Alec barked back. "I don't want to vaporise her!"

Alec's words just made Mark angrier. He wasn't going to stand there and do nothing for one more second.

"I've had enough of this crap," he muttered, and started walking forward, slapping away Alec's hand when he tried once again to stop him.

The men didn't so much as glance at him as he approached. They were all digging deep in their pockets for something, their bodies turned in a way that blocked most of Mark's view.

"Hey!" he shouted, his weapon held out before him. "Get away from her or I'm going to shoot. You won't know what hit you, believe me!"

267

They didn't hear him, or pretended not to. The next thing that happened was so quick and shocking that it made him stumble, almost fall down. In a blur of motion, one of the men pulled out a switchblade and stabbed Lana. Her screams sent a jolt of horror thudding through Mark's bones. Then he was rushing forward, slinging his weapon to his back, diving. He leaped and tackled the man closest to him, sending them both rolling away from Lana.

He heard Alec yelling his name, but somehow he ignored it. His only thought was that he had to disarm this guy quickly enough that he could stop the others. At least get them far enough away from Lana that Alec could take care of them. The man he'd tackled was strong, but Mark had taken him by surprise and was able to pin him to the ground with his knees and snatch the switchblade out of his hands. Without thinking, he stabbed him in the chest and ended it.

Mark fell off, crashing on to his back and scrambling away. Staring in horror at what he'd just done. But just as quickly, the world around him came back into focus and he jumped to his feet. Alec ran up and swung the butt of his weapon down with both arms, slamming its end into one of the attackers' heads. He crumpled and slumped to the ground.

There was a group of people charging in from the other side of the street. Mark had no idea where they'd come from, but there were at least seven or eight of them. All men. All with knives or hammers or screwdrivers, their faces lit up in rage.

"Watch out!" Mark yelled to Alec.

But the men weren't interested in them. Instead they all went after Lana, who was still being attacked by the lone man left of the three who'd originally dragged her outside. Alec took a few stumbling steps backwards and Mark ran to stand beside him. As they watched, Mark realised that they were powerless to stop the madness unless they started using the Transvices. He was filled with a sudden doomed uncertainty.

Alec seemed to suddenly harden, a visible change that

spread through his body. His face went still, hard as a rock. He straightened and stood tall. Then, without a word to Mark, he lifted his weapon and aimed it at the group of people attacking Lana.

He fired a shot. The quick stream of pure white bolted forwards and hit the closest man, who'd just been pulling his arm back, a bloodied hammer gripped in his hand. He transformed quickly into that shimmering flag of grey, then exploded into a cloud of mist, whisked away by an unfelt wind. Alec was already firing another burst at the man next to him. Mark knew they couldn't win this battle, though Lana had been brave and true and strong since the day they'd met back in the tunnels of the subtrans.

Mark lifted up his own weapon and started firing. He and Alec picked off the attackers one by one: Pull the trigger. On to the next.

Soon the monsters were gone and only the pitiful, wretched form of their friend lay on the ground. Alec didn't hesitate for a moment. He aimed and shot one more burst from his Transvice.

Lana's suffering ended in a spray of grey mist.

56

Mark's eyes drifted up from the bloody patch on the ground and fixed on Alec. The man had a look on his face that said a thousand things. But laced through it all was a profound sadness. Though Mark never fully understood what kind of relationship the two veterans had shared, it had been deep and full of history.

And now she was gone.

Alec's expression cleared in a few seconds, but it felt like a lifetime to Mark. He'd never seen his friend so sad before.

Suddenly Alec was all business again. He pointed at the house in front of them. "That's where they dragged her out. And that's where we're going in. I'm sure Trina and the kid are in there right now."

Mark turned to look. A mansion by any account, three storeys and all gables and massive windows – many of them broken now – and fancy brickwork. But with a scorched roof and filthy walls and a weed-choked, yellow lawn, it looked ancient. Mark was terrified at what they might find inside it.

And people were gathering around them.

Less than a minute had passed since they'd vaporised their friend and the violent thugs attacking her, but the crowd milling about in the yard and street seemed to have doubled in size. Men and women, children. Most of them marked with bruises and scratches, some with worse. A man with a huge section of his shoulder missing was slowly ambling towards them; it looked like someone had taken an axe to him in a fit of rage. There was a woman with an entire arm gone, the joint a bloody mess. Most disturbing of all, there were a couple of kids with brutal injuries, and they didn't even seem to know they were hurt.

Without fail, the people started to inch closer, surrounding Mark and Alec. Tattered and grimy clothes, dirty hair, hollow gazes – the crowd's attention was entirely fixed on the two newcomers.

Alec started walking slowly towards the front door of the large house. Mark mimicked his wary movements, as if any sudden action would trigger the budding insanity in those who watched their every step. They inched closer, weapons held firm. Mark wasn't taking even the slightest chance any more. If someone came at him, they were getting shot.

The crowd pulled in tighter around Mark and Alec, gathering like spectators at a parade. There had to be dozens of them now, maybe over a hundred. Then several men broke from the larger group and cut off the path to the front door. As soon as they did it, others followed suit, completely surrounding Mark and Alec now, a tightening noose.

"I don't know if you people can understand me," Alec bellowed. "But this is a one-time offer. Get out of our way or we start shooting."

"We've got friends in this house," Mark added. "And we're not leaving without them." He raised his Transvice just for show.

The looks on the faces all around him were changing. That

blank indifference was clearing. Eyes were narrowing, foreheads furrowing, lips curling up in slight snarls. A couple of women actually hissed at them, and a kid gnashed his teeth like some wild animal.

"Get out of our way!" Alec yelled.

The crowd surged in a few inches, pressing closer, tightening their circle. Mark felt that familiar break inside of him again, as if he was losing control. A rush of something like hatred burned through him.

"Forget this," he muttered.

He aimed his Transvice at the closest man between him and the front door and pulled the trigger. A blinding stream of white light shot from the weapon and into the man's chest, quickly turning him into a wall of grey, then an explosion of particles that disappeared. Mark didn't hesitate. He immediately aimed at the next man, pulled the trigger, watched him turn to vapour. Next to him was a woman. Three seconds later she was no longer there.

He'd half expected Alec to stop him. But the former soldier wasted no time. The woman had barely disassembled when Alec was firing away as well. They concentrated on clearing a path to the house, slowly sweeping their weapons back and forth as they picked the people off one by one. Flashes of light filled the air as their Transvices heated up, unleashing a wave of destruction. All without a single drop of blood.

They'd eliminated about a dozen people, cutting through half the crowd standing in front of them, when the rest of the infected seemed to finally catch on to what was happening. A violent scream filled the air, a piercing, horrible sound, and suddenly every last person there was charging forward, rushing at the two men with their death-dealing weapons.

Mark moved his weapon left to right, pulling the trigger in short bursts, not even bothering to aim. Streaks of white connected with a few women. One stray shot hit a small boy, vaporised him. Still they barrelled towards him at full speed.

Mark turned to face the people behind him. He fired again, then gripped the Transvice and swung it up to smash its butt end into a man's face, sending him sprawling, shrieking in pain.

Mark stumbled backwards but caught his balance. There were people all around him, hissing, baring their teeth, dancing about on their feet, all wild eyes and hysterical laughter. Mark held the Transvice tightly against his chest again and fired randomly, turning in a slow circle as he vaporised whoever was closest. Then he swept the weapon back the other way, all the while careful of where Alec stood.

The next few moments were complete madness. Mark felt a hitch of panic. He kept firing, swinging left, then right. He elbowed and shoved and broke through and fired and started all over again, pushing his way ever closer to the house. He killed at least ten more people before he was suddenly tripping over the steps of the porch.

He fell, twisted the Transvice around and fired it directly into the chest of a man who'd leaped into the air towards him. The grey mist washed over Mark's face and disappeared. He spotted Alec a few feet away, jamming the end of his weapon into a woman's face; Alec then broke into a run, jumping on to the steps and passing Mark, heading for the door.

Mark got off one more shot before he began to crawl backwards up the stairs. At the top he got to his feet and reached the door just as Alec was stepping through. He ran past Alec into the house and his friend slammed the door. Alec had barely tripped the lock before the thump of bodies hitting it sounded from the other side. Mark doubted it would hold for long.

Then they were running. Down a hallway, a right turn, another hallway. Two people came at them – they'd been guarding a door. Alec got both of them with shots from his Transvice. Mark slipped past him, opened the door – there were steps. A man was at the bottom, pounding his way up, his eyes all fire set in a dirty, scratched face. Mark vaporised him.

Down the stairway, two at a time. A man and a woman

rushed at him with knives, swinging at him before he could bring his weapon up. He smacked them both away and dived towards the floor just as Alec appeared and shot his weapon twice. And then everything grew quiet except for the distant sounds of the people outside, who'd be coming for them soon.

They were in a basement. A stream of sunlight shone through a narrow window at the top of the wall to Mark's right. Dust motes danced in the air. And two people were huddled in the corner of the room, looking as frightened as anyone Mark had ever seen.

Trina and Deedee, clutching each other, arms wrapped around one another's bruised bodies. Mark ran to them, knelt in front of them, placed his weapon on the ground.

Deedee was crying and spoke first. "She's sick," she said in her trembling, little-girl voice. She squeezed Trina tighter, crying.

Mark reached out and took Trina's hand, squeezed it. "It's okay. We found you. We're getting you out of here."

Trina had been staring at the floor the entire time, but she slowly raised her head and looked at Mark. Her eyes were empty and dark.

"Who are you?" she asked.

57

The words hit him like a rapid series of thumps to his heart. He tried to convince himself that there were a million reasons she could've said what she did. Maybe the room didn't have enough light; maybe she'd been hit in the head; maybe her vision was blurred. But the reality of it was in those eyes. She had no idea who he was. None.

"Trina . . ." He searched for words. "Trina, it's me. Mark."

There was a crash upstairs, something breaking. Then a few thuds. Footsteps sounded from above.

"We've gotta get out," Alec barked. "Now."

Trina had not stopped looking at Mark, her face wrinkled in confusion. Her head was tilted to the side, as if in her mind she was running through the possibilities of who this guy in front of her could be. But there was also fear and panic, something unsettling.

"Maybe there's a treatment," Mark found himself whispering, in some sort of trance. The only person in the world he wanted with him safe and sound . . . "Maybe—"

"Mark!" Alec yelled. "Get them up! Now!"

He looked back to see his friend at the bottom of the stairs, weapon raised to shoot whoever dared try to come down first. There was more noise above them: people running and shouting. Things breaking. Then Mark caught a blur of movement out the window, a pair of feet that were there, then gone.

"We'll figure everything out," he said, returning his attention to the two girls. "Come on, we need to get out of here."

The rising volume of noise threatened to push his panic over the edge, but he knew he was treading on fragile ground with Trina. He had no idea how she might react if he tried to rush her.

"Deedee?" he said as gently as he could. He picked up the Transvice and rested the strap on his shoulder. "Come here, Deedee. Take my hand and stand up."

A loud bang cut through the air, coming from the stairs. Someone had just thrown a door open and slammed it against the wall. The shouts had reached a hysterical pitch. Mark heard the distinct power surge and zing of Alec's Transvice going off, heard the shocked gasps coming from above as people saw one of their comrades disappear in a flash of grey mist. Mark imagined the scene, all while holding his hand out and trying to look calm for Deedee.

The girl just stared at him for an agonising few seconds, a thousand thoughts going through her head, by the looks of it. Mark didn't let himself move, just kept smiling and holding that hand out. Finally she reached out and took it, let him pull her up. Without letting go, he leaned in and slipped his other arm under Trina's back, got a firm grip. He used all the strength he had left to lift her off the ground and set her on her feet.

She didn't resist, but Mark was worried she might topple over if he let go. "Who are you?" she repeated. "Are you here to save us?"

"I'm your best friend of all time," he answered, trying not to let her words sting. "These people stole you from me, and now I'm going to get you back to safety. Home sweet home and all that."

"Please," she said. "Please don't let them hurt me again."

An abyss yawned in his chest, threatening to swallow his heart. "That's why I'm here. I just need you to walk, okay? Walk and stay close to me."

More sounds from up above: a scream, a window shattering. Then footsteps on the stairs. Alec fired off another shot.

Trina shifted and put all her weight on her own two feet. "Okay. I'm okay. I'll do anything to get out of here."

"That's my girl." Mark reluctantly slid his arm from her back and then focused on Deedee, bending over to look into her eyes. "This is going to be really scary, okay? But then it'll be over. Stay close to—"

"I'll be fine," she said, cutting him off. A sudden fire burned in her eyes that made her seem ten years older. "Let's go."

Mark felt a small smile on his lips. "Perfect. Let's do it."

He took her hand and put it in Trina's and squeezed them together. Then he grabbed his Transvice and positioned it firmly against his chest, ready to shoot.

"Stay right behind me," he said, looking at each of them in turn to get confirmation that they understood. Trina seemed a little more lucid now, clarity coming back into her eyes. "Right behind me."

He gripped his weapon, rested his finger on the trigger, then turned to face the foot of the stairs, where Alec maintained his position.

Mark had taken two steps towards Alec, Deedee and Trina right on his heels, when the window to their left suddenly exploded inward, a chunk of brick crashing to the floor in a shower of glass. Deedee screamed and Trina jumped forward, stumbling into Mark's back. Mark lurched forwards but caught himself before he fell. He pointed his Transvice at the broken window, where a man's arm had snaked through the narrow gap and was groping along the walls.

Mark fired a burst from his weapon. The first bolt of white heat missed, drilling a hole in the wall that sent up a strange cloud of dust. He tried again and this time hit home. The arm dissolved into a grey mass, then whiffed out of existence. Two more people appeared where the man had been, but Mark could tell the strip of window was too small for a person to crawl through. He turned away and moved once again towards the staircase, where Alec stood firm. He took a shot at someone above even as Mark looked at him.

"Got no choice but to make our way up there," the man growled without taking his eyes off the door. "More of these psychos are probably arriving by the minute outside."

"We're ready," Mark replied, even though he had no clue how they were going to get their group of four through the horde of Flare-infected maniacs. "Maybe we should put the girls in between us."

"Exactly. I'll go first, you take up the rear this time. It's gonna be ugly pushing through these wackos."

Mark nodded and took a step back. Trina seemed more and more with it, though she hadn't yet given any sign that she remembered him. She grabbed Deedee's hand and guided her to stand right beside Alec. The man winked at the little girl, then started up the stairs. Trina followed with Deedee in tow. Mark went up backward, just in case someone figured out another way to get into the basement.

Step by step, they ascended towards the chaos waiting above.

"Get out of our way!" Alec yelled. "I start shooting in three seconds!"

The roar of activity increased, a cacophony of shouts and whistles and jeers and laughing. Mark abandoned the idea of guarding their rear and looked up to see five or six faces packed together at the door, waiting for them, wild-eyed and seemingly hungry for violence. He felt such a burgeoning fear in his chest that it was hard to breathe. But he knew that if they could just get outside somehow, they stood a fighting chance.

"Time's up!" Alec roared. Then he let out three quick blasts from his Transvice. Two women and a man were whisked away into neverland.

Suddenly everyone surged forward, screaming and yelling, pushing through the door in a mass of bodies. Alec got off another couple of shots, but then it was too much. Soon he had ten people on top of him, jumping and leaping and clawing.

Alec fell backwards into Trina and Deedee, who crashed into Mark. The entire group tumbled down the stairs in a tangle of arms and legs. And the infected came charging after them.

58

Mark's head slammed against a step, then the wall, then the floor. All while feet kicked and hands slapped and elbows jabbed at him. The world had turned into spinning, pain-filled madness. When everything stilled, Trina and Alec were on his chest and Deedee was on his legs, squirming to get up. Alec awkwardly tried to lift his Transvice to get off a shot but was suddenly tackled by a man who jumped from the fourth step up and smashed into his body, sending him flying off Mark.

Trina was reaching for Deedee; she grabbed her and pulled her into a fierce hug, leaping out of the fray just as more people rained down from above. Soon they were on top of Mark, a dozen or more, punching and kicking and seemingly trying to rip him apart. Mark was at a loss, all plans out the window, relying on sheer desperation. He twisted his body and tried to spin out of the mass, gripping the Transvice with both hands to swing it left and right to get people away from him.

Trina yelled in a loud, piercing voice, "Stop it! Everyone stop and listen to me!"

Her words sliced through the air and the cries and shouts and grunts coming from everyone in the tangled mass of bodies lining the stairs from top to bottom went silent. All movement stopped. Mark was stunned at the abrupt change – he scrambled out from underneath a couple of people who were staring at Trina, almost transfixed. His back hit the wall across from the lowest step. Trina was to his left, still clutching Deedee in her arms; to his right, Alec had freed himself, too.

All eyes were on Trina, as if she had some magical, hypnotic power. The silence in the basement was broken only by the breathing of the occupants.

"You all need to listen to me," she said more quietly. There was a wildness in her eyes. "I'm one of you now. These men have come to help us. But you need to let us go so they can do that."

This set off a chorus of mumbling and muttering through-out the crowd. Mark watched in sick fascination as they got to their feet, frantically whispering to each other, seeming to obey. The people were bloody and filthy, but they started to act in an organised fashion. Soon they were lined up on both sides of the stairs, leaving a clear path up the middle. Mark could tell that those at the top were communicating with other people in the house, spreading the word. It was all done with something like reverence.

Trina turned towards Mark. "Lead us up."

She still showed no sign of recognition in her eyes, and it stung in his heart once again. He had no idea what was going on or how she'd got this sea of maniacs to listen to her com-mand, but he wasn't going to waste the opportunity. He jumped to his feet and held his Transvice at the ready, without overtly showing it as a threat. He looked at Alec, who seemed as unsettled as Mark had ever seen him, doubt clouding his eyes. He nodded at Mark to go first.

Mark walked forwards to the stairs and turned to Trina and Deedee. "Let's go up, then. Come on, it's going to be okay." He'd never said anything in his life that he believed less.

They came to him, ready to follow. Trina had Deedee in front of her, gripping the little girl's shoulders. Alec moved to stand right behind them.

"Up we go," the man grumbled. His eyes were darting back and forth at the lines of people on both sides of the stairs. And the way he looked at them said it all – he thought for sure it was some kind of trap. His grip on his Transvice was a little tighter than Mark's.

With a deep breath that made him aware of the awful smells of the people around him, Mark turned and faced the stairs again. He took the first step. Every single eye above him was focused on his face. To his right was a woman with stringy hair and bruised cheeks, staring at him with a slight, knowing smile. To his left stood a teenage boy in tattered clothes, scuffed and dirty from head to toe. He also seemed on the verge of laughing. More people waited with similar looks, all eyes on him. All silent and still.

"Would you get on with it?" Alec whispered from behind.

Mark took another step. He was worried about rushing up the stairs, as if Trina had put the infected into some kind of trance and that any hurried movement might break the spell. He lifted his foot and went one step higher. Then another. A glance backwards showed Trina and Deedee right on his tail, and Alec behind them. The old man shot him a glare that said he was clearly unhappy with how slowly they were moving.

Mark took another step and then another, the strangers' stares sending a cold tingling across his skin and down his spine. The smiles were getting bigger and creepier.

They were two-thirds of the way up when he heard a woman's voice right behind him.

"Pretty. So very pretty."

He turned to see the lady patting Deedee's head, almost petting her like an animal at the zoo. The little girl's face was filled with horror.

"Such a pretty child," the woman said. "I could just eat you up. Like a turkey dinner. Yes. So sweet."

Mark faced front again, repulsed. There was a bulging feeling in his chest, as if something were trying to escape. He'd just taken another step when a man reached out and poked his shoulder with a finger.

"Good, strong young boy, you are," the stranger said. "I bet your mama's proud, eh?"

Mark ignored him, went up another step. This time people on either side of him put their hands on his arm – not in a threatening way, just a touch. Another step. A woman moved away from the wall and threw her arms around his neck, squeezed him in a quick and fierce hug. Then she released him and stepped back into her position to the side. A wicked smile distorted her features.

Revulsion filled Mark. He couldn't take another minute in that house. He threw caution to the wind and reached behind him, grabbed Deedee's hand, then started moving faster up the steps. He could hear Alec's feet pounding as he brought up the rear.

At first the infected seemed taken unaware, stunned by the sudden burst of motion. Mark made it to the top, across the landing, through the haunted faces that stared at them from both sides – and then he was in the hallway. The house was packed, people everywhere, some of them holding sticks and bats and knives. But there was a clear path down the middle, leading to the front door. Mark didn't hesitate, started sprinting towards the exit, pulling Deedee along behind him.

They made it halfway before order collapsed. All of the house occupants seemed to scream at once, and their bodies swarmed in, pressing against Mark and his friends. Mark lost hold of Deedee's hand and saw her disappear into the crowd, her sweet little cry like that of an angel among demons.

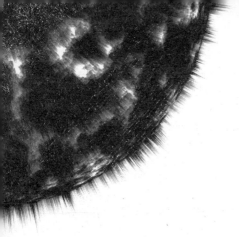

59

Mark lunged after her but lost his balance, slipping and falling. Bodies were on top of him in an instant, clawing and ripping at his clothes. He twisted and swung his elbows, felt both of them connect with bodies, heard screams. Hands were grabbing for his weapon, too many to fight off. He kicked out with his legs, squirmed on to his stomach so he could push himself up. Something hard hit him in the back of the head and he collapsed, his face smacking against the hard tile. Then there was a thin, painful tug on his neck – he realised with horror that it was the strap of his weapon. He was just trying to reach for it when it slipped past his chin and over his head. There were hoots and hollers and cheers.

His Transvice was gone.

All the focus in the room shifted to the stolen weapon, leaving Mark a few seconds to scramble back to his feet. The man who'd taken the thing from him was holding it up in the air with both hands and dancing in a slow circle. Those around him leaped up and down, their arms out-stretched so they could touch the shiny surface. They were slowly moving away from Mark, and more and more people were pushing in to see the new prize. The mass was heading towards the other end of the hallway, into what looked like the kitchen.

Mark knew he'd never get the Transvice back. He frantically scanned the room for signs of his friends. Deedee was being handled by three or four people. She was kicking and screaming as they tried to carry her up the stairs. Trina was right behind them, fighting to reach the girl. Alec was battling at least six attackers who seemed bent on getting their own shiny prize. Even as Mark glanced at him, his friend smashed the Transvice's end into one guy's face, shot a bolt of white light into another, vaporising him. But then there was a mad rush against the old man and he fell to the floor, people leaping on top of him.

Mark had no choice but to go after Trina and Deedee first.

He ran forward, pushing past people who didn't quite seem to know what they were supposed to be doing, and leaped on to the ledge running up the outside of the stairs. He knew his only chance was to climb along it. He held on to the railing and inched upward.

A man swung a fist at him and missed. A woman threw her body at him, oblivious to the possibility of hurting herself. Mark was able to duck and she sailed past, crashing to the floor below. Others tried to push him; some from below swatted at him, grabbed his legs, trying to pull him into the seething mass of bodies. He fought them all off, somehow keeping at least one hand on the wooden railing as he dodged and slapped and kicked away their attempts to stop his progress.

Finally he made it past the leading charge, past the man and woman who had Deedee in their arms. Mark grabbed the railing with both hands and heaved himself over, landing cleanly on a step almost at the very top of the staircase. The people didn't stop, kept heading straight towards him. Mark didn't know what else to do, so he dived forward, wrapping his arms around Deedee and squeezing tightly, letting the momentum of his body pull her free from her captors' grasps.

They rolled down the stairs, knocking people left and right until they bounced off the bottom step and on to the floor. He looked up from where he lay wrapped protectively around the little girl and saw Trina barrelling her way towards him, pushing others aside, her eyes afire and focused on Deedee.

Groaning from the pain that racked his body, he somehow got his feet under him and stood up just as Trina reached them. She grabbed Deedee from him, wrapped her arms around her tight. The little girl was sobbing. Their brief reprieve was over, however; people were coming at them from all directions.

Mark took a quick look around and realised their prospects were grim. The house was in chaos.

Alec was in the dining room, still fighting off a dozen attackers, firing his weapon when he could. Several of the mob gave up on him when they saw Mark, charging him instead. A surge of people also came from the other direction – from the hallway leading to the kitchen – and they came fast, as if they were fleeing something instead of attacking. More infected stood between Mark and the door, blocking any escape. And each one of them looked ready to kill or be killed.

Mark held his arms up to protect Trina and Deedee, backed up and pressed them against the wall by the stairs. The first person to reach him was a mangled old man with scratches and gashes covering his head instead of hair. He leaped into the air, coming straight for Mark, when there was a thumping sound from the kitchen. The man's body turned into a grey wall and then he was gone in a cloud of mist that washed over Mark.

Mark's entire body went cold. The sound hadn't come from Alec's direction – somebody had figured out how to use the Transvice.

The thought had barely formed in his mind before a bolt of white light shot past him and slammed into the chest of a woman standing in the group by the door.

"Alec!" Mark yelled. "Someone's shooting the other Transvice!"

The fear that prickled Mark's skin was like nothing he'd ever felt, even after all the hellacious things they'd experienced since that day when all went dark in the subtrans. A mad person was running around with a weapon that could vaporise a human in an instant. At any second, Mark's life might vanish before he even realised what had happened.

They had to get out of there.

Even with their diseased minds, the others in the house knew something extraordinary was happening. Panic rippled through the group, and every last person turned and ran for the front door. Screams and hysterical cries for help filled the air. The hallway was a surging river of arms and legs and terrified faces, all pressed together, straining towards the front of the house. More shots rang out from the rogue Transvice; more people disappeared.

Mark felt his sanity crumbling. He spun around and lifted Deedee into his arms, then grabbed Trina's shoulder and heaved her off the wall, pushed her away from the crowd and into the dining room, where Alec had been fighting. He was surrounded by a mass of people – too many to shoot.

Mark pushed Trina, this time towards the big bay windows – the few in the house that were still intact. He picked up a lamp and tossed it at the glass, shattering it into a million shards. Clasping Deedee tightly in his right arm, he ran forward, catching up with Trina and gripping her elbow with his left hand. Without slowing, he sprinted straight for the opening; then he let go of Trina and dived, turning his body at the last second so that his back went first. He hugged the girl tightly to his body, trying his best to protect her as he thumped against the hard-packed dirt of what had once been a flower bed. The fall knocked the wind out of him.

Gasping for air, he looked up into the bright sky and he saw Alec's head poke out of the house.

"You really have lost your mind," the man said, but he was already helping Trina climb out the window before he'd finished the short sentence.

He jumped down after Trina landed safely. Then they were both helping Mark to his feet and Trina took Deedee back into her arms. Some of the infected had seen their escape and were following; others were streaming out the front door. Screams and shouts filled the air. People were already fighting each other outside.

"I've had enough of this party," Alec grumbled.

Mark was finally catching his breath, and the four of them started running across the dusty yard, angling towards the street that would lead them back to the Berg. Alec tried to take Deedee from Trina but she refused, kept moving, her face showing the strain of carrying the burden. As for the little girl, her cries had been replaced at some point by silence. There weren't even any tears on her face.

Mark looked behind him. A man stood on the front porch, blasting away randomly with the Transvice, sending people to their wispy deaths. He finally noticed the group running away down the street and fired off a couple of shots. They came nowhere close, the white bolts smashing into the pavement, sending up puffs of dust. The guy gave up, returned to killing closer quarry.

Mark and his friends kept running. When they passed the house full of small children, Mark thought of Trina and Deedee and the future. He didn't stop.

60

Finally they saw the Berg once again. It rose up in the distance, more beautiful than Mark would've ever guessed one of the beat-up old things could look. Though each one of them was heaving like every breath might be their last, they didn't slow down, and soon the big hunk of scarred metal loomed above their heads.

Mark didn't know how in the world Trina had done it with Deedee in her arms the entire time. But she'd refused to let anyone else help.

"You . . . okay?" he asked her between deep breaths.

She collapsed to the ground, spilling the girl next to her as gently as she could. Trina looked up at him, still no recognition in her eyes. "I'm . . . fine. Thank you for rescuing us."

Mark knelt next to her, the pain creeping back into his heart now that the craziness of escaping was over. "Trina, do you really not remember me?"

"You seem . . . familiar. But there's too much in my head. We just need to get the girl – she's immune, I know it – we need to get her to people who matter. Before we're all too insane to try."

Mark felt something turn in his stomach and leaned back, away from his best friend. The chilling way she'd said those last few words . . .

He knew that there was something seriously wrong with her. And couldn't he say the same thing about himself? How long did he have until nothing mattered any more? A day? Maybe two?

The huge door of the Berg lurched into motion with a thump and a squeal, giving Mark an excuse not to respond. He watched as it lowered to the ground.

Alec spoke loudly over the grinding gears and hydraulics. "Let's get them on board, get everyone fed. Then we need to figure out what to do with ourselves. We might be like those kooks we just ran away from soon."

"Not the girl," Mark said, so quietly he wondered if his friend even heard him.

"What do you mean?" the man replied.

"The scar on her arm. She was hit by a dart months ago. Think about it. Trina's right. She's immune somehow. That's gotta mean something."

Trina had perked up at the statement, was nodding vigorously. Too vigorously. Mark's heart sank a little bit more. She just wasn't quite there.

Alec let out one of his infamous grunts. "Well, unless you wanna swap bodies with her, I reckon it won't do you a bit of good, now, will it?"

"But maybe it could help others. If they don't already have a treatment . . ."

Alec gave him a doubtful look. "Let's just get on board before some of them crazies catch up to us."

And blast us with my Transvice, Mark thought grimly. He appreciated Alec's not giving him a hard time about it.

Alec headed for the ramp, which was almost all the way

down, leaving Mark to deal with the two girls. Mark reached for Trina's hand.

"Come on. It'll be nice and safe on board. And there's food, somewhere to rest. Don't worry. You . . . can trust me." It hurt to even have to say such a thing.

Deedee stood up, her face still set in stone, and took Mark's hand before Trina could. The little girl looked at him, and even though her features didn't change, something in her eyes almost made him think she had a smile hidden inside somewhere. Trina got to her feet.

"I just hope the bogey man doesn't live on that thing," she said in a distant, haunted voice. Then she started walking towards the ramp.

Mark sighed and followed, Deedee in tow.

The next few hours passed quietly as the sun sped towards the horizon and darkness fell on the land outside the Berg. Alec flew the ship to the neighbourhood where they'd parked before – it still seemed deserted. Then they ate and prepared bunks for Trina and Deedee to get some sleep. Trina mumbled a lot, and Mark even caught her with a line of drool on her chin at one point. As he wiped it off, sadness once again welled up in his heart.

As for him, sleeping seemed utterly impossible.

He planned to talk to Alec, figure out exactly what their next move should be, but when he found him, the old bear was snoring in the pilot's chair, sitting straight up with his head lolling to one side. Mark was half tempted to throw a chunk of food in his mouth, and giggled at the thought of it.

Giggled.

I really am *starting to slip*, he thought. And his mood sank into a low and dark place. He desperately needed to do something to take his mind off things.

He suddenly remembered the workpads he'd seen in the cargo room – the ones he'd secured against the shelf with the straps. His spirits rose a bit at the hope that maybe something within those devices would shed some light on what they should do. Maybe, just maybe, there was a way to get rid of the virus somehow. Maybe there was a chance.

He banged his knee twice – and his head once – running through the dimly lit Berg towards the cargo room. He remembered halfway there that he'd need a torch and went back to get it out of his backpack. Then, finally, he was standing in front of the shelf. He quickly removed the workpads and sat down to read through them.

There were three. The first was dead. A password prevented him from getting into the second, but it flickered and would probably die soon anyway. Mark's excitement almost crashed to a halt. But the third came to life, its glow illuminating the large room so brightly that Mark turned off his torch. The owner – evidently a guy named Randall Spilker – had felt no need for a password, and the home station popped up immediately.

He spent the next half hour perusing useless information. Mr Spilker loved games and chat rooms. Mark was almost ready to give up, thinking the guy had merely used the device as a toy, when he finally discovered some hidden work files.

Folder after folder revealed nothing. But Mark finally hit the jackpot in a place most people would never have had the patience to find. It was a folder, marked as plainly as the rest, practically lost within a list of a hundred others that were empty.

It was titled *KILL ORDER*.

61

There were so many documents that Mark didn't know where to start. Each file had a number assigned to it and seemed to have been saved in random order. Mark knew he didn't have time to read every single file, so he decided to just start opening and see what he could see.

There was file after file of saved correspondence, memorandums and official announcements. Most numerous were the personal exchanges – all copied into a few files – between Mr Spilker and his friends, particularly one named Ladena Lichliter. The two of them worked for the Post-Flares Coalition, an entity people in the settlements had heard of but knew almost nothing about. From what Mark could gather, the group had brought together as many government agencies as they could from around the world. They'd gathered in Alaska – a location rumoured to have been only mildly affected by the sun flares – and they were trying to put the world back together again.

It all seemed very noble – and frustrating to those involved – until Mark came across an exchange between Mr Spilker and

Ladena Lichliter, who seemed to be his closest confidante, that sent an icy chill along his arms. He'd been skimming text after text, but he read this one twice:

To: Randall Spilker
From: Ladena Lichliter
Subject:

I'm still sick from the meeting today. I just can't believe it. I can't accept that the PCC actually looked us in the eyes and presented that proposal. Seriously. I was stunned.

And then more than half the room AGREED WITH THEM! They supported it! What the hell is going on? Randall, tell me what the HELL is going on? How can we even THINK about doing something like that? How?

I've spent the afternoon trying to make sense of it all. I can't take it. I can't.

How did we get here?

Come see me tonight. Please.

—LL

What in the world? Mark wondered. The PCC . . . The man named Bruce had mentioned them as part of the people behind the virus attack. Or had that been the PFC – the Post-Flares Coalition? Maybe the former was a division of the latter. Headquartered somewhere in Alaska. He kept digging.

A few minutes later, he found a series of correspondence spliced together into one file that almost made his heart stop. The icy chills from before turned into a cold sweat.

Post-Flares Coalition Memorandum
Date 217.11.28, Time 21:46
TO: All board members
FROM: Chancellor John Michael
RE: Population concerns

The report presented to us today, copies of which were sent to all members of the coalition, certainly left no room for doubt as to the problems that face this already crippled world. I am certain that all of you, like me, went to your shelters in stunned silence. It is my hope that the harsh reality described in this report is now clear enough that we can begin talking about solutions.

The problem is simple: the world has too many people and not enough resources.

We have scheduled our next meeting for a week from tomorrow. I expect all members to come prepared to present a solution, no matter how extraordinary it seems. You may be familiar with an old business saying, "think outside the box". I believe it is time we do just that.

I look forward to hearing your ideas.

To: John Michael
From: Katie McVoy
Subject: Potential

John,

I looked into the matter we discussed over dinner last night. AMRIID barely survived the flares, but they're confident that the underground containment system for the most dangerous viruses, bacteria and biological weapons didn't fail.

It took some wrangling, but I got the information we need. I've looked through it and come up with a recommendation. All the potential solutions are far too unpredictable to be usable. Except one.

It's a virus. It attacks the brain and shuts it down, painlessly. It acts quickly and decisively. The virus was designed to slowly weaken in infection rate as it spreads from host to host. It will be perfect for our needs, especially considering how severely limited travel has become. It could work, John. And as awful as it seems, I believe it could work efficiently.

I'll send over the details. Let me know your thoughts.
—Katie

To: Katie McVoy
From: John Michael Subject:
RE: Potential

Katie,

I need your help preparing my full proposal for the virus release presentation. We need to focus on how a controlled kill is the only way to save lives. Though it will make survival possible for only a select portion of our population, unless we take extreme measures, we face the eventual extinction of the human race.

You and I both know how hypothetical this solution is. But we've run the simulations a thousand times and I just can't see any alternative. If we don't do this, the world will run out of resources. I firmly believe it is the most ethical decision – the risk of race extinction justifies the elimination of a few. My mind is made up. Now it's a matter of convincing the others on the board.

Let's meet at my quarters, 1700. Everything has to be worded perfectly, so prepare yourself for a long night.

Until then,
John

Post-Flares Coalition Memorandum
Date 219.2.12, Time 19:32
TO: All board members
FROM: Chancellor John Michael
SUBJECT: EO Draft

Please give me your thoughts on the following draft. The final order will go out tomorrow.

Executive Order #13 of the Post-Flares Coalition, by recommendation of the Population Control Committee, to be considered TOP-SECRET, of the highest priority, on penalty of capital punishment.

We the Coalition hereby grant the PCC express permission to fully implement their PC Initiative #1 as presented in full and attached below. We the Coalition take full responsibility for this action and will monitor developments and offer assistance to the fullest extent of our resources. The virus will be released in the locations recommended by the PCC and agreed upon by the Coalition. Armed forces will be stationed to ensure that the process ensues in as orderly a manner as possible.

EO #13, PCI #1, is hereby ratified. Begin immediately.

Mark had to shut down the device for a minute. There was a rushing sound in his ears and his face burned with heat. His head throbbed.

Everything Mark had witnessed in the last week had been sanctioned by the acting government of the flare-inflicted world. It hadn't been terrorists or the work of madmen. It had been approved and executed with the intent of controlling the population. Of wiping out entire areas, leaving more resources for those who lived.

Mark's entire body shook with anger, intensified by the madness growing inside him. He sat in complete darkness, staring into a black void, but spots swam before his eyes. Spots that formed into shapes. Streaks of fire that made him think of sun flares. People's faces, screaming for help. Virus-laced darts shrieking through the air, thunking into necks and arms and shoulders. He began to worry at the things he saw dancing before him, wondered if this revelation had been the final push that sent him over the cliff of insanity.

He shook, and sweat covered his skin. He began to cry; then he screamed as loudly as he could. An avalanche of rage like he'd never known before crashed through him. He heard a loud crack. It had come from his lap.

He looked down but couldn't see anything. His attempt to power up the workpad proved worthless. He felt around beside him until he found the torch, then flicked it on. The workpad's screen had been destroyed, the entire flat panel of the device bent at a weird angle. In his anger, he'd broken the stupid thing. He never would have thought he had the strength.

Somehow he formed a coherent thought in the madness that pounded through his skull. He knew what they had to do, and that it was their last and only shot. If the people at the bunker were going to Ashville to face whoever gave them their orders, then Mark and his friends were going, too. Getting inside the walled city was the only way Mark could think to find the people who'd issued the kill order. He could only hope they had a way to stop the sickness. He wanted to be made better.

Asheville. That was where they had to go. Just like that thug Bruce had said during his speech in the auditorium. Except Mark wanted to beat them to it.

He stood up, feeling a little woozy from the images that had been swirling in his vision. The anger pulsed through him as if it, instead of blood, thumped out of his heart and through his veins, but even as he stood, he could feel himself calming. He shone the torch once again on the cracked workpad, then tossed the device to the other side of the room. It landed with a clatter. He hoped that someday he'd have a chance to tell this PCC what he thought of their decision.

Pain lanced through his skull, and a sudden wave of exhaustion washed over him, a heavy, dragging thing that was like a two-ton blanket draped over his shoulders. He dropped to his knees, then slumped on to his side, his head resting on the cold floor. There was so much to do. No time for sleeping. But he was so, so tired. . . .

For once, he dreamed of something pleasant.

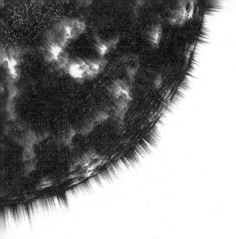

62

A crackle of thunder makes Trina jump in Mark's arms.

It's raining outside the cave, something they haven't seen in at least three months, since the sun flares struck. Mark shivers, the chill across his skin a fresh relief from the hellish heat that has become his life. They were lucky to find the deep recess in the side of the mountain, and he realises he doesn't care if they spend the rest of their lives in the dark, cool place. Alec and the others are further inside, sleeping.

He squeezes Trina's shoulders, leans his head against hers. Breathes in her smell, which is salty and sweet. It's the first time since they left the boat on the shores of New Jersey that Mark has felt calm. Almost content.

"I love the sound of it," Trina whispers, as if speaking too loudly might interrupt the drumming patter of the rain outside. "It makes me want to sleep. Snuggle my head right up in your armpit and snore for three days."

"My armpit?" Mark repeats. "Good thing we all showered up in the storm this morning. My pits smell like roses. Go ahead and get comfy."

She shifts and wiggles, then settles again. "I seriously can't believe we're still alive, Mark. I just can't believe it. Who knows, though. We could be dead in another six months. Or tomorrow, I guess."

"That's the spirit," he deadpans. "Come on. Don't talk like that. How could things possibly get worse than what we've seen? We'll stay here for a while, then go and look for the settlements in the south mountains."

"Rumours," she said quietly.

"Huh?"

"Rumours of settlements."

Mark sighs. "They'll be there. You'll see."

He leans his head against the wall and thinks about what she said. That they're lucky to be alive. Truer words have never been spoken.

They survived the weeks of solar radiation by hiding inside the Lincoln Building. Survived the relentless heat and drought. The trek across countless miles of wasted land and crime-riddled streets. The acceptance that their families were dead. Travelled by night, hid by day, found food wherever it presented itself, sometimes going without for days. He knows if they hadn't had the military skills of Alec and Lana, they never would have made it this far. Never.

But they did. They are still alive and kicking. He smiles, almost in defiance of whatever force of the universe threw such obstacles in their path. He starts to think that maybe, in a few years, all could be well again.

Lightning flashes somewhere off in the distance; thunder rumbling a few seconds later. It seems louder, closer than before. And the rain has picked up, pounding the ground outside the entrance to the cave. For the millionth time he thinks how lucky they are that they stumbled across the hidden haven.

Trina shifts to look up at him. "Alec said that once the storms started, they might get really bad. That the weather in

301

the world is gonna be screwed up big-time."

"Yeah. It's okay. I'll take rain and wind and lightning any day over what it's been like. We'll just stay in this cave. How about that?"

"Can't stay here for ever."

"Okay, then. A week. A month. Just stop *thinking*. Sheesh."

She tilts her face up and kisses him on the cheek. "What would I do without you? I'd die of stress and depression before nature killed me."

"Probably true." He smiles and hopes she'll just enjoy the peace for a while.

After shifting back down into a comfortable position, she hugs him a little tighter. "Seriously, though. I'm really glad I have you. You mean the world to me."

"Same to you," he replies. And then he grows quiet, not daring to let his mouth take over, say something cheesy and ruin the moment. He closes his eyes.

Light flashes, followed quickly by the boom of thunder. The storm is definitely getting closer.

Mark woke up, and for a few seconds he remembered the feeling of staring at Trina when things had begun to turn a corner and hope – the slightest trace – was in her eyes. Whether she would admit it or not on that day. For the first time in months he wished he could sink back into his dreams. The longing in his heart was almost painful. But then reality rolled in, along with the darkness of the cargo room. The storms had been bad, all right, he thought. Really bad. But they'd survived that, too, eventually finding their way to the settlements.

Where they might've lived in peace if it weren't for a committee called the PCC.

Groaning, rubbing his eyes, he let out a long yawn, then stood up. And fully remembered the decisions he'd made before succumbing to sleep.

Asheville.

He bent over, picked up the torch and flicked it on. Then he turned around to head for the door and was startled to see Alec standing there, filling up the frame as if he'd grown several inches taller. Because the faint light of the ship was behind him, his face was hidden in shadow, but there was something sinister about it. Something disquieting about how he'd been there for who knew how long without announcing himself. And still wasn't saying anything.

"Alec?" Mark asked. "You okay there, big guy?"

The man stumbled forward, almost fell down. But he righted himself and stood up straight and tall again. Mark hadn't wanted to shine the light in his friend's face, but he felt like he had no choice. He raised the torch and pointed it directly at Alec. He was flushed and sweating, his eyes wide and darting back and forth as if he expected a monster to leap from the shadows at any moment.

"Hey, what's wrong?" Mark asked.

Alec took another labouring step forward. "I'm sick, Mark. I'm really, really sick. I need to die. I need to die and I don't wanna die for nothing."

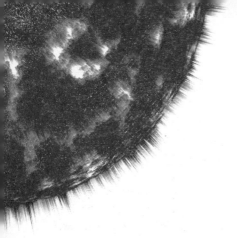

63

Mark couldn't remember ever having been at such a loss for words.

Alec slouched to the ground, falling to one knee. "I'm serious, boy. I've been feeling funny, my mind playing tricks. Seeing things, feeling things. I'm feeling a little bit better right now, but I don't want to be like those people. I need to die, and I don't wanna wait till morning."

"What . . ? Why . . ?" Mark stammered for the right thing to say. It'd been inevitable that this would happen, but it still shocked him to the core. "What do you want me to do?"

The man shot him a glare. "I've thought it—"

He spasmed, suddenly contorting into an unnatural shape, his head thrown back, his face twisted in pain. A strangled, choked cry escaped his throat.

"Alec!" Mark shouted, running up to him. He had to duck when the man suddenly swung a fist. Alec fell to the floor. "What's wrong?"

The old man's body relaxed and he got on his hands and

knees, labouring heavily to breathe. "I . . . I just . . . I don't know. Weird things are knocking around my noggin."

Mark ran his hands through his hair, looking around in anguish, as if some magical answer to all their problems might appear in a dark corner of the cargo room. When he turned back to Alec, the man had stood, holding his hands up as if surrendering.

"Listen to me," Alec said. "I've got ideas. Things are bleak, no doubt. But . . ." He pointed in the direction of the barracks where Trina and Deedee were sleeping. "We have a precious little girl in there who can be saved. If nothing else. We need to get her to Asheville, drop her off. Then . . ."

He shrugged, a pathetic gesture that said all too much. It was over for the rest of them.

"A treatment – a cure," Mark said, hearing the defiance in his voice. "That Bruce guy thought there might be one. We need to go there for that, too, and—"

"Oh, horse crap," Alec barked, cutting him off. "Just listen to me before I can't talk straight any more. I'm the only one who can fly this thing. I want you to come to the cockpit and watch me, learn as much as that head of yours can handle. Just in case. You're right – we're taking that girl to Asheville if it's the last thing I do."

A suffocating, dark feeling enveloped Mark. He'd be crazy or dead soon. But Alec's idea was much like his, and the only thing he could think to do was take action.

"Then let's go," he said, fighting back the sudden sting of tears. "Let's not waste one more second."

Alec twitched and his arms jerked outward, but then he clenched his fists and brought them back down, his face strained as if he'd fought off another attack with willpower alone. Clarity filled his eyes and he looked at Mark for a long moment. It was as if all of the past year – the memories, the horrors, even the laughs – passed quickly between them, and Mark wondered if either of them would ever be so grounded again. Madness waited in the wings.

The soldier gave a quick nod, and the two of them headed for the door.

* * *

They reached the cockpit without seeing any sign of Trina or Deedee. Mark had hoped they'd be awake – maybe by some miracle Trina would be better, laughing, remembering. It was a foolish thought.

As Alec got to work on the controls, Mark looked outside. A trace of dawn had brightened the eastern sky, the darkness fading into light purple over the houses and trees in the distance. Most of the stars had winked out; the sun would make its grand entrance within the hour. He had a heavy feeling that the day would end with everything changed for ever.

"I'm okay for a bit," Alec said, standing back to scan the instruments and screens of the control panel. "Why don't you go and check on the girls. We'll be off the ground in a jiffy. We'll do some flyovers and see what we see."

Mark nodded and patted him on the back, a ridiculous gesture but all he could think of to do. He was worried about his friend. He turned on his torch and left the cockpit, entering the short passage that led to the barracks room where he'd left Trina, resting peacefully in a bunk with Deedee.

Mark was almost to the door of the barracks when he heard a strange scratching noise above him, like rats scurrying across the panels of the ceiling. Then there was the distinct sound of a man giggling, only feet over his head. A shudder of horror passed through him. He ran a few steps down the hall and spun around, pressing his back against the wall. He looked up at the ceiling, shining the torch over the panels, but saw nothing out of the ordinary.

He held his breath and listened.

Something was up there, moving back and forth, almost rhythmically.

"Hey!" Mark shouted. "Who . . ." His question died when

306

he realised he hadn't checked on Trina yet. If someone, or some*thing*, had snuck its way onto the Berg . . .

He ran to the barracks door and flung it open, frantically shining his light on the bunk where he'd last seen Trina sleeping. For one split second his heart stalled – the bunk was empty. It was just rumpled sheets and a blanket. Then, out of the corner of his eye, he saw Trina on the floor, Deedee sitting right next to her. They were holding hands, and both of them had sheer terror on their faces.

"What?" Mark asked. "What happened?"

Deedee pointed a shaking finger towards the ceiling. "The bogey man's up there." She paused, visibly shaking – a sight that tore at Mark's heart. "And he brought his friends."

64

S he'd barely said the last word when the Berg burst into life and launched off the ground. The floor tilted and Mark stumbled and fell on to the bunk, then pushed himself to his feet.

"Just stay there," he said. "I'll be right back."

He wasn't going to hesitate this time.

He ran from the barracks into the hallway, piercing the darkness with his torch as he headed straight for the cockpit. He thought he heard another giggle coming from the ceiling in the same spot as before, and horrible thoughts popped into his mind: bloodthirsty men and women, infected and insane, leaping through the panels once he disappeared, attacking the girls he'd left behind. But he had no choice, and he'd be quick. Besides, if there *were* people up there, they'd waited this long without doing anything. Chances were he had some time.

He bolted into the cockpit, where Alec was manning the controls. He was sweaty and flushed, and concentrating hard on what he was doing.

"Where's the Transvice?" Mark shouted.

Alec spun around, fear crossing his face. But Mark didn't waste time with explanations – the man's weapon was propped up against the wall next to him. Mark ran to it, grabbed it and threw the strap around his shoulder, then made sure it was powered up and started back towards the barracks. Towards Trina and Deedee.

"Turn some lights on out here!" he yelled back to Alec as he slipped out of the cockpit – he'd dropped the torch at some point and the world was pitch-dark. Conserving power and fuel no longer meant a thing. He'd only gone a few feet down the corridor before the dim lights flashed on and illuminated his path, though shadows clung to the walls.

Sweat dripped into his eyes as he pounded down the corridor. It felt as if the heat inside the Berg had skyrocketed to a thousand degrees. The sweltering air combined with his shot nerves – the razor's edge of madness that cut into his psyche – put him on the brink of losing it. He just had to hold on for a little while longer. With every bit of effort he could muster, he focused only on the next seconds of his life.

He crossed under the place he'd heard the giggling. Even as he did, a cackle came from above. It was low and throaty, as ominous a thing as he could imagine. But the panel remained intact. He tore through the door of the barracks and saw with relief that Trina and Deedee were still huddled together on the floor.

He was just moving towards them when three sections of the ceiling suddenly collapsed, breaking apart in a crunch of plaster and metal. Several bodies fell among the pieces, crashing on top of the two girls. Deedee screamed.

Mark raised his weapon and rushed forward, not daring to shoot but ready to fight.

Three people were scrambling to their feet, shoving Deedee and Trina as if they were simply objects in their way. A man and two women. They were laughing hysterically, leaping from foot to foot and throwing their arms around like wild apes. Mark reached the man and swung the butt of his Transvice into the side of his head. The man cried out and crumpled to the floor. Mark used his momentum to turn his body and kick one of the women away from his friends. She shrieked and toppled on to the nearest bunk and he aimed the Transvice, pulling the trigger. A bolt of white heat hit her and she greyed, then dissipated into the air.

She'd barely disappeared when the other woman tackled him from the side – they both landed on the floor, and for what felt like the hundredth time in the past week, the air was knocked from his lungs. He twisted on to his back, pulling her on top of him as she struggled to rip the Transvice out of his hands.

He saw Trina and Deedee standing up, pressed against the wall, watching helplessly. Mark knew the old Trina would've joined in and helped somehow. She would have attacked the woman and probably beaten her senseless. But this new Trina, this sick Trina, just stood there like a frightened little girl. Clutching Deedee in her arms.

Mark grunted and kept fighting the woman. He heard a groan, looked over to see the man he'd knocked out crawling to his hands and knees. The guy's eyes were glued on Mark, full of hatred and madness. He bared his teeth and growled.

The man came at him on all fours, as if he had transformed into some kind of rabid animal. He pushed off the ground and leaped into the struggle between Mark and the woman like a lion attacking its prey. He crashed into the woman and the two were suddenly locked in an embrace. They fell off Mark, rolling across the floor as if playing some kind of game. Mark was still gasping for breath but he turned on to his side, then his stomach. Got his knees under him. His elbows. Pushed up. He leaned against a bunk and finally was able to stand.

He calmly aimed the Transvice at the man, then the woman, taking two clean shots. The noise shook the air like thunder, and the people were no more.

Mark heard his own breathing, heavy and strained. He glanced wearily over at Trina and Deedee, still huddled against the wall. It was close as to which of them looked more terrified.

"Sorry you had to see that," Mark mumbled, unable to find anything else to say. "Come on. Let's get to the cockpit. We're taking . . ." He'd almost said *taking Deedee*, but he'd caught himself. He didn't know how Trina might respond. "We're going somewhere safe," he finished.

A burst of deep laughing seemed to come from everywhere at once, the same horrible sound as before. It was followed by a hitched series of coughs that eased back into the haunted fit of giggling. To Mark, nothing sounded more as though it belonged inside a mental hospital, and goosebumps broke out across his skin despite the heat. Trina was staring at the floor, her gaze so empty that Mark felt another pang of loss. He stepped closer to the girls and reached out a hand. The man hidden in the rafters continued to chuckle.

"We can do this," he said. "All you have to do is take my hand and walk with me. It won't be long before we're all . . . safe." He didn't mean to falter on the last word.

Deedee raised her scarred arm and squeezed his middle finger, held on to it. This seemed to trigger some reaction in Trina, and she shifted away from the wall and put her weight fully on her feet. Her eyes didn't stray from that spot on the floor, and she was still clutching Deedee's shoulders with both hands. But it looked like she'd follow.

"Good," Mark whispered. "We're going to ignore that poor guy up there and walk nice and calm to the cockpit. Let's go."

He turned and started moving before anything changed in Trina's countenance. Tugging on Deedee's hand, he walked quickly towards the door of the barracks. A glance behind him showed Trina still attached to the girl as if they'd been glued together. There was the pitter-patter of footsteps above them, which almost made him stop, but he steeled his nerves and kept going.

They went through the door and into the hallway – they had nowhere else to go. It was even darker out there, the emergency lights just a pale glowing line running along the upper edges of the walls. After quick looks left and right, Mark headed off in the direction of the cockpit. He'd barely taken a step when there was a burst of sound and movement.

And then a thud directly above him. A fit of laughter. The sudden appearance of a man's face and arms, hanging upside down right in front of him. A cry escaped Mark's lips before he could help it, and shock froze him solid.

In his stupor, he was unable to react in time – the man reached out and tore the Transvice out of his hands, breaking the strap in the process. Mark grabbed for it, but the stranger had been as quick as a striking snake.

Then he disappeared back into the rafters above, laughing all the while. His thumping footsteps and cackles faded as he ran to another part of the ship.

65

Mark didn't think he could get up to the ceiling and climb after the man – and he could be hiding anywhere, with instant and certain death pointed right at whoever came his way.

"I can't believe it," he whispered. How could he have let the guy rip the thing out of his hands like that? It'd happened twice in less than a day. And now there was a crazy person in the ship somewhere with the most dangerous handheld weapon ever invented.

"Come on," he said tightly, then pulled Deedee and Trina along behind him as he started running down the hall. He looked up every few seconds, wondering if the man would suddenly appear, hanging down from the ceiling, ready to shoot. He also strained to listen for any sound other than the pounding of their own footsteps.

When they reached the cockpit the first thing Mark noticed was Alec slumped over the controls, his head buried in his arms.

"Alec!" Mark let go of Deedee's hand and rushed towards the man. But Alec shot straight up before Mark reached him, startling him so much he almost skidded across the floor. "Whoa. You okay?"

He didn't look it. His eyes were puffy and bloodshot, his skin pale and sweaty. "I'm . . . I'm . . . hanging . . . in there."

"You're the only one who knows how to fly this thing." Mark felt terrible for saying it – selfish. But he looked out the windows and saw the foothills above Asheville slowly moving past below them. "I mean . . . I don't . . ."

"Save your breath, kid. I know the stakes. I'm trying to find where the PFC is headquartered in the city. I just needed a rest."

Mark broke the news. "There's a crazy dude on the ship. He stole the Transvice."

Alec didn't say anything. Merely screwed up his face, which had become alarmingly flushed. He looked as if he might literally burst at any second.

"Calm down," Mark said slowly. "I'll get it back. You just find the place."

"I . . . will," the older man said through clenched teeth. "I need . . . to show you some of the controls soon."

"I'm scared," Deedee said, standing there with her hand in Trina's.

Mark saw that her eyes were focused on the windows – the poor thing had probably never been in a Berg before. He expected Trina to comfort the girl, but she did nothing. Just stood staring blankly at the floor again.

"Look, it's going to be okay," Mark said, squatting down to Deedee's height. He'd barely done it when the ship bounced in a pocket of air. Deedee screamed again, and this time she tore her hand free from Trina and ran, bolting out of the cockpit before anyone could grab her.

"Hey!" Mark shouted, already on the move. A flash of her being vaporised almost stilled his heart. He sprinted after the girl, just catching sight of her rounding the bend of the hallway outside the cockpit. In the direction of the cargo room. "Come back!"

But she was gone. Mark sped after her, but he'd only gone a few frantic steps when he caught sight of her again, standing completely still, staring at something in front of her. Mark didn't stop until he reached Deedee's side and saw what had her attention.

The infected man who'd stolen the Transvice was just outside the door to the cargo room, the weapon clutched in his hands. And he had it aimed at Deedee.

"Please," Mark whispered over the thumping of his icy heart. "Please don't." He held out a hand towards the man, put the other on Deedee's shoulder. "I'm begging you. She's only—"

"I know who she is!" the stranger shouted, a line of spit hitting his chin. His arms trembled and his knees shook. Matted dark hair hung down from his filthy head, framing a pale, scratched face that shone with sweat. He leaned up against the frame of the door as if he needed it to stand. "Sweet little girl? That's probably what you think she is?"

"What are you talking about?" Mark wondered how he was supposed to talk to someone this far past reason.

The man was obviously beyond any hope. His eyes said it all. "Brought the demons, she did." He stabbed the Transvice in the air to emphasise his point. "I was in the village with her. They came down on us like the flares themselves, lightning and rain of poison. Left us to die or worse, and look at her now! Even though she was hit. All fine and cute! Laughing at us all for what she's done."

"She had nothing to do with that," Mark said. He could feel Deedee quaking under his hand. "Not a thing. How could she? She's five years old at the most!" Anger seethed inside him – anger that he couldn't hide.

"Nothing to do with it? That's why she got shot and showed no sign of it? She's some kind of saviour to those demons, and

I mean to send her back to them!"

The man lurched forward. He took two long steps, almost lost his balance, but somehow stayed on his feet. The Transvice was shaking in his hands but still pointing at Deedee.

Mark's anger dissolved and was replaced by a huge lump of fear that lodged in his throat. Tears stung his eyes, he felt so helpless. "Please . . . I don't know what to say to you. But I swear she's innocent. We went to the bunker where the Bergs came from. We found out who's behind the disease. They aren't demons. They were just people. We think she's immune – *that's* why she didn't get sick."

"You shut up," the man answered, ambling forwards another couple of steps. He lifted the Transvice and aimed it at Mark's face. "You've got the look about ya. Pathetic. Stupid. Weak in the knees. Demons wouldn't even bother with someone like you. An utter waste of flesh." He smiled, pulling his lips further back than seemed possible. Half of his teeth were missing.

Something shifted deep down inside Mark. He knew what it was, even if he didn't dare admit it: that bubble of insanity that was ready to burst for good. A rush of anger and adrenalin flooded him.

Rage formed in his chest and tore through his throat, released in a scream so loud he didn't know he had the strength to create it. He rushed forward, leaping into action before the man could begin to process what was happening. Mark saw the man's finger move, close on the trigger, but somehow, as if his burgeoning madness had momentarily heightened all of his senses one last time, Mark somehow outpaced him. He dived and swept his hand upward, knocking the weapon away as it shot a bolt of white heat. He heard the shot thump against the wall behind them.

His shoulder slammed into the man next, throwing him to the floor. Mark crashed on top of him but was already righting himself, getting his feet underneath him. He grabbed the man's shirt and yanked him upward, tore the Transvice from his grasp and threw it to the ground. That was too easy a death for this psycho.

Mark started dragging him down the hallway, aware on some level that he himself had crossed into territory from which he wasn't sure he'd come back.

66

The man screamed and clawed at Mark's face, kicked blindly and tried to stand and run. But Mark didn't let any of it affect him. A universe of fury seemed to spin inside Mark, an impossible feeling that he knew couldn't last, couldn't be contained. His sanity hung by a thread.

He dragged the man on. Along the curve of the hallway. Through the cockpit door. Towards the broken window. Alec didn't even seem to notice, was sitting there with his hands clenched in his lap, staring blankly at the controls.

Mark didn't say anything, thought something might explode out of him if he dared open his mouth. He stopped next to the window, bent over and grabbed the man around the torso, then lifted him, holding him sideways. He twisted to pull the guy back, then flung him towards the window. His head cracked against the wall and the man fell to the ground. Mark picked him up, pulled back and tried again. Same result, the man's head thumping loudly.

Mark picked the man back up and once again threw him

towards the broken window. This time the guy went through – head, then shoulders, then waist – before he got stuck. Mark didn't let go, kept pushing and shoving, throwing all his strength into ending this man's life.

The ship lurched just as Mark shoved the man's hips through the open space, his muscles tensed as he pushed. The entire world tilted, his head spinning with a rush of blood through his system. Gravity seemed to disappear as well, and he was falling through the window along with the stranger. Where blue sky and wispy clouds had filled Mark's vision before, now he saw the ground straight in front of him. He was about to plummet to his death.

Mark kicked out and latched his legs on the lip of the window frame before he could fall all the way out. The rest of his body hung from the Berg, and the man hadn't let go of him. He clutched Mark's upper arms, gripping his shirt to keep himself from plunging to the earth below. Mark tried to push the guy away, but he was desperate and wild, climbing Mark's body like a rope, high enough that his legs now wrapped around Mark's head. Wind tore at both of them.

How could this possibly be happening again? Mark asked himself. Falling out of the Berg's window twice!

A jolt ran through the ship and suddenly it righted itself again. Mark and the man swung back towards the body of the Berg and slammed into the side, just below the window from which they dangled. Mark's legs screamed with pain from supporting two people. He flailed with his arms, trying to find something to hold on to. The outside of the Berg was littered with various boxy protrusions and handles for maintenance workers. He ran his hands along them but couldn't still himself long enough to get a grip.

Mark's fingers finally found a long bar, and he gripped it tightly. Just in time, because his legs had no strength left. His feet slipped from the window and the two bodies flipped over and slammed into the Berg's side once more. Mark felt the jolt through his entire body but held on, slipping his forearm into the gap between the handle and the ship so that his elbow took the weight. His stomach and face pressed against the warm metal of the Berg, the crazed man still clambering for some kind of position on his back. The man was screaming right in his ear.

Mark's mind jumped between clarity and foggy anger. What was Alec doing? What was happening inside? The ship had righted itself, continued to fly forwards – though at a slower speed – and no one was reaching out of the window to offer any help. Mark looked down and immediately regretted it, a wave of terror crashing over him when he saw how far away the ground was.

He had to get rid of this man or he'd never be able to climb back inside.

The wind gusted, whipping the man's hair into Mark's face and rippling through their clothes. The sounds were all too much – the wind, the screams, the roar of the thrusters. The closest spout of blue flame was just below them, maybe ten feet away, burning like the breath of a dragon.

Mark shook his shoulders, kicked off the side of the Berg with his feet and let himself slam back into it. Still the man held on. He'd scraped Mark's neck and arms and cheeks, leaving painful gashes everywhere. Mark ached, every part of him. A quick examination of the Berg's body showed several places he could wedge his feet. Going up seemed impossible with the extra weight of the crazy guy on his back. He decided to go down, a terrifying idea having formed in his head.

The gamut of options had run out. His strength was just about sapped.

He reached way down, grabbed a short bar, then let his body fall, planting his foot on a boxy metal outcrop he'd spotted. The man shrieked and almost let go of Mark's arms, slipping until he caught hold again, wrapping both of his arms around Mark's neck and squeezing just enough to make him gag.

Choking out a cough, Mark sought more places for his hands and feet, dropped another yard or so. Then another. The man had ceased his juddering movements. He'd even grown silent. Mark had never known such hatred for anyone, and in some faint part of his psyche he knew it wasn't quite rational. But he *loathed* the man, and wanted him dead. It was the only goal in his mind.

He kept descending. Wind tore at them, trying to rip them away. The thruster was so close now, just below and to his left, its roar the loudest thing Mark had ever heard. He stepped down again, and suddenly his feet were dangling in open air – there was nowhere left to put them. Another bar ran along the length of the Berg's lower edge, with just enough space for Mark to slip his arm through it.

Mark slid his right arm in and crooked his elbow, letting every pound of his and the man's combined weight rest on the joint once again. The strain was terrible – it felt like his arm would rip in two at any second. But he only needed a few moments. Only a few.

He twisted his body, craning his neck to look at the man who clung to his back. He hugged Mark with one arm above his shoulder and one wrapped around his chest. Somehow Mark got his free hand up, slipping it between their two bodies and up to his foe's neck. He slammed it into the man's windpipe and began to squeeze.

The guy began to choke, his greyish-purple tongue sticking out between his chapped lips. Mark's right elbow shuddered in pain, trembling as if the tendons and bone and tissue were coming apart. He tightened his fingers around the man's throat. The guy coughed and spat, his eyes bulging. His grip on Mark began to loosen, and as soon as it did, Mark acted.

With a shout of rage he pushed the man's body outward, snapping his arm straight and shoving him directly into the path of the thruster's blue flames, watching as the man's head and shoulders were consumed by the fire, disintegrating before he could even scream. What remained of his body plummeted towards the city below, swept out of Mark's vision as the Berg sped forward.

Madness crept through Mark's muscles. Lights danced before his eyes. Anger howled within him. He knew that his life was almost forfeit. But there was one last thing he had to do.

He started climbing back up the outer face of the monstrous Berg.

67

No one helped him through the window. Every inch of his body ached and his muscles were rubber, but somehow he managed to make it on his own, falling to the floor of the cockpit in a heap. Alec sat hunched over the controls, his face slack and his eyes empty. Trina sat in the corner, Deedee huddled in her lap. Both of them looked at him, but their expressions were unreadable.

"Flat Trans," Mark blurted out. Sparkles and flashes of light continued to cross his field of vision, and he could barely contain the unstable emotions that churned within him. "Bruce said the PFC had a Flat Trans in Asheville. We have to find it."

Alec's head snapped up and he glared at Mark. But then something softened in his gaze. "I think I know where to find it." As lifeless a thing as had ever come out of his mouth.

Mark felt the Berg descending. He leaned his head against the wall and closed his eyes, for a moment wanting nothing but to fall asleep and never wake up again, or to do the opposite and kneel, bashing his head against the floor until it was over.

But there was still that small sliver of clarity in his mind. He held on to it like a man clinging to a root on the side of a sheer cliff.

Eyes open again. With a grunt, he forced himself to his feet, leaning against the window. The small city of Asheville lay spread out before them. Walls had been constructed out of wood, scrap metal, cars, anything big and strong enough to protect what was inside: a mostly burnt-out urban centre. He saw a mass of people at a breach in one wall. Climbing over it. Surging into the town.

A man was waving them on with a red flag tied to a stick. It was Bruce, the man who'd given the speech back at the bunker. They'd come for the Flat Trans, too, just like he'd promised his co-workers. And by the looks of it, countless others who'd been infected had joined him – there were hundreds scaling the broken wall.

The Berg flew past them, over empty street after empty street. And then there was a small building with double doors hanging wide open. A hand-painted sign said PFC PERSON-NEL ONLY. A few people were lined up to go inside. They seemed calm and collected. Mark hated them for it and had a fleeting moment where he itched to find the Transvice to start firing away.

"That's . . . it," Alec muttered.

And Mark knew what he meant. If there really was a Flat Trans device, it would be there. The few people entering the building had to be the last of the PFC workers, fleeing the East once and for all. Leaving it to be claimed by madness and death. They looked up at the Berg with something like terror in their eyes, then, as one, they disappeared inside.

Mark fumbled around in a cabinet until he found some old-school paper and a pencil, stored there for power-loss emergencies. With a messy hand, he scrawled the message he'd been thinking about, then turned towards Alec. "Land," he breathed. His lungs felt full of fire instead of air. "Hurry." He folded the note and shoved it in his back pocket.

Alec's every movement was strained, his muscles tense, veins like ropes under his skin. He was flushed and sweaty. Trembling. But a few moments later the Berg landed with a surprisingly soft thump, just outside the entrance to the PFC building.

"Open the hatch." Mark was already on the move, the world a haze around him. He grabbed Deedee out of Trina's lap far more roughly than he meant to, ignoring the little girl's cries of protest. Holding her in his arms, he moved towards the exit, Trina on his tail. She hadn't said a word or lifted a finger to stop him.

At the cockpit's door, Mark paused. "You know . . . what to do . . . when I'm done," he said to Alec, words a struggle now. "If it's there or not, you know what to do." Without waiting for a response, he marched into the hallway.

Deedee calmed as he headed for the cargo room and the exit beyond that. Her arms tightened around his neck and she buried her face into his shoulder. As if understanding had dawned, even for her, that the end was here. Spots swam before Mark's eyes, flashing lights. His heart wouldn't stop racing, and it felt as if the organ pumped acid through his veins. Trina, silent, kept up with him.

Into the cargo room. Down the ramp of the hatch door, into the brightness of day. They'd barely stepped off it when squeals pierced the air and the slab of metal began to close. Alec lifted the Berg off the ground, blue thrusters roaring. Mark was barely holding on to his mind, but he felt a sudden, unbearable sadness. He'd never see the old bear again.

The sun sweltered in the sky. There was a rising rumble of shouts and whistles and marching. Groups of the infected were approaching from all directions. Far off, through the display of lights flashing before his eyes, Mark thought he could see Bruce and his red flag leading his own charge. If these people got to the Flat Trans before someone shut it down or destroyed it . . .

"Come on," he grunted to Trina.

The wind from the ascending Berg blew across them as he ran over to the entrance of the building, its doors still open. Deedee clung to him and Trina was right by his side. They went through the entrance into a wide room with no furniture. Only a strange object right in the centre – two metallic rods, standing tall, with a shimmering wall of grey stretched in between them. It appeared to be moving and sparkling, yet still and serene at the same time. It hurt Mark's eyes to stare at it.

A man and a woman were standing next to it, looking back at Mark and his friends with fear in their eyes. They were already moving towards the greyness.

"Wait!" Mark yelled.

They didn't respond, didn't stop. The two strangers leaped into the abyss and vanished from sight. On instinct, Mark sprinted to the other side of the grey wall, yet there was nothing there.

A Flat Trans. For the first time in his life, he'd actually seen someone travel through a Flat Trans. The noise of the approaching crowds outside seemed to tick up a notch, and Mark knew he was out of time. In so many ways.

He walked back over to the proper side of the Flat Trans and kneeled right before it, gently placing Deedee on her feet. It took every last ounce of his effort to remain calm and keep his swirling emotions and anger and madness at bay. Trina knelt as well, though she said nothing.

"Listen to me," Mark said to the girl. He stopped, closed his eyes for a second, fought off the darkness that tried to consume him. *Only a little longer*, he told himself. "I need . . . you to be really brave for me now, okay? There're people on the other side of this magic wall that . . . are going to help you. And you're going to help them. You're going to help them do . . . something really important. There's . . . something special about you."

He didn't know what he expected. For Deedee to protest, to cry, to run away. But instead she looked him in the eye and nodded. Mark's head wasn't clear enough to understand how she could be so brave. She *was* special.

He'd almost forgotten about the note he'd scribbled earlier. He pulled it out of his back pocket, read it one more time, his hand shaking.

She's immune to the Flare.
Use her.
Do it before the crazy people find you.

He gently reached out for Deedee's hand and scrunched the paper up into her palm. Closed her fingers around it. Squeezed her hand with both of his. The shouts and calls from outside grew to a crescendo. Mark spotted Bruce charging the door, a mass of people behind him. Mark's entire body washed with sadness. He nodded at the Flat Trans. Deedee nodded back.

Then she and Trina were hugging fiercely. Both of them shed tears. Mark was on his feet. He heard the unmistakable sound of the Berg's thrusters returning. Noticed a wind picking up outside. The time had come.

"Go, now," he said, fighting the emotions that tore through him.

Deedee pulled away from Trina and turned, ran into the grey wall of the Flat Trans. It swallowed her whole and she was gone. The roar of the Berg filled the air. The building trembled. Bruce arrived at the door, screaming something unintelligible.

And then Trina was rushing to Mark. Throwing her arms around his neck. Kissing him. A thousand thoughts flipped through his mind, and he saw her in all of them. Wrestling in the front yard of her house before they were old enough to know anything; saying hi in the school hallway; riding the sub-trans; feeling her hand in the darkness after the flares struck; the terror of the tunnels, the rushing waters, the Lincoln Building; waiting out the radiation, stealing the boat, the countless treks across ruined, sweltering land. She'd been there with him through it all. With Alec. Lana. Darnell and the others.

And here, at the end of the fight, Trina was in his arms.

Monstrous noise and quaking took over the world, but he still heard what she whispered into his ear before the Berg came crashing into the building.

"Mark."

EPILOGUE

TWO YEARS LATER

A single light bulb hung from the apartment's drab ceiling, buzzing every ten seconds or so. Somehow, it seemed to represent what the world had become. Lonely, noisy, dying. Barely holding on.

The woman sat in her chair, trying desperately not to cry.

She'd known the knock was coming far before it happened. And she wanted to be strong for her son. Make the boy think that the new life that awaited him was a good thing. A hopeful thing. She had to be strong. When her son – her only child – was gone, then she'd let it out. Then she'd cry a river's worth until the madness made her forget.

The boy sat next to her, quiet. Unmoving. Only a child, and yet it seemed he understood that his life would never be the same. He had a small bag packed, though the woman assumed its contents would be discarded before her son reached his final destination. And so they waited.

Their visitors tapped the door three times. There was no

anger behind it, or force. Just *tap, tap, tap*, like the gentle pecking of a bird.

"Come in," she said, so loudly it startled her. Nerves. She was on the edge.

The door opened. Two men and one woman stepped inside the small apartment, dressed in black suits, protective masks covering their mouths and noses.

The lady seemed in charge.

"I can see you're ready," she said, her voice muffled, as she walked forwards and stood before the woman and her son. "We appreciate your willingness to make such a sacrifice. I don't need to tell you how much this means to future generations. We're on the cusp of a very great thing. We *will* find the cure, ma'am. I give you my word."

The woman could only nod. If she tried to speak, it would all come out: Her pain, her fear. Her anger. Her tears. And then her efforts to be strong for the boy would have been for naught. So she kept it in, a dam against a raging river.

The lady was all business. "Come," she said, extending a hand.

The boy looked up at his mother. He had no reason to hold back the tears, and he didn't. They flowed down his face freely. He jumped to his feet and hugged her, shattering her heart a million times over. She squeezed him back.

"You're going to do great things for this world," she whispered, somehow keeping herself under control. "You're going to make me so proud. I love you, sweet boy. I love you so much and don't you ever forget it."

His only response was to sob into her shoulder. And that said everything.

Finally it had to end.

"I'm very sorry," the lady in the dark suit and mask said. "But we have a tight schedule. Truly, I'm sorry."

"Go on now," the mother said to her son. "Go on, and be brave."

He pulled back, his face wet, his eyes red. A strength seemed to come over him and he nodded, helping her believe he'd be okay in the end. He was strong, this one.

The boy turned away, never to look at her again. He walked to the door and went through it with no hesitation. No glance back, no complaints.

"Thank you again," the visiting lady said. She followed the boy out.

One of the men looked up at the dangling, buzzing light bulb, then turned to his partner. "You know who invented those things, right? Maybe we should call this one Thomas." And then they left.

When the door closed, the woman curled up into a ball and finally let her tears come.

ACKNOWLEDGEMENTS

All those who've helped make this series happen are well known by now, since I've mentioned them in every book so far. Especially Krista and Michael.

Therefore, I want to dedicate this space to all of my readers. My life has changed drastically since I first wrote about Thomas and the other Gladers, and I owe so much of it to you. Thank you for enjoying this story. Thank you for spending your hard-earned money on my books. Thank you for telling your friends and family. Thank you for all the enthusiastic praise you've sent me via Twitter, Facebook, my blog, etc. Thank you for allowing me to make a living doing something I love so much.

I've got a lot of books in my head, so hopefully we can be friends for a long time. With all my heart, mind, body, and soul . . . thank you!

THE STORY CONTINUES

BN 978-1-910655-10-8   ISBN 978-1-910655-11-5   ISBN 978-1-910655-12-2

KEEP UP-TO-DATE WITH THE MAZE RUNNER:

MAZERUNNERBOOKS.COM
WCKDISGOOD.COM
THEMAZERUNNERMOVIE.COM
JAMESDASHNER.COM
🐦 @MAZERUNNERBOOKS
f /MAZERUNNERBOOKS
t MAZERUNNERBOOK

TOP TEN THINGS I'D WANT DURING THE APOCALYPSE

by James Dashner

10. Very, very strong sunglasses.

9. Lots of plastic to wrap around my house.

8. A stranger taken in who happens to be the smartest, ablest doctor in a thousand years.

7. A server containing every show that's ever been on HBO and a nice entertainment system on which to watch it all.

6. An e-reader loaded with 5,000 books.

5. A generator and a gas refinery next door to provide fuel so I can watch all those shows and charge my e-reader.

4. Deodorant that smells like a rotting dead body so zombies think I'm just one of them.

3. Lifetime supplies in my basement of the following: hot dogs, Almond Joys, potato chips and Mountain Dew.

2. A cloaking device to hide my house from the tyrannical, evil, bloodthirsty government that will inevitably spring up.

1. Oh, and my wife and kids.

Paperback, ISBN 978-1-910002-06-3, £6.99 • ebook, ISBN 978-1-910002-07-0, £6.99

VENDETTA by CATHERINE DOYLE

For Sophie, it's a long, dull summer in the Chicago suburbs, until five mysterious brothers move into her neighbourhood. A chance encounter with one of them leaves her breathless. But as the secrets of Nic's Sicilian heritage emerge, Sophie's new world shatters. Now she realizes that the choice between love and family comes at a deadly price.

'The sexy bad boy and his distorted sense of honour will . . . have adolescent girls rooting for the wrong 'uns in this Romeo and Juliet of the underworld.'
DAILY MAIL

'. . . a novel that will keep its readers turning the pages.'
THE IRISH TIMES

Paperback, ISBN: 978-1-909489-81-3, £7.99 • ebook, ISBN 978-1-909489-82-0, £7.99